MW01703585

THE THERASAPIEN KICKED TROLL'S LEFT LEG AS HIS LONG BLACK TAIL LATCHED AROUND TROLL'S RIGHT LEG, KNOCKING HIM OFF BALANCE.

Troll fell onto his back and dropped his axe beside him, just out of reach.

The therasapien flicked it away with his tail and locked his left paw over Troll's right arm. "You don't know how to give up, do you? I've never had an opponent like you before. You are most impressive to be able to keep up with my every move. I'll kill you quickly, out of respect, but not yet—"

"What's stopping you?" Troll demanded bravely, trying to hide his fear. He locked eyes with the therasapien and gazed intently. *Will those be my final words?* Troll's breathing increased, but he kept poised.

"I'm done toying with you, *Niño.*" The therasapien leaped into the air and dropped his knee sharply into Troll's diaphragm.

Troll could feel the blow through his armor. It knocked the wind out of him. He tried to cry out in pain, but no sound emerged from his mouth.

The therasapien pulled out an extremely sharp knife and aimed it above Troll's heaving chest.

Troll looked at the weapon nervously. His lips trembled.

The therasapien looked into Troll's eyes. He finally saw the warrior's dread.

"Prepare to die!" he exclaimed and prepared to stab the blade deep into Troll's heart.

DESTINED EXISTENCE

THE UNIQUE CAMPAIGN

KRISTINA M. HOFFMAN

Brad + Lisa!

Kristina M. Hoffman

Never Give Up!

Cover design by Jay L. Hoffman

Paperback ISBN: 979-8-9893757-0-7
Hardback ISBN: 979-8-9893757-1-4
eBook ISBN: 979-8-9893757-2-1

Library of Congress Control Number: 2023924145

www.kristinahoffman.net.

Printed in the United States of America
First Edition

This book is dedicated in loving memory of
Johnny #5 Hoffman
Your love energized my heart and gave me strength to keep my dream alive.

To Jasper,
For helping me find myself again.

To my friends,
Shawn, Brendan, Dave, and Yanna,
whose personalities influenced the characters in this book,
is warmly dedicated.

To my friends,
Bett, Tara, Neva and Dawn.
For boosting my creativity and encouraging my motivation.

But especially dedicated to
Jay
for truly believing in me.
I love you.

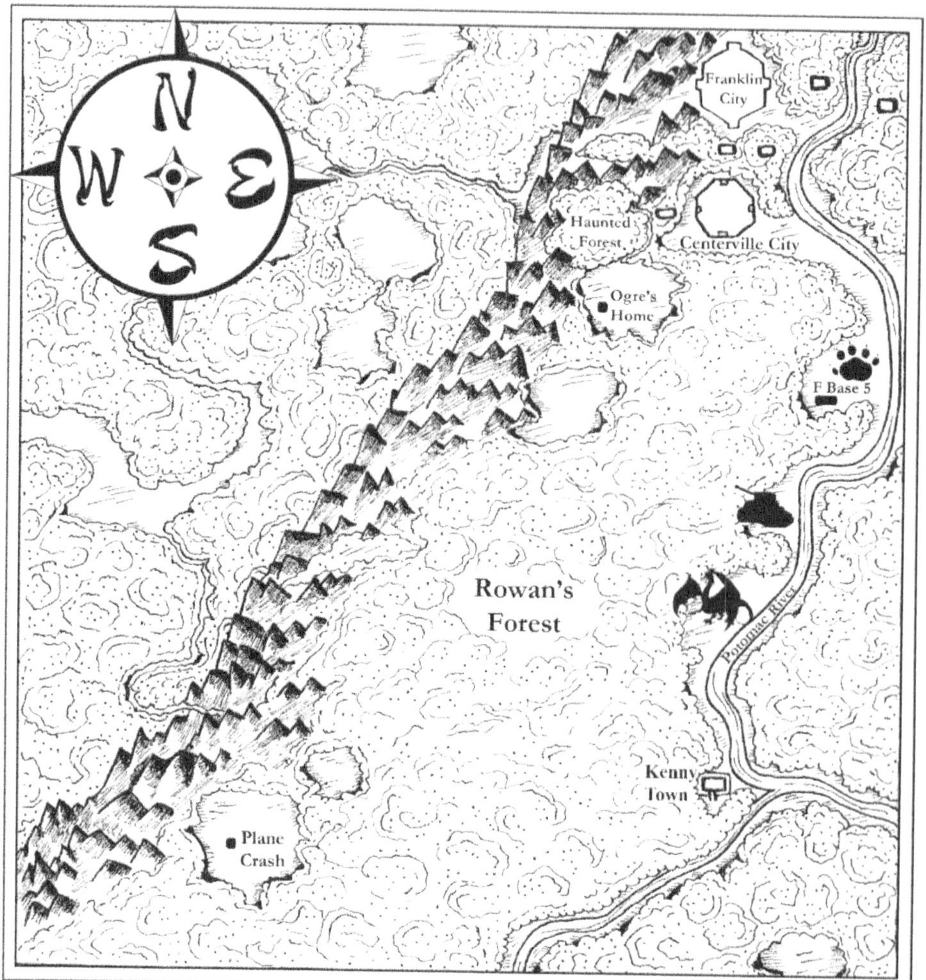

N
W
E
S
Franklin City
Haunted Forest
Centerville City
Ogre's Home
F Base 5
Rowan's Forest
Potomac River
Kenny Town
Plane Crash

ONE

The young, tawny-skinned warrior boarded the plane feeling tired and listless. He had not slept in five days and was irritated that he was being sent on a mission this early in the morning. His fingers glided through his long lavender hair as his unusually bright blue eyes observed the aircraft's cabin.

The aisle was narrow, and there were only eight seats.

Being six feet tall, he immediately felt claustrophobic. His throat tightened, causing him to gently tug on his blue choker. His skin felt restricted in his tight red and blue leggings and form-fitting dark blue athletic bodysuit. His feet sweated in his impressively large brown boots decorated with sharp spikes. His broad chest and stomach felt vulnerable, though they were protected by his light blue chest plate and yellow abdominal armor. Adorned in the center of his breastplate was a circular, smooth red gem secured by yellow clasps shaped like a star and an upside-down pyramid. The sweat on his brow and bulging muscles glistened. Attached to his thick brown belt were a canvas pouch and a small tan sack that he held gently.

I don't like limited space. It's difficult to move if there's an emergency.

"Passengers, T. Smith, and John Doe, welcome aboard the Junco 250 Transport. I am your robot pilot and ask that you get comfortable, fasten your safety belts, and keep your seats upright for take-off. Thank you," said a robotic voice on the loudspeaker.

"Can I have the window seat, Troll?" asked the excited voice of a shorter man behind him in a hooded, long black trench coat.

"Sure," Troll said.

John Doe grunted noisily as he struggled to get past him. "I think I'm caught on your spiky football shoulder-padded armor."

Troll smiled sleepily and stepped back, allowing John Doe to get by. "My armor doesn't look like football padding."

"Look in the mirror sometime, handsome," John Doe said, taking the window seat in the last row. "Now my attire is stylish. Pretty soon, everyone will be wearing decorative green tunics, sunglass-goggles, and long, red scarves over their faces. Then, I can proudly announce that they're wearing me, John Doe," he said, fluffing strands of dirty blond hair protruding from under his hood. His fair-skinned nose was the only part of his face exposed.

"That's disturbing, John," Troll said, sitting beside him. His battle axe was in its sheath attached to the back of his armor. He usually would've removed it before sitting down, but he was too tired and distracted by his discomfort to notice.

During liftoff, Troll's heartbeat quickened. He reached into the tan sack and pulled out a syringe with a hypodermic needle and a small vial. "Since the flight is going to be several hours, I'm going to get some sleep," Troll said, pulling the plunger back, removing the tip cap, and prodding the rubber center. Depressing the plunger pushed out the air before Troll turned the vial upside down.

"Do you think the people of Kenny Town will shower me with affection once they see we're there to protect them?"

"We'll find out once we arrive, John." Troll pulled back on the plunger, allowing the liquid to fill the syringe to the amount he needed.

"I bet they'll be impressed by my magic. I love being a wizard!"

Troll returned the vial to his sack and aimed the sharp tip at his left arm. *I don't want to do this. I want to be normal.* He breathed in deeply through his nose and then exhaled slowly through his mouth. *I want to be able to sleep, but I don't have that ability anymore. I can't allow exhaustion to render me helpless.* Troll hesitated. *This is the only way.* His racing pulse increased as he pierced the needle's sharp tip into his skin.

How did it come to this? Troll pushed the plunger on the syringe with a trembling thumb, injecting the tranquilizer. A tiny gasp escaped his lips as the elixir entered his bloodstream. The drug was very potent; his arm was already starting to feel numb as he carefully pulled out the needle. Troll put the cap back on the needle and placed the empty syringe in the small sack.

He swallowed hard as his breathing slowed. With his eyelids now heavy, he had difficulty focusing from blurred vision. The tranquilizer was working fast, probably due to being anxious. Troll's discomfort ended, feeling the plane's vibrations rock him gently, calming his heart. His back relaxed partially into the chair's soft cushion and his axe's hard handle. He closed his eyes and drifted into unconsciousness.

Troll was unarmed, bare-chested, and his long, lustrous hair cascaded over his shoulders. It was black, its natural color, and had yet to be dyed. He stood in a long, narrow room with incredibly high, decorated walls made of gold. There was a reflectively polished vinyl floor, turquoise drapery on tall windows, giant ornate pillars, and a grand chandelier hung from the ceiling. A long, slender red tapestry rug was at the foot of a large throne at the end of the room.

THE UNIQUE CAMPAIGN

The walls seemed to engulf him, creating an intimidating sensation as the back of the room faded, and darkness pressed down on him from all around. Very little light came through the windows, creating an unsettling atmosphere in the elegant space. Troll slowly approached the throne, and a chill went down his spine. He glanced at the walls but could not see a door that led out of this enormous room. He nervously ran his fingers through his long hair. Troll heard voices approaching and hid behind one of the pillars.

From the darkness emerged a group of soldiers dressed in black uniforms. They marched into the light, gathered around the front of the throne, and lined up along the edge of the rug. *I recognize their uniforms. These men work for the Restrain Corporation,* Troll thought.

A shorter man, wearing a black uniform with gold and red trim, decorated in ribbons and medals, and a medium-length red cape, walked to the throne and sat down.

He must be their leader. Troll noticed the man had dark hair, but his eyes and nose were concealed by a shadow. He could tell the man was frustrated by his clenched jaw and slouched shoulders. Troll winced when the leader suddenly let out a ferocious scream and pummeled his black-gloved fist into the mahogany arm of the regal throne. The booming sound echoed through the room.

The soldiers recoiled as if they had been struck.

"I was so close!" the leader bellowed, striking the throne with brute force again.

I have to get out of here. Troll inhaled sharply when he felt the ground quake from the powerful strike.

"I came so close to possessing it, and now it is gone again!" The leader's gloved hand squeezed the velvet-textured armrest as he reclined into the soft cushions. "I will have it," he said with quiet intensity. "Mark my words; it shall be mine. Mine!"

A symbol appeared in Troll's mind: a brain with an eye in the center. The vision made him shudder. He frantically looked for an exit before the feeling of being watched overcame him. Troll turned around slowly, and the Restrain Corporation leader stood before him and lunged for his throat. Troll fell to elude his grasp. A groan escaped his lips when he landed forcefully on his back. Looking up from his prone position, he could still not see the leader's face but recognized the insignia pinned to his uniform. It was the emblem from his vision.

The leader removed his glove, and a blinding yellow light emanated in the palm of his hand. The radiance was so bright it forced Troll to shut his eyes and turn his head to the right until his chin touched his shoulder. The leader's glowing hand descended slowly toward Troll's bare chest. Helpless and unable to see, Troll felt the sweltering heat ready to penetrate his skin and melt his heart. Troll screamed.

Suddenly, a cool breeze caressed Troll's chest. He opened his eyes, staring at the canopy of a forest. The soldiers, their leader, and the throne room were gone. He carefully sat up, preparing to stand.

He heard a twig snap. A low growl came from the trees before him.

His heart was hammering in his chest.

Another growl erupted behind him.

Troll smelled the intense aroma of musky animals. He slowly stood, ready to run, but was startled when someone grabbed his arms and locked his shoulders in a painful position. He shrieked in distress, struggling to escape the aggressor. While thrashing around, Troll managed to glance at his assaulter. He wasn't a human. His attacker was a mutant: half-man, half-tiger. "Hold still, boy," the mutant growled into Troll's ear. "You can't escape us!"

The other mutant, half-man, half-cheetah, emerged from the trees wearing black Restrain Corporation armor. The same emblem was carved into his shoulder plate. The mutant walked forward menacingly. His piercing gold eyes glistened with an intense desire to kill. His large claws were like knives. He aimed them at the center of Troll's bare chest.

Troll tried one final time to escape, but the overpowered tiger-mutant laughed at his feeble attempt.

Faster than Troll's eyes could follow, the cheetah-mutant's claws cut through his chest, effortlessly shredding his sternum and rib cage.

I'm about to die! He's going to rip out my heart! Squealing in fear, Troll could barely hear their sinister laughter as he lost consciousness from the searing pain.

Sometime later, Troll regained consciousness in a different part of the forest.

I'm alive? No. They killed me. Troll could feel his heart beating, but his chest was in excruciating pain. His shoulders also ached from being constricted. He slowly lifted his left hand and flinched from the agony in his arms.

What did they do to me? How did I survive? Apprehensive, Troll raised his trembling hand to his chest. He held his breath, swallowing back the pain. He expected to feel bloody textured flesh and bone. To his surprise, his hand brushed against a smooth surface. He yelled in terror, forgetting his pain, and sat up quickly.

Embedded in the very center of his chest was a large red amulet.

What is that? Troll inspected the ruby red gem, pressing it ever so gently. He screamed when he suddenly felt a rush of adrenaline surge inside him. His heart raced directly behind the amulet. His wounds healed miraculously, and he stood up.

Disoriented, Troll ran through the forest, dodging trees. His adrenaline overwhelmed him, and his speed increased. He was running as fast as the wind could blow. He had never run this quickly in his life. Troll misjudged evading a large shrub. He sprinted directly into it, grabbed the hedge, and ripped it from the ground, roots and all. Troll skidded to a halt, coughing bits of leaves and dirt from his mouth. Breathing hard, Troll walked back to where he accidentally uprooted the shrub. He returned the roots to the soil and sat beside the crooked bush. "How did I do that?" *This amulet has given me superspeed, superstrength, and rapid healing abilities.* Troll stood up but instantly became incapacitated and dropped to his knees. *If these are superpowers—then why does this feel like a punishment? The amulet is causing this, but I'm terrified to rip it from my chest. It might kill me.*

A foul odor irritated his nostrils as a ferocious yowl thundered behind him before someone knocked him unconscious.

Troll woke from the nightmare with a gasp, placing his left hand over his racing heart. His exposed skin shimmered with sweat.

John Doe was gazing out the window when Troll jolted awake, startling him. "Are you all right?"

Troll nervously moved his hand away from the center of his blue chest plate. He looked at the red amulet. He shut his eyes, threw his head back into the cushion, and exhaled with relief. He focused on calming himself. *That nightmare—the memory—is always intense. It's strange how the mind works—I can still smell that odor.* "It feels like I was sleeping on a log," Troll said, opening his eyes and adjusting his posture. *No wonder, Troll. You left your axe on your back.*

"You finally woke up from the coma you put yourself into. I've known you for two years and cannot get used to your sleeping habits. When you are out, you are *out*."

Troll's eyes looked far away as he swept his long lavender hair from his sweaty neck. "I had a disturbing nightmare."

"Another one? You seem to have nightmares every time you go to sleep."

THE UNIQUE CAMPAIGN

"I have this feeling—deep inside me—that something unpredictable will happen today. How long was I asleep? What time is it?"

"You've been asleep for about three hours. It's almost six-thirty. The sunrise is pretty," John Doe said. "We should be nearing Kenny Town, according to the robot pilot. He never shuts up, by the way. I don't know why the Eastern Regiment didn't just assign a human pilot."

"Time to destination estimated at forty-eight minutes," the robot pilot announced over the loudspeaker in its tediously mechanical voice.

"See," John Doe said, sighing. "I swear he estimates the arrival time every few minutes."

"Well, apparently, he's been programmed to annoy you, John." Troll chuckled. "Did anything exciting happen?"

"I saw a cloud shaped like a butt a few miles back. Nothing out of the ordinary unless you count that weird smell."

"You smell it, too?" Troll asked tensely, removing his seat belt and standing up. His nose led him to the closed cargo bay door behind his seat. *The cargo bay only has enough space for our equipment and parachutes. What's in there?*

"You're jumpy this morning," John Doe said, trying to shift in his seat to see better. His seat belt cut into him and prevented quick movements. "It smells like trash, honestly. I figured someone left dirty laundry in the cargo area."

"When did you first notice this smell?" Troll asked, carefully reaching for the handle.

"Shortly after you fell asleep," John Doe said.

Troll drew his hand back and slowly removed the battle axe from its sheath. He clutched it tightly and stared earnestly at the cargo bay door before turning to his dark-cloaked companion. "Get behind me," Troll whispered.

"What?" John Doe cried, struggling to unlatch his seat belt. "Hey, Troll, I'm stuck!" He pulled frantically on the strap, but it would not come loose.

"Don't move," Troll warned. He heard the faint sound of footsteps. The odor intensified. "We have a stowaway onboard. It's coming," Troll said, standing poised. He dared not move a muscle.

John Doe gulped and held perfectly still. He tried to clutch the leather seat belt, but his sweaty hands slipped down the strap. His hands were so wet they felt like they had been soaking in a tub of water. More sweat formed on his brow and ran into his eyes behind the large sunglass-goggles.

BANG!

Troll and John Doe jumped.

"Someone or thing is trying to get in!" John Doe yelled.

BANG!

Troll watched the door indent toward him. *That door is made of carbon fiber and aluminum, yet it is dented!* He swallowed hard and prepared to defend his friend.

BANG!

The horrible smell crept through stronger, making Troll's eyes water.

Another thump came from inside the cargo bay, but the door was not struck. John Doe yelped when he heard the noise.

Troll held steadfast.

BANG!

The door dented again.

"What's happening?" asked John Doe.

A disturbing sound transpired inside the cargo bay.

"That sounds like ripping metal," said John Doe.

"The stowaway is not coming through. Not through the door, anyway. It probably could have easily ripped the door off its hinges."

"It's toying with us." John Doe moaned.

Troll kicked the cargo bay door open and walked in. He sighed when he saw the large hole in the floor. "It peeled the metal floor like an orange," Troll said grimly. "It's under us."

"Outside the plane?" asked John Doe.

"No, it's in the undercarriage."

"What kind of creature is it?" John Doe asked nervously, trying to remove his seat belt again.

"It's a Magic-Eater. No other creature smells like that."

"I've heard of those! I have to get out of here, or I'm doomed! We've got to tell the robot to land the plane," John Doe cried, picturing a shadowy figure with massive, blood-stained claws.

"Try to stay calm, John. Need a hand?"

"Yes," John Doe pleaded, sighing hard. "I don't know why this seat belt won't come off."

Troll looked at the strap. He saw that the young wizard tangled it into a large knot. Troll sighed and pulled the belt away from John Doe's shoulder. He gently cut it with his axe, sawing back and forth, freeing his companion.

John Doe sprang to his feet and dashed through the aisle.

"John, wait!" Troll cried. "It could be waiting for you."

John Doe burst into the cockpit. "We need to land!"

"Negative. We must approach our destination on scheduled time, or you will be tardy," said the robot.

"I don't care about being on schedule. There is a monster onboard trying to kill us!" John Doe yelled. "You need to land the plane!"

"Destination will not be reached until forty-two minutes from current time," the robot said. "Please return to your seats in an orderly manner."

Troll cautiously entered the cockpit.

"Troll, this tin can is not going to land! How do we get that thing off the plane?" asked John Doe, panicking.

A sudden blast from under their feet caused the plane to shake and knocked John Doe off his feet. His rump struck the ground hard.

Troll managed to grab and support himself with the pilot's seat.

The robot activated the alarm system and announced, "Attention, passengers, I am programmed to report that the plane is rapidly leaking fuel. Estimated evacuation time is twelve minutes."

Troll tried to study the control panel but backed away the instant a fist punched toward him through the controls.

The clenched hand opened and revealed massive claws that began to slice through the panel.

The robot pilot reached for the radio, but the claws slashed through its arm.

Troll noticed the creature insert a small explosive device into the robot. He grabbed John Doe and retreated into the cabin.

The robot tried to make another announcement, but the bomb detonated.

Troll dropped to his knees, shielding John Doe.

The alarm continued to sound as a fire started in the cockpit.

Troll faced the licking flames.

Fire . . .

He could not move. He opened his mouth to speak, but no words would form.

The fire grew stronger, crackling and sizzling.

Troll could not take his eyes off of the threatening blaze. It was as if he were bewitched. The fire's mesmerizing dance kept the young warrior petrified.

Troll blinked, and his reality altered. He was a desperate child, crying hysterically in a field as he ran toward a burning farmhouse in the distance. He ran as fast as he could, violently pushing back his long black hair clinging to his tear-dampened face. He lost his footing and crumbled to the ground before reaching the farmhouse.

Troll gasped in surprise when John Doe touched his shoulder. Troll's conscious mind returned to the present.

"I'm getting our parachutes!" John Doe said, rushing into the cargo bay. He opened the trunk that should contain them—they were missing. John Doe returned to the cabin. "The intruder must've taken them. Troll, this plane is crashing, and we do not have parachutes!"

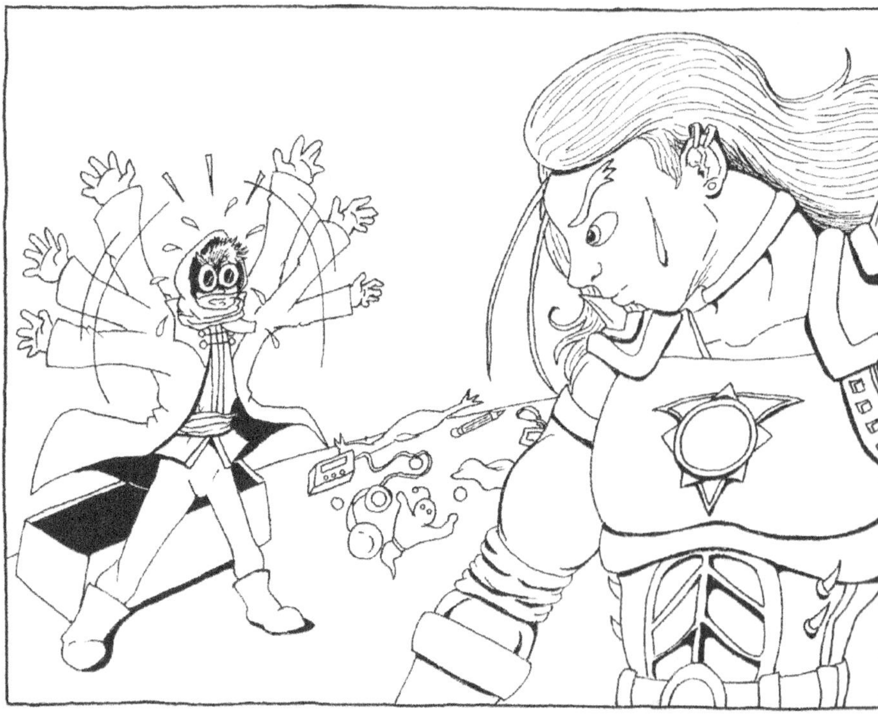

Still disoriented, Troll touched his forehead, trying to gather his thoughts. He struggled to stand and get away from the burning cockpit.

Another detonation under the plane knocked Troll and John Doe off their feet. Luckily, the seats caught them.

"That was close," Troll said. "Too close."

"Omnipotent and miraculous Thoth, protect us! We are crashing! We're going to die!" screamed John Doe.

Troll looked out the window and noticed the plane was heading into a heavily wooded forest.

Crashing was unavoidable.

"No, we're not going to die," Troll said, going over to John Doe. "John, you need to trust me. I'll carry you, and I'm going to jump."

"Jump? You can't jump! We're going to become pancakes! I love to eat them, but that doesn't mean I want to be one. Pancakes aren't my favorite breakfast anymore."

"Trust me," Troll told him as he looked out the window again.

The ground was approaching fast.

Directly under their feet, a massive explosion transpired. The floor beneath them rattled and cracked open.

Troll struck the red amulet on his chest. A surge of adrenaline raced through him. He grabbed John Doe. His legs became as fast as lightning. He ran into the cargo bay, taking hold of the plane's exposed steel beam strut. Troll's grip became a powerful vice as the floor ripped away, causing a giant hole under his feet. His eyes widened in alarm.

The pressure tried to suck them out.

Troll clutched John Doe even tighter. His muscles burned.

"Don't let go!" John Doe screamed.

"John, make a force field! Please, hurry!" Troll shouted, holding on for dear life.

"I'll try! Just don't let me go!" John Doe said. "*Ego creans custodies nos a scuto venti.*" His hands emitted a glowing white light that surrounded what remained of the plane.

The strong pull stopped as the glowing force field sealed the hole under Troll's feet.

"Good job, John." Troll exhaled sharply, keeping his grip on the beam but relaxing his muscles.

"It's difficult to hold! All of that stress . . . makes it hard to concentrate," John Doe said, his arms trembling.

"Do the best you can, and I'll handle the rest," Troll said, trying to sound confident. He gently touched the red amulet again before applying force to it. Another rush of energy swept through him. A small groan escaped his lips. Troll flexed his chest and biceps. He grabbed around John Doe's waist. "Hold onto me!"

The plane rocked violently after connecting with a tall tree, shearing off the right wing and breaking the magical force field like a necklace chain. The strands of magic blew in the wind as the rest of the force field held.

Troll's heart skipped a beat when he fell backward. He let go of the beam and collapsed onto the cracking hull beside the large hole.

"*Ego creans custodies nos a scuto venti!*" John Doe's hands glowed brighter, putting more magical energy into the spell.

The two broken pieces glowed intensely, came toward each other, fighting the wind, and swiftly reconnected.

"Keep the force field up!" Troll cried as he grasped the wizard.

"I'm trying!" John Doe said, straining. "I can't hold on . . . much longer!"

"I'm going to get us to the back door!" Troll got to his feet and hurried to the door. As soon as he clutched the handle, the plane hit another tree.

The impact destroyed the cargo bay around them.

Troll released the handle just as the door was ripped off its hinges. He kept a firm grip on John Doe as the young wizard kept the force field together. Troll glanced outside the plane and saw they were preparing to pass a tree that might support his weight. He could feel John Doe trembling. "We're going to be—" Troll's voice was cut off as the plane scraped against another tree. He was knocked off balance. "John, you must keep the plane hovering in a straight line! I'm going to jump into that tree! You can do it!"

Though John Doe was terrified, his will to live overcame his fear. "I might lose the force field! But I'll try! *Jube haec ego volitare contritum metallum. Glide quam ventus!*" He aimed his luminous white hands at the cracking hull directly under Troll's feet. "I got it! I can't believe it! We're hovering, and the force field is holding!"

"Good work, John," Troll said, clutching John Doe, leaping out of the plane, aiming for the tree.

John Doe shrieked and clamped around Troll's midsection. His hands stopped glowing.

The force field ceased, and the plane smashed into the ground yards behind them.

Troll's feet landed hard on a tree branch. It broke under his weight. He yelped but jumped onto another branch. It, too, broke under him. Troll leaped from the tree onto the ground, creating large boot imprints in the soil.

The plane exploded.

Troll shielded John Doe. The heat from the explosion was so hot his back felt like it was on fire. He screamed, picked up John Doe, and ran, putting distance between them and the crash site. He released John Doe after the bursts subsided. Troll took quick, short breaths to cool down his body temperature.

"You saved my life," John Doe said, relaxing.

"It was nothing," Troll managed to gasp over his hammering heartbeat. "We would've been goners if not for your magic."

"At least that stowaway went down with the plane," John Doe said happily. "Yuck! The blaze stinks like kerosene! I'll use my ice spell to stop the fire from spreading. I'll be right back."

"Be careful, John."

As John Doe walked cautiously to the burning remains of the airplane, Troll's nose caught a different scent on the wind, and the presence of a dark aura came over him. *No way! The Magic-Eater survived?*

The Magic-Eater emerged from behind a bush. It moved so fast that Troll could not determine its height, but it was broader than him. It had light gray skin, a sharp-beaked mouth, red eyes, long claws, and a muscular body sporting only a tan loincloth.

Troll gaped in horror as it swiped its long, sharp claws at his throat. He avoided being scratched by quickly stepping backward. Troll forcefully punched at the Magic-Eater's sternum, nearly losing his balance.

The Magic-Eater skillfully grabbed Troll's hand.

Troll could not pull away. He tried to touch the red amulet with his other hand, but the Magic-Eater grabbed Troll's left shoulder and pulled him to its beaked mouth.

"It would be a shame to kill such a fine warrior. My lord will be interested in your stupendous strength," the Magic-Eater whispered into Troll's ear.

The Restrain Corporation! Troll struggled to pull away from the Magic-Eater.

"Oh no, warrior. You cannot escape me. I have got you now. I don't eat humans who lack magical energy. They're disgusting! Although, your unusual strength piques my curiosity. I wonder if you taste as good as you look?" The Magic-Eater's tongue slithered out of its mouth.

Troll turned his head in disgust and shuddered when the forked tongue licked his neck.

"Hmm, not bad," said the Magic-Eater.

"John—" Troll whimpered when John Doe returned. He looked at John Doe as a sinking feeling gripped his heart.

John Doe watched his comrade struggle against the Magic-Eater's locked grip. *Is the Magic-Eater really going to eat him? I have to save Troll!* He rolled up his sleeves and aimed his hands at the Magic-Eater.

"No, John!" Troll shouted.

The Magic-Eater observed Troll's eyes and turned its attention to the wizard.

"Ice freeze! *Glacies congelo*!" yelled John Doe as a strong blast of ice-cold air shot from his fingertips.

The Magic-Eater laughed sinisterly and dematerialized as the ice spell struck Troll's chest.

I cannot move. I can't breathe! I'm so cold. It's getting hard to think—to focus. My heart is beating so fast! My heartbeat . . . my heart . . . .

TWO

I am not looking forward to today. It's early. I have been overworked, and I'm tired. I should stay in bed, but duty calls. I have to be on my ship at seven o'clock. I feel like a machine programmed to work non-stop, but this is the career I wanted. I love working in outer space, but I know nothing exciting will happen. Well, I'd best get to work.

—From the journal of Corin Degodi
June 10, 2215, 6:20 a.m.

As Corin Degodi's small spacecraft left Orion Three space station, a giant whirling tornado materialized behind him. His sensors picked up the anomaly. The alarm wailed. Corin activated the rear-view camera and hunched over his controls, surprised by what he saw. "Impossible!" Corin engaged his ship's thrusters, attempting to put as much space between him and the twister as possible.

A lifetime of living on the space station hadn't prepared Corin for such an encounter. He frantically ran his hands over his control pad, unintentionally flipping switches. He groaned in frustration as he activated the space-screen wipers. He tried to stay calm, firing the thrusters to their maximum setting and adjusting the gyroscope. Suddenly, his controls were deactivated, and Corin rushed to the emergency shuttle. He prayed that he could escape before his spacecraft was engulfed by the spinning void.

As Corin boarded the single-person shuttle, his ship endured a violent vibration emanating from the ground. He screamed, being thrown around in the shuttle by the pull of the severe storm. Corin climbed into the piloting chair and attempted to start the engine, breathing a sigh of relief when it activated. He raised the shuttle's gun and blasted a hole in the spacecraft's hull. He launched the shuttle into space as the ferocious tornado sucked in the dead spacecraft.

My poor ship, he thought, grinding his teeth and struggling with the controls to keep the little shuttle going. There was an explosion inside the tornado. Corin scanned for his spacecraft but could not pick up the signal. "Well, there goes my ship," Corin sighed.

The emergency shuttle vibrated uncontrollably. Corin gripped his controls tightly and monitored his life support. "Come on! I don't want to suffer the same fate as my ship!" The shuttle was reaching a critical stage.

Sweat dripped down his forehead. His hands were clammy, and his body trembled with fear. He gave the engines everything he had, but despite his efforts, the incredible pull of the vortex was just too much for the little shuttle, and the controls were deactivated.

The explosive wave of force from the detonation of the ship approached his shuttle.

Corin screeched in panic and closed his brown eyes. He braced for the impact. Visions filled his mind: an intense blow that threw him from his seat, the echoing alarm as the shuttle juddered, his life support system failed, and the walls were ripped to shreds as his body was hurled into darkness, and he became a victim to the vacuum of space.

Corin pushed the horrific visions from his mind and opened his eyes. He felt a gentle push from the blast, moving his shuttle away from the vortex. Once the shuttle was at a safe distance, Corin breathed a sigh of relief. He smiled, leaned back in his seat, and looked at the ceiling. "I'm safe."

He gasped sharply as he was suddenly forced out of his chair. It felt as if someone had fired at his shuttle. He quickly stumbled back into his seat and read his coordinates. "What was that?"

His shuttle had not escaped the vortex. It was coming.

Corin swallowed hard and gripped the arms of his chair tightly. Fear overcame him. His entire body shuddered, and he held on for dear life.

The metal ceiling of his shuttle ripped off. While screaming in terror, Corin exhaled all the air from his lungs. He was jerked out of the shuttle by the tornado. He closed his eyes tightly as his helpless body violently twisted inside the whirlwind.

I'm not going to make it. Corin's lungs were burning. *I can't take much more.*

The shuttle impacted the spinning wall of the vortex, causing it to explode as if it crashed into a solid surface. The sound of the explosion startled Corin, and he regrettably inhaled.

This is the end!

Expecting to suffocate, Corin was stunned when he breathed fresh oxygen. Breathing frantically, he opened his eyes, glancing at his surroundings. He noticed the shattered remains of his ship and shuttle while listening to the whistling wind circulating around him.

Is the tornado somehow protecting me from the vacuum of outer space? I'm not freezing to death! This isn't possible, Corin thought, feeling his spinning body suddenly slow until he was floating in the very center of the spinning vortex. The sound of the wind died down, and it became unnervingly quiet.

Corin tried to calm himself, but fear gripped his heart. Through his anxiety and confusion, he peered through the vortex at Orion Three space station. He saw his fellow Task Force Space Rangers walking through the corridors. *How has no one noticed this tornado?*

He inhaled when he saw a person standing on a ledge of the space station without a spacesuit, dressed in a hooded cloak. *It can't be . . .*

The cloak was dark as night, but the fabric had a slight shimmer—tiny stars appeared to shine upon it. It was like the figure was wearing a piece of outer space.

The dark figure's hands were purple, glowing brightly. The color inside the whirlwind matched the stranger's glowing hands.

Corin knew a tornado was a colorless vortex of air. *Is that person controlling the tornado? How? I wish I could see his face.* The thought was pulled from Corin's mind when his body floated away from the center mass of the twister and scuffed against the wall. His shuttle had been destroyed from colliding with the wall, but his impact was surprisingly gentle. His frail body was not harmed. *I want answers, but do I dare speak to this hooded figure?* "What is this?" Corin yelled nervously. "Who are you?"

There was no response from the stranger.

Nothing scientific can explain both of my crafts deactivating, the wind whistling, the sound of my shuttle exploding, that person able to stand in space, and all of the other factors that don't make any sense about that tornado. Unless . . . "Is this a portal?" Corin felt the air around him change.

The space station vanished.

Corin could no longer see through the vortex and was being pulled downward. He could see a bright light, and the air became warmer. Corin feared that this violet portal would drop him into the sun. He could now see the land and calculated that he was thousands of feet in the air. Below him was a rich forest.

The portal evaporated.

Corin fell, screaming.

He could feel the full force of the planet's gravity pulling him toward the ground. "So, this is how it all ends!" Corin screamed in horror, unprepared to watch his life flash before his eyes.

"No, this is how it all begins," a voice rang beside Corin.

"Help me! Who are you?" shouted Corin, feeling a small amount of hope.

There was no response.

Corin continued to fall headfirst at an incredible speed. His body became a missile.

THE UNIQUE CAMPAIGN

The wind pushed against his exposed face and helmet. Corin's cheeks flapped, and his mouth and lips became severely dry. The air felt thick like molasses. His ears were in agonizing pain. The wind encased him in a cocoon of noise that shrieked a continual reminder of his approaching demise. Corin never imagined falling through the air would be so loud. He could not hear his voice as he yelled at the top of his lungs. His heart was racing, and his mind had lost all focus. The only thing Corin could think about was his impending death.

The trees were approaching fast.

Corin stopped screaming, bizarrely able to manage his thoughts. His will to survive overcame his fear. He quickly brought his hand down to his leather utility belt and pressed a small green button. Instantly, his entire body was surrounded by a green light. Corin tried to swallow, but it wasn't easy due to his dry mouth.

In seconds, Corin would impact a thick tree branch.

He shut his eyes and shrieked again. His Task Force helmet broke through the first tree branch and then another. Branch after branch, one after another, his helmet broke through every single one. Corin continued screaming.

It was a miracle that his body remained unharmed.

He continued to fall, and the branches slowed his nosedive. Corin feared his lungs would explode from screaming.

Suddenly, his helmet failed to break through a strange, sticky, soft material. The force of his fall stretched the substance down, and then it sprang back up like a trampoline, trapping him inside.

Corin cautiously opened his eyes. He appeared to have landed in a large net. Thankfully, he had remembered his force field. It saved his life. He pushed the button on his belt, and the green light melted from his body.

Removing one of his gloves, he touched the net. It felt like extremely sticky silk. Corin returned the glove to his hand and saw the net was dangling from a tree.

"I feel like an animal in a trap, but at least I'm alive," Corin said, sighing with relief as he unbuckled his helmet and removed it from his head. He wiped away the sweat that had formed on his forehead and ran his fingers through his short brown hair.

"Hey!" yelled a voice below.

Corin looked down to see a strange woman staring at him. Her curly shoulder-length hair was the color of strawberries, her flesh was jade green, and she had pink dragonfly wings attached to her back. Her green skin was very exposed, with only a few flowers on a bikini covering her.

Corin's light-colored cheeks reddened as he looked her up and down, unable to pull his gaze from her exotic presence. *Her flesh and hair have been blessed with such beautiful colors. I'm used to pale skin and uninspiring shades of hair. Her wings are mesmerizing. I've never seen a humanoid like her before.* "I must be dead." Corin pinched his face. "Ow! I'm alive!" he said, relieved, putting his helmet back on and buckling it into place under his chin. "I was worried for a minute there."

"Don't you ignore me!" barked the green woman, putting her hands on her hips and tapping her barefoot.

Corin looked at her again. *Is this a dream?* He blinked several times to be sure he was awake.

"You don't look like a poacher," she said.

Corin, confused by her statement, looked side to side.

"Yes, *you*!" she shouted.

Corin's cheeks flushed. *My mind is jumbled after that terrifying ordeal. I don't know what's real.*

"Are you a poacher?"

"Um, no," Corin answered nervously.

"Then get out of my net!" she yelled, pointing her finger straight at Corin's nose before turning to leave him hanging there.

Corin struggled in the net. The more he tried to escape, the tighter the sticky fibers held him.

"Help!" he cried in panic. "Help me, please."

"What do you want?" asked the woman, turning to face Corin again.

"I can't get out. What is this net made of?"

"It's a spider's web. All of my arachnid friends are trying to help me capture poachers. I must protect my forest and all who live here."

"That is very fascinating, ma'am, but could you please help me get out?" Corin asked, trying to sound as polite as possible.

Her wings fluttered as she kicked off the ground and flew to him. "You seem suspicious, sir. You fell from the sky. Where did you come from?"

Corin swallowed hard and struggled to reposition himself. "This may be difficult to explain, but I'm not from here. I was pulled into a vortex . . . a portal. It dropped me here."

"A portal! I know what that is. Are you a wizard?" she asked, scrunching her nose.

"Not that I know of, ma'am. I'm a Task Force Space Ranger. I live and work on Orion Three space station," Corin explained. His gloves were stuck to the web at this point. He shook his hands in frustration, hoping to break free. It didn't work.

"You are a *what*?" she asked, narrowing her eyes.

"I work in outer space. Look, I'm wearing my job's uniform. A purple portal appeared when I was on my ship. It sucked me inside and brought me here. I swear that's all I know," Corin said, softening his eyes.

"What's your name?" she asked, her voice more relaxed.

"Corin Degodi. What's yours?"

"I am Rowan Fae, the eldest daughter of the Woodland Faerie King."

"I am pleased to meet you, Rowan." Corin felt like he had gained her trust. He shook his hands again, finally freeing his gloves. "If you would be so kind, ma'am, will you help me out of this net?"

Rowan smiled at him, humming to herself. She fluttered to the ground, landing gently, and looked at him. She stuck her tongue out and pointed her index finger to where the net was attached to the tree. "Sure!" A beam of gold light flew out of her fingertip and melted the webbing.

Corin landed hard on his posterior. "Ouch! Thank you, Rowan," he said, brushing the web off his uniform.

"You're welcome," Rowan said, walking around him, studying his uniform. "Why are you wearing gray pajamas?"

Taken aback by her question, Corin stood, letting out a small chuckle. "I'm not wearing pajamas. As I said before, this is the uniform for my job."

"It looks like a jumpsuit that people sleep in," Rowan said, gently tugging the material. "The helmet looks silly with your nightwear. At least the colors match. I like the tones." She circled him. "What are those colors? Denim, spruce, maybe stone? Kind of dull for sleepwear, don't you think?" She giggled and danced around him.

"I'm not wearing pajamas," he said sternly.

"Is it your union suit?" she asked, giggling through a wicked smile.

"This is not sleepwear," Corin grumbled as he stomped his left foot into the dirt.

"Long johns!" Rowan sang.

"They are not pajamas!" Corin yelled.

"I'm only teasing," Rowan said, stopping and sticking out her tongue.

Corin's blood pressure returned to normal.

Rowan crossed her arms over her chest. "Are you a human? You'd have to be with that temper."

He observed her skin and wings again. *At least she's changed the subject from my uniform.* "Yes, I am. And am I to understand that you are indeed a faerie?"

"I sure am," Rowan said, smiling. "But you can also call me an Antiquity. It's what we magical creatures call ourselves to separate us from humans. So, why do you think the portal brought you here? You know magic portals always transport someone from place to place with a purpose."

"I didn't know that," Corin admitted. "I honestly didn't know what the portal was. I thought a tornado materialized in outer space, but that's impossible."

"Anything is possible when you're dealing with magic." She pointed to a partially dead bush. "The poor thing was struck by lightning the other day. Watch this!" Rowan's hand glowed the same golden color. The bush's burnt branches began to tremble as a green, rejuvenating aura spread across the leaves and stems. A puddle of water appeared under the bush, and the roots gulped it greedily.

Corin was perplexed. "That's amazing!"

"Yeah, I know. I'm pretty amazing!"

"Um, I meant the plant," Corin said before being startled by a booming sound in the sky.

A dark cloud of smoke formed above the trees.

"What is that?" asked Rowan.

"That sounded like an explosion!"

There was another loud detonation.

Rowan screamed, dropping to her knees and trembling as she covered her long, pointed ears.

Corin pulled his laser pistol from its holster on his leg, aiming at the smoke. He positioned himself over Rowan, watching the burning aircraft fall from the sky. "Rowan, look!" he said, taking her hand and helping her to her feet.

"What is that?" she asked.

"A plane is crashing. Come on, we'd better go see where it hits. There could be survivors that need our help," Corin said.

"But isn't that dangerous?" Rowan whimpered.

They heard a loud rumble in the distance, followed by powerful vibrations under their feet. Many trees toppled.

"It looks like it landed over here. It isn't very far. Hurry!" Corin declared, dashing into the forest.

Corin and Rowan cautiously approached the burning remains of the plane.

"Let's investigate cautiously and see if we can spot any survivors," Corin advised, keeping his pistol ready. *I hope there are survivors, but I'm keeping on my guard in case this crash was not accidental.*

"Oh!" Rowan cried out, startling Corin's heart into his throat.

"Are you okay?" he asked.

"No!" she yelled angrily. "This is terrible!"

"What? What is it?" Corin asked, looking around.

Rowan was looking at the ground. "It squished that flower!" she said, pointing to a crushed dandelion.

Corin was mind-boggled by Rowan's reaction, but there was no time to discuss this. He heard something behind them. He turned around quickly and peered through the thick forest. "Look over here. I see someone," Corin whispered.

"Help! Help me!" John Doe yelled, running for his life into a clearing.

Corin huffed when the brawny monster burst through the trees after the man in the trench coat. He had never seen such a frightening creature. "Where in the universe am I?"

The Magic-Eater roared an ear-shattering sound from its sharp beak. Its large red eyes stalked its prey as its razor-sharp claws extended, intending to grab the human.

John Doe miraculously dodged the Magic-Eater's grasp as he tripped on an exposed tree root and faceplanted.

The Magic-Eater galloped past him, grunted in confusion, and slid to a halt.

John Doe got to his feet and ran.

The Magic-Eater flexed its bulging muscles and dug the sharp talons on its feet into the soil. It kicked up dirt as its long, powerful legs chased after John Doe again. "I will eat your soul!" the Magic-Eater bellowed.

"What is that thing?" Corin asked Rowan.

"It's a Magic-Eater! Oh no! That man must be a wizard, or else that thing would not be after him," Rowan explained. "Magic-Eaters only eat Antiquities or humans who have experience with magic. They were engineered that way by the Restrain Corporation."

"You can explain everything later. I need to help that man. You better stay here and keep out of sight," Corin said, raising his pistol and quietly stepping through the trees.

"You're not going out there, are you?" she asked him with fear in her eyes. Her bottom lip quivered.

"I don't have any magic powers, Rowan. He won't want to eat me," Corin explained. "But I *am* human, and that man is too. He needs help. Stay here."

I can't run forever and must take a stand, John Doe thought. He stopped, turned around, and aimed his hands at the monster. "Ice freeze! *Glacies congelo!*" They glowed like a white bulb and flashed with luminosity.

The earth before John Doe glimmered, becoming watery. It molded into a large wall of stalagmites and instantly froze.

The Magic-Eater slowly approached the stalagmite wall and chuckled evilly. It glared at the wizard through the ice barrier and licked its beak hungrily. "There is no possible escape. Do you truly believe this will stop me?"

Fear gripped John Doe, causing his fight or flight response to kick in. After a horrified gasp, he turned to run. He did not see the medium-sized sedimentary rock behind him and tripped. He landed on his sunglass-goggles, fusing them over his eye sockets like suction cups on glass.

The Magic-Eater easily kicked through the stalagmites and approached the wizard laughing. "Such a feeble attempt at protecting yourself. You are an inferior wizard, but poor skills won't sour your flavor. You're going to be delicious." The Magic-Eater stretched its flexible jaw ligaments like a serpent preparing to devour a large meal. Its mouth was wide enough to inhale the wizard.

John Doe lifted his head from the dirt and gripped his sunglass-goggles. He pulled them off and fell on his back. As his vision adjusted, John Doe sat up. He could see inside the Magic-Eater's lengthened mouth. *The Grim Reaper is here. He hangs from the Magic-Eater's uvula, reaching for me with his cold and bony hand. I want to run, but my legs feel like gelatin!* He swallowed hard and put on his sunglass-goggles, covering the lenses with his trembling hands as a whimper escaped his lips.

The Magic-Eater's beak was mere inches from engulfing him.

John Doe screamed.

"Hey! Over here!" Corin yelled, charging at the Magic-Eater from behind. He fired his pistol, and the laser blasted the Magic-Eater's back.

The Magic-Eater's eyes widened, and it howled in pain.

John Doe uncovered his eyes, noticed the Magic-Eater distracted, and jumped to his feet. He hid behind a tree.

"What the hell was that? Something bit me!" the Magic-Eater shrieked before collapsing.

"Come this way!" Corin yelled to the wizard as he blasted the Magic-Eater a second time.

The Magic-Eater howled again.

John Doe nervously left the security of his new hiding place and pumped his legs frantically to Corin's side.

"I must escape!" the Magic-Eater howled as it stood and looked at Corin with fury.

"Hey! Get lost, you bully!" Rowan yelled, flying out to them.

The Magic-Eater realized it was outnumbered and growled. It grinned evilly as its body faded away until it completely vanished.

"Where did it go?" Corin asked.

Rowan shrugged her shoulders. "I have never seen one just vanish that way before."

Corin apprehensively returned his pistol to its holster.

"Oh, thank goodness! Thank you so much, stranger. My name is John Doe. You saved my life!" John Doe shouted happily, grabbed Corin's hand from the holster, and shook it aggressively.

Corin's upper body jerked, and his helmet slipped over his eyes. He lifted his helmet and firmly held it as John Doe continued his tremor. Corin yanked to free himself from John Doe's grip.

"John Doe?" asked Rowan. "Um, you *are* aware that your name means—"

"Oh yeah, I know," John Doe said, not letting Corin have his hand back, continuing to wobble the spaceman. "But it's a good name I will never forget. I sometimes have memory problems, but don't we all? Who are you two? I must know the names of my rescuers."

"I am Rowan Fae, the eldest daughter of the Woodland Faerie King."

"My . . . name . . . is . . ." Corin finally pried his hand back. "Corin Degodi. I'm a Task Force Space Ranger."

"Wonderful to meet you, Rowan and Corin. I would have been eaten if not for you."

"John Doe, did you provoke that thing?" Corin asked, rubbing his wrist.

"Indeed not," John Doe answered. "It was on our plane and destroyed the controls. He is an obvious stowaway sent by the Restrain Corporation."

"Restrain Corporation? Rowan, you mentioned them. What kind of corporation is that?" asked Corin. "Why do they create monsters? What is their purpose?"

"The people who run the corporation are trying to own this region. If they manage to, there will be no stopping them from ruling over the other areas of this land. They hate magic and seek power. Some say they are direct descendants of the humans who previously abolished witches. They fear Antiquities, like myself and John Doe. They create Magic-Eaters out of fear."

"They're jealous of us," John Doe said, adjusting his hood and scarf.

"Wow! I'm certainly far from home." Corin gently exhaled. "Sir, you were a crewman on the plane that crashed?"

"Yes, I was," John Doe said, folding his arms across his chest. "It's a good thing that my magic made the plane glide. We managed to abandon ship before it—"

"We? Is there someone else in the forest?" asked Corin, startled.

"Yes, my partner. We're mercenaries for the Eastern Regiment. We are to report to the town of Kenny to protect the citizens from the Restrain Corporation. Their mysterious leader is staging forces to gain control of cities supporting the Antiquities. The mayor of Kenny fears his town is on their list."

"That is very interesting, John," Corin said.

"John Doe. Call me John Doe."

"Um . . . John Doe. I am confused. You used magic to make the plane glide, but how did you survive the crash?"

"Him," John Doe said, pointing through the forest.

Corin and Rowan looked and saw a human figure standing perfectly still. They approached cautiously and were horrified to see a person had been turned into an ice statue.

"Whoa!" Rowan cried. Fear gripped her. She slowly moved behind Corin. "What happened? Is he . . . dead?"

"Who is he?" Corin asked with wide eyes. *I'm astonished by how different the people of this world are compared to the individuals I know on the space station. I have never seen such a tall man with long lavender hair, olive skin, and massive muscles before!*

"That's Troll. He's a warrior. I accidentally zapped him with my freezing spell just before you showed up. I have really shitty aim! Anyway, he saved me when the plane exploded. He just scooped me up and jumped, and we landed over here." John Doe pointed to large footprints in the soil.

"He looks so strong," said Corin, admiring the large red amulet on Troll's chest plate. "His armor is most impressive."

John Doe glanced at Corin's attire, from helmet to boots.

"Is there a problem?" asked Corin, stepping away from the observing wizard.

"Why are you in night clothes?" John Doe asked.

"Oh, not this again." Corin sighed. "This is a uniform."

"It sort of looks like my onesie," John Doe said.

Rowan approached the statue cautiously. She stared at Troll's face. *I didn't know there was a Native American still on Earth. He's very handsome.* Rowan turned around, giving John Doe a concerned look. "He's not dead, is he? Is there any way to free him?"

John Doe didn't get to answer her because Corin suddenly screamed in pain as his helmet flew off his head. Corin's neck rammed into John Doe's face, and both men collapsed violently.

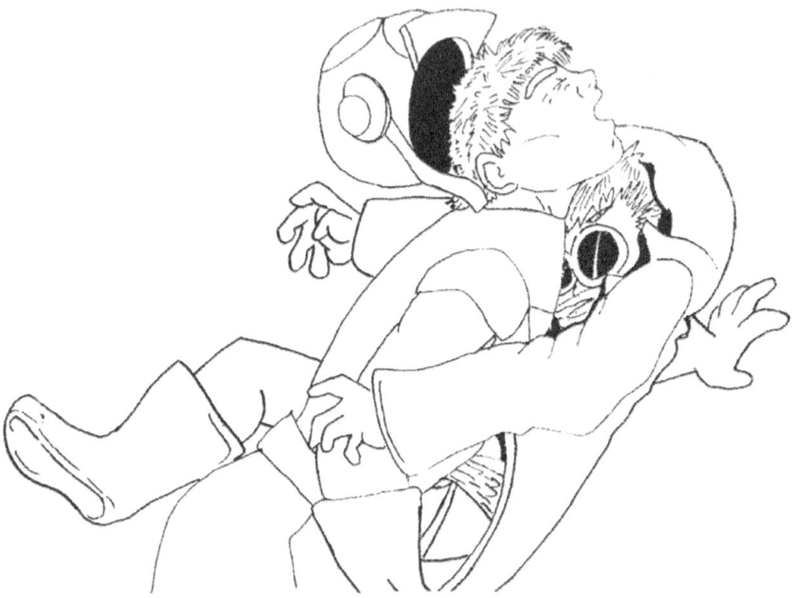

"The Magic-Eater is back!" John Doe shouted.

Rowan screamed and fearfully grabbed onto the frozen statue.

"I will kill you!" the Magic-Eater announced, reappearing over Corin. "How does it feel being kicked in the back of your neck? You deserve that after hurting me!"

Lying on his stomach, Corin was unable to respond. The pain in his neck had immobilized him.

John Doe swallowed hard and crawled away as the Magic-Eater focused on Corin.

"Where do you think you're going?" the Magic-Eater roared at John Doe.

John Doe got to his feet, running to a clearing at the forest's edge.

Corin managed to pull the pistol out of its holster, but the Magic-Eater noticed. It violently kicked Corin's side. Corin whimpered in pain and dropped his laser pistol. He feared his lung might have collapsed. Corin was desperate for oxygen and tried to breathe. Air could not enter his lungs. He reached for his pistol, but the Magic-Eater kicked it away.

"First, I will eat the wizard," the Magic-Eater told Corin. It looked at Rowan, who was still holding onto the ice statue. "You're next, my dear. You will make a wonderful dessert." The Magic-Eater laughed evilly. Returning its attention to John Doe, the Magic-Eater darted toward the clearing, eager to catch its prey.

Rowan pressed her forehead against the frozen warrior's chest. *What can I do to help stop that bully?* She closed her eyes and heard fluttering thumps. Her ears twitched. Opening her eyes, Rowan pulled her head away and placed her hands on the warrior's immense chest. Rowan gasped when she noticed the round, red amulet. She looked into the frozen warrior's eyes. "I can hear your heartbeat!"

Corin finally managed to inhale fresh air into his lungs. He coughed uncontrollably. *What a relief,* he thought, crawling to his pistol.

"Corin!" Rowan yelled to her hacking friend. "The warrior's alive! What should I do?"

"Stand back! Let's melt that ice, shall we?" Corin bellowed, aiming directly at Troll's heart.

THREE

Corin fired.

"Are you crazy?" Rowan shrieked, diving to the ground.

The laser blasted the ice barrier, melting it instantly before it struck the amulet on the warrior's chest.

My heart . . . feels like . . . it's burning. My heart is on fire! Troll's blue eyes grew wide, and he screamed, feeling the blazing heat.

Hearing Troll's scream, Corin withdrew his finger from the trigger and ceased firing.

Troll tightened his powerful arms, causing the ice to crack. He flexed his chest, and his icy prison shattered. Troll protectively put his hands on the amulet in the center of his chest. Steam rose through his fingers. He sighed with relief as the amulet cooled. He relaxed his shoulders and rotated his neck.

"Wow!" Rowan announced, captivated by his good looks.

"Impressive," Corin said as he retrieved his helmet and buckled it securely on his head. "Are you all right?" he asked Rowan.

Rowan was speechless but nodded as she stared at the purple-haired warrior.

Corin's mouth dropped open when he saw Troll up close, and he stepped back. *Whoa! He's the strongest-looking man I've ever seen!*

Troll shut his eyes, drew deep breaths, and exhaled sharply. He raised his nose, sniffing the air. "I smell the Magic-Eater's scent on the wind."

Corin and Rowan continued to stare at him.

Troll could feel their eyes on him. He opened his eyes and faced them. Troll grinned, giving them a friendly nod, and then looked to the clearing at the forest's edge.

John Doe's panicked cries erupted from the same direction.

Troll flexed his muscles again and sprinted to the clearing.

Rowan and Corin ran after him.

There wasn't any cover for John Doe. He tried to cast his ice spell but became tongue-twisted.

The Magic-Eater scratched John Doe's leg with its sharp claws.

The young wizard yelped and fell on his side. John Doe clutched his injured leg, trembling with fear.

The Magic-Eater licked its lips. "And now, I dine!"

Troll saw the Magic-Eater looming over his cowering companion. He reached over his shoulder and removed his large battle axe from its sheath. He gripped the axe's handle before stepping forward, aiming, and then, with great force, threw it.

The Magic-Eater stretched open its mouth again, wide enough for John Doe's head to fit inside.

John Doe squealed, covering his sunglass-goggles.

Just as the Magic-Eater lunged, the large axe's blade slammed into the ground. The Magic-Eater's face smashed violently into the side of the axe. It yelled in pain, kneeling and grabbing its face.

Corin and Rowan gasped simultaneously.

Rowan covered her mouth to hold back her laughter.

"What an amazing throw!" Corin cheered.

Troll smiled and marched to the Magic-Eater.

Corin and Rowan followed behind him cautiously.

John Doe uncovered his sunglass-goggles and saw the giant blade between him and the Magic-Eater. *The axe . . . if it had been any closer*—John Doe gulped and fainted.

The Magic-Eater patted its injured nose and wiped away tears in its eyes. It looked up, swallowing loudly.

Troll loomed with a menacing look. He pulled his gleaming razor-edged axe out of the ground and aimed it at the Magic-Eater's pulsing nose. "I missed on purpose, but my next slash will end you."

I am no match for the human warrior! "Please don't kill me!" the Magic-Eater begged, letting out a pathetic whimper as it bowed. "I'll leave your friends alone! I promise!"

Troll crouched. "Get out of here," he said in a deep, scary voice.

The Magic-Eater screamed in terror, but Troll punched it in the face before it could flee. The powerful strike sent the Magic-Eater cartwheeling through the air.

Corin and Rowan cringed as the Magic-Eater's body slammed into a tree with a sickening smash.

Troll returned his axe to its sheath, picked up a small stick, and walked over to John Doe.

The young wizard was snoring.

Troll rolled his eyes and gently poked John Doe's side with the stick.

John Doe groaned and scratched the spot where he was poked.

"Get up," Troll told him, throwing the stick away.

"Okay," John Doe said, hopping to his feet. "Thank you for saving me again."

Rowan and Corin slowly approached them.

"I guess we should introduce ourselves now that it's safe. Hi! It's nice to meet you, Troll. My name is Rowan Fae," said the green faerie with a friendly smile.

Troll smiled back at her.

Rowan's pupils dilated, and she just about swooned with delight.

"I'm Corin Degodi," Corin said, offering Troll his hand.

Troll gently took Corin's hand and shook it.

"Thank *you* for saving me," Troll said gratefully.

John Doe groaned again, stepping on his injured leg.

"The Magic-Eater clawed you, John," Troll said.

"I'll take care of that," John Doe said, clapping his hands. His fingertips glowed like little white flames. He touched his injury, and the wound healed. "That's much better. Thank you for noticing."

"That's amazing!" Corin exclaimed.

"So, what kind of a name is Troll?" asked Rowan, batting her eyes at the young warrior. "Is it a nickname?"

"It's a code name," John Doe answered for Troll, rubbing his hands together after completing his spell. "He's called that because he is so good at killing trolls. He has been fighting trolls since he was a child."

Troll blushed and faced his partner. "John."

"Yes?"

Troll gently flicked John Doe's nose.

The force of the small strike caused John Doe to fall backward. He let out a squeak and struck the ground hard.

Troll chuckled. "That's for turning me into an ice sculpture."

John Doe giggled as he stood up, rubbing dirt from his backside. "Sorry about that," John Doe said, lightly itching the side of his nose.

"It's okay," Troll said.

"It is?" asked John Doe, scratching his head.

"Yes, it is," Troll said, walking to John Doe and patting his shoulder.

"What is?" John Doe asked, briefly lifting his sunglass-goggles. His green eyes were perplexed.

Troll smiled, then sighed hard. He put his arm around John Doe's shoulders and led him back into the forest.

Rowan and Corin followed them.

"What's wrong with him?" asked Rowan.

"This happens sometimes. Remembering isn't John's strong suit. Why do you think they call him John Doe?" Troll explained. "We need to get back to the plane."

"Troll, I hope you don't mind me asking this, but what exactly are you? Are you superhuman?" asked Corin, barely keeping up with Troll's pace. "Did a magic spell make you super strong?"

Troll chuckled heartily. "No, I am not superhuman. No magic spell, either. I'm human, just a little different."

"Why do you have purple hair? It's so pretty . . ." Rowan huffed, trying to keep up with him. "My goodness! You're fast! Are you sprinting?"

"I like purple," Troll said as he stroked his hair. "And no, I am merely walking."

"I'm almost out of breath trying to keep up with you." Rowan exhaled noisily.

Troll made eye contact with her and smiled kindly.

"You have beautiful blue eyes," Rowan whispered, winking at him.

Troll's eyes widened, and he blushed. He gently rubbed the back of his neck as Rowan giggled.

They reached the crash site and observed that the wreckage was still smoldering and the area had filled with thick smoke.

Rowan coughed and stood back as the boys approached the remnants.

"It looks like the cargo bay is all that remains," John Doe said, peering in.

"John, we need to find our map," Troll said, carefully climbing inside.

"I'm not going in there!" said John Doe.

"A map?" asked Corin.

"It's for our mission," John Doe said. "It leads to the town of Kenny."

"You told them about our secret mission?" Troll asked, stumbling through the plane.

"It was a secret?" John Doe asked.

Troll sighed but could not help smiling. He lifted scraps of metal and shuffled through the debris.

"Was there anyone else aboard?" asked Corin.

"Just the robot pilot," said John Doe. "The Magic-Eater destroyed him."

"I'm glad no one else was with us," said Troll as he continued to search. "I don't know if I could've saved more than John and myself."

"Do you see it anywhere?" asked John Doe.

"Here it is," Troll said, climbing out of another large hole. In his hand was a small metal box. He opened the box and removed a folded-up piece of paper and a tiny compass.

"Great!" John Doe said, taking the map and compass from Troll. "Now we can be on our way."

Troll threw the box down and quickly ran to Rowan. He gently pulled her behind him with one hand and grabbed his axe with the other, taking a fighting stance.

Rowan's pulse fluttered when she felt how warm Troll's big hands were. She was impressed that he could be so gentle with her since he was so strong.

"Everyone, get down!" Troll ordered.

"You better listen to him," John Doe told Corin, nose-diving to the floor.

Rowan dropped to her knees and crawled to them.

"Rowan, stay here with John Doe," Corin told his faerie friend. Keeping as low to the ground as possible, Corin cautiously snuck over to Troll. "What is it? What do you see?" he whispered.

"Take a look," Troll said, pointing to the clearing where they had saved John Doe.

Over the hill strode a massive, seven-foot-tall metal man. His metallic body glistened with reflected sunlight. His wide feet sunk into the soft earth where he stepped, and his arms and legs made whirring and hissing sounds with each movement. Slung over his broad shoulders was the limp form of another smaller metal man, who was missing limbs and leaking fluids.

"They look like they've been through a war zone. Troll, what are they?" asked Corin.

"Cyborgs," Troll responded.

"I can't make it, Jack. Just leave me here." The small, damaged cyborg's voice cracked as he coughed up a few loose bolts and smelly green fluids. "Please let me lie down there." He pointed to a patch of beautiful wildflowers.

"Troll," whispered Corin. "I can hear them. I think we're too close. Won't they be able to hear us?"

"Well, they won't if you stop talking," Troll whispered back.

Corin blushed and bit his bottom lip.

"Kenny, you have to hold on. We are so close to your town. You said it yourself; the mechanic there can repair you," Jack spoke with a strong German accent. He gently placed his companion in the soft bed of flowers. "*Sei stark und geben Sie nicht auf.*"

"What?" asked Kenny, breathing heavily.

"Sorry, my German . . . Kenny, I said . . . be strong and don't give up. You are going to be okay," Jack said calmly.

"Thank you for saving me, my friend. If not for you, I never would have gotten to see the fair beauty of our planet one last time. The final days of spring truly are beautiful. May you always enjoy days such as this. Continue to be strong and fearless, Jack." The small cyborg's brain suddenly began to malfunction. "Goodbye, my friend."

"No, Kenny, it's only an error—" Jack dropped to his knees and held his friend's hand tightly. "You're my best friend."

"You . . . are . . . my friend," Kenny said as the yellow light of life in his eyes turned gray and his brain and body shut down.

"Kenny?" Jack lowered his head and gave his friend a moment of silence. "*Auf Wiedersehen.*" He stood, gently cradled his friend's motionless body, and walked toward the forest.

Troll's heart ached for this metal man and his fallen comrade, but he remained stock-still.

"The poor guy," Corin said, choking back tears.

"Most cyborgs are known to be ruthless killers, but this one seems different."

"John Doe said you were going to the town of Kenny. Do you think that the dead cyborg was the founder? The big one said they were close to *his* town. Should we say something to him?" asked Corin.

"I don't know. Kenny Town isn't far from here."

"I think we should try making friends with him. I'm fascinated to see how a cyborg functions," Corin said with sudden excitement, ready to enter the clearing.

Troll quickly blocked his path.

"What's wrong?" Corin asked.

"Be careful. You can't be so naïve."

"I—I'm only curious if we can help him," said Corin.

"That is noble, but please be cautious. You're not from this world, and I don't want others to take advantage of your trusting spirit. I will go with you. Some cyborgs cannot be trusted," Troll advised, tightening his grip on the axe. "I'll go first. Stay behind me."

"Where are you going?" asked John Doe, noticing Troll's action.

"You two wait here. We're going to check out that distressed cyborg. If we need you, we'll call," Corin said.

They carefully walked into the clearing.

Rowan fluffed her hair and sat comfortably, turning her attention to the wizard. "So, John Doe, you are a wizard?"

"I am, indeed. I am an Antiquity, just as you are," John Doe said, stuffing the map and compass into his pocket.

"If you don't mind me asking, what are you wearing?"

"Do you like my outfit? I came up with this look myself. Troll helped . . . a little. I know it's not your typical wizard's attire, but my unique style suits my personality."

"Suits your absurdity if you ask me," Rowan muttered under her breath.

"What?"

"That's great! So, do you like plants and animals?"

"I love forest fires and barbecues!" John Doe said happily.

"Well," Rowan said, her nose in the air. "I don't like you."

Jack stared at the ground. He was uncomfortable being alone with his grief. His body felt heavy. Jack's mind wandered through the memories of when he first met Kenny: historical stories, witty jokes, and inspiring words of freedom. *Nothing matters now. I could take apart my metal body piece by piece, remove all my weapons, gears, plates, and wires, and give up.* Rustling in the forest interrupted Jack's pondering. *Someone is here.*

Startled, Jack pressed a button on his left wrist. His hand transformed into a small energy gun. Keeping Kenny's body close, he turned around and saw Troll. Jack aimed at the red amulet on Troll's chest.

Troll's body tensed, but the towering cyborg didn't intimidate him.

"Excuse us, sir," Corin said, poking his head out from behind Troll. He gulped when he saw how massively tall Jack was. Corin raised his hands and cautiously slinked past the warrior. "We mean no harm. We overheard you speaking. We're sorry about the loss of your friend. Do you need help?"

Jack's eye compartment stared at them blankly. "That is very nice of you, but I do not know you. Are you friend or foe?"

Troll held the tension in his shoulders as he lowered his axe. "Friends."

Jack lowered his energy gun.

Troll let out a long sigh of relief.

Jack tapped the button on his wrist again, and his hand returned. "I don't know where I am. Forgive my edginess. I am not hostile, but I'm not used to kindness. Perhaps you can help me? I was following Kenny's directions to his hometown. Without his guidance, I'll be lost in the forest. I'd like to take his body home," Jack explained in his thick German accent. He did his best to sound gentle and trustworthy. *I'd better make sure they're not hiding anything.* Jack switched on the sensors in his temple and activated his virtual head-up display to scan them. He scanned Corin first.

"Well, my name is Corin Degodi. I am a space ranger, and I'm not from around here either," said Corin, slowly approaching the cyborg.

Jack completed his scan. The human was not a threat. Next, he scanned Corin's laser pistol. It was a fascinating hand-held gun made of iron, nickel, and unearthly materials with an unknown power source.

Corin smiled, offering the cyborg his hand.

"I am Jack Geyerwulf," Jack said, tenderly laying the corpse of his companion down in a small patch of grass beside a molehill. He accepted Corin's hand and shook it gently. "Tell me, friend Corin, why are you wearing pajamas?"

Corin sighed hard. "I'm not wearing pajamas." Corin could not help but smile as he explained again that he was wearing a uniform. *I might want to consider getting a new outfit to stop any more of these irritating conversations.*

Jack observed Corin's uniform. "I mean, it looks like something a person would wear to sleep comfortably in . . . I hope I did not offend you."

"No, it's okay."

Jack's sensors next scanned Troll. As his robotic eyes swept over the warrior, they picked up an unusual auric energy field emitting from Troll's broad chest, causing high fluctuations in his metabolic rate. The man was human, but the readings showed low-grade copper ore and malachite traces in his chest. Jack had never seen anything like it before. His scanner showed that Troll had multiple grenades in the canvas pouch attached to his belt. Next, he scanned Troll's axe. It was a standard battle axe. *I wonder . . . how strong is he?* Jack thought, completing his scan of Troll.

"My name is Troll. I am a warrior," Troll said, giving Jack a friendly smile. He returned his axe to its sheath but remained where he stood, loosening his uptight shoulders.

"That's an interesting name," Jack said, shutting off his sensors. "You are an intriguing person, Mr. Troll. Strange name, purple hair, and you claim to be a warrior. I believe there is more to you than meets the eye, but I will not press you to share your secrets."

Troll looked at Jack's metal body, lingering on the many dents and scratches. "What happened to you?"

"Kenny and I were slaves forced to work in the mines with other cyborgs."

"There are mines around here?" asked Corin.

"Yes, deep underground," Jack explained. "I was captured and brought there four years ago. Kenny had been there for a long time, possibly fifteen years. Together, we planned our escape. It took us over a year to map out the mines and store all the new data in our memory logs. Six days ago, after stealing weapons and attachments, we put our plan into action and escaped. Kenny was severely damaged when the Dro attacked us. I was lucky to take minimum damage and save him from the slaughter. I promised to take him home, but it was all for nothing. My best friend . . . is d-dead."

"No, you saved your friend," Corin said. "If he spent fifteen years in that hell and you managed to break him out—even for a little while—he got his freedom before his end. That's what is important."

Jack looked at Corin, tilted his head to one side, and nodded. "Wow, I had not considered that." Jack carefully kneeled, becoming unbalanced briefly before becoming stable. He sat beside Kenny's body and cleared his throat. "Forgive me, but do you gentlemen know where the town of Kenny is located?"

"What is your business with Kenny Town?" asked Troll.

"The town is named after my fallen comrade. I assume Kenny was a very popular cyborg long ago. He never told me how he came to have a town named after him. I was helping him to return there. I regret he won't be returning the way he had intended."

"Well, Jack, we are also on our way to Kenny Town," Corin informed.

Troll was surprised by Corin's comment. "You wish to venture to the town of Kenny also?"

"Well, yes. I am a stranger to your world and don't want to be alone. Traveling with you makes perfect sense until I discover a way back home."

"That sounds logical," Jack said, standing to his full height.

"Welcome to our group, Jack. Now you won't have to be alone. I'll introduce you to our other friends," Corin said, heading back to where Rowan and John Doe were hiding.

Jack picked up Kenny's body and followed Corin.

Troll watched them head into the forest. He looked at the dirt where Kenny's body had rested and crouched down.

Footprints, large and cat-like.

Troll growled softly in the back of his throat, and his brow became sweaty. Standing, he drew his axe from its sheath. He didn't see anyone, but his nose caught a familiar scent: musk. Troll shivered. *It's unnerving that just a smell has made me this anxious. My heart is pounding.* He gently touched the red amulet.

The musky aroma became lost to the wind.

Troll stared at the footprints again before he returned his axe to his back and trudged into the forest.

Corin and Jack walked to where Rowan and John Doe were hiding in the shrubbery. They could hear them arguing.

"The animals I know personally are my friends, not food!" Rowan yelled.

"I don't know, all animals taste pretty good . . ."

"Technically, you're an animal, John Doe! Do you taste good?"

"I don't know. Do you want to tenderize my meat and find out?"

"You're disgusting!"

Corin cleared his throat.

John Doe and Rowan screamed, embracing each other.

"It's just me, Corin! I didn't mean to startle you, but you can get up now. I have someone to introduce," Corin said.

Rowan forcefully pushed John Doe away and stood up.

Corin gestured to the cyborg behind him. "This is Jack Geyerwulf, and he is also on his way to Kenny Town."

"Isn't that where Troll and I are going?" John Doe pondered, scratching his head.

Rowan gasped at Jack's height and cautiously stood beside Corin.

"Jack, this is Rowan," Corin introduced.

"Nice to meet you," Jack said kindly in his strong German accent.

Rowan smiled bashfully at him.

"And the wizard is John Doe," Corin said.

"*Guten Tag!*" Jack announced.

John Doe awkwardly stood up, waving his hand. "What does that mean? Are you speaking German?"

"*Ja*, sorry about that. It means good day," Jack replied.

"I also want to accompany you and Troll to Kenny Town," Corin told John Doe. "I need to learn more about your world and find a way to return home."

"Four is better than two," John Doe said.

Rowan flapped her wings. "I wish to come along. My forest and animal friends may be in danger, and I must protect them!" She walked up to Jack and smiled sweetly. "Hi, I'm Rowan Fae. You sure are a handsome hunk of metal."

Jack's circuits made a whirring sound of surprise. He cleared his throat and could hardly say, "Thank you, miss."

"Five is better than four," John Doe said with exuberance, reaching his hand to Jack.

Jack took the wizard's hand, shaking it gently.

After their handshake, John Doe took out the map and compass. "We need to be on our way." He fiddled with the map, turning it numerous times.

Troll rejoined the group and looked at Jack, giving the cyborg a friendly smile.

Jack gently rested Kenny's body over his right shoulder and extended his left hand in friendship.

Troll took his hand, and they shook. Troll was not surprised to notice that Jack's strength nearly matched his own.

Let's see how strong you are, Mr. Troll, Jack thought as his sensors ran another scan on Troll's strength. He saved his new analysis to his data core. "You are a powerful man. I do not believe I have ever met another man with your strength. How did you come to be this way?"

"I exercise a lot," Troll said.

Jack could tell Troll was lying, but he honored his privacy. "Well, you seem like a strong man who loves a challenge. Perhaps we can arm wrestle sometime?" Jack asked.

Troll smiled with enthusiasm.

"Well, are we ready to go?" John Doe asked, sounding impatient. "We mercenaries have a job to do. I think we had best be on our way. Does anyone have the current time?"

"There is no such thing as time." Rowan giggled. "What kind of wizard are you? You can't possibly believe in time."

"I believe in being late!" John Doe said, gulping.

Troll looked up through the trees and noted the position of the sun. "It's around eight o'clock," he said, walking over to John Doe and looking at the map. "We are here in Rowan's Forest, and it looks like we'll reach the town in four hours."

"We would've been there by now if that Magic-Eater had not given us trouble." John Doe groaned.

"There's nothing we can do about that now," Troll said. "Besides, if it had not caused our plane to crash, we would never have met our new friends."

"Very true," John Doe said. "I'm glad we have company."

"Um, John Doe, I have a question about your mission—" Corin said.

"You must talk as we walk," John Doe interrupted, covering his face with the map. With his vision obstructed, John Doe walked toward a tree.

Rowan grabbed his trench coat, stopping him from colliding with the tree.

"Please do not touch my valuables," John Doe said. "I know where I'm going."

Rowan sighed hard but kept her grip as Troll approached John Doe.

"John." Troll exhaled.

"Yes?"

"You have the map upside down, and you're being rude."

"Right, I apologize," John Doe said, pulling his cloak away from Rowan. He uncovered his face and showed the map to Jack. "Which way are we going?"

Jack looked at Troll for help.

"Give me the map." Troll sighed.

John Doe gave the map to Troll.

"Corin, what is your question?" Troll asked.

"John Doe told me that the Eastern Regiment assigned you two."

"That is correct."

"He mentioned that you both were to report to the town to protect the citizens from any attacks from the Restrain Corporation. But if they only hate Antiquities, why attack this town?"

"Kenny Town supports Antiquities," explained Troll. "Many live there."

"That's why we're on our way now to protect the people." John Doe rolled up his sleeves and balled up his fists. He began to confidently march toward the direction of the clearing.

Troll sighed and gently grabbed John Doe's trench coat. "This way, John," Troll said, pointing in the opposite direction.

"I knew that." John Doe chuckled, turning around. "Hey, do you guys know why I was given this assignment? It's because I received excellent grades at Supernatural High School. Apparently, someone thought I had good magic skills."

"Don't you?" asked Jack.

"Not really," John Doe admitted. "I know my ice spell, but my specialty is opening portals."

"Portals?" asked Corin.

"Specialty, indeed. Every time John opens a portal, he pulls out multiple creatures ready to eat us," Troll mumbled.

"That is not true," John Doe said sternly. "It's usually just *one* creature, not multiple."

"John Doe, is there any way you would've opened the portal that brought me here?" Corin asked.

"Where did it drop you?" John Doe asked. "How large was it?"

"From the sky, it was a large tornado," Corin said.

"He fell into my net set up for poachers," Rowan explained.

"That was not one of my portals," John Doe said. "I only open them from the ground; mine are not very big."

"Don't worry, Corin. We'll find out how you got here, and we'll find a way to send you home," Rowan said, giving him a hug and a gentle kiss on the cheek.

"Thanks," Corin said, blushing. "It looks like we are going to make a great team. Let's go!"

FOUR

The four-hour trek through Rowan's Forest was pleasant. It didn't feel prolonged as she happily educated them about her territory. "My forest is about three million acres and home to over forty different species of common trees, multiple understory shrubs, herbs, and flowers.

"My forest is thick with maple, basswood, yellow buckeye, spruce, and pine trees. I'm so proud of the canopy! It is impressive, undisturbed, and immense. I've taken extra special loving care of my forest, keeping it lush and healthy, as countless animals live here. It feels homey and upbeat, never frightening or gloomy.

"The soil is rich with nutrients. I love planting new seeds and watching my flora friends grow. It pleases me even more when I watch my animal friends *eat* the plants! It's a bit ghastly, but that's nature's way. Knowing my animal friends are fed and healthy makes me a very happy faerie. So, what are your hobbies and interests? Do you have any fun experiences you'd like to share?"

John Doe told them about his time at a Supernatural High School, Jack shared growing up in Germany, and Corin described his job in outer space. Troll was quiet. He smiled and listened to their conversations but was determined to safely lead them to Kenny Town.

"I want to learn more about this world. I have so many questions! What do you call your planet?" asked Corin.

"Our planet is named Earth," Rowan told him.

Corin swallowed hard and stopped dead in his tracks. He feared his heart might stop.

The others noticed his pause and turned to face Corin, bewildered as they gazed upon his shocked expression.

"What's the matter?" asked Rowan.

"This is Earth?" Corin asked, almost breathless.

"Yes," answered Jack. "We're in the Northern States."

"What are the Northern States?" Corin asked.

"Well, this part of the continent used to be called the United States of America, but that was over one hundred and eighty years ago," John Doe answered.

"The Free States is what everyone says now because the United States fell apart after the last World War," Jack explained. "That was a long time ago, when this place was full of cities, pollution, and the magic was all dried up. Since I'm a history buff, let me give you some backstory on our world, Corin. The aftermath of World War III, during the twenty-first century, ended civil societies. The planet Earth herself grew tired of human scientific knowledge and futile attempts at improving the quality of life through technology. Creatures that mankind had labeled as mythical or legendary could sense human beings losing their evolutionary status, so Antiquities decided to return. They began to appear out of the vast forests, cave dwellings, underground prisons, and mountaintops where they had been forced to remain hidden for centuries while humans transformed the world.

"Magic flourished and could be felt coiling around all living things when it had once been nearly extinct. Many people embraced the new magical energy they could feel encircling them. These humans were the descendants of wizards and witches from long ago. Science and technology had controlled the planet for too long, so it was challenging to stop depending on them. After the war, all the technology and industry of the old world were rendered useless. We had to relearn how to build and fix everything. Today, we restore vintage vehicles and power them with clean nuclear energy."

"The airplane Troll and I traveled in was built in the twentieth century," said John Doe. "Although it's rubble now."

"The surviving humans who still believed in their scientific laws built a meritocratic culture where only the smartest and strongest could lead. This led to the rise of the Restrain Corporation. The divergence between magic and science became more extreme. Eventually, the Restrain Corporation set out to destroy all the Antiquities. It is a shame because most Antiquities want to live peacefully with humans," Jack explained.

"Wow! That's a lot of information to take in. My parents were born on Earth and then taken off the planet as young children," stated Corin, exhaling.

"Has your family encountered the Dro?" asked Jack.

"No," Corin said, shaking his head from side to side.

"What on Earth is *the Dro*?" asked John Doe.

"What on *Earth,* indeed," Jack said, his voice a low growl. "They are aliens foreign to Earth. Their kind resembles giant humanoid mollusks with hard-back shells. They are horrifying if you have never encountered one before. They kidnap cyborgs from their homes and force them to work in the mines. Before I became a cyborg, my late wife, Emily, and I were thirty-three years old when the Dro attacked our home. The Dro killed her when she refused to give up my location. They wanted to know where I was to convert me into becoming a trader with them. Emily and I were metal workers. We traded with many towns, but after the aliens invaded, we gave up the business to care for one another. I had one remaining client that I kept in touch with. I was at his establishment the day they attacked, and when I got home, I found Emily dead."

"I'm so sorry for your loss," Troll said mournfully.

"Thank you. I knew involving myself with the Restrain Corporation wasn't wise, but I was *desperate* to avenge her. I sold our house and valuables, then went to their headquarters in Franklin City. The scientists there turned me into the cyborg you see before you. Their officials offered me employment, but I could only focus on revenge and hunting the Dro.

"Oh, *Mein Gott*! I was completely unprepared! My cyborg body was not equipped for battle. I rushed in too quickly and was not adjusted to my new form. My arms and legs were so heavy, and I had no experience in fighting. The Dro outnumbered me. They tortured me for several months. I became unfamiliar with time. My human name and age became a myth. I wanted to give up until Tyrone *purchased* me. He is one of their leaders. He knew I was tough, so he entered me into several arena battles taking place in the cities. I won him millions in gold. I didn't think there was any escape until, one day, I snapped. I attacked Tyrone and his men and destroyed an entire arena. I killed a lot of innocent people. With my spirit broken, I realized I could no longer fight. Tyrone sent me to work in the mines, and that's where I met Kenny four years ago."

"How tragic," Corin said.

"I must apologize," Jack said. "I had no right to fill you all with despair about my past. After all, we only just met."

"It's quite all right," Corin responded. "It's good for us to have knowledge of these aliens in case we encounter them. I've never heard of them, and I was raised on a space station visited by aliens frequently. My parents told me they lived in a mysterious place called Roswell. I was born on the planet Danea in the Andromeda Galaxy."

"Roswell?" asked Jack. "That used to be called New Mexico. It's not a very friendly place. There's a rumor that the Restrain Corporation has an underground base there strictly dedicated to creating monsters and running strange experiments on them. Bigfoot moved to Roswell last year."

"Bigfoot?" asked John Doe. "Why did he move? He doesn't like the Restrain Corporation!"

"He wanted a permanent vacation. He likes warm weather and decided to move there."

"This may be an unusual question," Corin interrupted. "But what is the year?" he asked as sweat trickled down his hairline.

"It is the year 2215," answered John Doe. "Today is June tenth. You're not from another time, are you?"

"What a relief." Corin sighed, wiping away the sweat from his brow. "When the portal took me, it was also the year 2215 on June tenth. I thought I was in another dimension."

"By Thoth, you possibly still could be. We must learn more about how we can get you home."

"Thoth?" asked Corin.

"He's the Egyptian god I pray to," John Doe said.

"Are you familiar with Earth's history of ancient Egyptian gods?" asked Jack.

"I learned a little from my parents," said Corin.

"They ruled for centuries until the Antiquities went into hiding, but around the time Antiquities came back, the gods of Egypt emerged again," said Jack.

"It's the magic in the air," said John Doe. "Did you really have no magic on the station?"

"No magic, just science," Corin stated. "My dad works as a Task Force Commanding Official and is a skilled inventor. My mother is a teacher at the institution where I was raised."

"Interesting," said Jack. "Just like Bigfoot."

"It has nothing to do with Bigfoot," said John Doe.

"He has a bachelor's degree in science education," said Jack.

"Really?" asked John Doe with curiosity.

"*Ja*," said Jack.

"Oh . . ." John Doe fiddled with his scarf. "I don't know if I should believe you."

Rowan felt bored with their conversation and yawned loudly. She stretched her arms above her head and rested her hands behind her neck. "I'm a princess!" Rowan announced over their talking. "My father is King Clash, the Woodland Faerie King of England."

"Oh! I had no idea, Your Highness." Jack bowed to her.

Rowan let out a hearty laugh. "No need for the bowing," she said, waving her hand at Jack. "Just call me Rowan, but if you want to show my royal lineage loyalty, simply respect my forest."

"I think we can do that," Corin said, smiling.

"Now, back to our discussion," said John Doe, putting his arms around Corin and Jack. "Bigfoot enjoys the finer things in life, like lingerie."

"How the hell would you know that?" asked Jack with interest.

"I have sources," said John Doe.

Rowan rolled her eyes at their unusual discussion about Bigfoot. She turned her attention to Troll.

His blue eyes were focused on the map and compass.

"Troll," Rowan sang, drifting over to the young warrior. Her wing gently brushed against his left arm.

Troll inhaled sharply when he felt the gentle flutter tickle his skin. He held back a giggle as his cheeks slightly reddened. He looked at Rowan and smiled.

"You're so quiet. Is everything all right?" Rowan asked.

"Yes," Troll said.

"I thought all Native Americans left this realm," Rowan whispered.

Troll gave her his full attention, a surprised look on his face.

"That's right, Troll," she said. "I know what you are, but fear not; I will not tell anyone if it is a secret. Is that why your hair is lavender?"

Troll grinned shyly at her and then looked down at his boots. "It's not a secret," he said, returning his gaze to her eyes. "I didn't think anyone would notice. I like having my own style."

Rowan's cheeks became rosy as she gently ran her fingers through his long hair. "I like it," she said, locking her hands behind her back.

Troll cleared his throat, noticing their location. "We have arrived."

"Great! I was hoping it wasn't much farther," Rowan said.

"—but Bigfoot does not wear a loincloth," John Doe said.

"I didn't say loincloth," said Jack. "I said a business suit."

"Guys, we've made it," Rowan said, interrupting them.

They looked ahead and saw sunlight shining in a glade. They walked to it, welcoming the sun's warmth. They stopped. The path ended. Before them, the ground dropped several feet into a large, murky moat.

"Yuck," said Rowan, smelling the foul aroma from the stagnant water. "That is disgusting! Why is this in my forest?"

"Look across the moat," Troll said, pointing at a massive wall.

"Whoa, that has to be around twenty-four feet high," said Jack.

"This wall surrounds the entire town," Troll said.

"Where's the front door?" asked John Doe.

"I guess we need to circle the moat until we find a bridge," Troll said, handing the map and compass to John Doe.

John Doe put them into his trench coat pocket. "Which way should we go, Troll?"

Troll looked to the right and noticed a narrow and treacherous path along the muddy ledge. Straw had been put on the dirt path, but it was wet and old. He looked at the trees growing along the glade to see if they could avoid using the dangerous path. The trees had grown incredibly close together, competing for the sunlight. It would take them hours to navigate carefully.

Looking to the left, Troll could not see a safe path around the moat. The tree line was right along the moat's edge, leaving no room to walk. He swallowed hard and knew their only option. "This straw path is very narrow. We go one at a time. Follow me and try to stay close. It is wet and very slippery. Watch your footing and be careful."

John Doe followed close to his partner. Next in line was Jack, then Rowan, and finally Corin.

"Why is this giant wall surrounding the town like a fortress?" asked Rowan.

"It may seem a bit old-fashioned, but I believe it is for protection," Jack said.

"Well, I say they put it here to be annoying. We should convince the mayor to demolish it," John Doe said jokingly. He nervously watched where he stepped. John Doe didn't expect the mud under the straw to be unstable, as his weight caused the soggy soil to give way. It began to pick up speed and turned into a miniature avalanche. "I really don't like this!" John Doe's left foot began to slide toward the path's edge. "Troll, help!" he screamed, thrashing his arms wildly, unable to balance himself.

Troll swiftly turned around and grabbed John Doe's scarf with his left hand.

John Doe gasped as Troll's grip stopped him from sliding into the murky water. He locked both hands around Troll's muscular arm for support. John Doe tried to gain stability by putting pressure on his right foot, but he slipped again. He let go of Troll's arm and fell backward but grabbed his scarf and nearly choked himself. John Doe held on for dear life as he looked down and saw his boots were centimeters away from touching the disgusting water.

As Troll focused on holding onto John Doe, out of the corner of his eye, he saw ripples in the water. Something swam under John Doe's feet. Troll did not want to find out what was in there. *Don't look at the water,* he thought. His boots began to slip. Troll's heart skipped a beat. He tried to stabilize himself and closed his eyes. He inhaled sharply through his nose and breathed out through his mouth. Troll found his balance, opened his eyes, and sighed with relief. "Are you okay?" Troll asked, carefully pulling John Doe on the path.

"I think so. That was close!" John Doe said, digging his hands and knees into the mud and pulling himself up. "I almost had a bath. A *very disgusting* bath."

"Troll, you move so fast," Jack panted, carefully making his way to them. "I wanted to reach for John Doe, but by the time I took a step, you had him. You're very impressive."

"Thanks," Troll said.

"Hankie!" John Doe exclaimed, snapping his fingers. A handkerchief appeared in his right hand. "Thank you for saving me, Troll," he said, wiping the mud from his hands, pants, and boots. "This moat is unnecessary! We can't even walk here. I want to complain! I almost died!" John Doe shouted angrily.

"I don't think you would've died, John," Troll said. "I'm sure this wall and the moat give the townspeople comfort and stability. The path just needs tending to. Come on, let's continue around."

They cautiously walked until they came to a stone bridge. It led to a sally port, secured by a locked steel gate—the entrance to Kenny Town. Behind the gate, seated at a small wooden desk, was a tall man wearing a tuxedo and top hat. On the desk was a record book made of parchment, a quill, and an inkwell.

"Here we go," John Doe said, stepping onto the stone bridge. "Follow me!"

The tall man picked up the feather and twirled it between his middle finger and thumb before he saw them approach the gate.

"Excuse me, sir. We are mercenaries sent to patrol your town," John Doe informed the gentleman.

"Are you expected?" the man asked.

"The mayor should know of our arrival," John Doe said. "I'm John Doe, and this is my partner, Troll. Our commanding leaders at the Eastern Regiment sent us at the mayor's request."

"Very well, John Doe, I am the gatekeeper of Kenny Town. Your party consists of two mercenaries and three guests. For entry, I must write your names in the record book. Let's see, a human, a faerie, and—" His eyes narrowed when he looked at Jack. "—a cyborg? You are an interesting band of travelers."

"These are our friends, Corin, Rowan, and Jack," said John Doe.

The gatekeeper steadily wrote their names with the feather.

Wow! His handwriting is impressive! John Doe thought.

"Usually, metal men are dangerous and forbidden from entering our town unless registered with a trustworthy company," the gatekeeper said, eyeing Jack cautiously. "You do not work for the Eastern Regiment?"

"No, I don't. I am simply traveling with my companions. I assure you that I am different from other cyborgs. I have an honorable deed to fulfill in your town."

"And what would that be?"

"I am returning my friend to his home."

"Out of you five, who among you is originally from here?"

"Technically, there are six of us," said Jack, gently resting Kenny's body in front of the gate. "This is the body of Kenny Turbo; I understand he once lived here. I have brought him home."

The gatekeeper gasped in astonishment. "Impossible. Master Kenny . . . we recently received news of him being on a new adventure. What have you done to him?"

"I don't know who told you that. Kenny was captured and trapped in the Dro's mines for many years. He wanted nothing more but to get home. I tried to rescue him during our escape, but . . . he didn't make it. His final wish was to be buried among his people."

"Master Kenny . . . I must call the mayor. It will only take a moment." The gatekeeper sniffed as he quickly grabbed his communicator and phoned the mayor. "Sir, urgent news from the sally port. Master Kenny's fallen, and his body has been brought by the Eastern Regiment and guests. Yes, sir. Right away!" The gatekeeper put his communicator on the desk and swiftly unlocked the gate. "Please, come in. The mayor will be here soon. I apologize if I was so abrupt before."

"No need to apologize," said Jack as they entered.

"What a beautiful town!" Rowan exclaimed, flying above them and glancing around. "I see many wildflowers growing around a cute blacksmith shop and a dry goods store! They're so pretty! Hey, there's a lovely chestnut oak tree!"

"That tree was planted by Kenny when he founded Kenny Town. He felt the most dominant tree should sit in the town square to represent our home and remind us of our place in the natural order. That's why more than half of our town is surrounded by woodlands. That mighty tree is from one of his favorite varieties," said the gatekeeper.

"Planted? Do you mean transplanted?" asked Rowan.

"No, ma'am. Kenny planted the acorn himself."

"That can't be," Rowan said, puzzled. "That tree is well over three centuries old."

Troll noticed her distress. "Rowan, are you all right?"

Rowan landed and grasped Troll's hands. "Troll, that tree is ancient," she whispered. "The gatekeeper's story doesn't make sense."

A well-dressed, tall, stocky man with curly brown hair and a few silver strands near his temples arrived with two men in pantsuits. Behind them approached two larger men wearing brown service uniforms.

The taller of the two men in uniform had thick blond, spikey hair, gold lace on his cuffs and sleeves, and gold shoulder ornaments. He fluffed his thin, dastardly mustache and tilted his head. He elbowed the other man with no stripes or ornaments on his service uniform and gestured toward Toll and John Doe.

The shorter man with red hair huffed when the elbow struck his ribcage. He glanced at them, rubbed his full mustache that was slightly beyond the corners of his mouth, and smirked.

"Welcome to the town of Kenny, friends. I am Mayor Stanley Caser. Thank you so much for returning our beloved founder, Kenny," said the stocky man with a strong British accent. He smiled and offered his hand to each of them. "We occasionally would hear rumors that he was traveling or on holiday. He left our town over fifteen years ago. Many of us feared Master Kenny had passed on, and apparently, this is what has happened." He ran his fingers over his pronounced widow's peak.

"He was a prisoner in the Dro's mines with me," Jack explained. "He passed this morning. He wanted to come home so badly."

"I had no idea," said Mayor Caser. His forehead wrinkled as he frowned intensely, causing his cheeks to sag. "This is a mournful day. Thank you for bringing him home."

"You're welcome," Jack said. "Kenny was my best friend. He was quite a guy."

"Oh, yes, he was. He's the one who built this town for us to be safe. We owe everything we have to him. He shall have the best burial ceremony we can offer. You have my word," the mayor promised, wiping a small tear from his eye. The mayor held his hand toward the men who had arrived with him. "These are my two councilmen, Derrick Mann and Alexander Feather. This tall fellow is Junior Officer Norman Shell, and this is Private George Craig. These gents are mercenaries sent to us by the Eastern Regiment."

"What?" Troll asked with disbelief.

"But *we* were sent by the Regiment!" said John Doe. "We began our journey no more than two days ago. This is *our* assignment!"

"Yes, you *thought* this was your assignment. Our commanding officers said they'd set up two decoys for us," George said, laughing as he pointed at John Doe and Troll.

"Aren't you eager to learn *why* our commanding officers assigned you a robot instead of a human pilot? It's because they're expendable," Norman said.

"Just like the both of you," George added.

"You two made wonderful distractions. We didn't run into any difficulties on our way here. Did you *really* think you two were qualified to do this job?"

"We're here, aren't we!" Troll declared.

"Wait a minute, I have heard of *you*," Norman said, approaching Troll. "You must be that *rogue* who calls himself 'Troll.'" He slowly circled Troll, studying his stature as the young warrior stood poised. "Purple hair, toned body, and a red ornament on your armor that might as well be a bullseye for a sniper."

Troll grinned. "Well, at least you have heard of me."

Norman chuckled with an insulting sneer. "Why do you dress so strangely? We wear our uniforms with pride. You misfits aren't good enough to wear the regimental insignias? No one in the regiment dresses like this." His hand motioned from Troll's neck to his belt.

"I'm not worried about other people's thoughts," Troll admitted. "How I dress is no one's business but my own."

"Well, you look bizarre."

"I'm sorry, *Mom*. Maybe I'll dress more appropriately to suit your *childish* personality tomorrow."

Norman's face flushed, and he prepared to strike Troll.

"Gentlemen, control yourselves. Please," Mayor Caser said, quickly stepping in between them.

"Just stay out of our way! There's no room for an ignoramus like you on *our* mission!" Norman yelled at Troll.

"You, sir, are not very nice!" Rowan objected.

"Is your *girlfriend* standing up for you?" George laughed.

"How immature," Rowan said. "You two should be ashamed of yourselves!"

"Rowan—" Troll began.

"Troll is a fine warrior who saved our lives. He's not an ignoramus . . ." Rowan looked at Troll with sad eyes. "Why would they call you that?"

"According to records based on where I received my education, I am not a very smart person," Troll said, sighing.

"You do not deserve this."

Troll smiled gratefully. He took Rowan's hand, brought it to his lips, and planted a gentle kiss.

Rowan's cheeks turned a bright shade of red.

The two men laughed wickedly.

"What is that racket? I can barely hear my hammer," said a voice in the blacksmith shop. A bald-headed dwarf blacksmith with a thick white beard wearing a leather apron poked his head out of the shop. He observed their argument.

Corin had heard enough. "You leave Troll alone!" he said sternly. "He's obviously stronger than both of you put together."

"I do not want this argument to be about strength," Troll said, gently moving Rowan aside.

"Indeed," said Norman. "It's about intelligence, and he does not have any. I heard they don't even carry a knife!"

"A knife!" John Doe exclaimed, stomping his boot. "That would've been helpful back on the plane. I bet I could have cut the seat belt off."

"You just wait and see," said Norman, ignoring John Doe's comment. "If you continue to work with Troll, all your plans will fail because he will sabotage them. This warrior rogue has a code of *honor* he's always trying to uphold. Trust me. It gets you into trouble!"

"Sometimes, following your heart is sensible compared to following irrational orders," Troll said. "I have saved lives where men following orders have taken them."

"In the line of duty, sometimes lives must be lost," said George.

"Their lives didn't matter," said Norman. "They were not important—"

"Every life is important!" Troll shouted.

"That's the kind of attitude that will get you killed someday," George told Troll with a serious face. "Mark my words."

"Now, now," said the mayor. His eyebrows were so high on his forehead that they were practically at his hairline. "Chaps, let's not be hasty," Mayor Caser said, raising his hands at chest level while facing George and Norman.

"You're right, Mr. Mayor. He's not worth the trouble," said George. "If he were smarter, we'd be more interested."

"See here, many people do not appear intelligent, but that does not make it right to insult them. Our beloved Kenny was, in fact, daft at times, yet that did not mean we had the right to slander."

"Look, we're not trying to sound like we don't like Troll just because of that. We just do not like him in general. Keep him away from us, and keep that lame wizard away, too!" Norman bellowed.

John Doe pulled his scarf down and stuck his tongue out at the mercenaries.

George slapped his knee and laughed as he tapped Norman's shoulder with the back of his hand and pointed at John Doe.

Norman snickered and rolled his eyes at the young wizard.

John Doe crossed his arms over his chest.

Once the mercenaries stopped their cruel laughter, they cleared their throats, straightened their backs, and adjusted their uniforms.

"We have to present ourselves professionally," said George.

"Absolutely," agreed Norman.

"Mayor, with your permission, we'd like to return to our posts," said George.

"The Restrain Corporation could be at your walls before you know it. We need to set up and shouldn't waste any more time," said Norman.

"Quite so," said the mayor. "Off with you then."

As the mercenaries walked past the blacksmith shop, the dwarf blacksmith watched them. He raised a brow and glanced at the mayor.

"I do apologize for their behavior," said Mayor Caser. "I will do my best to make you comfortable. I wish I could employ you fine young gents, but unfortunately, the town only needs two mercenaries."

"It's all right," Troll said with a long sigh, bowing his head and closing his eyes.

"Is it?" John Doe asked sadly. "But that was our job."

"I know," Troll breathed as he stood tall and opened his eyes. "John, we now understand that our commanding officers were never serious about our performance. Our lives didn't matter to them. They used us as bait in a trap."

"We could have been . . . to be blunt, *I* could have been killed!" John Doe exclaimed. "This is not fair!"

"What do we do now?" Troll asked. "My heart feels heavy."

The dwarf blacksmith removed his leather apron, set it down on his anvil, and walked to the saloon beside his shop.

John Doe scratched at the blond hair sticking out from under his hood. "I don't know. We cannot collect unemployment since that hasn't existed for hundreds of years."

"This is horrible," Corin said.

"Well, luckily, we have been through worse," Troll said lightheartedly.

"It's true," said John Doe. "I met Troll before he was a mercenary. I had left Supernatural High School and already joined the regiment. After a week of training, my commanding officer ordered three other men and me to ambush a convoy of ten enemy Restrain Corporation soldiers."

"What?" Jack gasped. "Why in the world were you to ambush them?"

"The officer in charge was dirty," John Doe explained. "I did not know it until he abandoned us. He was trying to start a war with the men we were to ambush. He did not like them, and he did not like us either. He wanted to dispose of me and the other three men because he considered us *bothersome* after a week of training. We just didn't match his standards. He forced us to attack them, but we were outnumbered. My magic was not strong enough to protect us. I remember crying out to my commanding officer to help us, but he left! I watched the other three men die as the soldiers came for me.

"Troll appeared out of nowhere and saved me. He fought the soldiers, taking out all nine except their commander. Troll announced that the battle was an act of trickery. The Restrain Corporation commander surprisingly believed Troll, possibly because he was not a military man. The Restrain Corporation commander still hunted down my commanding officer. Out of fear, he told him the truth. He said, 'I want those four bothersome men out of my way! If I start a war with the Restrain Corporation, I will impress my higher-ups and earn a higher rank.' The Restrain Corporation commander killed him. The Restrain Corporation does not show mercy. Troll and I were lucky."

"The Eastern Regiment was so impressed with my abilities when I saved John that they offered me a job. That was when we became a team," Troll included.

"Through our time together working for the Eastern Regiment, we realized that we were disliked by many of the other mercenaries. I was the only wizard in the regiment, and Troll had grown up in the forest and did not have the best social skills to communicate with the other men. We honestly felt neglected and were often hazed by the other men. But we stuck together through the harassment and became like brothers. We always hoped that the head officers would see potential in our abilities one day.

"I had a lot to offer, being a wizard and knowing magic spells. If only I had a better grasp of my abilities. I was a good student in magic school, just not the best at getting my spells right. I love opening portals! Something about opening doors to other worlds is so neat and makes me really excited! I just reach in and grab creatures to assist in battles," John Doe said.

"Or try to kill us," Troll muttered under his breath, cleared his throat, and crossed his arms over his chest.

"My techniques are useful, but unfortunately . . . sometimes—"

"Most of the time," coughed Troll.

"It's a total disaster!" John Doe said, grabbing the top of his hood and hiding his face.

"John Doe has had a tough time *controlling* the creatures he has summoned, and they end up causing more problems," Troll said.

"The main point is I was disliked due to my inability to use magic spells well. But you see, I am still a wizard or an Antiquity by other human standards." John Doe uncovered his goggles and played with his hair. "I think Troll was disliked because he disagreed with terms set by our employer. The regiment's rule was the loss of civilian lives was acceptable so long as the mission's objective was achieved. Troll always disobeyed that rule because it went against his personal code. He instead would rescue as many innocent lives as possible, risking his own life in the ordeal. He luckily always made it out alive. He was continuously written up for disobeying orders. Troll, I always thought you were amazing because of that."

Troll blushed and scratched the back of his head. "Thanks, John."

"We were honestly surprised when we were assigned to protect Kenny Town. We hoped our boss had finally seen our potential and given us a private assignment. We knew this day would come and were excited and honored to accept the mission. Troll and I have worked together for two years, and in my mind, we've become an unstoppable force! I always wanted our commanding officers to respect us. Have them think that maybe we were too good. But that was a fantasy. We went against orders and took risks." John Doe sighed and shrugged his shoulders.

"It sounds like someone was just jealous," Rowan said, crossing her arms over her chest.

"Jealous or not, it does not sound like you two can trust them," Jack said, shaking his head back and forth.

"Never again," said John Doe, punching his fist upwards. "I quit!"

"Me too." Troll smiled. "I have wanted to for some time now. We must move on."

"We could start a new job together," John Doe said excitedly. "But what about helping Corin get home?"

"I feel so bad about what has happened," said Corin. "Let me help you find new employment before I go home. It's the least I can do to repay you for being kind to me."

"Perhaps you can get new jobs here in Kenny Town?" Jack suggested.

After hearing their story, Mayor Caser clapped his hands together and smiled. "I can talk to the townspeople about available jobs. I will hold a Town Meeting in half an hour and speak to everyone about Kenny's death. I will have my men prepare Kenny's grave, and we'll have his funeral this evening. I hope you all will attend. Until then, I promise you will receive the best food and hospitality here. I will prepare free and comfortable accommodations at our finest hotel, the Hotel Kenny. When you've finished your meals, come to the Town Hall. I should be done with my meeting. I want to give you a tour of the town."

"Thank you, sir," Corin said.

Mayor Caser turned to his councilman, who had reddish-brown hair, a pale complexion, and a pointed nose. "Alexander, go to the Hotel Kenny to reserve five of their best rooms," ordered Mayor Caser as he faced his other councilman with dark brown hair, thick eyebrows, and slightly crooked ears. "Derrick, please take our guests to the Ken Café for a good meal."

"Mayor Caser, may I please ask where Kenny will be buried?" asked Jack.

"Kenny will be buried like a king under the beautiful chestnut oak tree in the town square."

"The tree!" Rowan exclaimed. "Mr. Mayor, is it true Kenny planted the old oak? I am very familiar with trees, and it looks like it was planted before Kenny's lifetime."

"I assure you, Master Kenny did plant the tree here," said the mayor. "It may look older to you, my dear, because magic energy surrounds it. Kenny said that Antiquities placed a spell on it to bless the town for his generosity and for allowing their kind refuge here."

"Oh, well, that's very nice," said Rowan.

"Kenny was a good man. Please excuse me, but I must return to my office to prepare my speech."

"I'm sure you all would like to have a warm cooked meal," said Derrick as Mayor Caser and Alexander departed. "The Ken Café has the best food. I will speak to the owners personally so that you can enjoy a free meal."

"Thank you," Jack said. "Oh, boy, I have not had a freshly cooked meal in a long time!"

"Didn't they feed you in the mines?" asked Rowan.

"Sure, but let's face it, melted gallium, stoneflies, and rat stew isn't considered good."

Troll's eyes lit up. "Did you say rat stew?"

"Yes, it was horrid!"

"I haven't eaten rodents in a couple of months," Troll said, biting his bottom lip. "Man, that makes me hungry."

"What?" Rowan shrieked.

"That's disgusting," Jack said. "How can you enjoy it?"

"Troll doesn't exactly eat like other people," John Doe said.

"No kidding," Jack said. "What kind of stomach do you have, Troll?"

Troll shrugged his shoulders. "Maybe I have the iron stomach? I thought *you* were the cyborg, Jack." He laughed.

Jack laughed heartily and playfully smacked Troll's shoulder.

Troll gasped when he felt the blow. It didn't hurt, but it did surprise him. *Jack is strong, no doubt about it.*

"Well, to each his own," said Corin, shrugging.

"Sorry I'm late," said a grave caretaker, pushing a metal wheelbarrow. "The mayor called me to pick up Kenny's body. I'll get it prepared for burial."

Derrick nodded and assisted the grave caretaker in lifting the metal corpse into the wheelbarrow.

"What are you doing to Kenny? I thought he was your founder . . . why do you treat him this way? You have nothing but a wheelbarrow to cart him off to the graveyard? I'm appalled!" Jack yelled, carefully lifting his faceplate.

"You ripped off your face!" John Doe screamed.

"This is my *real* face," Jack said, latching his faceplate onto the top of his head. Soot residue from the mine coated his beige skin. His brown eyes glanced at Derrick before his metal finger gently rubbed away some of the debris on his pronounced forehead. Jack's straight nose was quite the schnoz, and a soot-filled dark brown goatee decorated his upper lip and chin.

"It does seem disrespectful," Rowan said.

"We don't have an undertaker available in our town," said the grave caretaker. "Just me and the wheelbarrow. I have a significant job, and I do it well. Now, if you'll excuse me." He attempted to cart away Kenny's remains.

"Wait just a minute!" Jack cried, blocking him. "I want to—say goodbye to Kenny."

"Okay," said the grave caretaker.

"Let's give him a moment," said Derrick to the grave caretaker.

They stepped away.

John Doe tapped Jack's metal body. "Hey, Jack—"

"Yes?"

"Nice goatee," John Doe said, admiring Jack's facial hair.

"Thanks," Jack said. "I try to keep it nice. Forgive the soot on my face. I need to wash."

"You're bald!" John Doe yelped, noticing the top of Jack's head. "So, do you have other human parts in there?"

"What? Oh, my body? *Ja*, my human head, brain, organs, and spine. I may have a few ribs in there somewhere as well."

Troll elbowed John Doe. "Don't be disrespectful."

"I don't mean any disrespect," John Doe said, chuckling. "I am just used to hair."

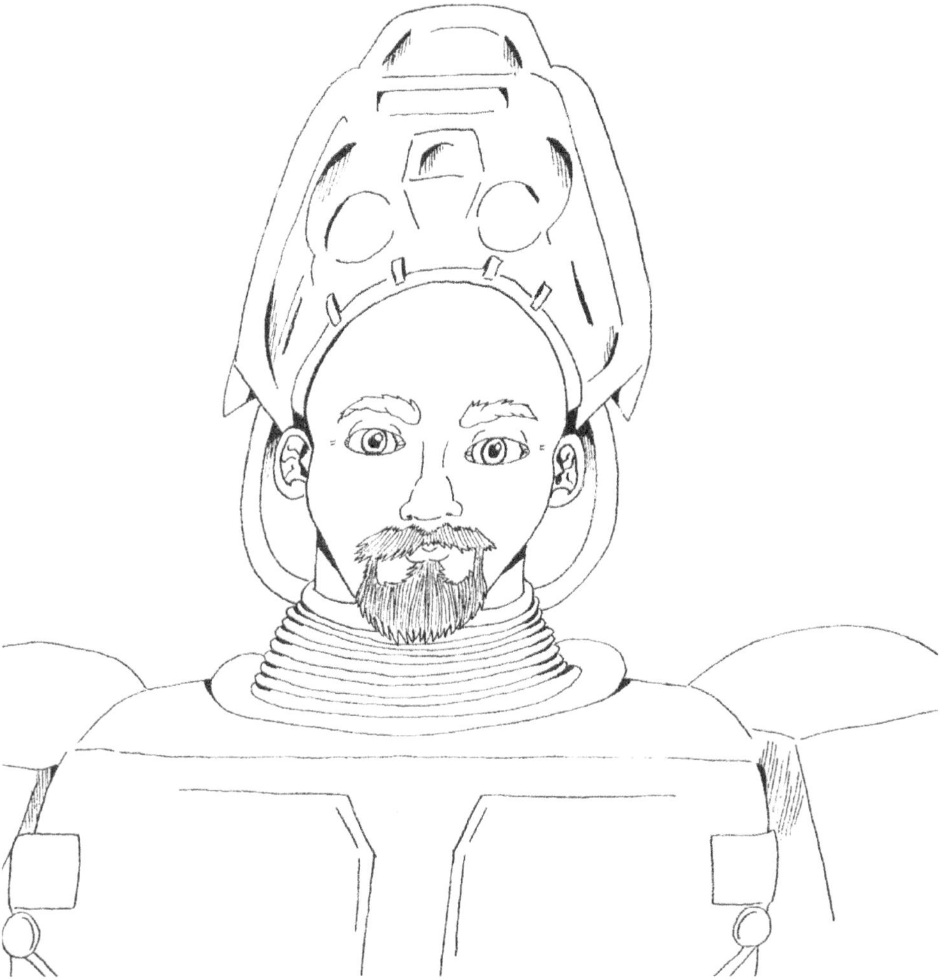

"Oh, I cannot grow hair on my scalp anymore. I thought I would look dignified with a beard and mustache," Jack admitted.

"It looks good, Jack," said John Doe. "But why did you only now reveal your face to us?"

"To avoid moments like this," Jack said, laughing. He patted John Doe's back as gently as he could.

John Doe grunted, collapsing to the ground. A tiny moan escaped his lips.

"Now, all joking aside," Jack said, "I'd like to look upon Kenny with my true eyes and say a few words before he is taken to be buried."

Troll walked over to John Doe and helped him to his feet. "John, you deserved that," Troll told him.

"I know it." John Doe nodded.

"Come on, give Jack a few minutes."

"Okay."

Jack gazed at his fallen friend with his human eyes. "Oh, Kenny. You're finally home, just like you wanted." Tears formed in his eyes. He quickly shut his faceplate. "I am a cyborg and must not show any weakness, not even tears for you, my friend. I shall speak at your funeral and tell everyone about your bravery. I promise." Jack nodded at the grave caretaker. "I am finished. Thank you."

The grave caretaker nodded at Jack and then at Derrick before wheeling Kenny's corpse to the town morgue.

"Follow me, everyone," said Derrick. "Let's get you something to eat."

"I can't wait to get a tour of this town," said Corin.

"Lunch first. You all need nourishment before venturing through the town," said Derrick as they followed him. They walked past the blacksmith shop and saloon.

Looking out an open window in the saloon was a tall man wearing a white cowboy hat, maroon western-styled button-up shirt, and black jeans. He puffed on a cigar as the dwarf blacksmith stood next to him. The cowboy stared at the newcomers, humming a melody.

THE UNIQUE CAMPAIGN

FIVE

They followed Derrick to the Ken Café. It was a rectangular brick building with a tan, rustic door and mounted shutters around big, square windows. Four white bistro tables and chairs sat in front of the café under red umbrellas, but no customers ate outside. Upon entry, the inside of the café looked more extensive than the outside had led them to believe. It smelled like coffee, freshly baked bread, and vinegary salad dressing. The walls were a cool slate color with a hardwood floor. The foam-padded upholstery in the bench seating was red. The plentiful natural sunlight that came in through the windows gave the place a very welcoming atmosphere. Derrick informed the owner that their meals would be on the house. At first, the owner argued, but once the councilman explained about Kenny, the owner agreed. The café wasn't busy. Two waitresses served six tables as three customers sat at the bar counter eating cakes and drinking coffee. Derrick led the travelers to a large, fancy booth usually reserved for the mayor's dinner parties. The table was slightly larger than the others, and the seats were made of fabric instead of vinyl.

Jack went to the washroom to clean his face.

"Wow! A large table made of marble, with soft, pillowy feather-stuffed seats! I feel so important!" John Doe exclaimed.

"Don't forget to please stop by the mayor's office when you've finished your meals. It's located in the Kenny Town Hall. When you leave, turn right and follow the road, then make another right, and you'll come to an intersection. You'll turn left because if you go right, it'll just loop you around to a different road that connects back to the street you were currently on."

"What kind of roads are these?" asked Jack when he returned from the washroom and heard the puzzling instructions.

"Keep going straight until you can turn right," Derrick continued. "Then you'll come to the Town Hall."

"I'm lost," said John Doe.

"Sir, please give me the directions, and I'll download them. This is a confusing place," said Jack.

"Of course," Derrick said as he repeated the bearings to Jack.

"I'm glad Jack's with us," John Doe said aloud.

"Thank you," said Jack to Derrick. "The upload is complete."

"All the arrangements for your hotel rooms will be ready before nightfall," Derrick assured.

"Thank you," Corin said.

"Enjoy," Derrick said, nodding, then left.

"Can I have the window seat?" Rowan asked Corin. "You can sit next to me."

"Sure," Corin said, letting Rowan sit in the booth first. He sat beside her.

Jack sat across from Rowan. Troll sat down across from Corin, and John Doe sat on the end next to Troll.

A beautiful blonde waitress walked over in a pink uniform. Her hair was in a ponytail, and she had rosy red cheeks and bright green eyes. She smiled, greeting their party.

John Doe gawked at her.

She handed John Doe a menu, but he passed it to Troll, who took it willingly as the waitress passed out more.

John Doe lifted his sunglass-goggles and smiled at her as his green eyes studied her curvy body.

She smiled back.

John Doe stretched the elastic tight until it slipped in his fingers and slapped forcefully into the middle of his face. "Ow!" he yelped, rubbing his nose and between his eyes. He readjusted his sunglass-goggles and elbowed Troll's side. "Hey, check her out," John Doe whispered.

"Not interested," Troll said, reading the menu.

"Come on, big guy, you could have her for one hour. I won't be greedy."

Troll ignored him.

"My name is Kat, and I will be your waitress for this evening. Can I get you anything to drink?" the waitress asked.

"Oh, Kat," John Doe said, leaning toward her. "What a beautiful name. Meow! Let me feel how soft your pretty fur is." He extended his hand to pet her like a house cat.

"Oh, my!" she cried.

Troll set the menu down and effortlessly put John Doe in a headlock. "I am so sorry, ma'am."

John Doe flailed his arms about, trying to scream from under Troll's muscles.

"He's just a little overexcited," Troll said. "Could you get us two glasses of water, please?"

"Certainly," Kat said, blushing at Troll. "What would the rest of you like?"

"Herbal tea for me, please," Rowan said.

"Ginger soda, please," Corin said.

"*Mineralwasser* mixed with apple juice!" Jack exclaimed. "Please, tell me you have that. I have not had a delicious *Apfelschorle* to drink in years."

"Oh, you poor dear," Kat said to Jack. "I will get you that sparkling water with apple juice immediately."

"You're a gods-send!" Jack chirped happily.

As Kat left to get their drinks, Troll released John Doe.

"Are you going to behave yourself?" Troll asked him.

"I didn't want water," John Doe said with disappointment as he adjusted his trench coat.

"Yes, you did," Troll said, glancing at the menu again.

"Can't argue with that," John Doe said, hastily snatching the menu from Troll and holding it close to his face to read.

Troll was perplexed, staring at his empty hands. He blinked, rested his elbows on the table, and looked at John Doe. He sighed and could not help but smile at his ridiculous friend.

Jack, Rowan, and John Doe began discussing the menu as Corin stared at Troll. He was very curious about the young purple-haired warrior. "Troll, what kind of job do you want? I think the mayor can find something worth your time."

Troll turned to Corin. "Honestly, I don't want to reside here and am unsure about another job. I *am* a rogue warrior when you think about it. I mean, I've been addressed by that title for so long. I think I'm finally starting to believe it. Before I met John, I was alone, saving people in the forest. I was known as a warrior and nothing more, and I really liked being a warrior. I never thought of myself as a rogue."

"I don't think you're a rogue," Corin said.

"Thank you," Troll said, placing his hands in his lap. He briefly glanced at Rowan. Her smile was mesmerizing. She was laughing about something Jack had said. Troll grinned.

Rowan noticed Troll's face. *Is he looking at me?* She made eye contact with him.

Troll's heart trembled. He wanted to speak to her, but something out the window caught his attention.

Is he all right? Rowan thought.

"Hey, Rowan," said Jack, regaining her focus.

"Oh, sorry," she said, joining their conversation again.

Troll did not say a word. He continued to stare out the window. His eyes filled with hurt, and his expression became troubled. He clenched his hands tightly into fists and shut his eyes.

Corin looked out the window, hoping to glimpse at what had Troll's interest. He noticed a father and son playing catch across the street in a quaint little park, townsfolk walking the streets, and a merchant selling fresh farm eggs in a medium-sized basket. Nothing appeared out of the ordinary from what he understood of terrestrial life.

Troll inhaled deeply through his nose and then exhaled gently through his lips.

Corin listened to the way Troll breathed.

Troll opened his eyes and glanced at the others.

They continued to talk and laugh.

Troll humbly smiled.

"Troll, are you okay?" Corin asked, concerned.

Troll's tension melted away, and he ran his fingers through his long hair. "Yes, I am all right. I will be right back. John, let me out, please."

"Oh, sure thing," John Doe said, standing up.

Jack and Rowan stopped talking and watched Troll get out of the booth.

"Where are you going?" asked Rowan.

"Are you going to get Kat's communicator number?" John Doe asked.

"No." Troll laughed. "I'm just going to step outside to think for a moment. I need some fresh air."

"Okay," John Doe said, sitting beside Jack.

"Don't take too long," Corin said. "We're going to order when Kat comes back."

"I will place my order before I head out. I already know what I would like," Troll said, going to the counter where the owner stood.

They watched Troll intently as he spoke to the owner, who looked surprised, scratched his head, and nodded before he entered the kitchen as Troll exited the café.

"SOMEONE ORDERED WHAT?" the head chef exclaimed so loudly from the kitchen that everyone heard him.

Corin, Rowan, and Jack looked at John Doe for answers.

"I did mention that Troll has an exotic food diet? Yes? No?" asked John Doe with a chuckle, shrugging his shoulders.

Corin sighed, peering out the window. *I want to tell them about my conversation with Troll, but I should respect his privacy.*

Kat returned with their drinks.

Corin glanced at Kat. "I'm ready to order."

"Okay, what'll it be?" Kat asked.

They told Kat their orders and the pretty waitress wrote each one down. After gathering the menus, Kat returned to the kitchen.

Corin thought about what the mercenaries had said to Troll and then thought about his job. *I doubt my coworkers will care that I'm missing, but my parents will be worried when they find out I am no longer on the station. They call every weekend. What will my commander tell them?* Corin put his elbows on the table and rested his chin in his hands. He glanced at his new friends. *No one back home would believe I'm on planet Earth, sitting in a café with a faerie, a wizard, and a cyborg. I didn't know this world existed. I didn't know magic was real. I am a stranger to their world, yet they took me in, and we've become friends. I never imagined having such amazing friends. Are they more than friends? Are we becoming a family? I really like Earth. It's beautiful and feels homey. The space station had charm, but not like this planet.* Corin blinked. His thoughts were interrupted by John Doe.

"Troll might leave. He does have his other mission . . . I'd hate to lose my partner," John Doe contemplated, pulling his scarf down and carefully sipping his water before covering his mouth with the scarf.

"What *other* mission?" Corin asked.

John Doe removed his hood and scratched his messy, dirty blond hair. "I'm not sure what it is. Troll is very private about his life. I only know that he always seems to be searching for something," John Doe said, putting his hood back on. "Troll has said it's an important mission, but I don't think he trusts anyone to know details. Even me and I've known him for a couple of years."

"Now that I think about it, Troll never talks about himself," Jack said. "John Doe, I know he calls himself 'Troll' because it is a code name, but I'd like to know his real name."

"I don't know his real name," John Doe admitted. "Do you honestly think 'John Doe' is my real name?"

"Your first name is 'John,' right?" asked Jack.

John Doe shook his head. "We all have our secrets," he stated, pulling down his scarf to take another sip of water.

"But you let Troll call you John," said Corin.

"He's like my brother," John Doe said.

"How old are you?" asked Corin.

"Twenty-two," John Doe said. "How about you, Corin? What's your age?"

"Twenty-seven," Corin said with a grin. "We're only five years apart. How about that!"

"What about Troll?" Rowan asked.

"I don't even know how old he is. I know he's younger than I am . . . at least, I think he is." John Doe brought his right index finger to his scarf, resting it on his chin. He snapped his fingers. "Yes, he's a year younger than I am! I'm fairly certain. My birthday is in August. Wait! His birthday was in May! It was last month on the twenty-seventh. He's twenty-four! He's older than me! He's two years older than me."

"Well, when Troll returns, we'll get to know him better," Rowan said.

"That's a great idea, Rowan," said Corin.

Jack stared at Rowan.

"What is it?" she asked him.

"How old are *you*?" Jack asked.

"I'm four thousand, four hundred, and twenty-seven years old," Rowan said.

They stared at her, stunned.

Corin's mouth gaped open, wide enough a fly could've flown inside.

John Doe choked on his scarf.

Rowan blushed. "You know, it's not nice to ask a woman her age," she kindly stated, giving them a cute and innocent look.

Jack cleared his throat. "Well, you look marvelous!"

"I know." Rowan giggled. "I have a great figure!"

Troll breathed fresh air into his lungs. He walked across the street to the park and saw that the father and son had left. The red amulet suddenly felt like a dense weight putting enormous pressure on his chest.

"My heart aches," he said, clutching the amulet. *I'd rip this from me and be normal again if I wasn't afraid. I need more time to focus on my private mission. My failure has become the dull blade constantly applying pressure to my chest. I feel the hopelessness trying to consume me. The betrayal from the regiment has sharpened the blade. It's attempting to pierce my heart! I can't let that happen. I have to stop these negative feelings. It's poison.*

Troll saw a beautiful tree providing shade from the sun. *That looks comfortable. I must meditate and calm myself.* Sitting under the tree, he looked at the Ken Café across the street. Troll relaxed his muscles and closed his eyes. He inhaled deeply and cleared his mind.

AH-WOOO!

Troll gasped and opened his blue eyes quickly. He listened carefully as he stood slowly, holding his breath.

AH-WOOO!

Troll's heart jumped in his chest. He stood perfectly still. *Did anyone else hear that?* He observed the townspeople. No reactions.

I was the only person who heard the howl? How can this be? He counted heartbeats as his long hair blew in the wind, tickling the back of his neck and cheeks. He listened intently. Troll exhaled gently, closed his eyes, and sat down. He crossed his legs and put his hands in his lap. *My imagination is tormented by so much on my mind.*

AH-WOOO!

Troll's eyes shot open, but he remained seated in his lotus position.

A wolf's face suddenly appeared to him. *Is this a vision?* The wolf's left eye was green, and its right eye was blue. Its face overlapped Troll's until their eyes aligned. Troll's eyes changed. His left blue eye blended with the wolf's green eye, becoming bright turquoise. His right eye shimmered, turning an even deeper shade of blue.

Troll blinked, and the wolf vanished. A warm sensation exploded in the center of his chest. Troll gently touched the amulet, and his heart quivered. He lay on the grass and closed his eyes. "What kind of vision was that?"

Troll opened his eyes and looked at the gorgeous blue sky through the slender branches and leaves of the tree. "Such beauty—"

He exhaled slowly and sat up. He rested his back against the tree. *I'm not a rogue, but am I a lone wolf? Is that why I had that vision?* "Is the wolf my strength?" he asked, raising his left hand. He removed the blue gauntlet cuff from his wrist and revealed the green aventurine bracelet. He touched the small stones, shut his eyes again, and meditated.

He focused on the park's sounds: birds chirping, the wind rustling through the leaves, and the melody of a bee's fluttering wings. Troll finally felt at peace and relaxed.

His serenity was interrupted by a low growl in the distance.

Troll opened his eyes and locked the gauntlet cuff back in place. He sniffed the air and panted in alarm as he detected the pungent smell of musk. *I'm not alone. Of course, you're not alone, Troll! It is a public place, but I recognize this from when we met Jack. Steady, Troll! Act normal.*

He slowly rose, rested his back against the tree, and pressed his hands against the trunk. It was rough under his palms. His body tensed. *The odor has grown stronger.*

The wind picked up, and the musky aroma mixed with the different fragrances of the city. Troll could not detect which direction the musk came from. As quickly as the wind increased, it died down, and Troll lost the scent entirely.

Sighing with relief, he rested his head against the tree and allowed his arms to dangle at his sides. A shudder raced through his spine as his tension melted away.

"This town is certainly an interesting place for visions and smells. Something is in the air. Antiquities blessed that oak tree in the town square? What other enchantments surround this place? Who *was* Kenny Turbo?" Troll looked over at the café. He saw his companions through the window. They looked like they were having a pleasant conversation. Troll smiled. "I believe I have gotten plenty of air," he told himself and walked back to the Ken Café.

As Troll entered the café, he saw Kat in front of him, carrying a large oval-shaped tray with five large, full plates of food on top of it. She was having difficulty grasping the large tray and lost her balance. Kat inhaled sharply as her body leaned to the left. She was unable to correct her posture and screamed.

"Look out!" Jack cried.

"Oh no, Kat!" John Doe shouted.

Corin and Rowan turned around in alarm.

Troll moved like lightning and caught her with his left hand and the tray with his right. He set the large tray on an unoccupied table and helped Kat regain her stability. "Need a hand?"

"Thank you!" Kat exclaimed, her cheeks turning red. "Forgive my clumsiness. You know, not many folks from these parts are as generous. Your act of kindness confirms you are from out of town."

"It's nothing, ma'am, really," Troll said.

John Doe growled.

"This tray of food is for your table," Kat said.

"Wonderful," Troll said, ready to help her carry the tray.

She touched his shoulder. "Thank you again, but I'm okay now. Please join your friends, and I'll come right over."

"Are you sure?" asked Troll.

Kat winked. "I'm sure."

Troll smiled and went to take his seat with his friends, who stared at him. He sat next to John Doe.

John Doe scowled at Troll and grumbled under his scarf.

Jack heard John Doe's muffled cursing.

Rowan also heard John Doe's foul language, thanks to her ears. She giggled. "I can almost see the steam coming off your head."

"Troll," John Doe said, crossing his arms over his chest.

Troll looked at John Doe with innocent eyes.

"You . . . big lug . . . you're a . . ." John Doe sighed, uncrossing his arms and smacking the table with his left hand. "Hell! I cannot get mad at you, Troll. Just you know this . . . your chivalry is not going to stop me from charming our waitress."

Kat overheard John Doe's comment and rolled her eyes.

"Of course, John," Troll said, smiling.

Kat set the large tray on a stand. "Okay, here is an order of herbs, spices, leafy greens, and turnips."

"That's mine," Rowan sang.

Kat passed her the plate and held up the next one. "Second is an order of ribs with a side order of potatoes and peas."

"Over here," Corin said, accepting his meal.

"Rowan, are you okay with us eating animals?" asked Jack. "I don't know if they might've been living in your forest."

"How nice of you to ask, Jack," Rowan said enthusiastically. "I am quite all right with the circle of life, but I hope I don't know any animals you eat today. I would be sad to lose a personal friend."

"Next, we have a large order of sauerkraut and bratwurst," Kat said.

"*Hier*," Jack said, lifting his faceplate. He licked his lips and rubbed his hands together. "I cannot wait!"

"You poor dear, you must be starving," Kat said, handing Jack his plate.

"You guys should time me! Let's see how long it takes me to eat these bratwursts."

"That sounds like fun!" John Doe said, rolling up his sleeves and glancing at his bare wrist. "Someone stole my watch!"

"Time does not exist," Rowan reminded him.

"Oh yeah," said John Doe. "Where's my food?"

"Broiled salmon steak with baked apples on the side?" asked Kat.

"Yes, that's mine!" John Doe said, taking his plate. He put it on the table and made eye contact with Kat. "Oh, kitty cat, my taste buds crave this delicious meal. Are you also interested in having something scrumptious? I guarantee you've never tasted anything like John Doe before!"

Troll grabbed John Doe in another headlock.

John Doe thrashed his arms, trying to free himself.

"I apologize again for him. John does not have an off-switch."

"That's okay. I've heard worse. Is this your order?" Kat asked Troll, gesturing to the last plate of food. "Tell me you're not eating this."

"Why not?" asked Troll. He felt John Doe's struggle subside and released him.

John Doe inhaled sharply, sucking his scarf into his mouth.

"This is like cat food," Kat said, disgusted. "A well-done rabbit with a side order of roasted crickets and a glass of boiled bees."

"It's a fresh young hare, right?" Troll asked.

"I think so," Kat said. Her cheeks began to match the green of her eyes the longer she stared at the food. "Do you always eat like this?"

"Like what?" Troll asked, taking his plate. "There are plenty of insects in the world, and they're a great source of protein."

"It's an acquired taste, no doubt," Jack said.

Troll nodded in agreement.

"Our chef thought this meal was for an Antiquity, but you're human. Well, enjoy your meals," Kat said, returning to the kitchen nauseated.

"Troll, she found you attractive . . . until she discovered your eating habits," Rowan said.

"I don't see what all the fuss is about." Troll shrugged his shoulders and began to eat.

"Let us strike up a conversation," suggested Rowan. "Troll, you're powerful, fancy the color purple, and have an exotic diet. Is there anything else about yourself you'd care to share?"

"That's a horrible way to begin a dialogue, Rowan," Jack said, groaning.

Intrigued by her sudden curiosity, Troll glanced at Rowan with a forkful of roasted crickets. "Why do you ask?"

Rowan blushed and covered her face.

"Rowan means you don't talk about yourself much, and we'd like to get to know you. We have all shared details about ourselves," said Jack.

Troll was astonished. "You guys somehow got John to talk about his past?"

"Um, not . . . exactly," Jack said.

"I'm John Doe!" John Doe shouted, pulling down his scarf and devouring his apples.

"Yes, we know your name," Jack said, annoyed.

"It's understandable if you don't trust us. After all, we just met," said Corin.

"I trust you, but I'm uncomfortable speaking about such things. Dark shadows haunt my youth." Troll sighed, shutting his eyes. He tried not to think about his past. "I will share one day, but not right now. I hope you can understand."

"We don't want you to feel uncomfortable," Jack said.

"I should not have asked. It's none of my business, after all. I apologize," Rowan said.

"It's okay, Rowan," Troll said, opening his eyes. He smiled at her and began to eat again.

John Doe stopped eating and violently thrust his fork into the salmon fillet. He crossed his arms and pouted.

"What's wrong with you?" asked Rowan.

"Everyone is so interested in Troll! What am I? Don't you want to know more about John Doe?"

"Well, sure," replied Corin.

"Okay, I'm John Doe!" he said, wiggling his fingers.

They stared at him.

He stared back and continued his finger dance.

"Is that it?" asked Rowan, annoyed.

"Is what it?" John Doe asked with a blank stare.

"I could really hurt you right now," Rowan said, eating her herbs.

After they finished their meals, Kat and the owner waited for them at the door.

"How much do we owe?" asked Corin.

"Mayor Caser said your meals are on the house," said the owner. "I hope you enjoyed your stay. Please come back and see us again."

"Can we give Kat a tip?" asked John Doe.

"Oh, no—" Kat began, but John Doe gently took her hand.

"Kat, please accept our tip as a token of putting up with my rash behavior."

"Are you going to give her any coins?" asked Troll.

"Nope," John Doe said, pulling down his scarf and kissing Kat's hand.

"Yuck!" Kat exclaimed, pulling her hand away and wiping it on her uniform.

"Will I be giving her coins then?" asked Corin, sighing.

"You got it," John Doe said, turning out the pockets of his trench coat. They were empty.

"You're a rude man, John Doe," Jack said.

Jack was frustrated as they followed his downloaded directions. "I am curious who designed the town's urban planning," he said, analyzing the streets, logging the map in his virtual head-up display. The structure irritated him. It was below the floodplain and built into rugged terrain. "This town is small but built bizarrely. I have never seen a road layout like this; no street signs exist, and the pavement is too slender for vehicles."

"I haven't even seen a means of transportation," said Corin.

"True. Everyone seems to walk here," said John Doe.

Jack frowned. "I couldn't live here."

After a twenty-minute walk, they found Kenny Town Hall and entered the courtyard. In the center was a medium-sized circular fountain that sprayed water into the air and onto the yellow flowers surrounding it. The ground around the flowerbed and fountain was covered with brown pebbles, and green shrubs grew in a perfect square around the courtyard fencing off the entrance to Town Hall. The tall building was made of red, orange, and white bricks. It resembled a school and church structure, and a small tower was on the roof. It embodied the uniqueness of the town. A lanky reptilian man sat on the stoop. His eyes were bright gold, his skin was green, and his long, thick tail protruded out the back of his slacks.

Corin was flabbergasted.

"Greetings, friends," said the reptilian man, hopping off the stoop. "The mayor is expecting your party."

"Thank you," said Corin, trying his best not to stare. "Are you a lizard?"

"Indeed. I was created to be the mayor's bodyguard. My name is Tialp. Mr. Caser is my third mayor. I really like him. I think he is my favorite mayor."

"Your third mayor?" asked Jack, running a sensor scan on Tialp. "How old are you?"

"I am sixty-five," said Tialp. "My first mayor had my appearance programmed to be a lizard in 2150."

"You're a robot!" exclaimed Jack, finishing his scan.

"Correct! Now, if you please, Mayor Caser is expecting you. Please go on in and make yourselves at home."

"Tialp, how old is Kenny Town? I'm curious because of the unusual layout," Jack stated.

"The town was built over one hundred and seventy years ago on the ruined remains of a pre-war community."

"Thank you, Tialp. I'm used to a grid plan."

"There is a more common grid plan where homes are located. Pardon me, sir, but the mayor is waiting."

"Thank you, Tialp," said Jack.

"You are welcome," Tialp said as he sat back down.

Jack opened and held the door for the others.

To their left was the registration desk made of granite. The representative was not there, but they peered at a hand-drawn map of the entire town on the wall behind the desk before glancing at the rest of the Town Hall interior. It was stunning. In the center of the room was a giant, white spiral staircase. Behind it was an elegant meeting room, a shiny metal elevator, and a luxurious powder room. The lights on the ceiling were bright and warm. The marble tile floor accommodated the mint color of the walls. Antique mirrors were hung on the walls facing each other. The old mirrors were misshaped and had a transparent appearance. They were unnerving and made the ground floor appear like a haunted house of mirrors.

"This room has rigid energy," Troll said.

"I don't like it," said Rowan.

"Gentlemen and lady," Mayor Caser announced, walking down the spiral staircase with his councilmen. "You don't need to worry about dinner. My council has taken care of it. Each of you has a hotel suite for tonight, and your breakfast will be free. Just meet at the dinette on the first floor after you wake up. Your rooms come complete with a basket of fruit and soap. I met with the townspeople and agreed that Kenny's funeral service would start this evening at five o'clock."

"Soap?" asked Troll.

"Yes, they are shaped like swans," said Mayor Caser, smiling. "They were my late wife's idea."

"She had great taste," said Rowan. "I love swans! It's a shame that there are so few remaining. What a graceful and splendid creature."

"Eventually, all species will go extinct. Perhaps with my help!" John Doe exclaimed.

Rowan growled at him.

"John, please be careful of what you say," said Troll.

"Why?" John Doe asked.

"Because our faerie friend is going to maul you," Troll said, pointing at Rowan as her skin turned red with anger. She looked terrifying.

"Is she transforming into a chameleon?" John Doe gulped.

"I think you should apologize," Troll suggested.

"Good idea," John Doe said. "Rowan, I'm sorry . . . that one day all of your animal friends will cease to exist."

Rowan screamed and charged at John Doe.

"John, I'm not saving you this time," Troll said, rushing outside.

"Leaving so soon, sir?" asked Tialp, nearly bumping into Troll.

"Troll, wait for me!" John Doe screamed, running after him.

Rowan burst through the door.

"Not a chance," Troll said, positioning himself behind Tialp. "You are on your own this time, John. You've dug your own grave."

"I don't want to be in a grave!" John Doe shrieked, running for his life as Rowan flew after him.

"But you are living, sir," said Tialp. "The only person in a grave today shall be Master Kenny."

"Kenny might have company if Rowan gets her hands on him," Troll explained.

"Company is nice," Tialp said happily.

"Not this kind," Troll said.

John Doe wanted to cast a spell but was too busy running.

Rowan aggressively flapped her wings to keep up with him. *"Amicae radices funes flunt!"* she shouted, raising her glowing arms.

Tiny, thin grass roots spiraled through the soil and wrapped around John Doe's ankles. He screamed and fell to the ground as the roots wrapped around his legs and torso like an ancient Egyptian mummy.

Mayor Caser, Corin, and Jack ran out of the building to see Rowan sitting beside the bound John Doe. Her red flesh changed back to jade-green as she calmed herself and gently patted John Doe's shoulder.

John Doe tried to speak, but with the roots wrapped across his mouth, the only sound he could make was a muffled squeak.

"You deserve that, you know," Rowan said, snickering. She stood and danced her way back up the stairs. "Sorry for my horrid display of anger, Mayor Caser. I'm not usually so cross. That guy just gets to me."

"You're entitled to feel what you need to and have the right to be upset," he said. "You didn't injure the boy, just wrapped him up with my lawn. I see no harm done."

"Ice freeze! *Glacio congelo*," John Doe muffled. The thin roots froze, and John Doe balled up his fist, punched through the ice, and freed himself. "Good thing for my ice spell! That was a terrible experience. Don't let me make her mad ever again."

"That's a good idea." Jack chuckled.

"Now, back to the point at hand. All of you will be well taken care of for the honor of our beloved Kenny," said Mayor Caser, smirking.

"Thank you," Corin said. "We appreciate it."

"Come, we have nearly three hours until the funeral, so there's plenty of time for a private tour of Kenny Town."

"Who designed your streets? Whoever did, tell them I hate them," said Jack.

"Why Kenny was part of the urban designer team," said Mayor Caser.

"Oh," Jack gulped. "Well . . . it's not so bad . . ."

For the next few hours, they saw many historical places in the small town: ruins of an ancient church, a retired railroad, the remnants of an ancient power plant, an old musket factory, a four-hundred-year-old mill and lock, a stone fort, and antique homes.

At five o'clock, all the townspeople met at the heart of the brilliantly decorated town square to bid farewell to their beloved founder, Kenny Turbo. The beautiful oak tree glowed with white lights. A red carpet lined with white chairs on both sides led to the open grave under the tree.

Mayor Caser invited Jack to have a seat in the front row. Jack was hesitant, but his friends encouraged him to sit upfront. They sat a few rows back.

Tialp, the tall cowboy, the dwarf blacksmith, and Derrick walked onto the red carpet carrying a beautiful mahogany sarcophagus with gold trim, carved and painted with the likeness of Kenny's human face before his cyborg conversion. Mayor Caser and Alexander stood beside the open grave.

Mayor Caser led the service, and everyone had wonderful things to say about their founder and friend. The blacksmith shared how Kenny hired him to make the town's finest irons, the Ken Café owner bragged about how Kenny loved his menu, and the school teachers spoke highly of their school designed by Kenny.

Jack was the last to speak. "Hello, I am Jack, a personal friend of Kenny. I am sorry that I do not know any of you, but Kenny was my best friend. He helped me stay alive when all hope seemed lost. He was a very honorable cyborg. Kenny taught me that there is still goodness in this world of bias and prejudice. I will miss him. Thank you for all you have done, Kenny. Goodbye, my friend."

The townspeople applauded.

After Jack's compassionate speech, he tapped the button on his left wrist. His energy gun emerged. He opened his right leg compartment and pulled out a small orange rocket. Jack inserted the rocket into his energy gun, aimed at the sky, and fired. An orange spark flew into the air. It burst, creating a grand fireworks display. The crowd cheered at the sky's beautiful array of light and color. Jack returned his energy gun to his hand and walked to his friends.

When the fireworks ended, Tialp and Derrick carefully lowered the sarcophagus into the grave. Once securely in place, Alexander poured dirt, covering it completely.

At the crowd's edge, the dwarf blacksmith stood with the tall man wearing a cowboy hat. He glanced at the taller man and nodded.

The cowboy nodded back and lit a cigar, breathing a puff of smoke away from the crowd.

"You want to get a beverage at the Ken Café?" asked the dwarf.

"Sure, we might as well discuss over a good drink of whiskey."

"It's on me, old friend. This funeral was a rough one."

"Indeed." The cowboy's eyes glanced over at Corin.

"Who do you think those young kids are? They brought Kenny back, and the mayor seems to trust them."

"Caser trusts too easily. We'll keep an eye on those boys until they leave town."

"And the faerie?"

"She does not concern me. That little fellow in the gray helmet and onesie sure does bring up a red flag, though."

"*Is* he wearing night clothes?"

"I have no idea."

"What do you think of the German?"

"Kenny befriended him, and I trust his judgment."

"What about the boy with the lavender hair?" asked the dwarf. "I heard him speak outside my shop. He was virtuous."

"He's no threat to us. He *is* strong. You can tell just by looking at him! Virtuous, eh? That's interesting."

"The little one is a wizard."

"He looks about as harmful as a cute jumping spider."

"Jumping spiders *are* cute, aren't they?"

"They sure are . . . we're getting off-topic!" The cowboy cleared his throat. "Bottom line is, we stay alert. I have a feeling about them. I don't know what it is yet, but I reckon we'll soon find out."

"Thank you all for attending," announced Mayor Caser. "Yes, this is a funeral, and we are saying goodbye, but that does not mean we cannot celebrate Kenny's life and legacy. Food and music will now be provided. Please enjoy yourselves and help us to celebrate our founder!"

The mayor's council brought out a buffet potluck dinner, and an instrumental band began to play Baroque music.

After a hearty meal and mingling with the townspeople, the five friends departed to the hotel to rest for the night. They were exhausted, except for Troll.

"Good night, my friends," said Corin before entering his private hotel room. "Enjoy your rooms, rest well, and we'll see each other again in the morning."

After a relaxing shower, Corin took a tiny notebook from his pouch attached to his utility belt. It was his journal. He opened the small book and turned a few of the pages. Corin smiled and took out a pen, and began to write.

Today has been one of the longest days of my entire life. I never thought anything like this would ever happen. I got out of bed just like every morning, ready to work, feeling programmed to only do the job I am best at. Now, I feel almost like I'm on vacation! I was forced into a portal and fell from the sky by an unknown figure wearing a cloak. Then, I met some incredible new friends:

Jack—a cyborg from Germany—is the one I feel closest to,

Rowan—a forest-protecting faerie—is very flirtatious but benevolent,

John Doe—a young, unskilled wizard—is extremely forgetful but an interesting person,

Troll—a brave man—is the strongest person I have ever met. His intelligence was insulted, but I find his actions quite admirable. I am curious how he feels toward the rest of us.

I miss home and hope to return there, but I cannot help craving the adventure. I don't know what's in store for me tomorrow, but I'm excited to find out! I've never been so thrilled before.

Earth is fascinating. Antiquities don't believe in time, but others like me who value science still follow the time of day. That's interesting and weird, but I'm too sleepy to judge. I am turning in early.

—From the journal of Corin Degodi
June 10, 2215, 8:55 p.m.

"I'm exhausted." Corin yawned, returning the notebook to his pouch and preparing for sleep. He brushed his hair with a small comb from his utility belt and looked in the mirror, smiling. He shut off the lights and got into bed, snuggling his head into the pillows. Corin closed his eyes, and sleep found him quickly.

"I desperately need to shut down," Jack said. "I carried Kenny's body so far through the forest, but it was well worth the exhaustion." He approached the bed. "I have not slept in a bed in years." He smiled and climbed in. After lying down and becoming comfortable, Jack turned to his right and glanced at the empty space beside him. *Emily . . . she always slept on the right side.* Sadness overcame him. Jack whimpered and turned on his left side. He could not bear to look right. He didn't know if he could even remain in bed. Knowing it would be the only way sleep would find him, Jack set the alarm in his chest and shut down his power sequence adapters to shut off his brain.

As soon as John Doe walked into the hotel room and locked the door, he collapsed. He was drained from his day of fright, disappointment, and hiking.

"Sleep will be just the solution to calm my overworked nerves," he mumbled, losing consciousness and snoring loudly.

Rowan danced around her room for an hour. Time had no meaning to her, and she began to sing as she pirouetted into the bathroom and groomed herself. Rowan yawned and skipped to the bed. She lay down and stared at the white ceiling. *What a dull room. There are no paintings, bright colors, or even a patterned blanket on this squishy bed. How boring.* She swiftly fell asleep.

Troll was the only one who did not sleep. He made himself comfortable in a chair and stared out the window, looking up at the night sky with a serious expression. He sighed and placed his right hand on the red amulet in the center of his chest. "The stars are beautiful," he said, shutting his eyes. Troll inhaled deeply and focused on his heartbeat, drifting into deep meditation.

SIX

I slept in! I can't believe it. I have not been allowed to sleep this long in forever. It felt great! I feel awake and rested. I only got up twice to use the bathroom. Man, this hotel room is nice. I almost wish I could live here. I can't wait to eat breakfast. It's been great having free meals. I hope the others slept comfortably. I can't wait to start the day.

—From the journal of Corin Degodi
June 11, 2215, 7:00 a.m.

Jack was awakened promptly at seven by a loud buzzing in his chest. He deactivated his alarm and was groggy for a moment before feeling awake and refreshed after sleeping on the comfortable bed. He stood up and walked to the door. "I hope there's coffee. I have missed the magnificent caffeine beverage of the gods."

Everyone met in the dinette. Only Troll was attentive even though he had not slept all night. They ordered food at the breakfast bar. Corin ate two plates of scrambled eggs with ketchup, Jack drank three cups of coffee, John Doe dined on a plate of sausage and bacon, Rowan enjoyed a kale smoothie, and Troll ate a bowl of fruit, an avocado, two hardboiled eggs, and a cup of spinach.

"Did any of you have interesting dreams last night?" asked Rowan. "Humans have some of the best dreams."

"I dreamed of home last night," said Corin. "Do you think I'll ever find my way back?"

"We're going to try and help you get back, Corin," said Jack.

"I appreciate it, but if I can't return to my space station, then at least this planet is nice. I wouldn't mind living here if the conditions were to my liking," Corin admitted.

"Troll, you seem comfortable here. Are you going to stay in Kenny Town?" John Doe asked, trying to put aside his fear of losing his partner.

"Well, I want to help Corin, but once I accomplish that goal, I may return here one day. I don't mind this quaint little town."

"I've always wanted to go to Centerville City to see if it's the type of city I'd like to retire to," said John Doe. "I heard of a warlock who resides there. He is known to be very powerful and smart. He may know of a way to get you home, Corin."

A powerful warlock? Could his magic help me to understand this amulet? Troll thought, gently touching the red gem. *Perhaps he could figure out a way to remove it without killing me? But I would lose my powers. Would I still be a warrior without it?*

"What's his name?" Corin asked.

"Heeb," said John Doe.

"I wouldn't mind meeting Heeb," Corin said.

"As long as we stay close to my forest, I want to help and go with you guys," said Rowan.

"Well, friends, I believe we've decided. Today, we leave Kenny Town and venture to Centerville City," said Jack.

They finished breakfast and trekked to Kenny Town Hall, but the door was locked.

Corin knocked on the door, and Tialp answered. "Hello, everyone."

"Hello, Tialp. We'd like to see the mayor, please," said Corin.

"Mayor Caser is at home. It is Sunday, and he attends a house of worship at ten o'clock."

"Oh! We are going to head out of town today and want to say goodbye," explained Jack.

"I will contact him on my communicator and have him meet you at the main gate. He lives close. It will not take him long to get there."

"Thank you!" said Corin.

"Let's go," Rowan cheered, flying to the main gate.

"This is great! Just the thought of meeting Heeb is so exciting!" John Doe proclaimed.

"Where is Centerville City on our map, John? Is it far?" asked Troll.

"That's a good question!" said Jack.

They walked into the sally port and saw the cowboy conversing with the gatekeeper as he smoked a cigar. He noticed their arrival, tipped his white hat, and nodded. "Good morning."

"Good morning," said Corin, Jack, and Troll simultaneously.

"Hello, are you leaving?" asked the gatekeeper.

"Yes, but we're meeting the mayor here first," said Corin.

"We want to say goodbye," said Jack.

The mayor arrived carrying a medium-sized box. "My honored friends, thank you again for bringing Kenny home to us," Mayor Caser said. "I am sad to see you leave, but please return soon. You are always welcome here."

"It's been an honor," Jack said.

"I'm sorry about what your old employer did to you both. It wasn't right," the mayor said to Troll and John Doe.

"That's quite all right," John Doe said. "We're on a new mission now. We're helping our friend Corin get back home."

"That's an honorable mission. I spoke to the townspeople, and if you wish to live in Kenny Town, there are positions our community agreed on just for you."

"The sheriff and marshal," the cowboy said, puffing smoke into his mouth, shaping his lips like an O, and slowly blowing a smoke ring.

"Wow!" John Doe exclaimed, watching the smoke ring fade. "You're good at that!"

"Thank you, Mayor Caser," Troll said. "We will consider that."

"I'm a wizard. I won't make a very good sheriff or marshal."

"Well, I am interested," Troll said.

"Wonderful! Well, I wish you well on your journey. Oh! Centerville is just a six-hour walk from here if you need a friendly place to stay."

John Doe took out the map. "That's where we want to go next! I bet Centerville City is on here somewhere."

"If it's not on your map, cross the moat bridge, head east until you get to the Potomac River, and follow it north. You can't miss Centerville City. Before you go, take these food rations and radios," said Mayor Caser, opening the box and revealing a dozen tiny radios. "These belonged to Kenny. He stylized them himself to fit in your ear. Before you use them, you need to personalize your radio. To do that, press this large button and record your name. To contact someone, gently tap your communicator and state the person's name. The transmitter uses waves to match the recorded name and contacts their radio. These two-way transceivers were Kenny's most famous invention."

"That's amazing," Jack declared.

"Thank you for everything," Corin said, ensuring everyone received a radio.

Jack stored the food rations in his back compartment.

Corin shook the mayor's hand and gasped when he felt something hard, flat, and smooth between their fingers.

"There's one for each of you," Mayor Caser said, smiling.

In Corin's hand was a large gold coin.

"That one gold piece is worth one hundred silver," Mayor Caser said, handing out coins to the others. "Now, off with you. Safe journey, young ones."

The gatekeeper opened the main gate, and they exited the sally port.

"Farewell, friends," the mayor said, waving.
"Goodbye!" Rowan sang, blowing a kiss.

Mayor Caser patted the cowboy's shoulder. "I'll see you at worship service?"

"I might be a little late."

Mayor Caser nodded and left.

Troll felt eyes on him. He turned around and noticed the cowboy looking at them.

The cowboy tipped his hat at Troll, puffing on his cigar.

Troll nodded and turned around. "Watch your footing, John. Remember, it's very slippery out here."

"There's no wet straw on the bridge," John Doe chirped. "What are the chances of me almost falling into the moat again?" Before anyone could answer, John Doe walked off the stone bridge and onto the muddy path. His boot immediately slipped, and he fell backward, screaming.

Troll charged forward and grabbed John Doe's coat. His heart skipped a beat as his boots slid. He tried to stabilize himself but lost his sense of balance.

"They're going to fall into the moat!" Rowan yelled.

Corin grabbed Troll's left leg. "Jack, help me pull!"

Jack clutched around Corin's waist and pulled them back to safety.

"That was close," John Doe said with relief.

"I thought I was going to fall," Troll said, trying to catch his breath. "Thank you."

"Don't mention it," Corin said, grinning.

"Um, guys . . . is it just me, or is the water moving?" Jack asked, pointing at the water.

They looked at the water and saw movement.

It's back, Troll thought.

"Boys, something big is swimming in here," Rowan said, hovering over the moat.

"What is it?" asked John Doe, leaning over the muddy bank to look closer.

A giant reptile jumped out of the water, nearly biting John Doe's face.

John Doe yelped and lost his balance again.

Troll quickly grabbed him.

"It's an alligator snapping turtle!" shrieked Rowan. "It's ginormous!"

The turtle's large beak snapped at John Doe again.

"Troll, pull me up!"

Troll tugged but slipped. "I can't. It's too slick."

John Doe screamed.

Jack grabbed under Troll's arms, stabilizing him. "Pull now. I've got you."

"You boys need some help?" asked a voice behind them.

Corin turned to see the cowboy standing at the moat's edge, looking at the turtle. He blew cigar smoke at the large snapper. "Moat monster, get back to patrol and leave these young men alone."

The turtle peered at the cowboy and hissed.

Jack and Troll pulled John Doe to safety.

"John Doe, you're not allowed near any ledges ever again," Jack stated through a frustrated groan.

"This turtle is almost sixty-two years old. He's just an old, cranky mess," said the cowboy as the alligator snapping turtle growled before sinking into the murky water. "You go on now! You folks don't need to worry. He won't bother you anymore. You can go about your business."

John Doe wiped the sweat from his brow, smearing mud onto his forehead.

"Thank you, Jack, and you too, stranger. We appreciate your help," Troll said.

"Don't mention it, kid," the cowboy said, tipping his hat. "You seem to have everything in order. I'll leave you, boys," he said, pulling a handkerchief from his pants pocket and handing it to Troll. "You all clean yourselves up and take care now." He headed back to the sally port.

Troll cleaned his boots with the handkerchief and passed it to Corin.

Rowan landed beside them. "Well, there's never a dull moment with you four. I love it!"

"I wish every riveting moment did not have to deal with me almost dying!" John Doe said, crossing his muddy arms across his chest.

"At least we're all safe," Jack said, unscrewing his left index finger. He pointed it at John Doe, and a stream of pressurized water spewed out with great force, soaking the muddy wizard's coat.

"No! This coat is leather," John Doe cried, coughing as water splashed through his red scarf and into his mouth.

"It was ruined leather before you met me, John Doe," Jack said, laughing as the water stopped, and he screwed back on his finger.

Corin finished wiping the mud from his boots. "Let's head out," he said, flicking the dirty handkerchief.

"I'll hold onto that, Corin," said Jack, opening a small door on his thigh. He dropped the handkerchief in and closed the compartment. He tapped a tiny button next to his hip, and his friends gazed in confusion at the immediate sound of rushing water.

"What is that?" asked Corin.

"Washing machine," Jack said.

"Sure, why not!" Corin chuckled, shrugging his shoulders. "Are we all ready to go?"

"I'm wet!" complained John Doe, wriggling his damp arms.

"I'll blow you dry," Jack said. "Just let me take off my right hand—"

"No, no, no," John Doe squealed, running and hiding behind a tree.

"John, wait for us," Troll yelled.

The cowboy entered the sally port, and the gatekeeper shut the gate behind him. "I guarantee we will see those youngsters again," said the cowboy. "Mark my words; they'll be back."

"They seem well-intentioned and did return Master Kenny to us," said the gatekeeper, watching them go after the hyperactive wizard.

"Indeed," said the cowboy, crossing his arms.

Jack attached a hair dryer to his hand, aimed it behind the tree, and turned it on.

John Doe screamed as the forceful hot air blew him out of his hiding place. He landed on his backside a few feet from the tree.

"Sorry, John Doe! I had it on full blast."

Troll helped John Doe to his feet.

The cowboy shook his head, watching the unusual team depart. "I just know they'll be back."

"So, we just head east to the river. John Doe, do you have the map?" asked Jack.

"I do. I'm glad it didn't get wet," John Doe said, pulling out the map and compass without missing a step in his stride. "Didn't the mayor say it's a six-hour trip? That's a *long* way to walk."

"We might need to purchase a vehicle," said Corin. "Besides the coins from the mayor, I always have universal money on me. Do you think it will be considered valuable here on Earth?"

"Let's take a look at it." Jack held out his hand.

Corin tugged on a tiny wallet attached to his belt as they walked. He opened it and removed a thin silver coin. He gave the coin to Jack.

Jack raised the coin to his eye components and took a reading. When his scan was complete, there was a shrilling *BEEP!* from his stomach compartment. "Oh, pardon me!" Jack said, patting his stomach before handing the coin back to Corin. "It's definitely a silver coin. I'm certain this currency will work for our needs. It can always be melted down for the value of the silver."

"Terrific!" Corin said, returning the coin to his pouch. "Maybe we'll come across a storehouse with a vehicle we can purchase?"

"There is nothing on the way there, according to this map. Hey! I bet I could pull something out of a portal that will help us," John Doe said, cracking his knuckles.

"That's a *bad* idea," Troll said nervously.

"How exactly do you reach into the portals?" asked Rowan. "Is it similar to the legends of amateur magicians? The performer would pull a rabbit out of a magic hat."

"Sort of. Would you like to watch how it's done?" John Doe asked, handing the map to Troll. He rolled up his sleeves and wiggled his fingers.

Troll's eyes were distressed, but the others eagerly watched John Doe. "We'll watch from a distance if you're that interested. We *need* to take shelter first," Troll said, putting the map into the small tan sack and getting his axe ready. He took cover behind a large tree.

"Let's see . . . how does that spell go again? Oh yes, here we go," John Doe said, stretching his arm out. He hummed, and his fingertips glowed. *"Oscail doras misticiúil, tabhair amach mo bhealach isteach."*

"That's not Latin," Rowan declared. "What language is that? What kind of joke are you playing, John Doe?"

"Jack, can you translate it?" asked Corin.

"I can try," Jack said, scanning his data banks.

John Doe repeated the spell, and his fingertips glowed brighter.

"Oh, it's Gaelic," Jack said when he finished scanning.

"Interesting. The only human languages I speak are English and Latin. My native language is not spoken by mortals."

"You're immortal?" asked Corin.

"I didn't say that. More importantly, I have no idea what kind of spell John Doe is casting."

"You guys should hide!" Troll yelled, but they weren't paying any attention to him.

John Doe finished chanting. He balled up his fists and punched forward. His hands vanished.

"Whoa!" Rowan exclaimed.

Corin and Jack gasped simultaneously.

"Watch this, guys!" yelled John Doe.

"His hands are *really* in another dimension!" Corin said gleefully.

"I wonder what he's going to pull out?" Rowan asked sunnily.

Something brushed by my hand. Can I find it? There it is! Yes! "I caught something!" John Doe shouted, pulling vigorously. "Here it comes! It's heavy!"

There was a crackling sound, followed by a whispering hiss like gas escaping from a pipe.

John Doe leaned back as he yanked a long, scaly red tail through the portal, followed by hind legs and forelegs with sharp claws, wings, and—

Jack, Corin, and Rowan screamed in terror when John Doe pulled the head through. Before them was a red, thirty-foot-tall dragon.

John Doe shrieked, letting go of the dragon's tail. His legs trembled, and he lost his balance, collapsing.

The portal closed, and the realm it had come from was no longer accessible.

"Who dares abduct me?" the red dragon asked crossly.

"Its voice is high-pitched. Is it a female dragon?" asked Jack, quivering.

"I think so," said Rowan.

The dragon looked at John Doe hungrily. She bared her fangs and lowered her head to strike.

John Doe could see bits of rotting flesh in between each sharp tooth. "Why does this always happen?" he asked fearfully. "You're supposed to be my follower."

She chuckled at him and licked her lips. "I follow no one!" she roared.

John Doe whimpered softly when he felt the dragon's breath upon his face.

"Everyone, get down!" Jack yelled, pressing the button on his wrist, activating his energy gun. "I have to make my arm gun more powerful!" He opened his leg compartment and rummaged through his weapon accessories.

The red dragon looked at Jack as Corin and Rowan hid behind a thick tree.

John Doe wanted to run, but his legs would not function.

Jack grabbed his beam enhancer, but the dragon smacked him with her powerful tail. His built-in speaker system exclaimed a loud stock scream sound effect as his metal body plunged into a tree. The metallic clang of his body striking the wood was deafening. The beam enhancer landed beside the dragon.

The tree began to uproot immediately, falling toward the tree Corin and Rowan were behind. The ripping and tearing sound of the falling tree was frightening.

Rowan screamed.

Corin pulled out his laser pistol and blasted the tree. The sizzling laser ripped through the tree, causing it to hiss and pop before exploding. Corin reflexively threw himself over Rowan as wood chips and splinters rained on them. He kept her close, retreating into a thicker grove of trees.

The dragon returned her attention to John Doe, opening her mouth to devour him.

John Doe covered his sunglass-goggles with his hands and folded into a fetal position.

Troll's heart was pounding. "I knew this would happen. I blame myself. I could've stopped John. It's up to me now." He maneuvered around the tree and confronted the dragon. "Dragon, face me!" Troll yelled, gripping his axe. "If you are looking for a challenging meal, look no further!"

The dragon glared at Troll.

Troll threw his axe. It sliced into her snout, immediately drew blood, and became stuck.

She backed up, roaring in pain. She shook her head, trying to dislodge the axe.

Troll ran over and pushed John Doe, sending him flying through the air and into a rose bush. "Stay in there!" Troll yelled.

"Okay!" John Doe moaned as several thorns dug into his flesh. "Ouch, the thorns are in my spleen!" *But this is better than being eaten.*

"That was extremely foolish, purple man!" the dragon bellowed, her thunderous voice echoing. She speedily approached him.

Troll gently applied pressure to the red amulet. *Please grant me the strength to save my friends.* Immediately, raw power surged to every part of his body. Troll inhaled sharply, grinding his teeth. He pushed his chest out and flexed his muscles. He waited until the dragon's mouth was directly in front of him. He felt her hot breath. Troll reached out with his left hand and grabbed her upper jaw as his right hand seized her lower jaw. With all of his strength, he kept her mouth wide open.

The dragon was shocked, and she roared ferociously.

Troll didn't flinch, though his eardrums hummed in agony, and his stomach turned from her putrid breath. He saw the decaying remains stuck between her teeth. "You need to floss!" he shouted, barely resisting nausea.

The dragon pushed Troll, trying to destabilize him.

THE UNIQUE CAMPAIGN

He pressed against her, and his boots dug a trail in the dirt. *I wonder how much longer I can last. Please, don't breathe fire. Please . . . don't burn me alive!* Troll clenched his teeth, and sweat ran down his face.

Jack recovered from his collision with the tree. He shook his head and heard something rattling around in his neck. His face shield was loose. "Damnit! That crash must have broken something." He stood and looked for his beam enhancer. He saw it beside the dragon that Troll had by the mouth. *How on Earth is he holding his own against that dragon? How did he even manage to grab her?*

The dragon inched forward, causing Troll's boots to dig deeper, finally throwing off his balance.

Troll whimpered as his body painfully shifted into a skewed position, but he didn't let go. He fought his discomfort and used his strength to push on her mouth.

Jack knew this was the perfect opportunity to grab his enhancer. He raced toward them. *If I can get just the right shot at the dragon's head, I might be able to kill her.*

The dragon's enormous ears heard the pounding of Jack's feet. Her golden eyes darted over to the charging cyborg.

She's distracted! I have to keep her head down. Troll put his left foot on the dragon's lower jaw. With his right hand free, he grabbed the dragon's forked tongue and pulled as hard as possible. He kept his right foot secured on the ground.

The dragon roared out in pain.

Troll forcefully shut his eyes and scrunched his face as pain ripped through his eardrums. He feared his ears would bleed but kept his grip.

Jack grabbed his enhancer and attached it to his arm. He aimed just below her eyes and fired. There was a loud *SHUUNN!* as his energy beam blew a hole in the dragon's face.

She painfully howled as her purple blood gushed from the wound.

Troll wished he could shut his ears. The temperature in her mouth elevated. He moaned, cautiously opening his eyes and looking down her throat. He saw a red light approaching her tonsils. "Oh no." *I'm going to be barbecued.* Troll began to panic, and his muscles went slack. "Help me!" he yelled as the dragon's tongue slipped out of his hand, and his left foot fell into her mouth.

In that second, the dragon put enormous pressure on Troll.

He yelped in alarm, digging both feet into her gums and pressing his hands on her upper jaw. Her top teeth hovered directly over his chest, and her bottom teeth were aimed at his back.

The dragon chuckled, lifting her head and flapping her wings.

"Troll!" Jack yelled, distressed.

"Please, no!" Troll cried, struggling to keep her from biting him in half. His muscles burned. *I'm vulnerable in this position!* He put all his strength into his right hand to keep her jaw open. His left hand avoided her sharp fangs and moved to the roof of her mouth. *I never thought I'd ever climb into a dragon's mouth willingly like this, but I have to avoid her teeth!* Troll could feel the heat in her throat increasing, and the red light became brighter. He straightened his posture and carefully brought his right hand to the roof of her mouth. Sweat poured from his brow as he panted loudly.

The dragon spread her wings and flew into the air.

"No! Come back here!" shouted Jack.

Her tongue licked Troll's neck, sending chills down his back.

Troll looked away in disgust and tried to focus on his strength.

She gave the bare skin of Troll's left arm a gentle lick.

He exhaled sharply, bit his lower lip, and clenched his eyes shut as the dragon continued to lick his left arm and then his right. *She knows what she's doing! Eventually, I will let go. I'm ticklish and can't resist forever. Then she'll have her meal.*

She thoroughly enjoyed playing with her food.

Troll's arms and legs trembled. *I hope I've been a worthy opponent. I never thought my life would end this way*—"Please . . . someone . . . help me!"

Jack heard Troll's cry of desperation. "He's still alive!" He fired his energy gun again, striking her left ear.

The dragon's eyes appeared on fire in her pain and anguish, changing colors from bright gold to a burning red. She did not shriek in pain but exhaled black smoke as more violet blood spewed out of her new wound.

Troll coughed several times in the dark, thick smoke. His arms trembled even harder now. He was weakening and knew the dragon was winning. She was going to crush him, burn him, and then consume him.

"We need to save Troll," Corin said to Rowan.

"Are you insane?" asked Rowan, crying. "*That* is a dragon! We're no match for her! There is nothing we can do!"

"I don't believe that," Corin said, clutching his pistol tightly. "I'm going to help him." Corin dashed out of his hiding place and fired at the dragon's face. "Maybe my laser will blind her, and Troll can escape?"

Jack saw Corin firing at the dragon. He knew this was the moment to create a diversion. He aimed for the dragon's ear and fired his energy gun again.

SHUUNN!

The impact from Jack's blast completely ruptured the dragon's eardrum. Her eyes opened wide in pain as she was unable to hear.

Corin fired his pistol at the same moment and blinded her.

The dragon threw her head back with immense force, opening her mouth as wide as she could, letting out a blood-curdling bellow.

Troll's axe flew out of her snout, and the blade impacted the ground.

Troll screamed as he was expelled from the dragon's mouth into the air above her.

The dragon kept her head back as an explosion of fire erupted inside her jaws. The blaze surged into the air, heading for Troll. Gravity pushed Troll toward the line of her fire.

The flames . . . the haunting flames . . . Troll screamed again and shut his eyes. There was no way he could save himself. *I don't want to burn to death!*

Rowan saw Troll falling. There was no time to fly and attempt to catch him. He would've been too heavy for her anyway. *"No!"* Rowan screeched as tears poured down her cheeks. She closed her eyes and cried hysterically.

"Jack, can you save him?" Corin asked.

"I can't reach him in time!" Jack said, panicked.

John Doe sat up in the rose bush, covered in sharp thorns. He saw Troll falling to a fiery death. He rolled up his sleeves and aimed his glowing fingertips at Troll. *"Concussas undam manibus creo, percurro aerem—velocior soni velocitate!"* A clear hypersonic wave of solid energy discharged from his fingers. The wave approached the fire as Troll was about to fall into the blaze, but instead of being burned alive, he landed on the wave.

"John Doe saved him!" Corin cheered in delight.

"I can't believe it!" Jack exclaimed.

On impact, Troll grunted and opened his eyes, astonished that he was still alive. He looked through the sturdy wave of energy. It was like looking through a crystal. It carried Troll away from the dragon and her fire, but before he could relax, he saw the wave was going to collide with a gargantuan tree. Troll screamed and jumped.

John Doe watched in horror as the top of the tree shattered into pieces. The bottom part of the tree uprooted and fell over. He gulped and released the magic. His fingers stopped glowing, and the wave disappeared.

"Troll jumped from that thing!" Jack yelled.

Troll was all right but had a very rough landing. He crawled out of a large sticker bush and had tiny, sharp thorns stuck in his arms and legs. Troll growled with annoyance, looking at John Doe.

"You're welcome!" John Doe called happily, waving at Troll before abruptly dropping his hand. "Ouch! It hurts to move!" John Doe exclaimed as thorns continued to jab his flesh.

Troll sighed hard and started pulling thorns from his skin.

"You vile creatures! How dare you bring me here and maim me! I will have my revenge," the dragon screamed, emitting a displeasing sound. Thrashing her head back and forth, now blind and nearly deaf, she stumbled into the forest, heading north. She continued shrieking and cursing them, smashing trees in her path.

"I guess we won. I'm glad Troll is still in one piece," said Jack, removing his beam enhancer from his energy gun and returning it to his leg compartment.

"Yes," agreed Corin. "It's amazing. He's so strong!"

"You're an excellent shot, Corin," Jack said as he turned his gun back into his hand.

"Thank you, Jack. So are you."

They shook hands, then made their way over to check on Troll.

"Troll is alive?" Rowan gasped, drying her eyes. She danced from her hiding place and was the first to reach Troll. Rowan frowned when she saw the thorns had pierced him. She gently blew on his neck.

Troll shuddered.

The thorns fell from his flesh.

Rowan hugged him.

"You blew the thorns from my skin?" Troll asked, gently embracing her.

Rowan nodded and closed her eyes, allowing tears to run down her face again. "I'm so glad you're okay. I feel terrible. I wanted to help you!"

Troll touched her shoulders and gently pulled himself from the hug.

She opened her dark honey-colored eyes, looking into his baby blue eyes. "Your eyes are so beautifully blue. But how? How are they so heavenly?" Rowan asked, gently touching his cheek, becoming lost in his eyes.

He touched her hand, smiled, and gently kissed her forehead.

Rowan smiled shyly as her cheeks turned a bright cherry color. She quickly covered them with her hands and giggled.

Troll started pulling out thorns again.

"Let me help," Rowan said, assisting him.

John Doe walked over to Troll's axe and picked it up. He had a difficult time lifting it but managed to drag it.

"Are you all right?" asked Corin, walking with Jack to Troll and Rowan.

"Yes," said Troll. "That was close. Thank you for saving me."

"You held your own against a dragon," said Jack. "I'm impressed! We must face each other someday. I am curious to see what else you can do."

Troll smiled and ran his fingers through his lavender hair. He nodded, then noticed John Doe dragging his axe.

"Troll, are you injured?" John Doe asked, struggling to pull the axe along.

"John Doe, how many languages do you speak for spell casting?" asked Jack.

"Latin and Gaelic," said John Doe. "The Gaelic spells are for my portals. Latin is for normal incantations," John Doe explained, handing the axe to Troll.

"Maybe you should not speak Gaelic . . . ever again," Jack suggested.

"Why on Earth not?" asked John Doe. "My Irish ancestors were witches."

"You have witches in your family?" asked Corin.

"Who?" asked John Doe.

"You," said Corin.

"I do?" John Doe asked, scratching his head.

"You just said that you have ancestors who were witches from Ireland," said Rowan.

"I wouldn't know about witches in Ireland, but I also wouldn't mind having a sandwich," John Doe said, feeling his stomach rumble. "Is anyone else hungry?"

Troll said nothing. Instead, he extended his index finger and poked John Doe's forehead. The force of the poke flung him into the same sticker bush Troll fell in.

"My spleen!" John Doe yelped, thorns piercing his skin again.

"I feel better now," Troll said, smiling, and he returned his axe to its sheath.

SEVEN

John Doe summoned a large red dragon into this world, and now it is on the loose. He just wanted to help us find transportation, but after that experience, walking never looked so good. It's going to be a very long trip. I wonder . . . would Jack give us piggyback rides?

—From the journal of Corin Degodi
June 11, 2215, 10:15 a.m.

They continued their journey and finally saw the Potomac River in the distance.

"We just need to head north from here," Troll announced.

"We need to rest soon," said John Doe. "I'm bushed!"

"Already?" asked Corin.

"I could carry you," suggested Jack.

"I'm not a baby," said John Doe.

"No, John, you're not a baby," agreed Troll. "You're just a whiner."

"You can only say that because you know me so well!" John Doe yelled sternly.

"Hey, guys, I hear something ahead," said Rowan. "I'll go check it out." Her jade-green body became transparent.

"Whoa, neat trick," said Jack. "Can you turn invisible whenever you wish?"

"Sure," said Rowan. "I'll be right back."

"We can't keep stopping," said Troll. "We're wasting time and do not want to be out here when night falls."

"Troll has a good point," said Jack. "I can power up my security lights and build a fire, but that may not be enough to keep away dangerous animals."

"Boys," Rowan called to them.

They looked around but could not locate their faerie friend.

"Where are you, Rowan?" asked Corin.

"Oh, sorry," Rowan said as she appeared beside Jack. "I forgot!"

"What is it?" Corin asked.

"There is a giant metal machine ahead!"

"Another cyborg?" asked Jack.

"No, it's a machine with wheels! I could hear voices coming from inside of it."

"It must be a tank," said Jack with excitement. "Do you think we should go check it out?"

"I'm game," said Troll, drawing his axe.

"Let's not attack them. I'll try to talk to them first," Corin said. "Maybe they'll be willing to give us a lift to Centerville."

"I'm not planning on attacking, Corin," said Troll, chuckling. "The axe is for protection in case they're hostile."

"It's over here. Come on!" Rowan said, leading the way.

They followed her cautiously through the woods.

"Don't let the people see you. I can hear them talking within the metal mechanism," Rowan whispered, stopping at a large row of overgrown shrubs. She carefully pulled back a few branches. "This is red twig dogwood. It'll be an excellent concealment. Get in and look."

They delicately crept into the giant shrubs, looking through the branches. They gasped in unison.

"It *is* a tank!" cheered Jack. "I can't wait to see what kind of weapons it has!"

"We are not going to attack them," said Corin. "We don't even know who they are."

"No one mentioned attacking, Corin," said Jack. "You're really hung up about that. Let us go and introduce ourselves. We'll kindly ask if we can *steal* their ride."

"No!" Corin announced. "There will be no stealing. We must gain allies."

"Corin, I am kidding." Jack laughed.

"You can never be too careful," Corin said embarrassingly. "Let's allow them to see us." He began to dig through the branches, preparing to walk out to the tank.

"Um, they *are* in a tank," Troll said.

"Yes, so what?" asked John Doe.

"Well, if Corin makes them mad, they are going to blow him up," Troll stated truthfully, clutching his axe.

Corin stopped dead in his tracks and swallowed hard when he saw the large gun barrel of the turret. The hatch opened, and Corin quickly sat back down. Three men and a beautiful blonde woman emerged from the tank mere seconds after his abortive attempt at being courageous. Corin stared at Troll nervously. "Troll, would you like to go first?"

Troll laughed and shook his head. "I'm not stupid."

The four individuals wore matching jumpsuits. The three men began to clean the tank as the woman reviewed their surroundings.

"Let's take this path," the woman announced, pointing at a dirt road through the woods heading north. "The city should not be much farther. We can take a much-needed vacation once we arrive with our cargo."

"Do you think the Centerville military will like those bags of spuds?" asked a tall man with green eyes, thick brown hair, and a mustache. Across his chest was a large, wide leather strap holding a medium-sized assault rifle against his back.

"They had better if we want to get paid," answered the woman. "Ace, how's the transmission?"

"She's in great shape, lass," said the second man with a Scottish accent. He wore a tight piloting cap with goggles attached to the front, grease covered his hands, and his clothes were bulky.

"RJ, are the treads clean?" she asked.

"Yes, Jessica, we are ready to go!" The final man looked up from the tank's treads. Caked into his messy sand-colored hair was dirt and grease. In his hand was a grimy rag and hook.

"Were you lighting up over there again?" Jessica asked, walking over.

"Oh, Jessica, I don't touch those anymore."

Jessica put a supporting hand on his shoulder. "You need to break the addiction."

"I have," he admitted. "I have not used it in three months. You should be proud of me!"

"I am proud of you . . . just stop collecting the junk."

"What junk?" he asked innocently.

She looked into the treads and noticed several candy bar wrappers, old documents, a dirty baby diaper, and empty cans. Jessica grabbed one of the candy wrappers and held it to RJ's face.

RJ sighed hard and shrugged.

"RJ, you can fight this addiction. You don't need to collect junk, and you know it. I'm so proud of you for giving up the drugs, but collecting trash is just as bad. I know you can beat it."

"I just feel like I need to collect things," RJ confessed. "Since I went straight, I've felt like I'm missing a piece of myself."

"Healing takes time. You need to be confident. I'm so proud of you for stopping the pill popping."

"Those were vitamins," RJ said, laughing.

Jessica rolled her eyes at his joke. "Okay, funny man. No more trash, and work on the jokes," she said, giving him a friendly wink.

"Yes, sir, boss!" RJ said, saluting. He ran over to Ace. "Ace, I don't do drugs anymore, right? I'm not a junkie."

"You could have fooled me!" the man with the mustache yelled, boarding the tank.

"No one is asking you, Finnegan!" RJ barked. "No more pills! I'm not a junkie!"

"Yet you collect trash," said Ace. "Trash is junk, RJ."

"Oh! You're right," RJ said. "I'm still technically a junkie."

"Aye, lad."

"Load up, guys!" Jessica ordered. "Prepare to leave."

The three men rushed to their stations and worked on completing their tasks before starting the tank.

Jessica sighed, looking down the road. "Will we arrive before dusk?" She heard something moving in the bushes behind her. She turned around and noticed some branches were moving. Jessica listened very carefully. She could hear voices.

"They're leaving," said Rowan, pushing through limbs.

"That tank is gorgeous!" said Jack.

"I think we should keep our voices down," suggested Troll.

"I think you should go first," said Corin. "We don't know what these people are capable of."

"Corin, I am not going out there," Troll replied.

The bush rustled even more. Jessica approached it slowly, looking directly into the shrub. A pair of oversized black sunglasses-goggles looked back at her.

"I th-th-think she can s-s-see us!" John Doe stuttered.

Corin continued to argue with Troll as Jack and Rowan observed the tank.

"Weapons officer," Jessica summoned.

"Yes?" asked Finnegan, poking his head out of the tank.

"Could you come here for a moment? Bring your firearm," Jessica ordered, pulling a knife from her boot.

Finnegan's face hardened as he swung his assault rifle off his back and held it ready. He flicked off the safety as he quietly stepped to Jessica's side.

"Aim for the bush," she ordered, pointing with the knife.

"They know we're here!" John Doe panicked and grabbed at Jack.

"How do you know?" Jack asked.

"Someone besides me, please look!" John Doe cried, pointing out of the bush. "We're about to die!"

"Come on out of there!" Finnegan shouted.

Corin parted his lips, but no sound emerged. He became tense and stared at Troll, frightened. He looked like a terrified, lost child.

"Who are you, and why are you spying on us?" Finnegan shouted angrily. "Come out now. This is your last warning!"

Corin was very nervous about engaging with the angry man holding the rifle.

Rowan hugged Jack while John Doe kept his head down.

Troll squeezed the handle of his axe.

Finnegan became impatient and fired the rifle into the air. The startling roar of the weapon forced Rowan, Corin, and John Doe to scream. "The next bullet won't miss!" Finnegan threatened, aiming the rifle into the bush.

Troll swallowed hard and put a comforting hand on Corin's shoulder. As their eyes met, his blue eyes told Corin everything would be all right. Troll slowly stood, emerging from the bush.

"No, Troll," John Doe wailed. "Come back!"

Finnegan and Jessica gaped at Troll's size. Jessica pulled a small pistol from her leg holster and aimed it at him.

"Calm down," Troll said nervously, throwing his axe on the ground. He raised his hands above his head and slowly walked forward. "We mean no harm. My friends and I saw you, and we want nothing more but to talk."

"Bullshit!" Finnegan declared, pressing his firearm onto the red amulet.

Troll froze in terror. "Please don't—" His voice cracked as his entire body trembled. *I know I can get the gun from him, but I don't want to endanger the others.* He felt vulnerable with the hard steel over his shuddering heart. Troll shut his eyes and didn't budge.

Finnegan's eyes grew wide, and he quickly pulled his gun away. "What the hell is that?" asked Finnegan, backing up and pointing at Troll's chest.

"What's wrong?" asked Jessica.

"It's the strangest thing . . ." Finnegan said. "I thought it was a spell! I swear I could feel his pulse through my weapon!"

"Are you an Antiquity?" Jessica asked Troll.

"No, ma'am," Troll said as he opened his eyes and kept his hands in the air. "I'm just a warrior protecting my friends."

Finnegan smiled menacingly and pressed the firearm onto the amulet again.

Troll gasped but held his ground. Sweat formed on his brow.

As strange as it was to feel the strong pulse of the young warrior through a weapon, Finnegan kept the firearm poised. "Everyone in that bush, I suggest you come out, or handsome here dies!" Finnegan warned.

"Let's go!" Rowan panted with tears in her eyes.

"We're coming out," Corin said nervously. He cautiously led the others. "Please lower your weapon. That man is my friend. His name is Troll. He's telling you the truth. We don't mean your group any harm. Please, don't hurt him. My name is Corin Degodi, and my other friends are Jack, Rowan, and John Doe."

Finnegan narrowed his eyes with suspicion as Corin spoke and applied tremendous pressure on Troll's amulet.

Troll closed his eyes as Corin's eyes darted from Finnegan to Jessica to see what she would instruct. The sweat from Troll's brow ran down his cheek.

"Why are you spying on us?" Finnegan demanded. "Either you answer my question, or I'll shoot your purple-haired friend!"

Troll moaned and slowly opened his eyes. He felt dizzy as he looked at Jessica.

She felt their eyes on her. Her body tensed, ready for combat. Jessica glanced at Troll first and noticed his wide, pleading eyes. Meeting his gaze, she felt sorry for him, and her tension began to ease. Jessica looked at Corin. They made eye contact and inhaled sharply. They instantly felt a charge, like being struck by a powerful lightning bolt. Her teal eyes twinkled at his brown eyes. Corin could not take his eyes off her. The right side of his mouth quirked upwards. Jessica's mouth gaped open, and sweat formed on her neck.

Finnegan saw Jessica's reaction. He became confused, jealous, and flustered. "Jess, what do you want me to do?"

Jessica blinked. She tossed aside the momentary feeling and looked at Troll again. He had not moved. Jessica finally realized that a man his size and physique could have fought Finnegan and gotten the rifle away with no problem. Troll did not appear to be a danger to them. She considered Corin's words and could see he was genuine. Her tension melted away. She looked at Corin again and gave him a dazzling smile. "Let him go," she ordered Finnegan.

"But, Jess—"

"I said, let him go!"

"Yes, boss," Finnegan said dejectedly, pulling his firearm away from Troll's chest and slinging it back over his shoulder.

Troll breathed a sigh of relief.

Rowan and John Doe ran to Troll and hugged him tightly. She glanced at John Doe angrily, and he glared back at her with jealousy.

"He was my best friend first!" exclaimed John Doe, folding his arms across his chest and pouting.

Rowan and Troll rolled their eyes.

Troll hugged Rowan tightly.

The jade-colored faerie blushed, running her fingers through his soft, lavender hair. "I'm so glad you're all right," she whispered into Troll's ear.

"Hey!" yelled John Doe, waving his arms. "I'm John Doe!"

Troll sighed hard but smiled. He let Rowan go and put John Doe in a headlock.

John Doe moaned loudly and rapidly tapped on Troll's enormous forearm.

"Yes?" asked Troll.

"I need air!" John Doe cried.

Troll chuckled, releasing John Doe from the headlock and patting his back. "Are you okay?" Troll asked innocently.

"Why can't I stay mad at you?"

Jessica smiled at them. *His friends were worried for his life. They're not thieves. Had they been a threat, they would've attacked us.* "Hate to interrupt, but why were you spying on us?" Jessica asked boomingly to gain attention. She looked at Corin again. *Is he the leader?*

"We didn't mean to," Corin said. "We're on our way to Centerville City, and wanted to ask you and your men if we could perhaps join you for a—"

"Ride?" Jessica interrupted. "You wish to ride with us since we're *also* going to Centerville? Is that it?"

"Yes, ma'am," Corin replied.

"Well, we don't have much room. We have a large shipment of potatoes in the back cargo compartment, and you're traveling with a rather big cyborg that'll never fit inside my tank."

"*Verdammt*," Jack swore. "I was hoping to look inside it, but that's okay. I can walk and keep up with the tank. I don't need to ride inside it."

"I can keep up on foot as well," said Troll.

"Really?" asked Jessica, curling her finger on her chin. Her eyes glimpsed at the red amulet, then returned to his eyes. She smiled and put her hands on her hips. "You must be quite fast?"

"Yes, ma'am," Troll answered.

"Hmm. You're fast and strong. You can come if you help protect my cargo."

"Certainly," said Troll.

"Good, I need a strong man around."

Finnegan overheard. "I'm the strong guy here. What's so special about him?"

"Oh, Finn, he's not your competition!" Jessica said. "He's just big enough to keep bandits away."

"Why do you need to worry about bandits?" asked John Doe. "You're driving a tank. You're unstoppable!"

"Well, our tank has a problem," Jessica admitted.

"What?" Jack asked.

"It doesn't fire," Jessica said, shrugging her shoulders.

Jack peered into the barrel of the large tank gun. He noticed it was filthy and clogged. "I might be able to fix this. How did it become clogged?"

"We used it a month ago when a creature in the forest attacked us. It fired at us with a lightning weapon. We never saw our attacker, but after that, the gun never fired again. We assumed it was a spell preventing us from firing. Everything else works perfectly."

"Give me five minutes," Jack said, preparing to work on repairs.

"I'll give you a hand, lad," Ace told him. "I'm the mechanic here. So, what appears to be the situation?"

"Well, first things first. Is this a 1940s M4 Sherman?" asked Jack.

"Aye," said Ace. "Beauty, isn't she? She's completely restored and upgraded. We cut out the old petrol engine and fuel systems. We replaced 'em with a miniaturized nuclear engine with about five hundred horsepower. Ol' girl purrs like a kitten and drives like a hot rod! She used to fit about five people, and they'd be like sardines squished together in a can."

"Why on Earth are you using such an old tank? Its last use was in the 1970s."

"Well, it's Jessica's tank. The lass loves antique weapons. This tank is her favorite thing in the world." Ace smiled. "Even though she had the inside updated, she had to keep that classic look on the outside. It's important to her."

"Are you mercenaries or in a military faction?"

"We're a martial delivery company." Ace chuckled. "We deliver supplies to military bases in civilian populations, like Centerville City."

"Interesting! Let's see now . . . we'll need my ultrasonic cleaner."

"What'll that be?" asked Ace.

"I'll show you." A small plate on Jack's chest lifted, and he hit a few buttons. He closed the plate and opened his leg compartment. He dug around inside, making many banging noises from within his leg. "You know, my father always said I have a hollow leg. I was a serious eater, and he could never figure out where all my food went. The crazy old man! Who'd ever thought that old fart would be right after I became a cyborg? Aha! I found it. This should do the trick!" he said enthusiastically. Jack pulled out what appeared to be a small hose nozzle. "I hook this baby up to my left index finger. I use it to clean my circuits and weapons. It should work for the tank. I'll have to recharge my ultrasonic cleaner later, but that's okay."

"Isn't this going to take forever?" Ace asked, watching Jack attach the nozzle to his finger.

"Nah, this is going to be fun," said Jack. "Now, get some rags."

"I have long applicators as well," said Ace. "I haven't been able to insert one since that battle."

"The clog must be huge," said Jack, spraying his cleaning solution inside the gun opening.

"We should give them room to work," Corin suggested. "Look, we all got off on the wrong foot. How about I make a good second impression since we ruined the first?"

"Okay," said Jessica. "Impress me."

"Hello, my name is Corin Degodi. I'm a Space Ranger from the Andromeda Galaxy. I'm *visiting* from out of town." He took Jessica's hand in his and kissed it gently.

Jessica's cheeks turned bright red.

"I'll introduce you to the rest of my group. The faerie is named Rowan. She protects and owns the forest."

"The entire forest?" asked Jessica.

"I'm not certain," said Corin. "She rules over a large portion, though."

"That's impressive."

"The cyborg's name is Jack Geyerwulf. He's German."

"Oh, I could tell." Jessica laughed. "His accent is quite strong."

"The human in the black coat is John Doe. He's a wizard, and you already met Troll."

"So, why are you on your way to Centerville City?" Jessica asked.

"We're on an adventure. I'm trying to get back home, and John Doe knows a warlock who may have the power to get me there."

"How did you come here?" Jessica asked.

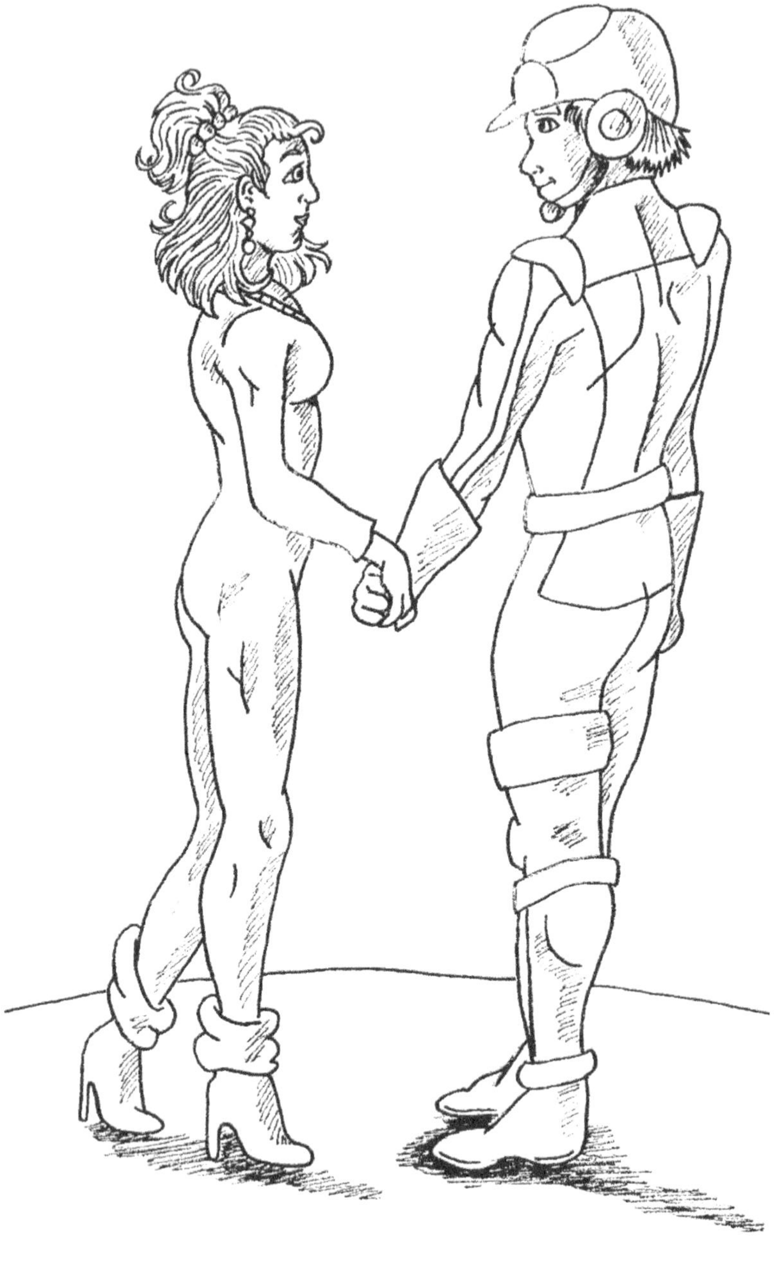

"A purple portal," Corin said. "It sounds crazy, but I don't know where it came from or why it chose me."

"A portal doesn't just appear out of thin air for no reason, trust me. It sounds like someone brought you here. Do you have any enemies?" Jessica asked.

"No," Corin said. "I don't think so."

Corin and Jessica's eyes met again.

"Your eyes are like two frozen comets glittering in the star's light like gemstones," Corin said, gulping.

Jessica blushed and then laughed out loud. "Where on Earth are my manners?" She slapped her wrist. "I'm so sorry, Corin. My name is Jessica Dove."

"Jessica Dove," Corin said. "What a beautiful name!"

"My weapons officer is the man over there with the mustache. His name is Finnegan White. The man we call a junkie is named RJ. Please don't ask me what those initials stand for. I have no idea. He is my driver. And Ace Kenmore is the grease monkey helping your cybo . . . Jack."

"Hey, Ace. Do you need any help?" Finnegan asked, trying to distract himself from Jessica's interest in Corin.

"Finn, get in the tank with RJ," said Ace. "I want ye to press the red button I installed last week."

"All right, all right," said Finnegan, sighing in frustration. He climbed inside. "Move over, junkie!"

"Jessica, thank you for allowing us to ride with you. We appreciate this," Corin stated.

"The pleasure is all mine," Jessica said, leaning forward.

They brought their lips close and—

BOOM!

Corin shrieked, jumping into Jessica's arms.

"Get down!" Troll cried, diving on top of Rowan and John Doe.

"Is someone shooting at us?" asked John Doe.

"That tank burped," said Rowan. "Disgusting!"

"Is everyone okay?" Troll asked, realizing the tank had fired. He stood, helping Rowan and John Doe stand.

"She fires!" Ace cheered, covered in thick, black tar. "I love this cyborg!"

RJ and Finnegan poked their heads out, also covered in the black residue.

"What is this stuff? It stinks! Ace, I didn't know the red button fired this damn thing!" shouted Finnegan.

"Don't you love it? I originally thought I'd use it to cut power quickly if we needed an emergency stop. But after thinking about it, I decided to install it for emergency firing instead," explained Ace.

"Ace!" Jessica yelled, putting Corin down. She marched to her tank. "You're supposed to clear the area before test firing! There could have been casualties! I should beat the shit out of you! But instead, I'll cut your rations for one week. No fish and chips for you!"

"Oh, don't do that, lass," begged Ace. "I need me fish n' chips!"

"Clean up this mess! All of you!"

They let out a chorus of sighs, looking at the filth.

Finnegan growled, peering into the hatch. "It smells horrible, Jess!" he whined, repulsively covering his nose and disappearing into the turret. He returned momentarily, handing Ace and Jack a pair of mops.

"We're going to need baths," RJ groaned, passing Finnegan a rag.

"I'm going to hate working for this woman," Jack sighed.

"How are we going to clean all this?" shouted RJ from inside the tank. "This smell is unbearable!"

"What am I stepping in? It's like shit!" yelled Finnegan.

Rowan's ear twitched when she heard Finnegan's comment. She gasped and covered her mouth. She remembered a significant disturbance destroying her tree friends about a month ago. She shot lightning at the enemy and cast her fertilizer spell.

Troll noticed Rowan's reaction and raised an eyebrow. "What's wrong?" he asked.

"Nothing," said Rowan, giggling. "Nothing at all."

After three hours of cleaning and becoming better acquainted, they were ready to continue their journey. Troll and Jack walked briskly beside the tank as it rolled along the path. John Doe and RJ sat atop the tank, animatedly discussing their plans for the future. A musky scent briefly wafted by Troll's nose. *What's this, then?* Troll thought, a serious look pasted on his face. He glanced around. *This odor is different from the one in Kenny Town.*

"Troll, is something on your mind?" asked Jack.

"I thought I smelled something," Troll said. "But it's probably nothing."

"Don't look at me," Jack said, lifting his hands. "I can't technically fart anymore."

Troll laughed.

"It wasn't us either," said RJ from the top of the tank.

"It could be your collection of junk," John Doe said.

"No, I keep that sealed tight."

"So, RJ, if you aren't going to be a junkie anymore, what do you want to do with yourself?"

"I want to be the best engineer on the planet," said RJ, "but I want to live in the woods. John Doe, have you ever lived in the wilderness?"

"Not exactly," John Doe said. "Troll has! He grew up in the wild."

"Really?" asked RJ. "He didn't go to school?"

"Troll had schooling, but I'm unsure where he went."

"So, what do you want to do with yourself, John Doe?"

"I want to be a god," John Doe said quietly.

"What? I could not hear you."

"I'm getting tired," John Doe said, snapping his fingers. A small portal opened beside them. John Doe reached in and pulled out a lawn chair. He snapped his fingers again, and the portal closed.

"What was that?" asked RJ.

"My bedroom," John Doe said, unfolding the lawn chair.

Jessica drove the tank, showing Corin the controls while Rowan and Ace sat in standard seats. Finnegan was seated at the primary weapon in case of an emergency.

"I can't tell you how happy I am that your cyborg fixed this thing," Finnegan said to Corin. "I've been waiting to fire this bad boy again."

"Don't mention it," Corin said.

"We should reach Centerville by tomorrow afternoon," Jessica said.

"Why should it take that long? I thought we'd get there much sooner," Rowan said sadly.

"Sorry," Jessica said. "We'll have to stop and camp for the night. My men need to rest. Plus, my tank's nuclear engine needs to cool."

"I was hoping we would not need to camp," Rowan said, sighing deeply.

"We'll be all right," Corin said. "We'll take turns keeping watch."

"RJ can stay up all night," Finnegan said. "He's wired that way. Do you ever sleep, RJ?"

There was no response.

Finnegan tried again. "RJ?"

Again, no response.

Annoyed, Finnegan raised his voice. "RJ!"

RJ and John Doe had cuddled up like kittens and were fast asleep on the lawn chair.

"The thermal cooling vents are starting to glow," Ace said, checking the controls.

"What does that mean?" asked Corin.

"The engine is too warm," explained Ace. "We've been on the road for four hours now. We'd best halt."

"Troll and Jack probably need to rest," said Rowan.

"This looks like a nice spot," Jessica said as they rolled into a clearing. She stopped the tank.

"This area looks recently used," Corin said. "Maybe we should find another location?"

"If anyone was here, they're long gone now," Finnegan said, opening the hatch. "Come on, let's get a fire started."

"Hey, why did we stop?" Troll asked.

"We're camping, boys," Finnegan told Jack and Troll. "Who wants to take the first watch after the sun goes down?"

"Wait a minute; we can't stay out in the open like this," Troll said. "Something could find us very easily here. Someone cleared this area for a reason. It's not going to be nightfall for a few more hours. We should continue."

"Let me take a look at our surroundings," Jack said, walking into the center of the clearing. He noticed food wrappers, previously gathered wood and a shallow pit from an older fire. He analyzed the land with his virtual head-up display and saw footprints. "Troll, I think we'll be fine. These tracks are about a week old, and the wood is rotten. No one has been here for several days."

"I know we're eager to get to Centerville, but we need to rest," Jessica said. "It will be easier to camp here for the night. We'll arrive at Centerville bright and early, then we can get to know the citizens and explore the city."

Troll pulled out the map and studied it. He noticed a neighboring city less than six miles from Centerville. The map read FRANKLIN CITY. *Isn't that where Jack said he became a cyborg?* Troll's breathing increased as he walked over and looked at the tracks in the dirt. He sighed in relief when he saw they were human tracks. "Okay," said Troll, nodding. "I'll keep watch tonight."

"I'll take the shift after you," Finnegan volunteered.

"No," Troll said. "You rest with everyone else. I can stay up all night."

"What?" Jack asked. "You need to sleep sometime."

"I haven't slept since the morning we met," Troll said. "I won't need to again for a while."

"What? What did you do last night in your hotel room?" Jack asked.

"I was thinking," Troll said, gathering firewood.

"You mean you don't sleep like normal people? What are you?" Finnegan asked roughly, following him.

Troll exhaled, putting the firewood in a pile. He rubbed his hands together and turned to Finnegan. "I'll explain—" Troll paused.

The smell was back.

Troll's eyes widened and darted around the tree line. He sniffed the air; a tiny breath escaped his lips. He placed his right hand over his heart.

"Are you okay?" Jack asked.

"Yes," Troll said softly. "I'll be right back. I need to check on something." He slowly backed away from them, disappearing into the woods.

"What's his problem?" Finnegan asked.

"Maybe he needs to use the bathroom? He'll be back," Jack said and shrugged his shoulders.

"Well, I don't care what he's doing. All I care about is sleep. If he can stay up all night, then that makes me happy."

John Doe and RJ continued their nap as the others set up camp.

Jack filled the pit in the middle of the clearing with the firewood Troll had gathered.

"I bet you can't light a fire without using your gizmos," dared Rowan.

"I'll show you," Jack said, rubbing two sticks together. "Come on, work!"

Rowan giggled and winked. "I'm about to be unladylike," she said, spitting on the wood.

"Ugh, Rowan, that's—"

A fire immediately ignited.

"Scheisse!" Jack hollered, falling backward into the dirt.

Rowan laughed and danced away.

Jessica grabbed a large pot as Finnegan opened a compartment inside the tank and pulled out bowls, utensils, and cans of beans. When they emerged from the tank, there was rustling in the trees above them. They paused, looked up at the trees, and listened carefully. The rustling stopped.

"Do you see anything?" Jessica asked.

"No, ma'am," Finnegan said. "Might have been the wind or a bird. Come on. I'm starving."

They joined the others at the campfire.

"Where's Troll?" asked Corin.

"He went off into the woods," Jack said. "He said he needed to take care of something."

"What?" Corin asked. "That doesn't make any sense. Wake up, John Doe!"

"Hey, John Doe," Jack yelled, walking over to his sleeping friend. He gently shook John Doe's lawn chair. "Hey, John Doe, wake up."

"Are we there?" John Doe asked sleepily.

"No, what—where in the hell did you get this lawn chair?" Jack asked, baffled.

"My bedroom," John Doe said.

"Huh?" Jack squeaked.

RJ woke up and looked around. "Where are we?"

"We need to camp for the night, boys," said Jack. "John Doe, Troll, just wandered off alone. Do you know where he may have gone?"

"He what?" John Doe shouted, snapping his fingers and opening the portal to his bedroom again. "Something must be wrong." He folded the lawn chair, returned it to his bedroom, and shut the portal.

"Nothing's wrong. We're all here," Rowan said. "We're going to make some food, relax, and then go to bed."

Finnegan looked at the surrounding forest. "It's not safe being in the woods alone."

"Finn, will you cook the beans?" Jessica asked.

"Sure," he said, opening a few cans with his Swiss Army knife.

"Do you think we'll see any wild animals?" Rowan asked Corin.

"We may," he said. "This forest is full of creatures."

"I hope so!" Rowan said, smiling. "I've met most of the creatures born in my forest. But we're getting far from my territory. I'm sure I will—"

"Die!" yelled a sinister voice from the trees above.

"Who in the hell—" Finnegan pulled out his rifle and aimed at the trees.

Corin also drew his pistol as Jack transformed his left hand into his energy gun.

"Who's there?" Jessica called out.

"What do you want?" Rowan cried, hiding behind Corin.

"You all will die! *Forasteros,* I hope you enjoy your final night," said the evil voice in a heavy Spanish accent.

"Show yourself!" John Doe screamed.

"No, I don't think so. You will all know in due time who I am."

"If this is your land, then we will leave," Jessica said. "We're not looking for trouble. We didn't mean to trespass."

"It's too late to leave. Even if you try to escape, I will find and destroy you all! I give you this night, but tomorrow, you will perish!" The evil voice laughed.

The trees rustled as the invisible spy leaped from tree to tree.

"I'll be back in the morning. *Adios*!"

"He's leaving," Rowan said with relief. "Who was that?"

"I don't know, but we should leave," Jack said.

"Where's Troll?" John Doe shrieked, waving his arms around with agitation.

EIGHT

The evening sun was starting to set, making the forest floor darker. Troll used this to his advantage and crept through the darkness, keeping low to the ground. He made each step slow and precise. He didn't want a twig to break or a leaf to crunch. Troll spotted a shadowy figure jumping from branch to branch with proficiency. It perched on a thick branch, looked around, and sniffed loudly. Troll froze, swallowing hard. *That's who threatened my friends. I'd better hide my scent.* He dug his hands into the dirt and rubbed it on his exposed arms.

The shadowy figure jumped from tree to tree again. Troll carefully resumed his pursuit. The shadowy figure stopped abruptly and growled.

Did it hear me? Troll took a step back, and his boot snapped a twig. His heart skipped a beat.

The shadowy figure turned around; two golden glowing eyes looked directly at Troll.

Troll grabbed his axe, tapped the amulet, and charged.

The shadowy figure sprang from the tree, roaring ferociously. As soon as its feet touched the ground, it pounced.

Troll let out a loud battle cry as the power in the amulet surged. He raised his axe and brought it down before him as the creature brought up his large paws with long, razor-sharp talons ready to strike.

Back at the campsite, Rowan sat with her elbows on her knees and her hands on her chin. *I'm worried about Troll alone in the forest with that crazy stranger on the loose. I like Troll. He's not an Antiquity, but I can't stop my feelings. Could I be smitten? Oh no! This is so unlike me. I usually flirt with any male.* Her large ears twitched. She heard the dreaded roar of the stranger and Troll's bellow. "I can hear Troll! He's in trouble!" Rowan yelled, standing and balling her hands into fists. "I think he's fighting whoever was just here!"

"He shouldn't have gone alone. What an airheaded decision," Finnegan said, throwing a piece of wood on the fire.

"Which direction, Rowan?" asked Corin.

"We've got to help him," John Doe said with desperation.

"Follow me," said Rowan, spreading her wings and kicking into the air. She flew toward Troll's voice as John Doe, Jack, and Corin followed her.

"Should we help them?" asked RJ.

"No," said Finnegan. "We won't endanger ourselves just because their friend did something stupid."

"What's stupid about it?" asked RJ.

"You should never separate from your group in the wilderness."

"But John Doe told me Troll grew up in the forest."

"Then he might have a fighting chance. If he's lucky."

Troll swung his axe, and the sharp blade penetrated the shadowy figure's armor.

"*Niño estúpido*!" roared the shadowy figure in agony.

"Who are you?" Troll demanded, pulling his axe out of his opponent's armor. Blood splattered as Troll brought his axe around for another attack.

The shadowy figure dodged, but razor-sharp talons scraped against the side of Troll's chest plate.

Rays of the evening sunlight pierced through the canopy.

Troll noticed an emblem on the shadowy figure's armor. *I have to see that logo!* He kicked the shadowy figure's abdomen, forcing it to stumble into a sunbeam. Troll was thunderstruck, and his heart beat like a drum as he gazed at the creature from his nightmare.

Muscles bulged under black and red armor, crowned with pointed ears, golden eyes, sharp claws, a long tail, short, fine black fur, and a jaguar's face.

I knew it! Troll thought.

"I'll kill you! How foolish of you, *hombre*, to track a therasapien such as I! What is that look you are giving me, *niño*?" asked the jaguar-man, noticing Troll's wide-eyed expression. "Have you seen another like me in these parts?"

"No," Troll said. "Not around here."

Troll's response engrossed him. "Where have you come into contact with another?"

"That's not what this fight is about," Troll said, keeping his axe ready. "Why did you threaten my friends? Why did you follow us here?"

"You're good. You *knew* I was following you."

"I could smell you a mile away."

Troll's comment interested him even more. The therasapien slowly circled Troll, looking him up and down.

Troll studied the therasapien's movements.

"You could *smell* me? How? You look like a normal human. There does not seem to be anything special about you! However, you were able to follow me without my realizing . . . no one has ever been able to track *me* before. In my experience, no one has *ever* been able to track my kind. Who are you?"

"I'm not important," Troll said.

"No, you're not," said the therasapien, laughing. "But I *am* fascinated. I want answers before you die. If I must treat you as a disobedient *niño* and beat what I wish to know, I shall! *Niño* is what I will call you and write on your grave!" He pounced, hovering over Troll's head. His maniacal laughter scattered in different directions.

Troll raised his axe to block, but the therasapien sunk his sharp claws into Troll's exposed biceps. He yelled in pain but didn't drop his axe. His blood trickled down his arms. *I need to get this heavy guy off of me!* He used all his strength and lifted his axe to strike.

The therasapien roared when he saw the sharp blade coming at him and sprang from Troll's arms. His leap forced Troll to collapse.

Troll groaned and barely caught himself with his left hand as his right clutched the axe.

The therasapien lunged, but Troll felt his approach and somersaulted out of the way. The therasapien cursed under his breath when his fist punched the dirt where Troll had been.

Troll swiftly kicked the therasapien's head before swinging his axe sideways, striking his abdominal armor.

The therasapien staggered, one hand grabbed at his face as the other clutched his midsection.

Troll sliced at his throat.

The therasapien dodged and roared ferociously. He kicked Troll's left leg as his long black tail latched around Troll's right leg, knocking him off balance.

Troll fell onto his back and dropped his axe beside him, just out of reach.

The therasapien laughed maniacally again and jumped onto Troll, landing vertically on his torso.

Troll tried desperately to reach his axe, but the therasapien flicked it away with his tail and locked his left paw over Troll's right arm.

The therasapien grinned maliciously, showing all of his fangs. He licked his right forefinger's sharp claw and brought it down to Troll's throat under his blue choker. "You don't know how to give up, do you, *Niño*?" he asked, tracing his talon along Troll's throat. "I've never had an opponent like you before. You are most impressive to be able to keep up with my every move. I'll kill you quickly, out of respect, but not yet—"

"What's stopping you?" Troll demanded bravely, trying to hide his fear. He locked eyes with the therasapien and gazed intently. *Will those be my final words?*

The question caught the therasapien off guard, but he became infuriated when he saw no fear in Troll's eyes. His face sweltered, and his entire body heated like fire. He wanted Troll to die with terror in his heart. He put his fingers on Troll's carotid artery and felt his pulse. It was strong, swiftly throbbing.

Troll's breathing increased, but he kept poised. He squeezed his free left hand into a fist and punched the therasapien where his axe had bit through the armor into his flesh.

The therasapien coughed up blood and caused a slight abrasion across Troll's throat.

Troll exhaled sharply, grabbed the therasapien's neck, and violently slammed his face into the dirt. Unfortunately, Troll didn't use enough force to knock the therasapien off him.

"You're so strong," said the jaguar-man, lifting his head from the soil, coughing and choking on his blood. He stood but kept a foot on Troll's abdomen, his golden eyes filled with loathing. "I'm done toying with you, *Niño.*" The therasapien leaped into the air and dropped his knee sharply into Troll's diaphragm.

Troll could feel the blow through his armor. It knocked the wind out of him. He tried to cry out in pain, but no sound emerged from his mouth.

The therasapien pulled out an extremely sharp knife and aimed it above Troll's heaving chest.

Troll looked at the weapon nervously. His lips trembled.

The therasapien looked into Troll's eyes. He finally saw the warrior's dread. "Prepare to die!" he exclaimed, prepared to stab the blade deep into Troll's heart.

"No!" shrieked Rowan as a massive gale struck the therasapien, knocking him off Troll and into a tree. She flew out of the woods and landed next to Troll. "Help me, roots!" she beckoned, hands glowing green.

The trees animated and loomed over the therasapien.

He let out a terrible roar when tree roots burst from the ground, slithered around him, and pinned him against the tree. The therasapien sliced through the roots with his sharp claws, but more erupted, enveloping him.

"Troll, get up!" Rowan cried, kneeling beside him and gently running her fingers through his purple hair.

Troll's shell-shocked blue eyes met Rowan's frightened honey eyes. "I need my axe," he said weakly.

"Oh, Troll!" Rowan exclaimed, flying to the axe. "It's so heavy!" She strained to lift it. Her eyes teared up, looking at the man she adored.

Troll struggled to his feet and noticed the therasapien was almost free from the tree roots. He saw Rowan tugging on his axe. Swallowing hard, Troll took a deep breath and slowly trudged toward her.

Rowan managed to drag the axe closer to Troll. She wanted to tell him not to move, but she couldn't find the words in her fear.

The jaguar-man fought away the roots and faced Rowan. He roared ferociously, running toward her.

Rowan screamed in terror. Her mind blanked. She closed her eyes and fell to her knees, cowering behind the axe.

The therasapien attempted to swipe at the sweet faerie, but Troll swiftly side-tackled him, using the force of his entire body to knock the jaguar-man off his feet. They crashed into a tree, damaging the trunk.

Rowan trembled but opened her eyes. She watched in horror as the two warriors wrestled.

The therasapien rolled on top of Troll again, overpowering the young human. "I hate you! *Niño*, you are dead!"

Troll coughed up blood. It splashed onto the therasapien's face.

The therasapien snarled, got up, and continuously kicked Troll's chest plate, attempting to crack it under the red amulet.

"No!" Troll pleaded.

"Save him!" Rowan screeched desperately. "Please! Please save him!"

Corin, John Doe, and Jack ran out of the woods. Corin and Jack had their weapons aimed at the therasapien. John Doe's hands glowed with magical energy.

The therasapien looked at them and snorted.

"Get away from him!" John Doe shouted.

"Your *amigos* have come for you, *Niño*," said the therasapien, slowly stepping back.

"Who are you?" Corin demanded, keeping his finger on the trigger of his laser pistol.

"You'll find out in the morning," the jaguar-man said, leaping into the trees. "You were lucky this time, *Niño*, but I'll be back! You will all die when the sun rises!"

Rowan rushed to Troll's side. "Troll, are you all right?"

"Come back here, therasapien," Troll moaned like he hadn't heard Rowan. He struggled to stand, watching the trees where the therasapien had vanished. "You coward," Troll breathed, dropping to his knees. He gasped sharply and pressed his hands on the amulet.

"Troll, what's wrong?" Corin asked, running to him.

"Troll! Answer us, please!" Rowan bawled, her voice trembling.

His blue eyes widened, his breathing increased, and a cold sweat broke out on his forehead. He gulped, then inhaled sharply. His pupils shrank. Troll tightly closed his eyes before screaming. His hands pressed harder onto the amulet, and he collapsed.

"Oh, Heka, the magic god! What happened to him?" Rowan shrieked.

"Was that a heart attack?" asked Jack.

"I'm not sure," Corin said, rolling Troll onto his back.

Troll's wounds instantly healed, and he opened his eyes. "Hi, guys. Thanks for coming." Troll looked at the red amulet on his chest and sighed with relief. He sat up slowly, brushing dirt off his arms.

His friends stood motionless, astonished to see him behave like nothing had happened.

Troll saw minor cracks in his chest plate. "Well, that just won't do," he said, carefully removing the yellow star and upside-down pyramid clasps locked around his amulet.

"I thought that was part of your armor," Jack said.

"It is. It protects my amulet," Troll said, stripping off his chest plate, revealing a perfectly circular hole in the center.

His four friends simultaneously drew in deep breaths of surprise. The red amulet was not part of his armor but embedded into Troll's chest, directly over his heart.

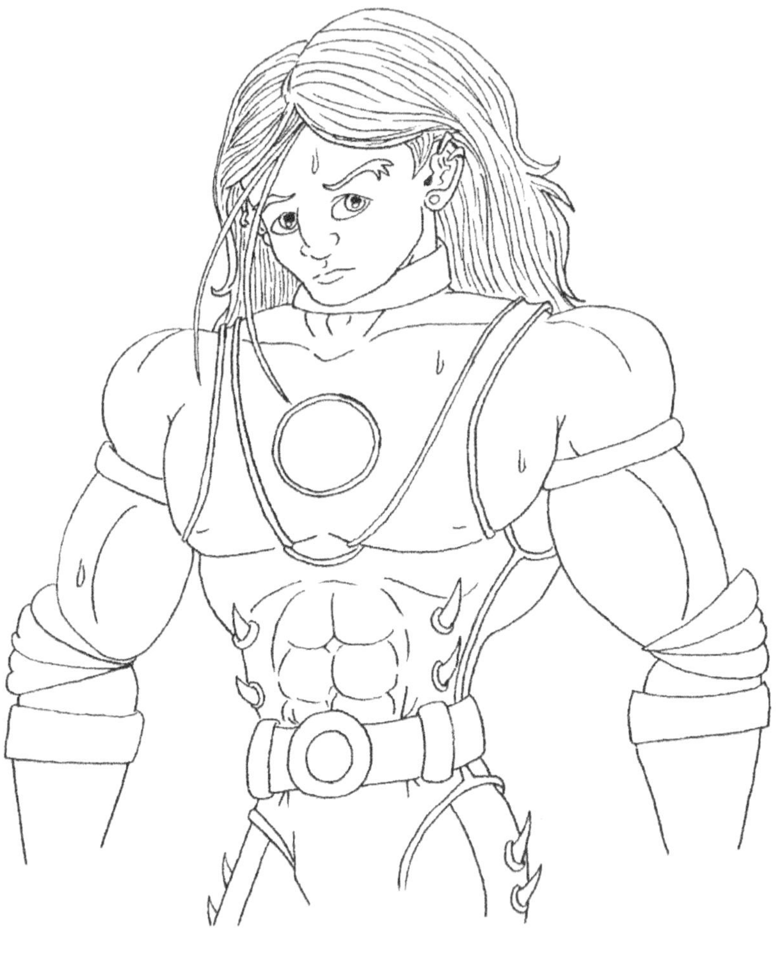

NINE

Troll opened the sack on his belt and pulled out a vial of blue polish and a stained rag. He removed the cap, tipped the bottle, and a tiny drop of the polish fell onto the discolored cloth. Troll gently rubbed the liquid on the small cracks in his armor. Like magic, his armor mended. "That's much better." Troll sighed as he donned his armor once again. He reattached the clasps around his amulet and smiled.

Troll's companions stared at him, speechless.

"What are you guys staring at?"

"Troll, that thing . . . in your chest . . . is . . . a part of you?" Corin asked nervously.

"Were you born with this?" Jack asked with concern. "Or is it some kind of implant?"

"No," Troll said, gently touching the amulet. "I was not born with it. Five years ago, after a battle, I woke up, and there it was. I have no memory of how this became a part of me. It's why I can't sleep."

"Your wounds have healed . . . like magic," Rowan said, feeling his biceps where the jaguar-man had cut him.

"That's one of the effects of this amulet," Troll explained as he returned the vial and rag to his sack. "It protects me. It also makes me run at incredible speeds. I don't know all that it can do. It somehow knows when I need it and activates by my touch. It will also act on its own sometimes, and it . . . scares me every time."

"Does it have anything to do with your secret mission?" asked John Doe.

"If it did, I would not tell you all this."

"John Doe, he's your partner! You didn't know about this?" Rowan angrily asked.

"Hey, I don't hang out with Troll when he's naked!" shouted John Doe.

"I wonder why that mutant left? It's so unusual. First, he threatens us, attacks Troll, and then runs away. I don't get it," Jack stated.

"Yes, it's pretty strange behavior," Troll said, standing slowly.

"We're glad you're safe, Troll," said Corin. "Do you know anything about that creature?"

Troll swallowed hard and retrieved the axe where Rowan had left it. *I am not ready to talk about this.*

"Let's head back to the tank and think of a strategy in case he comes back," Corin suggested when Troll remained silent.

"He *will* be back as soon as the sun comes up," Troll said quickly as he returned his axe to its sheath.

"How do you know?" Rowan asked, concerned.

Troll breathed in deeply, sighed, and gently touched the amulet. He looked at it and then at his friends. *I need to tell them.* "Once we return to the campsite, I'll explain," Troll said. "I'll keep watch tonight in case anything else happens."

"Someone else will stand guard with you," Corin said, walking beside Troll.

John Doe, Rowan, and Jack followed behind them.

"He will not return tonight, Corin. Trust me," Troll said. "You guys need to rest so you'll be able to get up before dawn."

"Let's get the tank ready and get the hell out of here," Jack suggested. "Come tomorrow, we'll be gone, and that lowlife can have that clearing all to himself."

"He's not watching the clearing," Troll said. "It doesn't matter where we go . . . he'll follow us until he destroys us."

They entered the clearing. The tank crew had prepared dinner and were seated around the small campfire, passing out the bowls and utensils.

"Oh, good. You found him! I can't have the protector of my precious cargo going missing," Jessica said, smiling at Troll. "I'm glad you're safe."

"Thank you," Troll said, sitting near the campfire but keeping his distance from the flames.

Jack sat beside Troll, resting a supportive hand on his shoulder.

"He looks apprehensive," Jessica whispered to Corin. "What happened?"

"He found the guy who threatened us, and they fought. No one won," explained Corin, sitting beside Jack. "Gather around, everyone. Troll, are you ready to talk? Do you need a minute?"

Troll breathed in deeply, glancing at the canopy. He watched the sun setting in the distance. "As some of you may know, all big cat apex predators have been extinct on Earth since the twenty-second century. Scientists had stored their DNA to revive their species; however, the DNA fell into the wrong hands. The Restrain Corporation felt engineering genetic cat mutants would be more fitting of the big cat DNA than attempting to bring back the extinct species. They mixed human DNA with the big cat DNA, and therasapiens were born.

"Therasapiens are bred to hunt a target they are assigned to unless they're guarding a location. I caught his scent earlier; he's been following us since Jack and Ace repaired the tank. More than likely, we've accidentally gotten too close to his hidden base. We are now considered a threat, and he will destroy us. He'll attack at dawn. He's gathering reinforcements tonight, so we should have some supper and form a plan to protect ourselves."

"Troll, how do you know all of this?" asked Jack.

"I just have—personal experience—purely coincidental."

"I'll fill you all in on my plan as we eat," Corin said, spooning beans into a bowl.

"You've come up with a plan already?" asked Finnegan. "That was fast."

"I'm a skilled planner," said Corin. "Jessica, does your team have radios? If not, the mayor of Kenny Town gave us some. We'll share them to keep in constant communication."

"Yes, we have communicators. Corin, no offense, but I want to know more about my enemy before I hear your plan. Troll, does this therasapien consider us a large threat?" asked Jessica, gulping.

"He knows I cannot beat him on my own. He also knows we have a tank, which means we could be considered a large threat. He'll either attack with a bomb or send his troops. He may fire explosives at us before attempting to confront us. Therasapiens do that if they believe they can't handle an enemy."

"What do we do now?" asked Rowan, sitting across from Troll. She glanced over the campfire and saw Troll's tense posture. She nervously chewed on her bottom lip.

"Well, the first part of the plan is that we'll need a distraction," Corin said. "We'll need someone to distract the therasapien while we move into action."

"Who can we get to do that?" asked Finnegan. "I'm not doing it. That creature is strong and crafty."

"I could try to hold him off," Troll said bravely, making eye contact with Rowan.

A concerned look flitted across her face, but she remained silent.

"No," Corin told Troll. "You can't fight him alone again."

"Lads, can our wizard not summon something to distract him?" asked Ace.

"That's not a bad idea," Rowan said, hopeful. "He summoned a dragon earlier!"

"A dragon?" Finnegan choked in surprise.

"It was an accident," John Doe said, fiddling with his scarf.

"Well, that's perfect! Have him do it again," advised Finnegan.

"Oh! Thoth, be merciful!" exclaimed John Doe. "Do I have to?"

"Yes, you'll need to," said Corin.

"Oh, that is going to be a mistake," Troll grumbled. "Everything he summons tries to kill us."

"That doesn't sound promising," said Ace.

"It'll have to do," said Corin. "A distraction must be made somewhere in this battle to get the therasapien off his guard—something he won't expect. Now, myself and two others will stay at the camp. Everyone else will be off in the distance. Stay hidden. While in camp, we'll stay back-to-back to judge which direction the attack will begin. Once we know, then we fall back to the others."

"I'll stay," Troll volunteered.

"I guess I will stay as well," said Finnegan, looking at Troll. "Two strong men are better than one."

"All right," said Corin. "Now, after we fall back, Jack will have us covered and use his energy gun to defend us. Ace will operate and fire the tank. I have a few weapons I can use as well."

"I have a larger attachment for my energy gun, Corin. I have a feeling you'll like it. I also have some little missiles which I can activate," said Jack. "I haven't used them in forever, but they should be in working order."

"That's great, Jack," said Corin. "Rowan, it'll be your job to rescue any wildlife if a fire starts."

"Oh my! Will there be fires?" Rowan asked, becoming agitated and playing with her hair.

Troll saw Rowan's discomfort.

"It's possible," said Corin.

"Oh no!" Rowan cried, pressing her hands onto her cheeks.

Troll inhaled through his nose and stood up. He maneuvered over to Rowan. His friends watched him drop to one knee and place his hand on Rowan's shoulder, comforting the fearful faerie.

Rowan smiled gratefully at Troll.

Corin raised an eyebrow, then cleared his throat. "While John Doe's dragon distracts the therasapien, we'll be able to capture him."

"What about his reinforcements?" asked Troll.

"We kill them . . . all of them," said Corin coldly.

TEN

Today was full of excitement. I never dreamed of ever meeting someone as beautiful as Jessica Dove. She's so temperamental yet angelic. I have a weird feeling in the pit of my stomach. She's a dangerous woman, and I like danger.

Troll proved his loyalty today. He protected us from a mutant jaguar-man known as a therasapien. I have never seen a creature like that before. Even though he told us about the therasapien, I can't help but think that Troll is still hiding something.

I devised a brilliant plan to kill any of the therasapien's reinforcements. No one threatens Corin Degodi!

—From the journal of Corin Degodi
June 11, 2215, 10:35 p.m.

Corin looked up from his journal at the others sleeping around the fire.

"You should get some rest. Come dawn, you'll need your strength," said Troll, sitting under a tree beside their wood pile.

"I won't be long," promised Corin.

"What is that?" asked Troll, pointing at the notebook.

"I'm keeping a log of our journey. You never know when someone may want to read about our adventure. This book could become famous one day." Corin closed his journal and returned it to his pouch. He yawned, hitting a small button on his belt. A chamber opened, and a blue blanket unfolded.

Troll lifted an eyebrow as he watched Corin remove his helmet and put it on the ground.

"I have no pillow packed," Corin said, shrugging his shoulders. He laid his head on the helmet. "This will have to do."

"Good night, Corin," said Troll. "At least you're already wearing pajamas."

"*Humph!* Good night. This outfit isn't even comfortable," Corin muttered under his breath, knowing getting cozy would not be easy. He drifted to sleep.

It's going to be a boring night. I know nothing will happen, Troll thought, leaning against the tree. He listened to the creatures of the forest: crickets chirping, frogs croaking, the hoot of an owl, and the gently cry of the—

"No, n-n-no . . ." John Doe whimpered.

Troll looked at his sleeping friend.

"No, Mommy! Don't put the burnt cheese on that flapjack! The rancid gas will kill my potato!" John Doe whined, his legs twitching.

Maybe the night won't be as boring as I thought.

After his strange-sounding dream, John Doe grew silent.

Troll looked at the night sky through the canopy. His mind raced, and he knew meditating was the only way to tame it. He took deep breaths, relaxed his muscles, and eventually lost track of time as the night dragged on.

Hours later, upon waking to complete darkness, Rowan became increasingly nervous. Her eyes needed to adjust. The campfire smoked eerily, and she heard strange noises like a symphony of demons snorting. She gasped and looked around. She sighed with relief when she noticed John Doe, Corin, Finnegan, and Jack were snoring.

"Are you okay?" asked Troll from behind her.

Rowan squeaked and flew into the air, her wings flapping fiercely. She quickly grabbed a tree branch and held on before looking down at Troll.

"It's all right, Rowan. I'm still on patrol. No one has come or gone."

He looks so sincere and innocent. I would like to have some fun with him, she thought with a smug expression as she yelled, "Don't do that!"

"Do what?" he asked, confused.

"Scare me!" she stated as she let go of the tree branch. Rowan intentionally kept her wings together and fell.

Troll rushed to his feet and caught her.

"Oh!" Rowan gasped when she felt his strong arms around her. "Th-thank you."

"You're welcome." Troll chuckled heartily. "I didn't mean to startle you."

Rowan blushed as he gently put her down. She quickly cleared her throat, put her hands on her hips, and gave him a stern look. "I bet you think you're funny!" she exclaimed, giving him a little growl.

Troll crossed his arms over his chest, leaned against the tree, and smiled. "Not at all. I promise it wasn't intentional."

"Good, because I do not need someone deliberately pulling pranks on me, mister! And I didn't ask you to catch me." *Oh, gods! We're flirting! Well, I'm teasing . . . he's so handsome! Now, Rowan, say something nice to him.*

"I take it you're not a morning person?"

"What makes you ask that?" Rowan asked as she stuck out her tongue and rolled her eyes.

Jessica woke up in her sleeping sack and threw a baseball-sized rock at Rowan.

"Hey!" Rowan shrilled as she dodged the rock heading for her head.

The rock soared toward Troll. He caught it with his bare left hand and gently tossed it away.

Rowan stood up straight, glaring at Jessica. "Why'd you do that?"

"You need to shut your mouth, faerie!" Jessica said. "Do you want to let that therasapien know we are awake? I suggest you keep silent if you want to keep that pretty little head of yours! I'm sure he'll do much more than throw a rock at you."

John Doe groaned and lifted his head from a large, hard stone. "Great, two women who woke up on the wrong side of the bed." He yawned and stretched. "Ow! Why does my head feel like I used a rock as a pillow?" He noticed the stone. "Oh, it's because I *was*." He laughed, holding his neck painfully.

Rowan grunted but sighed hard, "I'm sorry," she said, walking over to Jessica, who was packing her sleeping sack. "I hope I didn't put us in more danger."

"I think we're okay for now," Jessica told her. "Troll, have you seen anything?"

"No," he answered. "No smells either. Our friend will return with the dawn, not before. We have some time left until the sun is up."

Finnegan woke up beside John Doe. Tiredly, he began to roll up his sleeping bag and mumbled about something to eat for breakfast besides beans.

Rowan made her way over to where Corin was resting. "Wake up, Corin," she said, kneeling beside her friend and gently nudging his back.

Corin yawned loudly as he slowly turned onto his back and sat up. His hair was a complete mess, and his brown eyes had red lines around them.

"You look awful!" Rowan told him.

"Thank you," Corin moaned. "What time is it? I didn't sleep well. My helmet is not the perfect pillow. At least I had a decent blanket," he said, pressing a button on his belt. The blue blanket around his legs sucked into a little notch on his belt.

"That's a neat gizmo," said Jessica, referring to Corin's belt.

"Thanks. My father invented it. He's always developing interesting ways to store important things." Corin chuckled. "Are we ready?"

"It's around five o'clock, lads," said Ace, climbing out of the tank from where his small bunk was. "We'll be able to see the sunrise from here in about forty-five minutes."

"We are all not awake yet," Troll said, pointing at Jack.

Jack was in sleep mode. His eye sockets were black, and a small radio monitor was sticking out of his chest compartment. A small red light glowed as a muffled snore emerged from the speakers.

"Someone wake him," Corin ordered. "We have to get ready. It's almost dawn."

"Junkie!" John Doe cried. "Junkie? Where is my best bud?"

"His name is RJ," said Corin.

"Well, he answers to Junkie, so that's what I'm calling him."

RJ woke up inside the tank, on the floor beside Ace's small bunk. He looked around and noticed that he was alone. He knew he was never supposed to be left alone. He smiled ridiculously and got up, looking at the driver's seat. "Now's my chance to be the hero!" RJ announced as he sat in the chair and glanced at the control panel. He felt something was missing. Something RJ craved against his better judgment. "Screw it!" He reached into his pocket and pulled out a caffeine pill. He popped the delicious tablet into his mouth, and with every suck, his eyes lit with excitement. The caffeine pill tasted like coffee and contained more energy than three cups of espresso. Though it wasn't the strongest drug he'd ever consumed, he became hyper quickly. He guessed this was because he had not been taking pills regularly. He laughed maniacally and started the engine with the ignition key.

Outside, everyone looked at the tank when it miraculously started.

"It's possessed!" screamed John Doe, panicking. He hid behind Corin, locking his hands around his waist.

"Don't be ridiculous, John Doe!" shouted Corin, trying to pull apart John Doe's hands. "You're like a stubborn belt buckle! Let go!"

"Who's in the tank?" asked Jessica.

"Where's RJ?" asked Ace.

"Junkie!" John Doe bellowed. He released Corin and dashed to the tank. He quickly climbed up the turret. "I'll save you from the spirit! Here I come."

"Oh no," Finnegan said, running after John Doe. "Stop him, John Doe! Don't let him take off!"

John Doe opened the hatch and fell into the tank. He saw RJ running his hands over the controls.

"Hi, John Doe!"

"Junkie, where's the spirit?"

"What are you talking about? There's no spirit in here. I'm leading the charge! We're going to catch the enemy by surprise!" RJ's voice was high-pitched, like an eight-year-old boy.

John Doe climbed into the seat beside RJ. "I thought the tank was possessed. Finnegan said not to drive."

"RJ! Stop!" Finnegan yelled outside the tank as he grabbed onto the hull.

"We can't let the enemy win! Let's roll!" RJ proclaimed, hitting the gas, and the tank accelerated.

Finnegan screamed when he felt the tank move. He let go, dropping to the dirt. He knew Jessica would not be pleased, but he was terrified of the tank dragging him. The tank could kill all of them.

RJ balled his hand into a fist and pounded on a black square button.

A jarring horn blared.

"What is that sound?" asked Rowan, covering her large, vulnerable ears. "I'm going to go deaf!"

"That's my doing, lads," said Ace. "I installed a horn sometime back. I thought it could scare away intruders."

"It makes *me* want to run away," said Corin. "It's too loud!"

Jack's audio monitor detected the loud horn as everyone chased the tank away from the campsite. The commotion activated Jack's internal alarm, which forced him out of his sleeping cycle. He let out a muffled yawn from behind his faceplate. Power surged into his eyes. He looked around, but no one was there. Even the tank was gone. Jack noticed fresh tread tracks and footprints. "What did I miss?" he asked sleepily. His robotic eyes scanned the prints for more data. The stride length and deep imprints in the heel and toe sections indicated that his friends had been running. He lifted his faceplate and could hear yelling in the distance. "Oh shit!"

"RJ, Stop!" Jessica screamed.

"What is he doing?" asked Corin, breathing hard.

"I take it you're not an athlete?" asked Finnegan, passing Corin.

Corin did not respond; in fact, he *could not* respond. *Even though my space station has artificial gravity and I work out regularly, I'm not used to the pull of Earth's natural gravity. Not getting comfortable sleep has also taken its toll. I feel light-headed and out of breath. How long can I keep up with the others?*

"We're never going to catch them!" Rowan grumbled, flying beside Corin.

"We must not lose heart," said Troll, pressing the amulet in his chest.

Finnegan was dizzy and hungry. He suddenly lost his balance and tripped over his own feet. His face met the ground.

No one expected Finnegan to collapse, and everyone tripped over him except Troll, who moved like the wind and dodged their crumpled bodies. Their eyes couldn't keep up with him.

"I have never seen anything like that," Finnegan exhaled.

"Wow!" Corin breathed. "Everyone else saw that, right?"

"What was that?" asked Jessica.

"I think it was Troll," said Rowan.

Troll effortlessly caught up to the tank with his enhanced speed, gracefully jumped on board the turret, and opened the armored hatch. He looked inside and saw John Doe and RJ were having the time of their lives. They failed to notice Troll had opened the hatch.

"We're going to chase him down!" John Doe hollered.

"Yeah!" cheered RJ.

"Then we'll show him that he can't threaten us!"

"Not us!"

"I'll use my magic!"

"Magic!"

"No one can sneak up on the mighty John Doe!"

Troll loudly cleared his throat.

John Doe and RJ embraced, screaming like terrified school girls. Their high-pitched screams were mind-numbing.

"Stop that!" Troll yelled. He reached in and grabbed RJ's shirt collar.

"Hey," said RJ. "What are you doing?"

"Get out here!" Troll shouted, pulling RJ outside.

"I can't drive!" John Doe squawked, taking hold of the controls.

"Where do you think you're going?" Troll asked, keeping RJ balanced on the turret.

"We're going to surprise our enemy. Dude, we will kick in the head of the mutant!" RJ said.

"Well, I have news for you, dude. You're going in the wrong direction, which isn't part of Corin's plan."

"I am? I was? It isn't?"

"Yes! Now turn this thing around!" Troll ordered, dropping RJ into John Doe's lap.

"My spine!" John Doe exclaimed.

"You caught me! I didn't know you cared," RJ said, hugging John Doe.

"Get off of me!"

"Watch where you're going!" Troll shrieked into the tank.

"Take the controls! Take them!" John Doe cried when he noticed they were twenty feet from an enormous tree.

Can the tank knock over that tree? RJ thought.

"Do something! You're going to crash!" Troll bellowed at them as he held on for dear life.

We're going twenty-eight miles per hour. Do I have time to turn? We're going to get hurt if I hit it.

John Doe firmly clutched the chair. "I can't look!" he yelped, pulling his hood over his sunglass-goggles.

RJ took the tank's controls. "I'm stopping!"

Troll prepared to save them if RJ failed to turn or stop the tank.

RJ engaged the brakes.

Troll vice gripped the steel rim of the hatch.

RJ clasped his hands onto the control panel, white-knuckled. He shut his eyes and braced himself.

The tank stopped . . . just short of colliding with the massive tree.

John Doe lifted his hood slightly. "Oh, I'm alive! Thank you, lords, I live!"

RJ opened his eyes and looked at John Doe. "So, I'm a lord?" he chuckled with a goofy smile.

"No way!" John Doe yelled. "You scared me! You nearly gave me heart failure!"

"That makes two of us," Troll said, looking into the tank.

John Doe slapped RJ in the face.

"Ow!" RJ barked, placing his hand where he was struck. "Take it easy, man."

John Doe slapped RJ again.

RJ grunted and grabbed John Doe. He attempted to put him into a headlock.

"Knock it off, both of you. RJ, come out here, and I'll show you how I discipline John."

"Don't compare him to me! I didn't encourage this!" John Doe said.

"Oh, you weren't the one I heard yelling with him about attacking the therasapien? That wasn't you? I guess there is another John Doe in the tank?"

"Maybe?" John Doe laughed sheepishly and shrugged his shoulders.

"You know what? You're both off the hook. I won't be the one that disciplines you. Corin will. You disobeyed his orders, and we're probably going to be murdered by the therasapien," Troll declared.

The others finally caught up.

"Where are they?" Jessica screamed angrily, leading the charge.

"Actually," said Troll, laughing. "I think she might pulverize you before Corin gets a chance."

Jessica climbed the hull and pushed Troll's shoulder. "Get out of my way!" she yelled.

"Nice knowing you!" Troll said to them, jumping off the tank.

"What were you two thinking?" Jessica screeched, climbing inside.

RJ and John Doe clung to each other, trembling.

She slammed the hatch shut to lecture them in private, but even through the thick metal hull, everyone could hear her shrill voice.

Troll frowned and leaned against the tank. He looked beyond the trees and crossed his arms over his chest. He inhaled through his nose and exhaled out of his mouth.

"Good job, Troll," Corin said, patting his shoulder. "I'm glad you caught them."

"It didn't help us," Troll said, pointing into the distance. "It is nearly dawn. The therasapien will be upon us before we know it."

"We need to get back to the campsite," Corin said, panicked. "Everyone needs to get into position if this plan will work! Turn on your radios now."

"We might be too late," said Finnegan. "But I sure hope not. I don't want to die this morning."

After the intense lecture, Jessica opened the hatch and climbed out carrying a rucksack. She growled as she joined the others. "So, what are we doing now?" she asked Corin, handing the rucksack to Finnegan.

"John Doe," Corin called, facing the tank.

John Doe cautiously poked his head out of the tank.

"Come here," Corin said.

John Doe looked over at Jessica and shook his head back and forth.

"She's not going to bite you. Get down here!" Corin stated. "We need you!"

John Doe nodded and quickly emerged. His body was shivering like he had been left out in the cold.

Jessica sighed hard, glancing at the trembling wizard.

"Hi, Corin," said John Doe nervously.

"Here's what I need you to do—" Corin said, pulling off John Doe's hood and whispering into his ear.

Jack finally managed to catch up with his companions. His large, metal body clanked loudly with each step. He walked up to Ace, who was leaning against the tank. Lifting his faceplate, Jack asked, "What happened?"

"Nice of you to join us, laddie. It seems our neighborhood junkie decided to lead the charge without us," Ace said.

"But the enemy is in the other direction," Jack said, confused.

"That's what I found out!" RJ shouted from inside the tank. "I made a big boo-boo!"

"I'll say you did. What did Jess say?" Jack asked.

"She said many mean things," RJ said, poking his head out. "Then she gave John Doe and me what for."

"John Doe did it, too?" asked Jack. "What the hell?"

"It's okay. John Doe is going to solve our problem. Remember, I'm the one who suggested he summon a distraction," Ace said proudly, placing his hands on his hips and nodding.

Jack cocked his neck, producing a whip-like snapping sound. He inhaled sharply and lowered his faceplate to hide his worried expression. "Oh, shit. I know it's part of the plan, but Troll's right. John Doe can't control his creatures. I'm nervous."

I sure hope we're ready for this. I know I'm ready. No matter the cost, I'll make that mutant pay. I hope John Doe does what I told him and doesn't do anything stupid. I remember what the Eastern Regiment mercenaries said about Troll. I hope they're wrong about him, and he won't put us all in danger. He hasn't let us down yet.

—From the journal of Corin Degodi
June 12, 2215, 5:57 a.m.

Corin, Troll, and Finnegan returned to the campsite. There was no sign of the therasapien.

"He's not here," said Finnegan, taking the rucksack off his back.

"We have ten minutes until sunrise," Troll said.

"I don't like this," Corin said.

"I bet he chickened out," said Finnegan.

"I doubt it." Troll sighed.

"Rowan, come in," Corin said through his communicator.

"Yes?" rang Rowan's sweet voice.

"Rowan, change in plans. You stick to the air. If you see the therasapien or anyone coming to his aid, you let us know immediately. We won't stand a chance if they surround us."

"B-but what about the animals?"

"Do you understand?" asked Corin gruffly.

"Yes, over and out," Rowan said crossly.

"Corin, what *about* the animals?" asked Troll with a serious tone. "A fire could happen in this bat—"

"That's secondary," Corin said curtly.

Troll didn't like Corin's attitude and especially didn't approve of how he spoke to Rowan. He knew he could not focus on that now. Their lives were all in danger.

"Make sure your radios are on," reminded Corin.

"Calm down. They're on," said Finnegan with his assault rifle drawn.

Troll had his axe ready.

"Let's get busy," Corin said.

They moved quickly, watching each other's backs as they attached the sleeping bags to the rucksack and cleaned the area.

"Is that everything?" asked Troll.

"Yes, everything else was in the tank before RJ's escapade," said Finnegan.

"Okay, let's go," Corin said.

"Not so fast, *amigos*," roared the jaguar-man from above.

"Show yourself!" Finnegan yelled, aiming at the treetops.

A grenade landed in front of Finnegan.

"Watch out!" Troll shouted, throwing himself on top of Finnegan and hitting the deck.

Corin also hurled to the ground.

The grenade exploded.

Once the fragmentation ceased, Corin dashed for the trees and cried, "Take cover!"

Troll covered Finnegan in case the therasapien threw another grenade. They took shelter in the trees.

The therasapien laughed at them.

"That was a cheap shot!" Corin stated. "Why don't you face us?"

"I do not need to," the therasapien declared.

Troll and Finnegan cautiously joined Corin. "Keep back-to-back until we know which way they are coming from," Troll ordered.

They braced for battle.

Ten large human soldiers, equipped with advanced weapons, wearing black uniforms and armor, emerged from the shrubs. The insignia on their uniforms was the emblem of a brain with an eye.

The Restrain Corporation! Troll thought, tensing.

"Now, where are your companions?" asked the therasapien, remaining out of sight.

"Wouldn't you like to know," Corin said.

"No matter. We will find them. *No muestres piedad*!" the jaguar-man announced.

"Sir?" asked a soldier.

The therasapien rolled his eyes. "I said, show no mercy!"

The soldiers roared a battle cry, startling Corin and Finnegan.

Troll stood poised.

"Now! Soldiers of Franklin City, attack and kill them!"

"Franklin City?" Corin breathed.

I knew it, Troll thought. *We're too close to their base and headquarters.*

Two of the men held small remote controls. They pressed a few buttons, and two large jets materialized above. Each had an energy gun similar to Jack's and was ready to fire.

"They have cloaking devices!" Corin cried out in shock.

"What's that?" Finnegan asked.

"Never mind, just run for it!"

Finnegan and Corin covered their heads and ran for their lives as the energy guns fired deadly lasers.

Troll used his axe as a shield and reflected some of the lasers off his enormous blade.

The soldiers tapped a few more buttons, and the jets came down. The men boarded and flew after Corin and Finnegan as four soldiers wearing helmets tapped the symbols on their uniforms. Their insignias shimmered, and four hoverbikes de-cloaked. They boarded the bikes and took off after Corin and Finnegan as well.

The therasapien pounced on Troll.

Troll screamed in surprise and lost his balance. He fell forward into the dirt and dropped his axe.

"We meet again, Mr. Troll!" said the jaguar-man as he sat on Troll's muscular back. "That is what your *amigos* call you, isn't it, *Niño*?"

"Yes," Troll said, struggling to knock the therasapien off him.

"Why is that?" the therasapien asked.

The four remaining soldiers ran over and aimed their rifles at Troll.

"Don't stop, you idiots! Incompetence! Go after them! *This* one is mine."

The soldiers nodded and ran after Corin and Finnegan.

"*Hermosa*," said the therasapien, showing all his teeth in a sinister smile as he stroked Troll's purple hair.

Troll swallowed hard. "Wh-what?"

"Beautiful . . . your locks of hair, *Niño*," the therasapien said, chuckling. "What a shame."

Troll elbowed his gut.

The therasapien shrieked in surprise and fell off Troll's back.

Troll rolled over, sat up, and punched him in the face.

The therasapien hollered, tumbling over.

"Troll is my code name," said Troll proudly. He backflipped to his axe and tapped the amulet. "It is good to have a strong code name that will make an attacker think twice before initiating combat."

"You think you're so tough," said the therasapien. He stood up and approached slowly.

"I *am* tough," Troll said, his adrenaline surging. He took a fighting stance. "So, what do I call you?"

"*Que*?"

"What's your name?" Troll asked, flexing his muscles.

"That's not important, *Niño*."

"I need to know my opponent. I plan on fighting you again after this."

"What makes you think that?" asked the therasapien. "I plan on killing you right now! There won't be a future battle."

"You enjoy fighting with an opponent worthy of your time, and I'm the first challenge you've ever had. It's your way of playing cat and mouse."

"How do you know?" the frustrated therasapien roared as he unsheathed his large knife and charged at the young warrior who had gotten under his skin.

Troll forced a smile onto his face to look braver than he felt as his heart pounded wildly. He counter-charged with a massive swing of his axe.

ELEVEN

Corin and Finnegan ran to their next position.

"What happened to Troll? We need him!" Corin yelled.

"He can handle himself! Jessica, are you ready?" Finnegan asked through his communicator.

"We're in position!" Jessica replied.

A knot formed in Finnegan's throat as he spoke slower than usual to keep his voice clear. "There are four on foot, two in small jets, and four more on hoverbikes."

"Roger. Ace has the tank ready. He'll take care of those jets when they are in range."

"On my signal," Corin said. "Jack, are you ready?"

"Maybe," Jack responded nervously.

"Jack?" Corin hollered.

"Yes, yes!" Jack said, lacking confidence.

"Now!" Corin exclaimed.

They dodged into the shrubs as Jack emerged from behind a thick tree.

Jack's left hand was switched out with a bazooka attachment. Jack quickly aimed at the hoverbike closest to him. He fired. The rocket streaked out of his launcher and slammed into the bike.

The rider tried to bail out, but the bike exploded under him.

Jack looked away as Corin and Finnegan opened fire on the four men on foot.

The soldiers screamed and dove behind the trees for cover.

The jet pilots fired at Jack but missed. One of the hoverbike drivers drove toward Jack as the others retreated.

"Ace, fire now!" Jack ordered, standing his ground as lasers rained around him.

Ace had the tank hidden on Jack's left. He aimed the big gun at one of the jets and fired.

The tail assembly of the jet exploded, causing it to lose control. The pilot took evasive action as the shock wave nudged the other jet, throwing it off course.

"Nice shot!" Jack exclaimed, cheerfully extending his right fist. He opened his palm, and a tiny missile propelled at the hoverbike driver.

Managing to dodge the missile, the livid driver circled back.

"Is he in range?" Jessica radioed Jack.

Jack used his scanner to measure the biker's distance. "On my signal," Jack said. "Three—"

The biker scowled at Jack.

"Two—"

He reached for the gun controls.

"One—"

He fired at Jack.

"Now!" Jack commanded, dodging behind the same large tree.

Jessica and RJ stood beside the tank and fired their rifles. Their shots hit the biker's engine. The driver screamed as the hoverbike lost control and smashed into the tree Jack was behind.

"Whoa!" Jack cried when he felt the explosion against the tree. "That was close. Good job!" Jack praised, lifting his faceplate and kissing the bark.

"That's two bikes down," Jessica said. "Where did the other two go?"

"They left," Jack said, removing the bazooka and opening his leg compartment. "I need to reload this."

"What happened to the jets?" asked RJ.

As if on cue, the damaged jet de-cloaked. It was severely unbalanced, with flames dancing on the hull and tail. The pilot was frightened.

The second jet de-cloaked directly above Jack, and the pilot fired at him.

"*Verdammt!*" Jack bellowed, shutting his leg compartment, stumbling as he ran. "I forgot about them! Ace, I need cover."

"Copy. I'm on my way," Ace said as RJ and Jessica jumped on board.

Hidden in the safety of the trees and shrubs, John Doe watched his friends fighting for their lives. *I know what I must do, and I'm worried. I have never successfully commanded those I summon. Corin told me to flatter and be a lackey to whoever comes through the portal, but I'm not an ass-kisser, and I don't like manipulators. Plus, I would shame my wizard school if word got out that I sweet-talk and suck up to my servants. I'm a trained wizard, but I'll feel like a novice if I listen to Corin. My spells could be better, so I need more power. If I live long enough, I'll achieve my goal of godhood and be like Thoth. If I'm ever going to be like Thoth, I must take command! Sorry, Corin. Here goes nothing.* He sighed hard, gathered his courage, and rolled up his sleeves. *"Oscail doras misticiúil, tabhair amach mo bhealach isteach."*

A medium-sized portal opened.

He carefully reached in and felt something furry. "This can't be a dragon," *Unless it's a pretty dragon with a mane like a unicorn!* "Oh, boy!" Smiling, he grabbed the fur tightly and pulled it through the portal.

As the creature came through, its back leg struck John Doe, knocking him facedown into the dirt. The portal closed.

John Doe sat up coughing. He removed his dirt-covered sunglass-goggles and cleaned them on his trench coat. Once they were clean, John Doe gazed at what he had summoned. *That's not a dragon!* John Doe thought as his eyes widened in alarm.

"Where am I?" growled a large brown dog with beautiful white eagle wings.

"You're in my world now. You will work for me if you ever wish to return home," John Doe ordered, trying to sound intimidating to the dog.

"You dare to threaten me? I am a brute demon; I'm like a god. My race inhabits the Reyes Domain, where my kind enslaves. It is not the other way around."

"I respect that," whimpered John Doe. "I want to be a god someday. But my friends and I . . . we could use your help. Please?"

"*Why* should I help you?"

"Because you need to return to your realm. Right?" John Doe gulped. *That's it, John Doe! Bargain with the beast!*

The brute demon looked condescendingly at the cowardly wizard and laughed. *He's pathetic. I almost feel sorry for the pitiful fool! He's no threat to me and certainly has no way of controlling me. I shall humor him and lead him to believe I willingly obey to boost his silly little ego. The instant he opens a portal to send me home, I'll drag him through and devour him.* "So, what do I call you, and how do you require my help?"

"My name is John Doe. A mutant cat called a therasapien is attacking my friends. Can you help us defeat it?"

"A cat? *That* is why you summoned me? You thought I would automatically agree to beat up a cat because I am a dog?"

"Yes?" John Doe smiled. *I had no idea he'd be a dog. I was expecting a unicorn dragon.*

I can't believe this, the demon thought. "Fine! Whatever! As long as I go home. By the way, I am known as Magnum, but you will address me as Sir."

"You're supposed to call *me* that," John Doe said and snapped his fingers.

A portal opened beside him.

"Don't count on it." Magnum laughed. "So, where is this cat?"

"Come here," John Doe said as he pulled a rope and saddle out of the portal.

"Just what the hell is *that*?"

"I'm going to ride you." John Doe smiled, snapping his fingers again.

The portal shut.

"Where did you acquire that thing?"

"My bedroom."

"What makes you think I will allow this?"

"Because . . . you are mine?"

Magnum paused and stared at John Doe before bursting into hysterical laughter.

John Doe sighed hard and slowly approached the demon dog.

Magnum saw him and stopped laughing. "What do you think you are doing?"

"If I can get this on you . . . then you must promise to help us. After we win, I will let you go."

"And what if you cannot put that on me?"

"Then I will send you back and pull out someone else to help us."

"You're not very good at confrontations, boy."

"No, I usually leave my friend to that. He's big and strong."

"And you can do nothing."

"Oh, that's not true," John Doe said, smiling before taking off his sunglass-goggles. He put them into his trench coat pocket and charged toward the demon. "I can do some things."

Magnum roared and extended his large claws.

Corin and Finnegan concealed themselves in the shrubs, firing at the soldiers taking cover in the trees.

"We can't hit them this way," Corin stated. "If we move, they'll get us."

"Cover me," said Finnegan. *This is a risky move.* He stood tall and aimed.

A soldier saw him and aimed at Finnegan's head.

Finnegan fired his rifle. His bullet struck the soldier's shoulder, and he collapsed.

Another soldier aided the injured man while the other two continued to shoot.

Finnegan took cover beside Corin. "We can't keep this up. We need help!"

"I have something that may give us a chance to get better cover," Corin said, opening the pouch on his belt. He pulled out a small, round silver cylinder. "When I give the signal, you run as fast as possible." Corin pulled on the cylinder and then twisted the device. Five yellow lights appeared in the center. After flickering twice, one of the lights went out. There were now four lights. Again, after blinking twice, another light went out.

"What is that?" Finnegan asked.

"A countdown," replied Corin.

"Is that a bomb?" Finnegan asked nervously.

"Run!" Corin threw the cylinder toward the soldiers.

Corin and Finnegan ran as fast as they could to where their allies had taken shelter.

The enemy soldiers saw them rush out of their hiding place and prepared to fire at them. They didn't notice the tiny silver bomb land next to them. It detonated in a blinding flash. The four men vanished, the trees they stood behind shattered into splinters, and everything nearby instantly started burning.

The powerful blast threw Finnegan and Corin to the ground.

"Come on, we need to help Jack," said Corin as he made it to his feet and helped Finnegan stand.

"I didn't know you had a bomb!" said Finnegan. "You never mentioned that in your plan."

"I'm full of surprises," Corin admitted.

"I just bet you are," said Finnegan in a low voice.

The jet pilots had Corin and Finnegan in their sights and fired with anti-personnel weapons.

Corin and Finnegan ran, screaming.

Jack stopped running when he heard their cries. He turned around and saw them in the line of fire. "Ace, hurry!" Jack barked into his communicator, racing toward Corin and Finnegan.

The pilot in the unbalanced, smoking jet began to cough and vomit as he lost control and soared away from the battle. The other jet pilot ruthlessly fired, toying with Finnegan and Corin.

Finnegan collapsed and curled into a fetal position as bullets and lasers rained around him.

Corin stood over Finnegan, aiming his pistol at the jets. *I don't like him, but I'll do this for Jess!* Bullets ever so closely whizzed past him. Corin shrieked in fright. *This was a bad idea!*

The jet pilot sneered as he put Corin's head directly in his gun's crosshairs and pulled the trigger.

Jack leaped in front of Corin. The rounds struck him, and he accepted the damage. Jack could not allow another friend to die. He knew a mechanic could repair his metal body, even if finding one would be annoying.

"Jack!" Corin cried out.

"Take cover!" Jack yelled, pulling back a hatch on his left pinkie. It revealed a tiny red button. He pressed it, and his shoulders opened. Small missile launchers emerged from inside his shoulders. He aimed and fired.

The two men on hoverbikes returned to the therasapien. The jaguar-man saw them and pointed at Troll with an evil smile. The drivers activated heat-seeking missiles, targeted Troll, and fired.

Troll saw the heat-seekers heading for him. He took a sharp intake of breath and ran to the therasapien, putting his arm around him. "They take me out, and you're coming, too," Troll said cunningly.

"No!" the jaguar-man screamed. "Get away from me!" He violently pushed Troll away, but it was too late. The missiles headed toward the therasapien. He choked on a roar and meowed like a kitten.

Troll quickly put distance between them.

The therasapien managed to dodge the missiles and returned to a fighting stance. He activated his radio and yelled, "Be careful, you *idiotas*! Do not fire when he is close to my location."

Troll front-flipped toward the therasapien and attacked him with his axe.

The jaguar-man roared ferociously, blocking with his blade. "Little *Niño*, you will not defeat me! You are a mere rodent!"

"Tell me your name!" Troll yelled, swinging his axe at his midsection.

The therasapien dodged. "You are trying my patience," he hissed, tightening his grip on the large knife. "Come down here!" he yelled into his radio.

The drivers brought their bikes to the ground.

"Yes, sir, what is it you request?" asked one of the soldiers.

"I request your vehicle," the therasapien announced, kicking him off the seat.

The soldier landed face-first in the dirt.

The therasapien mounted the hoverbike. "Get back to the base and call for reinforcements on the double!" he commanded, taking the controls and soaring into the air.

Troll could not let him get away. He somersaulted onto the other hoverbike. His boot struck the soldier's face and knocked him into a bush. Troll pursued the therasapien.

"Should we go back to base?" asked the soldier, climbing out of the bush.

"Nah, he started this escapade. Let him cook in his own stew," said the other man, brushing dirt off his face and uniform. "Come on, let's have a coffee break."

"Oh, coffee sounds great!"

The fire caused by Corin's bomb rapidly spread throughout the forest. Panicked animals abandoned their homes, fleeing through the blaze, trying to find safety.

Rowan was invisible until she heard their squeals. She materialized and carefully landed on the branch of a tall tree that was not on fire. She wanted to cry. "Corin told me to stay up here and ensure no one comes to aid the therasapien. My friends won't stand a chance if more soldiers come, but my animal friends are frightened!"

She heard more desperate animals wailing. She tried to cover her large ears and shut her eyes but could not stop her tears.

Rowan suddenly heard the shriek of a fawn. She opened her eyes and spread her wings. Rowan flew as fast as possible toward the defenseless baby animal. "The hell with you, Corin. I'm coming, little one!"

She found the fawn but spotted twenty-two more baby animals in despair: raccoons, rabbits, chipmunks, squirrels, fawns, weasels, marmots, opossums, birds, and one box turtle. Rowan called to them, "Follow me, children! I shall lead you to safety! Do not be frightened!" She picked up the turtle, hugging it to her chest. "Come on!" Rowan fled the burning forest, and the other twenty-two baby animals followed. She guided them to a dirt path.

Driving down the path was a large, unusual forest-green-colored vehicle driven by a handsome, brown-skinned fellow wearing fine garments with well-kept black hair on his head and face.

Rowan flew into the side of the man's car and crashed through the window. She clutched the turtle, who had taken shelter in its shell.

"What the . . ." screamed the fellow, gasping in alarm when the faerie landed in his lap. He slammed on the brakes, stopping his car.

"Forgive the rude entrance," Rowan said, her eyes fluttering as she handed the turtle to the startled man. "Here, you hold this little guy. Don't let him out of your sight."

"Huh?"

Rowan climbed out of the window and opened the back door.

"Hey! What are you doing? Close my door!" yelled the driver. "This is an antique! You damaged my 1969 Chevrolet Caprice!"

"Hurry, my woodland friends. Get into this vehicle, and it shall bring us to safety!"

"Who are you talking to?"

The twenty-two baby animals charged the classic automobile and jumped into the backseat.

"No!" shouted the owner. "I need to get to my job! I have an important meeting to attend! What is this about, strange woman? Get these wild animals out of here!"

"Don't worry," Rowan said as she closed the back door, keeping the babies secure. She returned to the front door, pushed the man into the passenger seat, and sat down.

He clutched the turtle in shock.

"I will do the driving," Rowan said, shutting the door. She adjusted the mirrors and asked, "How does this thing work?"

"What?" he yelled. "Oh, no, crazy lady! Get out of my car! I tried to be nice, but this has gone far enough."

"I must get my little friends to safety! It is my duty. This is *my* forest, you know," Rowan said proudly.

"Who are you exactly?"

Rowan looked at the human and smiled. "My name is Rowan Fae . . . and we're on our way!" She put the vehicle into drive and slammed her foot onto the gas pedal, and the car took off.

The man screamed in horror as she quickly drove the car off the path and back into the woods.

"I will get us there!" Rowan announced, dodging flames and driving toward an open clearing.

"Where are we going?" asked the panicked owner as he clutched the turtle tightly.

"I don't know," she sang, driving incredibly fast.

The terrified baby animals climbed to the front and piled on the man.

"No!" he shrieked. "What are they doing?"

"They want you to comfort them."

"I'm the one who's not comfortable!" he screamed, setting the turtle on the passenger seat. He carefully climbed into the back.

The antique automobile smelled terrible from having so many frightened animals inside.

As soon as he buckled his seat belt, more baby animals cuddled onto him.

Rowan drove over an area covered with rocks of all sizes. The jarring motion startled the babies so intensely that a few of them lost control of their bodily functions.

"NOOOOOOO!!!" he cried in horror as they urinated all over his backseat and attire.

Jack's missiles struck the jet, knocking it off course.

The sick pilot continued to cough. He was suffocating on the jet fuel vapors and smoke. He was terrified yet amazed his jet still functioned. He returned to the skirmish, flying toward them.

Jack was losing control of his motor functions. His body had taken too much damage. "Corin, try to get to cover," Jack ordered.

"I won't leave you here to be destroyed!" Corin yelled.

eyes grew wide, and his heart throbbed. Troll's breathing grew rapid as the flames mesmerized him. His consciousness fell into his dark memories as his mind ripped from the present. He wasn't on the hoverbike anymore . . .

He was a young boy. He sobbed and ran to the burning farmhouse in the distance. His vision was fuzzy, and breathing was difficult. His legs wobbled, and his muscles screamed. Fear ripped through him, making his body feel weak.

His wobbly legs gave out, and he fell to his knees.

"No," Troll whimpered, his long, black hair covering his eyes.

His heart was beating like it was trying to escape his chest.

A loud explosion below startled Troll, causing him to nearly drop the grenade.

The therasapien was still ahead of him.

Troll pulled the pin and spat it into the flaming forest. He threw the live grenade to the front of the therasapien's bike with all his might.

The grenade detonated, and the jaguar-man screamed. He pressed his back into the seat and lifted the front end of the hoverbike, heading to the canopy.

Troll shifted his weight, forcing the front of his bike to rise, and drew closer. He pulled his hoverbike beside the therasapiens as they burst through the treetops.

A wave of relief washed over Troll when he was away from the fire. He could focus now. Troll pulled the pin on the second grenade and tossed it into the therasapien's lap.

The therasapien squeaked, grabbed the grenade, and threw it back at Troll.

Troll reflexively used his left gauntlet cuff like a baseball bat and hit the grenade back to the therasapien.

The grenade landed at the jaguar-man's feet and rolled under his accelerator pedal. He leaped from the hoverbike just before the grenade exploded. He fell toward the burning forest, arms and legs spread wide.

Troll forced the hoverbike to nosedive and accelerated as fast as possible. He grabbed the therasapien's armor and pulled him onto the hoverbike. Troll flew away from the flames and into the open forest.

The therasapien looked at Troll in confusion. "You are saving me, *Niño*?"

"I couldn't just let you fall to your death," Troll said.

"Well, I don't mind watching you fall to yours!" said the jaguar-man, punching Troll's chin and pushing him out of the seat.

Troll screamed but managed to grab onto the foot peg. He dangled helplessly and fearfully stared at the therasapien.

The therasapien laughed and stamped his foot onto Troll's hand.

"J-just one thing—I want t-to know—b-before I die," said Troll nervously.

"Yes, *Niño*?"

"T-tell me—y-your name."

"My lord named me Raw Brio."

Troll smiled. "Nice to meet you, Raw," he said confidently. "I hope you enjoy my present." Troll willingly let go of the foot peg and gave Raw an obscene finger gesture as he fell.

"Present?" Raw gulped as he looked under the seat. He saw the grenade ready to explode. Raw let out a blood-curtailing scream and desperately tried to jump clear of the bike.

The grenade exploded, blowing the bike in half.

Burning shrapnel peppered Raw as the force of the blast sent him cartwheeling into the sky like a rag doll. Gravity finally took him, causing him to fall at a perilous speed.

As Troll fell, he quickly determined the most appropriate trees to target to slow his plummet. He spotted a large one he felt could support his weight and aimed his body to impact its branches. "This is going to hurt," Troll whimpered, shutting his eyes. He tried to relax his muscles and ignore how the impacts would damage his body. Troll couldn't allow his thoughts of fear to overcome his strength. *Please, body! Don't tense up!* He slammed into the first branch, yelped in pain, and opened his eyes. He aimed for the next limb. It hurt almost as badly as the first. The third knocked Troll unconscious. Following several more impacts, his plunge slowed, and he landed on his back in a large, soft bush. Troll's eyes fluttered open as he regained consciousness and moaned quietly. He swallowed blood and tried to move. *I can't feel my body.* "H-help me—" Troll surrendered to his injuries and lost consciousness again.

The blazing wildfire licked at the trees and crept dangerously close to where Troll helplessly lay.

"Great Ptah, god of justice, please spare him!" Jack exclaimed. "Troll fell almost eighty feet! He couldn't have survived a fall like that—"

"Calm down, laddie," said Ace, trying to finish Jack's repairs. "Hold still, please. I'm nearly finished."

Finnegan parked the tank at the meet-up point. He climbed out and stood beside Jessica. "The forest fire is unstoppable now. The faerie is going to be angry."

Jessica didn't hear him. She stared at the sky where she had watched Troll fall. "Troll can't be dead," she said.

"Jessica, I don't think he—"

"No!" Jessica yelled. "We'll find him."

"What can we do? Even if we find Troll, *we* might not make it out alive. The tank's systems are starting to overheat. If it shuts down, we'll never outrun this wildfire."

"I won't leave him!" said Jack. "Get me off of this tank! I'm fixed!"

"Lad, you're not going anywhere until I finish your repairs. I'm almost done," Ace said, working on Jack's shoulder.

"I'll get him!" shouted John Doe from above.

They looked up and saw him on the back of the flying demon dog.

"John Doe to the rescue!" he exclaimed, pulling on the rope he had tied around Magnum's face.

"I cannot believe I allowed you to tame me," said Magnum angrily. "I am not some domesticated pet!"

"*Sir*, you're my minion for now." John Doe laughed. "Let's find my friend Troll!"

"Good luck, John Doe," said Jack quietly. "Find him."

"He wasn't wearing his goggles," said RJ. "His outfit doesn't work without his signature sunglass-goggles."

"What the hell is he riding?" asked Ace. "Looked like a dog . . . I thought he was supposed to summon a dragon?"

"Maybe it's a dog dragon?" asked Jack, shrugging. "I don't care what it is as long as they save Troll."

"Save Troll?" asked Corin, running to them. "What happened? Where is he?"

"Corin!" Jack shouted.

"All done, lad," said Ace, freeing Jack.

"I was worried about you," Jack said. As soon as his feet touched the ground, he ran to Corin and hugged him.

"I'm sorry. I didn't mean to worry you. I thought I heard more of the therasapien's men, so I investigated. My mind was playing tricks on me. Now, where's Troll?"

"He fell out of the sky," Jack said worriedly. "John Doe is going to go look for him."

"In there?" Corin exhaled, looking at the giant flames. "My gods! We need to get away from here! Where's Rowan?"

"I don't know," Jack said. "I just hope our faerie friend is safe."

"I hear a vehicle approaching," said Ace.

"I think I hear my stomach," said RJ.

"Oh, no," said Jessica. "Could more of the therasapien's men be after us?"

"I don't think so," said Corin. "Like I said, there was no one out there."

"It's just my stomach. Does anyone have a candy bar?" asked RJ.

"Well, someone sure is," said Ace, ignoring the junkie's comments. "Trust me, lad. I recognize the sound of an engine."

"I hear it, too," said Finnegan. "It's coming from behind us."

They all turned to see Rowan driving a dark green antique car.

"Rowan!" Jack cheered. "You're alive!"

"Hi, guys! Just follow us. I know how to get to a path. I'm going to put out the forest fire, too," Rowan said, smiling.

"You'd best douse the flames fast, lassie," said Ace. "Your friend Troll is in there and could be burned alive."

"What? No! Jessica, take the wheel." Rowan opened the door.

"*Ahh!* Put the car in park!" shouted the man.

"What's that? How do I do that?" Rowan asked.

He maneuvered up front and pulled on the automatic transmission shift lever, putting the vehicle in park.

"Thank you," Rowan said and flew out the open door. "I'll stop the fire. You guys get out of here!"

"I know where we can go. I'll lead us," said Corin.

Jessica entered the automobile and saw the turtle sitting in the passenger seat. "It stinks like urine," Jessica said, checking the backseat. She inhaled sharply when she saw the drenched man surrounded by baby animals. "Um, hello. Did Rowan steal your vehicle, sir?"

"How did you guess?"

Raw tore through the forest with his claws and knife. He bled heavily from his wounds caused by the blast and fall. "I deeply thank my animal resilience, being half-jaguar, or else I may not have survived," Raw said. "I know *Niño* lived. I can feel it." He longed for the satisfying sensation of thrusting his blade into Troll's beating heart. Determined to find Troll, Raw sniffed the air. It was challenging to smell anything over the burning forest, but he picked up Troll's scent and soon found where he landed. He smiled evilly when he saw that

Troll was still breathing and was unconscious. The flames grew dangerously close. Raw had to kill him before the fire would. "Perfect. *Adios, Niño.*" Raw raced to Troll, ready to stab his heart.

"Hey, cat," yelled Magnum.

Raw stopped mid-strike when he saw the demon dog flying toward him. He screamed, jabbing at Magnum but missed. His blood loss threw off his balance. His knees were weak, and his vision became blurry. Raw collapsed but remained conscious and dropped his knife.

"Troll!" John Doe cried when he saw him. "*Sir*, hurry to my friend!"

"Shut up!" Magnum said. "Stop calling me that!"

"You asked me to call you—"

"I hate you," Magnum growled, rushing over to Troll.

John Doe moaned and groaned as he strenuously pulled Troll onto the back of the demon dog. "Okay," John Doe said breathlessly. "I got him."

"Hold on," said Magnum. "I will get us out of here."

"Don't forget to grab our cat friend," said John Doe.

"How could I forget? Come here, kitty." Magnum gave an evil chuckle and flew over to Raw.

Knowing he was too weak to run or fight back, Raw grabbed his knife and returned it to its sheath. The demon dog bit into his meaty leg, and Raw roared in pain. He tried to scratch him, but Magnum laughed at Raw's feeble attempt.

Raw slipped into unconsciousness, and his body went limp.

"Let's go!" John Doe exclaimed.

Magnum flew them away from the burning forest and back to the tank.

Rowan flew into the sky. Her body glowed bright green. *"Im-mando pluviam, effundo in ignem feram! Im-mando pluviam, effundo in ignem feram! Im-mando pluviam, effundo in ignem feram!"* She sang her spell until her glowing skin changed to a brilliant yellow. Once she reached the puffy, white clouds, Rowan hovered and opened her arms over her head. *"Dominus tempestatis ego sum."* Lightning shot out of her glowing body and into the clouds. They turned gray, built moisture, and rain poured. Rowan was soaked from the cloudburst, but it was worth it to save the remaining forest, animals, and Troll. Once the flames were out, she flew to her friends.

Corin had led them to a nearby clearing with a giant crater surrounded by pieces of shredded metal of all different sizes and shapes.

What happened here? Rowan thought, landing next to Jack. "I'm glad everyone is safe." She shook her wet hair back and forth, attempting to dry it.

"Rowan, the man in that vehicle won't leave the backseat. He's mad at you," said Jack. "You ruined his antique."

"He'll get over it. It's just a machine."

"I don't know if I should take that as an insult," Jack said, shrugging his shoulders. *Attempting to argue about the importance of machines probably means very little to a faerie.*

My only concern right now is Troll, Rowan thought.

Jessica leaned against the Chevrolet, smiling at the man inside, who was being embraced by baby animals. "Please refrain from strangling Rowan," she said. "She took your antique for a good cause."

"This car is my baby," he said as a chipmunk curled in his lap, "but I guess these babies are pretty cute." He smiled.

One of the fawns passed wind loudly.

"Okay, they're not so cute anymore!" he grumbled, fanning his hand in front of his face. "That was nasty!"

"You could come out," said Jessica.

"I don't think so!"

"You're not a prisoner. I'm sorry if Rowan scared you."

"I don't know you people, and who knows what that faerie will do to my car next! I'm staying right here."

A bunny sneezed on his face.

"You're lucky you're cute."

Magnum flew over with John Doe, Troll, and the captive therasapien.

"We're back, guys," said John Doe.

Everyone stepped back, giving Magnum plenty of room to land.

He landed gracefully and folded his beautiful white eagle wings. He kneeled so John Doe could get Troll off his back.

Jack and Rowan rushed over to help.

Magnum spat Raw in front of Corin.

Raw fell on his head, and a grunt escaped his lips.

"What is this place?" asked Magnum. "What a mess. It looks like the earth threw up. Was there something underground here at some point? The land looks blown outwards."

"I'm not sure," said Corin, trying to refrain from telling the others he blew up the therasapien's underground base. *Oh no. I brought them here to keep everyone safe from the fire. I didn't know so much evidence of the blast would have come above ground.*

"Troll, please wake up," Rowan whispered into Troll's ear.

"Come on, buddy, open your eyes," said Jack.

"He'll come around soon," John Doe said, putting on his sunglass-goggles.

"I like your style, John Doe," said RJ. "I need a pair of those."

"I made these," said John Doe.

"You don't seem worried about Troll at all," said Rowan. "Don't you care, John Doe?"

"Of course, I care. Troll is like my brother," said John Doe. "I just know he's going to be all right. He gets injured like this a lot and has always recovered quickly. I'd give him five more minutes, and he'll be back on his feet."

"How's our boy doing?" asked Finnegan.

"He's going to be fine," said John Doe. "Trust me."

"Well, if you're wrong, then I'm eating him," said Magnum.

Rowan's eyes blazed red. "If you try to touch him, I shall fight you and rip out your fur!"

"Whoa!" gawked the demon dog. "Relax, lady! I was kidding."

"Do not joke about such things, you beast!" Rowan yelled. "John Doe, put that monster back into your portal!"

"Nah, I don't mind it here as much as I thought," Magnum said and snickered as he looked down at Raw, who was still unconscious. "It's a lot of fun beating up cats."

"*Sir*, is it a lot of fun being my minion?" asked John Doe.

"Don't push it," said Magnum. "And stop calling me that! You're enjoying it way too much. It's annoying."

"Welcome to our group," said Jack.

"My name is Magnum."

Troll suddenly regained consciousness as his body spasmed into a fit of violent coughing. He frantically gasped, desperate to fill his lungs with fresh air.

"Troll!" hollered Jack, startled. "Take it easy. Slow breaths, Troll. Breathe." He gently rubbed Troll's arms, trying to keep him calm.

Troll slowed his breathing, swallowed hard, and carefully sat up.

"You shouldn't sit up yet, Troll. You could have broken bones," said Rowan, panicking.

"I'm okay," Troll said, slowly standing.

"You're the most remarkable man I've ever met," Jack admitted. "I've never seen someone in your condition stand up like that, let alone wake up like nothing happened."

"I try not to make a habit out of that, believe me," said Troll, glancing at Magnum. "John, did you summon this creature?"

"I sure did!"

Troll looked at John Doe in bewilderment. "How in the world did you subdue such a ferocious beast? I've been trying to teach you how to fight for years, and you're still awful at it."

John Doe puffed his chest out and gripped his coat. "Well, you know how my girlfriend is a centaur, right? She taught me various cowboy rope tricks and ways to tie people up. I was really interested in learning all about it because that's the sort of stuff she likes when we get frisky and—"

"Stop! That's enough, John Doe," Troll said, his face bright red. "I don't want to know the details, please!"

"Oh gods, are you saying I've been tamed by a perverted buffoon?" Magnum groaned. *How embarrassing. I must regain my dignity and eat the wizard before he sends me home.*

"Where's Raw?" Troll asked.

"Who?" asked Jack.

"The therasapien," said Troll. "His name is Raw. Is he alive?"

"He is," said John Doe. "He tried to kill you when you were healing."

"I don't doubt it," said Troll. "Bring him forth."

Magnum tapped Raw's rump with his paw. "Wake up, kitty."

Raw's eyes opened slowly. He carefully stood and drew his knife when he saw that he was surrounded. His attention, however, was not focused on being outnumbered. *This area . . . was this my . . . the underground base has been destroyed!* "What the hell?" Raw roared in anger. "You *pendejos* destroyed my base!"

"Your what?" Troll breathed. He saw the rubble and giant hole. "Oh no . . . who did this?"

Corin pulled out his pistol and aimed it at Raw. "Calm down."

"I demand to know who has dishonored me!" growled Raw, clutching the knife and trembling.

"This wasn't part of the plan," Troll said. "Who did this? This was a huge mistake."

"*Niño* is correct, no matter how much I wish he was wrong!" said Raw, glaring at Troll.

"Jessica, you and your crew should get the tank away from here in case reinforcements come for this captive," Corin said.

"What about you guys?" asked Jessica.

"We're going to tie up this loose end," said Corin. "Then we will catch up."

Jessica nodded, understanding Corin's intentions.

"What about me?" barked the man sitting in the Chevrolet, still cuddled by the baby animals.

"I'll help you," Rowan said, flying to the vehicle. She jumped into the driver's seat, rolled down the windows, and smiled at him.

"Oh no," he said. "Not you again."

"No worries," said Rowan. "I'll follow the tank. You sit back and relax."

Jessica and Finnegan sat on the hull as RJ and Ace entered the tank. Ace started the engine, and RJ drove into the forest.

Rowan pursued them in the Chevrolet.

"Thank you for keeping the windows down! It's getting funky back here! I need a shower!" announced the man in the backseat.

"Magnum, you can go with them. Make sure they are protected in case there is an ambush," said John Doe as he removed the rope and saddle.

"An ambush should be fun," Magnum said, smiling. He spread his wings and flew after them as John Doe snapped his fingers and opened the portal to his bedroom. He shoved the rope and saddle inside, then sealed it with another snap.

Raw unsteadily faced Troll. "There is no saving yourselves or your friends now. You have dug your own graves at this point. *Niño*, you die first!" Raw said, aiming his large knife at Troll.

"Not today," said Jack, grabbing a piece of sheet metal from the base's remains. "Put that little butter knife away. I have a new outfit for you, a metal straight jacket."

TWELVE

Raw stared at the young human warrior with hatred-filled eyes before glancing at Troll's friends. Rage, shame, and pain overpowered his rational thought before Raw realized he had been defeated. His anger was replaced by helplessness, and the edge of his gleaming blade became an invitation as Raw's hope for escape faded. He wanted to kill himself but could not do so and slowly slid the knife back into its sheath.

Jack wrapped the large metal sheet around Raw's body. The metal shrieked, hurting Raw's ears.

Corin stepped up to Raw, and their eyes met. "Now tell us why you threatened and attacked us."

"It no longer matters," Raw told him with a grunt. "You destroyed F Base 5! I do not know why you chose to do that, but all that matters to me now is that I am a dead man!"

"Why?" Corin asked, his curiosity stimulated.

"It was my station," said Raw. "When my lord learns I failed to keep it safe; he will kill me. Why did you destroy it?"

"Why did you attack us?" asked Corin with a coy grin.

"You're a foolish boy," Raw roared. "I was trying to keep you away! You were trespassing into my territory, and if you had discovered my station, I would have killed you much sooner. I thought I'd have a good hunt before the slaughter. I enjoy a game of cat and mouse now and again if my prey has not stumbled upon my secret mission. It is my way."

Troll was right again! That's how he described the therasapien yesterday. Corin aimed his pistol at Raw's face, and the photograph in the underground base crossed his mind. "I'd hate to think of your cub ending up fatherless."

"*Eh?* I do not have a cub," said Raw, puzzled.

Troll gave Corin a suspicious glare.

That must've been a picture of Raw as a cub, thought Corin, putting his finger on the trigger. *No matter.* "I think I'll save your master the trouble of killing you," Corin said coldly, his eyes showed no mercy.

"No!" Troll exclaimed and stepped in front of Raw.

Corin gasped and pulled his pistol back. "Troll, what are you doing? I almost pulled the trigger!"

"I can't let you kill him, Corin," Troll said as he turned around and faced Raw. "I cannot let that happen."

"Do you take pity on me, *Niño*?" asked Raw with a chuckle. "*Gracias muchacho*!"

"No," Troll said, walking behind Raw. "Though I know exactly how to release you."

"Release?" Jack asked. "What are you talking about, Troll?"

"If we let him go, he will try to kill us again!" Corin said.

"No, he won't," Troll said with confidence.

"What makes you think that I won't?" asked Raw.

"You have no more men, and you are outnumbered. Corin, check him for a radio."

"What?" Corin asked with a confused look. "Troll, he's tied up!"

"I'm serious, Corin. Check him," Troll said. "It could be anywhere."

"You mean he could have one stuck up his ass?" asked Jack.

"Definitely," said John Doe. "I've seen that. It is not pretty."

"Just check him while I make sure he's put to shame," Troll said, grabbing Raw's long tail.

"What are you doing?" Raw suddenly cried out in panic. Beads of sweat formed on his brow and trickled into his eyes. "Do not touch that!"

"Troll, what *are* you doing?" asked Jack.

The young warrior grasped Raw's belt, and the therasapien tried to maneuver away, but he could hardly move. Troll pulled Raw's knife out of its sheath and studied the blade. "It's nice and sharp," Troll said, bringing it down to Raw's tail.

"Stop!" Raw roared out in horror. "Do not dishonor me!"

"I hereby punish you and show your cowardice!" Troll said as he sliced the long knife's blade across Raw's tail, cutting it clean off Raw's backside.

In shock, Corin, John Doe, and Jack all drew in their breath.

"I'm so glad Rowan is not here," Jack said. "She'd throw a fit!"

Raw wept and hung his head. "How?" he whispered under his breath. "How did you know to do that? How did you know to shame me? I'll never be taken seriously again."

"I don't think you were ever taken seriously," Troll told him. "Your master obviously could care less about you if he put you in command of watching an abandoned base in the middle of a forest."

Raw's eyes became rageful. He tried desperately to get free from his metal bond. He roared and bit at Troll. "You lie! *Como te atreves!* I am a leader! I will kill you, Mr. Troll! I swear, so help me . . . I will kill you!"

"Not today," Troll said as he attached Raw's tail to his belt. "Now everyone will know I defeated you and proved you to be a coward. Jack, release him."

"No, Troll, he'll attack you," Jack said with concern.

"No, he won't," Troll said, returning the knife to Raw's sheath.

"You're giving him back his weapon?" asked John Doe with confusion. "Why?"

"He'll need it on the way back to his master," Troll said. "He will use it to protect himself or take his own life before his master does."

"How do you know so much?" asked the therasapien. "No one knows this!"

"I just know it," Troll said. "That's all you need to know."

"If the cyborg frees me, I will use my knife to cut out your heart!" Raw threatened.

"I will take that risk," Troll said. "I am sparing your life. Jack, let him go."

"Okay," Jack said, loosening the metal. "I hope you know what you are doing!"

"I do," Troll said.

Jack freed Raw and threw the metal sheet to the ground.

"Did you check him for a radio?" John Doe whispered to Corin.

"No," Corin said.

Raw glared at Troll with hatred.

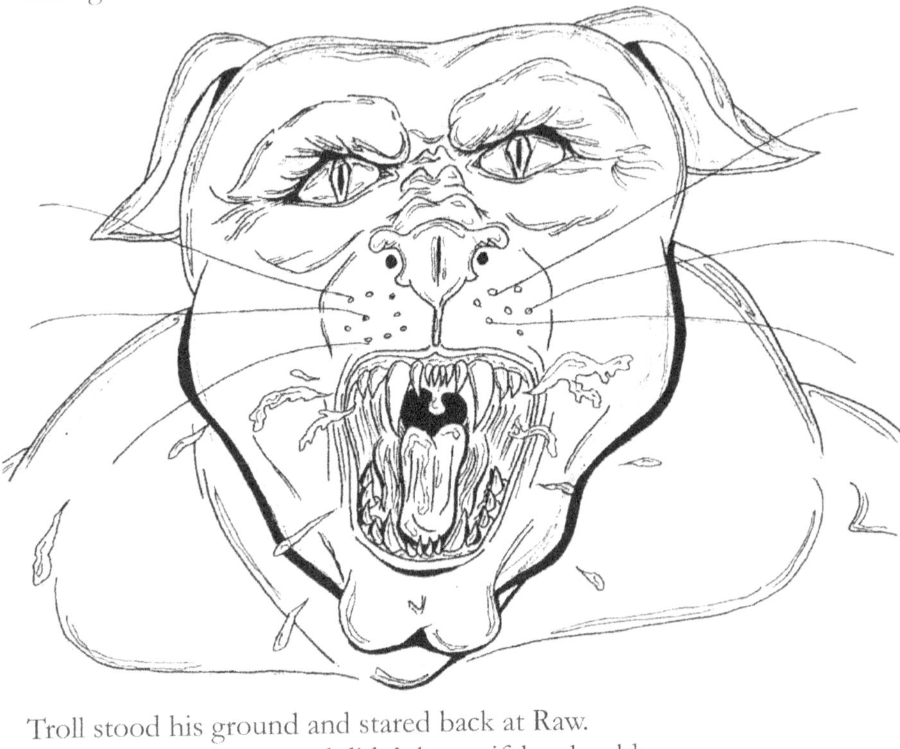

Troll stood his ground and stared back at Raw.

Jack was behind Raw and didn't know if he should move.

Corin and John Doe remained motionless as well.

Raw cocked his head at Corin and John Doe, then he turned to scowl at Jack. He spun around and faced Troll. "You are truly allowing me to just go?" he asked.

"Yes," Troll said. "It would be a wise decision."

"It would have been wise for you, *Niño*, if you had left me as your captive!" Raw roared as he drew his knife and charged at Troll.

Corin blinked.

Raw suddenly had Troll flat on his back. Though injured and tired, Raw had moved like lightning, driven by anger. He aimed his knife at Troll's heart.

Troll's blue eyes looked into Raw's golden cat eyes. His heart hammered vigorously. He felt it throughout his entire body. *"Oh gods, I think I made a mistake."*

"No!" John Doe cried.

"Corin, shoot him!" Jack yelled.

Corin lifted his pistol.

Raw peered deeply into Troll's stunned eyes.

Troll saw conflict in Raw's eyes. His heart continued to pound wildly. Troll felt dizzy.

Corin aimed.

Raw's hand trembled as he hovered the knife over Troll's chest.

No one dared to speak or take a breath. The silence increased their tension.

Corin put his finger on the trigger. He waited.

"You spared my life, Mr. Troll," Raw finally said, letting out a frustrated roar. He returned his knife to its sheath and stood. He loomed over Troll, then took two steps back. "I'll spare yours . . . for now." He felt tremendous pain from his severed tail. He remembered his other wounds. He needed aid soon. He glanced at Jack, then at Corin and John Doe. He snorted at them and returned his gaze to Troll. He growled at him softly, ran into the forest, and disappeared.

Troll sighed with relief and attempted to calm his pounding heart.

"Troll, I think that was very stupid," Corin said, walking up to him and offering to help him stand.

Troll accepted Corin's hand and shakily got to his feet. "I was scared for a minute there," Troll said, placing his hand on the amulet. "I didn't expect him to do that."

"Are you insane?" asked John Doe. "He's going to be back to kill you!"

"No, he won't," Troll said. "He won't come back here until we are gone. He cannot call for reinforcements so we can freely be on our way without worries."

"Reinforcements?" Corin asked, putting away his pistol.

"Yeah," Troll said. "He will call for backup if he needs to send out a convoy to attack. But we have his radio, so he won't be able to do that. Their cavalry is usually not far away. He may have another underground base somewhere close."

Corin swallowed hard and looked concerned. "Maybe we should leave?"

"There's no rush anymore," Troll said calmly.

"There might be," John Doe said with a sigh.

"What?" Troll breathed. "What do you mean?"

"Ask Corin," John Doe said.

"John Doe, you're not helping." Corin groaned with aggravation.

"Corin," Troll said. "You did get his radio, right?"

"Um . . ." Corin gulped. "No . . ."

"What?" Troll panted. "Why didn't you?"

"I don't—I didn't think he had one."

"Oh, Ra, god of light, protect me," Troll whispered, and his heartbeat increased again. "He's calling them now. We have to get out of here as quickly as possible! Try to cover our tracks, and whatever you do, don't separate from the group!"

"Are we going to die?" John Doe asked nervously.

"Maybe—" Troll said, looking at Raw's tail on his belt. "Or I might."

THIRTEEN

Raw ran through the forest, making sure they did not follow. *It was incredibly foolish of them not to listen to the one with the purple hair. Soon, they will discover I have my radio. Niño knew everything about my kind,* Raw thought. He jumped into a tree and nearly lost his balance because of his missing tail. His shame gripped him as he sat on a branch. Raw pulled his handheld radio out from under the armor covering his shin and turned it on. "This is number 7-3-0-1 at F Base 5. I need reinforcements right away! There is a band of ten travelers that have stumbled into my territory. They are armed and dangerous. They are equipped with a tank and a cyborg. They also have three Antiquities: one faerie, one demon dog, and one wizard. Those three must be put to death. Does anyone copy?"

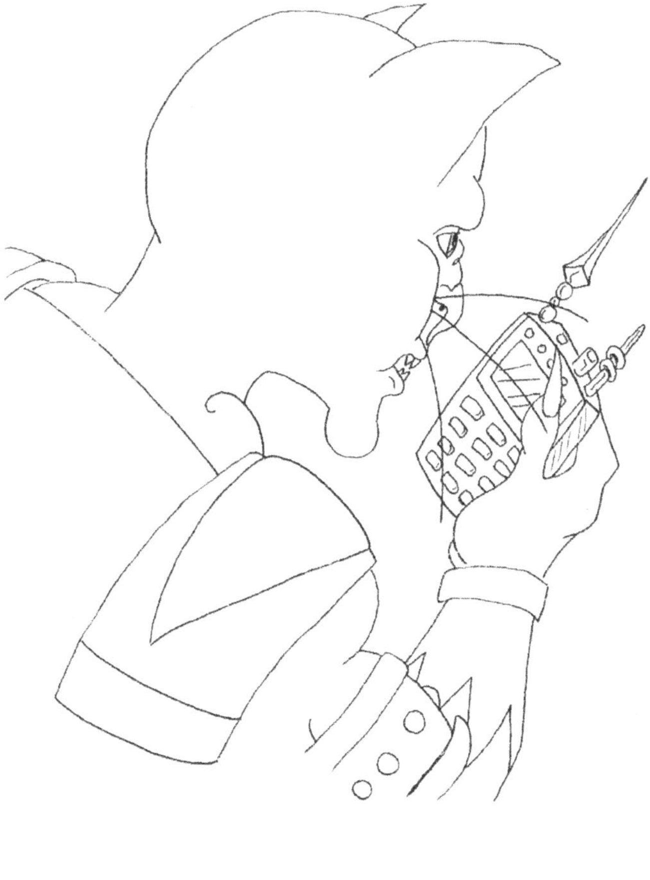

"This is number 1-1-9-8-9. I copy 7-3-0-1," a female voice replied. "My men are close to F Base 5. We'll be in your area within a few minutes. I want a full report on the trespassers."

"Captain Rinaldi, you have no authority to make such demands!" Raw roared into his radio.

"Number 7-3-0-1? That is the designation number of a therasapien. Correct me if I am wrong. Therasapiens must respect their human officers, like me, isn't that right, soldier?"

"Yes, but I am Raw Brio. I am second-in-command to our lord. You will show *me* respect!"

"I still have the authority as a human, like our lord! Why are the Antiquities not already dead? It's your duty—"

"Just get your men here as soon as possible!" Raw shouted nervously, turning off the radio and gripping it tightly.

I am unsure what came over me, but I wanted to kill that mutant! I was ready. I liked the feeling. I felt empowered and strong. I felt like a natural leader, but Troll ruined it. What does he know? I did the right thing by destroying that base. We've seen the last of Raw. I like being the guy in the shadows and blowing up things. I feel like a spy or comic book hero.

—From the journal of Corin Degodi
June 12, 2215, 8:36 a.m.

"Come on, Corin, we must get out of here now!" Troll shouted.

"Calm down, Troll. Look, you're obviously invincible. You have nothing to worry about," said Corin, putting away his journal.

"I'm mortal just like you are. Trust me . . . we will all die if Raw gets his reinforcements! Let's move!"

"Corin, please listen to Troll," said John Doe. "He's never been wrong about stuff like this."

"What do we do?" asked Corin. "Lead them to Centerville?"

"No, we just run," said Troll. "If we leave, they may no longer consider us a threat. Fleeing is our best option."

"*You* would run away from a fight?" asked Corin.

"I am talking about a fight no one will win," said Troll.

"Look, Corin, I'm going with Troll regardless of what you say," said John Doe. "He's my partner, and where he goes, I go."

"Fine," said Corin. "Go ahead. I thought you wanted to help me. This warlock is in Centerville, right? I can find him on my own."

"Corin," Jack said. "Be reasonable. They're not trying to leave you. We want to help you. Come on, friend. Join us. Let us be off."

Corin folded his arms across his chest. *I was expecting a different reaction. I better keep it a secret that I destroyed the base for now.* Corin shook his head to clear his thoughts. "Okay, let's go."

"Hurry," said Troll. "We must catch up with the others."

"Follow the tank tracks," said Jack. "Centerville City, here we come!"

RJ hit the seat adjustment lever and reclined his chair before the seat lunged forward. He giggled and pushed it back before it sprung into a seated position again.

Ace curiously looked at him. "Are you enjoying yourself, lad?"

"When do you think we'll arrive at Centerville?" RJ asked, reclining his seat a third time.

"It should only be another two-and-a-half-hour drive from here now," said Ace. "What's your hurry?"

"I'm bored," said RJ, thrusting his chair upward again. "I was hyper, and now I'm not."

"Thank the gods for that," Ace whispered.

"What was that?" asked RJ.

"Nothing, lad, nothing," said Ace with a smirk.

"Can I drive the tank with my feet?" asked RJ.

"Why don't ye radio John Doe and ask him if you can sit outside on his lawn chair? He would pull it out of the portal for you. That'd be fun, right?"

"Oh, I can't do that!"

"Why not?"

"The portal leads to his bedroom. It belongs to him. I can't touch it. It's a sacred object."

"RJ." Ace sighed.

"Yes?"

"I'm going to be completely honest, lad. Please go outside for a few minutes, or I'll lose my patience with you. I'll drive. Trade places with Jessica."

"Okay," RJ said as he unbuckled his seat belt.

Outside, Finnegan and Jessica sat on the hull, watching Rowan drive the automobile behind them.

"Look, Jess," said Finnegan. "About Corin—"

"Yes? What about him?" asked Jessica.

"I have seen how he looks at you and how you look at him," said Finnegan.

Jessica blushed and fiddled with her long blonde hair. "He's just an interesting guy. He's polite, charming, and smart."

"He might be *too* smart," said Finnegan.

"Finn, I know you're jealous," said Jessica. "Look, it's over between us. You and I . . . we had our thing, and now it's over. Besides, you're too old for me, and I'm your boss. There are too many conflicts."

"Only if you make them conflicts, Jess," said Finnegan. "We never had any problems. You just decided to end our relationship. By the gods, I would die for you!"

"Finn, my career is important, and you are a part of my crew. We cannot be a couple. It's unprofessional."

"I don't trust him," said Finnegan. "Please, I want you to be careful. Even if you no longer have feelings for me, I have deep feelings for you. Just be careful. I have a terrible feeling about Corin Degodi."

"I appreciate your opinion," Jessica said. "But I can take care of myself. I'm a cautious person."

RJ opened the hatch. "Hi, guys. Ace told me to come out here and trade places with Jessica. I'm being an annoying pest again."

"I will accept that offer, RJ. Thank you," Jessica said, carefully standing and walking to the hatch as RJ climbed onto the hull. As Jessica descended, she grabbed the hatch and glanced at her weapons officer. "Finnegan—"

He didn't look at her.

With sad eyes, Jessica sighed and shut the hatch.

RJ sat beside Finnegan.

"Don't ever fall in love, RJ," Finnegan said.

"Do you think John Doe's lawn chair has a demonic attachment?"

Finnegan looked at RJ.

RJ smiled.

Finnegan sighed.

"Do you know how many parts I had to find to put this car back together?" yelled the vehicle owner. "This is a 1969 Chevy! It's a rare specimen, and you have ruined it, Missy! I will make you pay for all the damage you have done to this car!"

"My animals like you," Rowan said, smiling. "You make them feel safe. You know, I like you too. Thank you for letting us borrow your car. Once we get to Centerville, you can have it back."

"Have you heard a word I have said?" the man asked, sighing. The baby animals cuddled against him and looked at him lovingly. "Get these wild animals away from me!"

"Aw, how cute!"

A large hole was suddenly blown into the earth beside the Chevrolet.

Rowan yelped in surprise. "Is everyone all right? What was that?"

"I hope it wasn't my tires!"

"I think something or someone shot at us," said Rowan.

"You mean like a cannon?"

"Maybe? I'm not very familiar with weapons. I live in the forest."

Another blast struck beside the vehicle.

Rowan and the human screamed, and the baby animals lost their bodily functions again.

"No! Not again!" he shrieked.

Another explosion struck near the tank.

"What the hell was that?" asked Finnegan. "I think someone is firing at us!"

"I thought we escaped the therasapien," said RJ.

"I guess he had friends," Finnegan said, opening the hatch. "Ace, get us out of here!"

"What's happening out there?" asked Jessica.

"Well, it's not some kid with cherry bombs," said RJ. "We're under attack! Floor it!"

"Pass up my rifle," said Finnegan. "Ace, take control of the big gun. Jessica, try to outrun them. RJ, get below and help Jess!"

"But—"

"Get below, kid!"

"What the hell is going on down there?" asked Magnum, soaring above the tank. "Someone is dumb enough to fire at us? Don't they know who I am? Oh, only the tank and car are being fired at. Well, no point in assisting if the fire isn't directed at me. Why should I help anyone?" Magnum smiled, flying calmly.

"They're attacking the tank too!" Rowan shouted. "It must be the therasapien's reinforcements. I think we are in big trouble!"

"Are they seriously trying to blow us up?" asked the vehicle owner as another blast struck directly in front of the Chevy.

The car plummeted into the freshly made crater.

"I'd say so," gulped Rowan. "We need help!"

"Put the Chevy in reverse. Try to get us out of here!"

Cannon fire echoed around them. Indentations appeared in the soil beside the Chevrolet before bits of shrapnel ricocheted off the car.

Rowan ducked her head and trembled in her seat.

"Save yourself!" the human ordered.

"No," said Rowan. "I cannot leave the baby animals, and what about you?"

"What about me? You should go!"

"I cannot do that!"

"But why?"

"Because I have honor . . . don't you know about honor?"

He stared at her compassionately. "I'm sorry I have been so angry with you about ruining my car."

Another blast rocked the vehicle.

"We're going to die!" Rowan cried.

"Not today, you won't!" yelled Jack, jumping into the crater behind the Chevy and pushing it out.

"Jack!" Rowan cheered.

"You're free. Take off as fast as you can. Head to Centerville and don't look back."

The cannon fire unexpectedly ceased.

"Good work, Jack," said Corin as he and John Doe caught up to him.

"Where's Troll?" asked Jack.

"He went into the forest to locate the shooters," said John Doe.

"Didn't he tell us that no one is to separate from the group?" asked Corin.

"He did, but he's close by," said John Doe. "He's done this before."

"What hasn't he done?" Corin asked curiously.

"Later, you two," said Jack. "We've got to move. John Doe, look at the map. How long will it take us to get to Centerville from this location?"

"I don't know where I am," John Doe said with panic.

"Give me the map," said Corin.

John Doe searched his trench coat. "I don't have it! Troll does."

"Oh shit," said Jack. "I hope he hurries back soon!"

"Hi guys," Troll said from behind them.

They screamed in alarm.

"You scared me!" shouted John Doe.

"That's nothing new," said Troll. "We need to keep moving. I stopped them for now."

"What'd you do?" asked Corin.

"I knocked them unconscious, but more soldiers will be after us. I believe Raw's men think we are going to the city of Franklin." Troll pulled out the map from his small sack. "Look, Franklin is the neighboring city to Centerville."

"The people of Franklin City hate Antiquities," said Jack. "They must think we're invading their headquarters because their base was destroyed during our fight."

"I don't know who could have done that," said Corin. "Maybe no one blew it up? It could've been a storage area for explosives, and one went off."

"I'll believe that story for now," John Doe said as he skipped along the path.

"What's that supposed to mean, wizard?" Corin barked, walking after him. "Do you have something to say?"

"You didn't take away Raw's radio," said John Doe. "You could be lying."

"Hey," said Troll, hurrying after them. "Knock it off, guys. Let's get to the tank! Centerville City is about two hours away. Raw's men should leave us alone once they figure out we're not going to Franklin City. Let's just keep moving."

"No problem, partner," John Doe said as he paced beside Troll. "If we run, we'll make it to Centerville in less than an hour."

"I bet I can catch up to the tank faster than you," Jack dared, running ahead.

"That's not fair. Your legs are longer!" John Doe bayed, trying to keep up with him.

"They're also motorized," Jack laughed as he caught up to the tank.

"I thought we were goners," said Finnegan.

"I think they just wanted to get us away," said Jack. "They don't seem to be following us."

"Well, stay alert, just in case."

"Jack!" squawked John Doe. "You get back here and carry me!"

Corin was nervous as he walked beside Troll. *Troll and John Doe suspect me. I know it. What should I say to him?* "You know, Troll, we're in a war zone . . ."

"It's not our war," said Troll. "We just arrived here accidentally and stumbled onto Raw's turf." He stared straight at Corin, his expression grim. "Corin . . . don't think I don't know."

"Know what?" asked Corin smugly.

"You destroyed the base."

Corin fell silent. *He's smart!*

"Admit it," said Troll.

"I will admit nothing," Corin said quickly. "What proof do you have?"

Troll looked at the dirt and sighed. "I thought you would confess," Troll said. He had no proof other than the feeling in his heart.

"Troll, don't be suspicious of me. We're on the same side! That base wasn't important. Raw was not important. Our goal is to get to Centerville. *That's* important. You're overthinking. Don't worry. I won't take your suspicion personally. Besides, we're friends. We need to get to know each other better," Corin said, feeling very smug and confident in his words. *Man, that was close!*

Corin thought. *I didn't know he was this intelligent! I don't want to make an enemy of Troll. I need him on my side if it'll assist me in getting back home and possibly rich along the way.*

Troll's heart was pounding in his ears. His cheeks were slightly flushed, and his skin felt clammy. *I can tell he is lying. Why would you destroy the base? Why did he think Raw had a cub? It doesn't make sense! He knows something we don't. He must not be left alone. What is he thinking right now? Who are you really, Corin Degodi?*

FOURTEEN

I want revenge! Niño, you will meet your end. No one gets the best of me. I am a powerful being of incredible strength and stealth! I must prove to my lord that I am still just as skillful as when he trained me. I will not fail him!

—From the log of Raw Brio
June 12, 2215, 9:37 a.m.

Raw roared ferociously as he threw his logbook into the forest. He heard voices coming from the same direction. He knew they were the reinforcements. He stormed through the trees until he found their location. Raw saw over thirty human soldiers in black tactical body armor, and around ten men wore robotic-powered suits. They were armed to the teeth with various deadly weaponry: rocket launchers, grenades, claymores, and rifles. There were also six therasapiens present: three humanoid tigers, two humanoid cheetahs, and one youthful humanoid jaguar of no relation. Raw noticed the youngster had spotted his logbook on the ground and went to pick it up. "Don't touch that!" Raw exclaimed.

The jaguar therasapien glanced at Raw, chuckled, and left the logbook alone.

Raw exposed his fangs and growled. "Who is in charge here?" he demanded, looking for the leader of their unit. "Why did you cease firing? Those trespassers need to die!"

"What happened to your base?" asked a human in black cybernetic power armor.

"What are you talking about? How dare you talk to me! I am the second-in-command of Franklin City, human!" Raw yelled, his voice trembling.

"Our group scanned your site. What was left of it anyway," chuckled a tiger therasapien.

"Everything was left in ruins by those rogues you're upset over," laughed the other jaguar-man.

"Don't have a hairball over the incident, Mr. Brio," said a human cleaning his rifle. "The captain is on her way."

"I don't care about your captain. F Base 5 was *not* destroyed. There was a freak accident!"

"Freak," said one of the cheetahs.

"I only see one *freak* here," laughed the other cheetah, and they high-fived.

"You are pathetic," spat Raw.

"What do you think the lord will say about your base?" asked the other jaguar-man.

Raw sighed hard and kicked the dirt, a motion that reminded him of his painful injuries. Suddenly, the world was spinning. He sat and closed his eyes, trying to gather himself.

"Whoa! Guys, check it out . . . Raw Brio, the second to our lord . . . has been dishonored!" stated a tiger-mutant.

Raw's eyes widened. He shrieked in his attempt to hide that his tail had been removed. He tried to get back on his feet but collapsed again and groaned. He could not stand. He needed medical attention. He reached for his logbook, and his pain spiked. He winced and panted. "No, you don't understand—"

"Your tail is gone—" said the tiger-mutant.

"I lost it in battle!" Raw interrupted. "I was fighting—"

"None of our kind has ever lost their tail in a battle," the other jaguar-man cut in as he kicked the logbook away. "The only way we can lose our tail is if we're captured and dishonored. Who did this to you?"

"One of my enemies," Raw growled. "A young man with purple hair. He knew everything about us."

"Really?" asked the human in power armor. "I have been working with you guys for almost twelve years, and I don't even know much about therasapiens besides being half-human."

"That is because we are very secretive," answered Raw. "The only human who knows our secrets is our lord of Franklin City. I don't know who that *niño* was, but his life will end at my claws. I will see to that! He and his *amigos* will not get the best of me again!" snarled Raw as he managed to sit up and punched his left fist into his right palm.

"Do you want to explain to me why they got the best of you in the first place?" asked a female voice behind them.

The humans and other therasapiens bowed to the female approaching them.

"Fall in, men," said the woman.

The soldiers and therasapiens lined up and stood at attention.

"We have a base to clean up. Make it look as if it never existed. Prepare a new location for F Base 5, under orders of Franklin City's Captain Unna Rinaldi. Fall out."

The men scattered all at once and began working diligently.

Raw turned around and looked up at the woman who spoke with authority. She was not what he expected, a petite woman who carried herself like a giant. She was smaller than him by nearly two full feet. Her Restrain Corporation black and gold uniform was a non-regulation style, with a short gold cape, a low-cut neckline that exposed her cleavage, and tight enough to show off her ample curves. Raw growled and hung his head.

"Do you want to explain this now, Raw, or do you want to take it up with our lord?" Unna coldly asked as she walked around him, picked up his log-book, and showed it to him. "You dropped this," she said, not giving it back.

She paced around him as she opened it and looked through its pages. "I need to know what happened here. Whoever did this kicked our corporation's ass! The weapons and computers destroyed here were worth millions! Do you know who did this?"

"It was a group of outsiders," Raw explained. "I have been listening to their conversations and learned that the cyborg escaped from the Dro's mines. The extraterrestrials owned him. There are three Antiquities: one is a human wizard, the second is a demonic canine, and the other is a faerie. There was also a human team of renegades with a tank, four of them total, one female and three men. There were also two unusual men. The first one I could smell was not from our world. I believe he could be an alien. The second, he has purple hair and knows how we therasapiens operate. He could smell me, and he knew how to find me. He is also strong, probably the strongest human I have ever encountered. I despise him!"

"So, these ten travelers just randomly showed up and decided that blowing up our base was their idea of a good time?" Unna asked, continuing to look through the pages as she circled him.

"I do not know, ma'am. I was only spying on them, as instructed by our lord. I was doing my job. My orders were to keep others away from the base and hunt those who posed a threat. I swore to kill them at dawn. The man with the purple hair fought me both evening and morning. Captain Rinaldi, I am here to kill our enemies!"

"Then why does this new enemy continue to exist?" asked Unna, anger in her voice. Her eyes suddenly brightened. She brought her hand to her chin, thought briefly, and smiled evilly. Unna threw the logbook before Raw, so it was within his reach. "Apparently, you are not qualified to continue this assignment. You were even dishonored by these outsiders. I will take over your mission."

"What?" Raw roared, returning his logbook to a pouch on his belt, "Captain Rinaldi, do not take away my mission. I *will* kill the outsiders!"

"You had your chance . . . twice! You fought them last night and this morning? You failed. There are no other chances. You will report back to our lord. He may have better use for you in his city."

Though in pain, Raw slowly stood up to face the petite woman. "Captain Rinaldi, we both know our lord may kill me. I ask that you do what the purple-haired warrior did not. Kill me."

She stared at Raw but said nothing.

"Ma'am," said a soldier, walking over. "I have a report from our scouts about the artillery position."

"Why did the mobile artillery cannons cease firing?" she asked.

"The entire unit was unconscious, ma'am. Someone attacked them. We found footprints. They head north."

"If our new enemy goes to Franklin, they will be killed on site. They must know this. I bet my fortune they are going to our enemy city to request help from that no-good mayor. Good work, lieutenant," Unna said as she pushed Raw out of her way. "Get out of here, Brio." She ordered, detaching her radio from her belt and holding it to her lips. "Come in number 7-8-9-0."

Raw growled ferociously and then confronted her again. "Captain Rinaldi, I gave you an order."

Unna ignored him and walked away, waiting for a response on her radio.

Raw snarled and then sat down.

A human medical officer ran to his side. "Do I have permission to help you, sir?"

"Fine," said Raw. "Be quick about it. I need to return to Franklin City."

"Yes, sir," said the medical officer. "I can escort you there myself on my hoverbike. Here, let me give you something for your pain first." He took out a syringe driver full of an analgesic drug. He cleaned a spot on Raw's shoulder with alcohol. It was easy to apply thanks to Raw's short, fine fur. The medical officer couldn't help but notice how miserable Raw looked. "I imagine this entire ordeal was arduous for you, sir."

"You can say that again," said Raw as he watched Captain Rinaldi indirectly. He smiled evilly at the woman before the medical officer took his arm and guided him toward a hoverbike.

Unna also watched Raw obliquely. She didn't trust him, nor any of her soldiers for that matter. That's just how things were in the Restrain Corporation.

"This is 7-8-9-0. What do you command?" asked a hissing voice over the radio.

"Are you stationed in Centerville?"

"Yes."

"Good, I have a new mission for you. A party of ten outsiders will enter the city within the next few hours. Your mission is to find them and report to me their profiles. Find out who they are. They threaten our ways, and you know what we do to threats. Beware of the man with purple hair."

"Purple hair? Hmm, I understand, ma'am. Thank you for this opportunity."

Unna locked her radio back onto her belt. She turned to face her soldiers, who stood around the remnants of F Base 5. "Continue to clean up the remains of this base. You will report to the headquarters once you have completed your sweeps. I am going to Centerville City alone."

"Ma'am?" asked one of her soldiers.

"No insolence!" Unna shouted. "You all understand the ancient aphorism: 'If you can't get something done right, you do it yourself!'"

"Did you not just give the mission to someone already posted in Centerville?" asked a private.

"Hold your tongue!" she yelled, breaking the private's nose with a swift punch to his face. "I am in command here, and I am going to perform this assignment! Now, do as you are told. I shall return with a full report and hopefully with the heads of our new enemies." She walked over to a silver-colored hoverbike and boarded it. She glanced at her men and nodded.

They saluted as Unna activated the hoverbike and drove toward Centerville.

FIFTEEN

After nearly two hours, they saw a great wall in the distance surrounding a city larger than Kenny Town. The wall was much higher, thicker, and made of concrete. They continued down the path until they came to a sign. Corin cleared his throat and read it aloud, "'NO THERASAPIENS AND NO PERSONS FROM FRANKLIN CITY ARE ALLOWED WITHIN THESE WALLS. IF YOU ARE OUR ENEMY, YOU SHALL BE SHOT ON THE SPOT. NO MERCY!'"

"Where are we?" asked John Doe. "This is not a friendly sign. I don't like it."

"Could this be Centerville City?" asked Jack, referring to the map.

"No, this is obviously New Jersey," said RJ.

"Really? Where's that Jersey Devil? He owes me thirty gold," John Doe said excitedly.

In disbelief, Jack's palm covered his brow, and he shook his head vigorously.

"Jessica, have we arrived?" Finnegan asked, opening the hatch.

"Gentlemen," said Jessica, emerging from the tank. "Welcome to Centerville City."

We're finally here. I like this world, but I don't fit in. I didn't think I'd miss the space station this badly. I love adventuring in outer space. I hope the warlock who lives here can help me return home. John Doe wants to meet him and receive training, and I hope he does. He's not a very good wizard. Maybe this Heeb can help him?

—From the journal of Corin Degodi
June 12, 2215, 11:15 a.m.

"Is this how we get in?" asked John Doe, studying an enormous, locked, decorative wrought iron gate. "Fancy."

On the other side of the gate, off to the left, was a small office desk where a dull green-skinned goblin sat. It admired a beautiful fountain behind the desk in the middle of a roundabout just beyond the gate. The fountain gracefully sprayed water into the air, making soothing splashing sounds like a magical waterfall. On the goblin's desk were a pair of glasses, a logbook, maps of the city, scattered sheets of paper, a small tub of ink, and a feather quill.

"That running water will make me need the lavatory," said John Doe.

The goblin heard John Doe and scowled. It picked up its glasses and adjusted them on its face as it glared at them, exhaled hard, and pushed aside random papers. The goblin grabbed a clean sheet, opened the logbook, and dipped the feather quill into a small tub of ink.

"Excuse me," said Corin.

"You'd best excuse yourselves!" the goblin hissed. "State your business, and what is that tank doing here? This better not be some trick set up by Franklin City. Jeer won't allow it in Centerville."

"Jeer?" asked Jack.

"That's me!" growled the goblin. "I am Jeer."

"This is my tank," Jessica responded, walking to her tank and placing her hand on the hull. "And no, sir, we are not members of Franklin City."

"You have papers?" Jeer asked, walking to the gate.

Jessica pulled a folded blue paper from her pocket and handed it to the goblin through the iron bars.

He looked at the paper carefully. "Oh, a delivery. Very well. You're legit, Ms. Dove. According to your documentation, this delivery to the South Gate is from you and your three employees. Which of these people are in your party?"

"Finn, please call out RJ and Ace," Jessica said, motioning to Finnegan.

"RJ, Ace, come out here for introductions," Finnegan commanded.

Ace and RJ quickly emerged from the tank.

"This is my crew," said Jessica.

Jeer nodded his head and returned to his desk. He wrote a few words on his sheet and hers with the quill. He returned to Jessica and handed her the blue paper.

She folded it and returned it to her pocket.

"I wrote the military location on your paper where you'll be delivering. Your tank must remain there until the mayor directs it to be moved or used for another mission. Now, any questions? I didn't think so." Jeer threw a map of the city and a brochure at Jessica.

"Wait a min—" Finnegan said as Jessica caught the map and pamphlet.

"Next!"

"What will we do?" whispered John Doe to Troll. "We don't exactly have documentation for being here. The mayor of Kenny Town just told us to come here to find work."

"Let's wait and see what happens, John," said Troll. "We can always find another town to reside in if necessary."

"But I'm tired," John Doe grumbled.

"Shh," said Troll as he placed a comforting hand on John Doe's shoulder.

"Now, what about that vehicle?" asked Jeer, adjusting his glasses to look at the Chevrolet.

"Oh," Rowan gasped. She stepped out of the vehicle and approached the gate. "I am returning this to my friend."

"What friend of yours lives here? No one in Centerville owns an antique vehicle like this," Jeer told her. "You must be mistaken!"

"He does not live in Centerville. I don't think. I don't know, actually, but he's in the car. He'll take it back now."

"Really?" Jeer asked. "The human in the backseat is the owner?"

"Yes, sir," Rowan said, dancing to the back door. She opened it, and her baby animals jumped out and stampeded toward the gate.

"What is this? A zoo? No pets allowed!" Jeer declared.

"They're not pets," Rowan said.

Magnum landed next to John Doe.

"What is that? That's *not* a normal dog!" screamed the startled goblin.

"He's my friend," said John Doe.

"He is my dinner," laughed Magnum as he tapped John Doe on the back with his tail.

"That's not funny," said John Doe, crossing his arms across his chest.

"He's an Antiquity but looks devious. He *is* allowed in; however, he must be someone's responsibility."

"Devious?" laughed Magnum. "I've been called worse."

"He is my responsibility," said John Doe.

"Very well," said the goblin. "Now, back to the matter at hand . . . that antique car cannot enter unless it has proper documentation. That's the law."

"I do not live here," said the human when he exited the backseat. As he shut the door behind him, he brought his face close to Rowan and smiled. "But I have an idea. And it's thanks to you and your escapade."

"Really?" she asked with enthusiasm. "What's your idea?"

"Oh, it's something that will be great. However, I never want to see you or your friends again. This experience has been quite . . . disturbing, detestable, and disgusting."

"Oh," said Rowan with a frown. "Three words beginning with the letter D, meaning something negative. Please accept my apologies, friend, and thank you for the getaway car."

The man nodded to Rowan, opened the driver's door, and sat down.

Rowan politely shut the door and handed him the keys to the ignition. "I am again very sorry that I stole your vehicle, but thank you for the use of it to save my dear little friends."

"Madam," the man said, taking his keys and handing Rowan her turtle. "I highly suggest you toilet train your 'dear little friends.' It will take me weeks to get this smell out of here. Plus, all the damage you caused driving like a maniac. It is going to take forever to repair this antique car."

"Well, I wish you the best of luck, friend," Rowan said as she hugged the turtle, oblivious to the man's complaints. She skipped back to the iron gate.

"Crazy lady," the man muttered as he put the key into the ignition and attempted to start the Chevy. The engine made a struggling sound and then sputtered and died. He tried again, but the same thing happened. He screamed and sobbed as he put his head down on the steering wheel and sounded the horn.

Jeer covered his ears and looked at the vehicle with annoyance. "I don't care what you guys do. Just get that thing away from this gate!"

"I'll take a look under the bonnet, lad," Ace said, hurrying to the car and lifting the damaged hood. He smiled at the old model and cracked his knuckles. He dug his hands into the engine and had a field day. "What an old beauty! Aha! I do believe I found the source of the problem." He plugged in a spark plug that had come loose. "Try your key now, laddie."

The man turned the key, and his engine started. "Oh, thank you."

"No problem! Have a safe journey."

"Wait!" yelled Rowan. "What is your name?"

"Phillip Walker," the driver said as he reversed the car. "Goodbye. I hope I don't see you ever again! This was an experience I will not forget." He put his green 1989 Chevy into gear and drove away.

"What a hot head!" Jack said. "I'd hate to travel with that guy. Rowan, how did you put up with him?"

"He wasn't *that* bad," Rowan said, grinning. "He would've liked us better if the animals had not urinated all over him."

Jeer grumbled under his breath after hearing Rowan's disgusting comment. He pounded on his desk. "Over here! Remember me, people? Give me your attention. Weapons are not allowed. You cannot take any firearms or hand-held weapons beyond this point. All weapons will remain here in a storage facility. So, do you still want to stay here?"

"Yes," Corin said. "We require room and board."

"There are plenty of hotels," said Jeer, clasping his hands together. "Now, are there any objections to the weapons law? There are usually complaints."

"I can't have my axe?" Troll asked.

The goblin shook his head.

Troll groaned and pulled his axe from its sheath on his back. He looked at his axe before he glanced at Jeer and then at Corin. "I cannot leave my best weapon here."

"It'll be safe here," assured the goblin. "Surrounding the entire city is our greatest landmark, the giant wall, protecting everyone and everything. No one can break in. The wall only has four main openings: the South Gate, which you travelers see before you; the North Gate, the West Gate, and the East Gate. These gates don't just embellish our city. They are like monuments that represent our culture. We are protected."

"What if I need it?" asked Troll.

"Civilian use of weapons is not legal inside Centerville unless they are chosen by our mayor for the arena. The police and military are the only exceptions."

"Well, that's just—" Troll paused and smiled. "Did you say there is an arena?"

"Yes, we have a large arena."

"How often are there battles?" Troll asked, excited.

"Whenever someone decides to have a challenge," answered the goblin. "There has not been a battle in quite some time. The last one, I'd say, was eight months ago. It's about time they have another."

"I'll say!" Troll said. "You can hold onto my axe. Just keep it safe. It was a gift. I also have my grenade pouch."

"Fine. After I let you in, put your weapons in this giant steel storage unit labeled C2 by my desk. I'll write your name and the description of your belongings in my logbook. If you exit the city, you have to sign out your things to have them returned to you. Now, have your identification ready."

"If you schedule an arena battle, put me in as your opponent," Jack told Troll. "I am interested in a real match with you."

"If you fight Troll, then I have to be an announcer for that battle," chuckled Corin.

"Get out your identification, Finn," said Jessica over their conversation. She wasn't interested in scheduling an arena battle. "Do you think RJ has his?"

Finnegan looked over at RJ.

The junkie was frantically searching his body for his I.D. badge. He looked in all of his pockets, his sacks, his boots, his socks, and even his hair. He finally found it after putting his hand into his undergarments.

Why did I watch him do that? Finnegan shuddered. *I'd hate to be that goblin right now . . . he's going to have to touch that.*

"Um, sir," said Rowan as she danced to the gate again and gently put her turtle down with the rest of the animals. "I don't technically have identification because I'm a faerie and live in the forest."

"Well then, because of your absent identification, you can't come in unless you are in your invisible state," the goblin said.

"What?" Rowan screeched, feeling insulted.

"That's the law here. Faeries with no identification must remain invisible."

"But why?" she asked.

"Faeries cause too much trouble and bring havoc while visible."

"Oh, that's hogwash!" Rowan spat. "I bring harmony!"

"Do you want to get in?" asked John Doe.

"Fine!" Rowan squawked as she became invisible. "This is going to stink! You're such a grouch!"

"I work all day long. Expect the grumpiness!" Jeer shouted. "I don't get to play in the forest all day like you!"

"Well, will my animals be safe?" she asked.

Jeer glanced at the baby animals.

"We have a large park area where they will be happy. No one is allowed to hunt within the city. The animals will be well treated and protected."

"Wonderful!" Rowan cheered. "I'm happy now!"

"Spectacular. Everyone else, have your identification ready," Jeer said. He nudged a sheet of paper and revealed a small button on his desk. He pressed it, and a rock beside his desk moved as a large lever rose from the ground. Jeer pulled the lever, and the gate opened. "All right, form a line. I need this to be orderly," he said as he sat at his desk.

"I'm not from here," Corin said, showing the goblin his badge.

"I don't care. This has your name on it, so that's all I need to see," said Jeer, taking the card in his hand and examining it. He jotted down Corin's name into his logbook and handed him back his badge. "Step aside. Next!"

Everyone showed their identification to the goblin one at a time and loaded their weapons into the storage unit as Jeer wrote their names and information into the logbook.

Troll had a dilemma and went to the back of the line. Sweat formed on his brow.

"You're last, handsome," Jeer said, finally getting to Troll. "I. D., please."

Troll swallowed hard and handed the goblin a small military-grade dog tag.

"This is not an official identification badge. Why don't you have identification?" asked the goblin.

"I did not grow up within a town or a city. Like Rowan, I was raised in the wilderness. The only thing I can show you is this tag given to me by the Eastern Regiment."

"Let me get a better look at this thing," said the goblin, opening a drawer. Jeer took out a magnifying glass and held it up to the tag. It read T. SMITH. "Your last name is Smith?"

"No," answered Troll.

"Then what in the hell does T. Smith stand for?" he asked gruffly.

"I have no last name, so they made one up," Troll explained.

"What's your first name?"

"People call me Troll."

"That is your *name*?"

"Yes?" Troll gulped.

"Who gave you that name?"

"I did," Troll responded.

"I give up!" the goblin screamed as he wrote the obscure name in the logbook. He then snarled at the purple-haired warrior, handing him back his dog tag. "I suggest you all go see the mayor. He will be in his office. Just turn right behind my station. That'll put you on King Street. Follow it, and Centerville City Hall will be on your left. He loves to meet new people, so I'm sure he'll just love you imbeciles."

"Thank you for your time," said Troll kindly.

"Yeah, yeah," grumbled the goblin. Jeer pushed the lever and closed the gate. He pressed the button, and the lever sank back into the ground and was covered by the rock. "I sit here all day, and what happens? The same thing! Every single day! I meet new people. *Argh!* I need to retire!" he groaned, pulling the lever.

SIXTEEN

Jessica took out the map and brochure of Centerville. She unfolded the blue paper Jeer had written the address on for the military base. *This city is bigger than I thought.*

"Wow!" said RJ as he glanced at Jeer's note. He pointed to a place on the map. "The military base is way over there. Does this mean we need to separate from our new friends?"

"Don't worry about splitting up for good. I'm going to find us all a hotel," said Corin, looking at the map. "We should go meet the mayor together tomorrow."

"Can we stay at the hotel close to the park?" asked Rowan, pointing to the park on the map. "I want to make sure my animals are happy and safe."

"That's a good idea," said Jack.

"Where do you see a hotel near there?" asked Corin, looking around the map.

"It's right here, steps away from the park," said Jack, showing Corin the location of the WAY O' WINGS HOTEL.

"Okay," said Corin. "Jessica, you guys come to meet us here. I will have rooms for you when you arrive after dropping off the tank. Let me hang on to the map."

"Thank you," Jessica said, giving the map to Corin. She kissed his cheek. "We'll be back soon. Come on, guys."

"We have spuds to deliver!" cheered RJ.

Corin blushed momentarily.

Jessica and her crew boarded the tank and drove to the military location.

Rowan appeared beside Troll and stared at him.

Troll felt her eyes and glanced at her.

When their eyes met, she winked and turned invisible.

Troll blushed and gently rubbed his cheeks.

Corin returned his attention to the map.

"Look!" John Doe exclaimed as he glanced over Corin's shoulder and pointed to a spot on the map that read HEEB'S HERBAL REMEDIES. In his excitement, John Doe nearly collapsed on top of Corin. "This is the warlock's place! Only a great warlock would have an herbal store. It even says 'Heeb.' That's him! That's his name!"

"That's great. We'll go there soon," Corin said, pulling away from the eager wizard.

"I sure hope this city has a good mechanic," Jack said. "I could really use some fixing up."

"I bet the mayor knows a mechanic," said John Doe. "Maybe we should meet him today? Jeer said he was at City Hall. Don't mayors live at City Hall?"

"I don't think he *lives* there," Rowan's sweet voice giggled. She danced invisibly around her friends. They could feel her breeze by them.

"What about the hotel?" asked Corin. "Don't we need a place to stay first?"

"Of course," said Troll, "but getting Jack to a mechanic right away may be best for him."

"I need to reload my weapons, and recharging will be easier for me once I am repaired," said Jack.

"I bet if we become friends with the mayor, he'll arrange for us to have cheaper hotel suites," said John Doe. "I'm such a cheapskate."

"Cheaper?" Corin asked excitedly. He looked at the map again before swiftly heading toward City Hall. "Come on, let us go meet the mayor first. Jessica and the others will be gone for a while. It's a long drive to the other side of the city, and they'll need to walk back. Let's go see the mayor now!"

"Is it just me, or does he really like money and the idea of being cheap?" whispered John Doe to Troll.

Troll shrugged. "I don't know what's wrong with him."

"We all have our weaknesses. Yours is women," John Doe said proudly.

"No, it's not," said Troll, brushing his right hand through his long hair.

"It's not?" asked John Doe, looking puzzled. "Oh yeah, that's *my* weakness!"

Troll chuckled as he put his arm around John Doe and gently tugged on the wizard as they followed Corin. "Come on, partner."

"Magnum, come, follow your master," John Doe told the demon dog.

"Oh, I am so going to eat you in your sleep tonight," said Magnum.

Golden glowing eyes watched them from the shadows of an alley.

Captain Unna Rinaldi arrived at Centerville's large warning sign. "Such disrespect," Unna huffed as she parked her silver-colored hoverbike. She glanced at the city wall in the distance. She grinned evilly, opened a compartment on her bike, and pulled out a medium-length brunette wig. She put it on her head and secured it with bobby pins before she pulled out a black leather jacket. She put it on to hide her uniform and casually walked to the sign. She spat on it, then walked to the gate.

Jeer's attention was on a magazine. As he turned a page, he noticed her approach.

Unna glared at the goblin gatekeeper. She knew he was not a threat, but she was wary because he could call guards to arrest her if he discovered her true identity. "Excuse me," Unna said to Jeer when she walked to the bars. "I am seeking shelter. Do you mind if I inquire about your city?"

"What is there to know?" Jeer asked with a barking voice. "It's a city. People live in it. We have hotels if you need a place to stay. That sums it up, ladies and gentlemen. I'm unfortunately here all day. Do you want to stay here or not?"

"I will require a place to rest," she replied expressionless.

"I need to see your I. D., and no weapons may enter here. You'll leave them with me, and that bike of yours must be registered; otherwise, it can't come into the city. Does it belong to you? Do you have papers for it?"

"Unfortunately, I do not, but I will go retrieve whatever documents are needed to enter your city," Unna said, swallowing hard. "I will return the day after tomorrow."

"I can put your name down in the logbook," said Jeer as he pulled out the large book. "Your name, please, miss?"

"Shana," Unna said.

"Okay, June fourteenth is your arrival date," Jeer groaned as he wrote her information.

"Thank you," she said, returning to her hoverbike. She gasped in surprise when she noticed a man wearing a brown and tan leather outfit admiring her hoverbike.

"This is very nice," the stranger told her. "My name is—"

"I didn't ask," Unna said as she marched up to her hoverbike. "You should take your leave, sir."

"I wouldn't mind leaving with you . . . you're a pretty lady with a nice ride! I'm impressed! I'm a Vicissitude member," the stranger said with a large smile as his eyes admired Unna's form. He leaned against the handlebars of her hoverbike.

"I'm not bothered to know what type of membership that is, and you disgust me," Unna said. She sat on the saddle and put her heeled boot on the stranger's chest. "You'll get my bike dirty, you filthy man. Be gone!" She kicked him as hard as she could. The man toppled back and landed hard in the dirt.

"Yes," admitted the man. "I have a filthy mind, but you get used to it. My entire group is like that. We appreciate the finer things in life, like drinking alcohol, eating carbohydrates, wearing leather underwear, and more drinking."

"Ugh," Unna's upper lip curled slightly in her dislike of the strange man. "Just go climb back into whatever hole you climbed out of!"

"How'd you know I live in a hole? Oh, my gods, you're psychic! I like psycho people. I think I love you!"

Unna started her engine and drove into the forest.

"Wait! Come back, angel!" yelled the stranger as he strode after her. He threw his arms up in defeat as she disappeared from his view. He sighed after he could no longer hear the roar of her engine. He walked over to Jeer and leaned on the decorative bars. "I think she's the one! Yeah . . . I am in love with her."

"That's disgusting," Jeer said, wrinkling his nose.

"I know," said the man. "We'd be absolutely revolting together. It's the perfect match."

"Well, she's coming back in two days," said Jeer. "Maybe you could impress her with your skills? If you have any."

"Really?" huffed the man in excitement. "I'll be ready."

"Which gate did you get out of this time?"

"West," he said.

"I have got to talk to the other gatekeepers about letting you out," Jeer mumbled.

"Why?"

"Because you always end up here and talk to me!"

"Can I come back in now?"

"Son of a—yes!"

Unna pulled out her radio as she drove through the forest. "Come in 7-8-9-0."

"Yes, madam," replied the hissing voice.

"I am informing you of my swift return to Franklin City. I must gather supplies before I enter Centerville City. I will rendezvous with you on the day after tomorrow."

"I have been watching the outsiders, as you commanded."

"Excellent! Have their profiles ready for my arrival. Continue your survey, but pay close attention to the purple-haired man. You may test his skills in any way you'd like, but don't openly engage him or cause a disturbance in the city."

"As you command, Captain Rinaldi, I hear and obey. Thank you for this opportunity of entertainment."

"Do not fail me."

Rowan let out an audible sigh, expressing her disappointment at having to remain invisible. The boys did their best to comfort her on their way to the mayor's office.

"Hey," said John Doe to Rowan. "Maybe the mayor will let you show yourself?"

"If what the goblin told us is true, then I am not permitted to show myself in this city, but I want to escort my animals to the park. I want them to be safe."

"I'll go with you," said John Doe happily.

"I'd rather not have you come," she grumbled. "No offense, but I don't like you."

"No problem," said John Doe. "Not like I was going to tell Magnum that the park was where he could find a midnight snack."

"You're horrible!" Rowan shouted.

"Okay," Troll said quickly. "I'll go. You two knock it off."

"Oh, thank you, Troll!" Rowan exclaimed.

"Oh, thank you, Troll," John Doe mimicked her. He felt a hard kick in his rear end. John Doe turned to face whoever struck him, but no one was there. He then received another strike in his buttocks. This strike was hard enough that he screamed and face-planted on the ground.

Troll sighed hard. "Rowan, stop it."

"Sorry," she hummed. "I was only playing."

John Doe sat up and looked around. "I did nothing to deserve such horrible treatment!"

"Sure, you did," said Magnum.

"Oh? Well then, I deserve this," said John Doe in surprise.

Magnum could not help but chuckle at the wizard. He disliked being his servant, but he enjoyed the entertainment.

Jack picked John Doe up by grabbing the fabric of his hood and scarf.

As soon as John Doe planted his feet, he turned and faced the cyborg. "Thank you," John Doe told Jack before he glanced at Corin.

The space ranger stared at a tall, brown brick building with a fancy door and clock tower.

John Doe rolled up his sleeves as he walked up to Corin. "What are you looking at?"

"City Hall," said Corin. "What kind of architecture is this?"

"That is the classical Greco-Roman style," said Jack. "Very popular on this planet."

"I like it. It's regal. So, John Doe, are we going in, or will you continue playing in the dirt?"

John Doe paused, thinking about Corin's question. He rolled his sleeves back down and looked at the impressive building. "No, I'm finished. Check out all these stairs! I'm in awe! We should count them as we run to the door!"

"Let's go," said Corin.

"One, two, three—" John Doe counted, heading up.

Jack turned to Troll. "We'll see you and Rowan soon. Well, you, at least. Rowan, I guess we'll *hear* you later," said Jack.

Troll grinned and nodded.

"Come on, my children. Follow my voice. I'll lead you," Rowan sang as the baby animals, and Troll followed her sweet voice.

Corin, Magnum, and Jack walked up the stairs quietly, allowing John Doe to count without distraction. "—Forty-two, forty-three, forty-four!"

The front door was resilient, made of wrought iron, and decorated with a complex pattern of leaves and vines. The craftsmanship was magnificent.

Corin put his hand on the Victorian-style knob and opened the door.

"Ugh, it's horrible!" John Doe declared. "That carpet is grotesque! Who would have picked that shade of color?"

The inside of Centerville City Hall was very different than Kenny Town Hall. The lobby was built into the main hall, which led to a big door marked COURTROOM. The reception desk sat off to the left in front of a steel elevator. Two potted trees sat on either side of the elevator door. Branched from the main hall were offices for the mayor, councilmen, executive assistants, fire chief, police chief, and finance director. There was also a marriage department and a security room. City Hall didn't feel welcoming with its unpleasant tan walls, antique sailboat paintings, and dark red curtain-drawn windows. The lights above them were dull and hummed loudly. Luckily, the annoying sound distracted John Doe's attention from the ugly burgundy carpet.

The receptionist sat at her desk, reading a fashion magazine, chewing pink bubble gum with her mouth open. The smacking of her lips and movement of her jaws was in comparison to a cow dining on hay. She was in her early thirties, had bright brown hair with blonde highlights, and wore blue glasses, which matched her blue suit and white blouse. She blew a bubble and looked at them. The bubble popped, and she lowered her glasses down her nose. "Can I help you?" she asked, high-pitched and nasally.

John Doe twitched. "Her chomping and voice are like a cheese grate shredding my nerves," he whispered to Jack.

"Hi," said Corin. "We're here to see the mayor."

"No one can see the mayor without an appointment," she said.

"Well, can we schedule an appointment?" asked Jack.

"That depends on his schedule," she said, gazing at the magazine.

"How can we see his schedule?" asked John Doe.

"You can't," she said, turning a page.

"Then how can we schedule an appointment?" asked Corin.

Annoyed, the receptionist looked at them again, put down the magazine, and opened a sizeable green logbook. She turned multiple pages until she located a blank slot. She took out a feather and inkwell. After dipping the feather into the ink, she began to write in the logbook. She blew another bubble. It popped onto her lips. She sucked the gum back into her mouth. She finished writing and slammed the book shut. She eyed the boys, then opened her magazine and continued to read.

"Did we get an appointment?" asked Corin.

"Yes," said the receptionist.

"Well, when is it?" asked Jack.

"When is what?" she asked, annoyed again.

"Our meeting to see the mayor!" yelled Corin.

"No one can see the mayor without an appointment," she said, turning another magazine page.

"Can I just eat her?" asked Magnum.

"No," said John Doe. "Wait until after we see the mayor."

"No one can see—"

"Yeah, we know!" Magnum interrupted the receptionist. "By the stars, I will go insane listening to her. Can't we just go find the mayor on our own?"

"The mayor is not in his office right now," squeaked another voice in the room.

Puzzled, they looked around but saw no one near the receptionist's desk.

"You guys heard that voice too, right?" asked John Doe.

"Yes," said Jack, Magnum, and Corin simultaneously.

"Good," said John Doe. "I thought I was going even crazier than usual."

"Down here, please," the voice squeaked again.

They looked down, and a tiny eight-inch person stood by their feet. He looked like a human who had been shrunk by an enchantment.

"What are you?" asked Magnum. "You look like you could be my in-between meal snack."

"That's rude," said the little fellow.

"Who are you?" asked Jack.

"I'm the mayor's advisor, Peter. He left me in charge. Rebecca made you an appointment to see him later today. I must apologize for her manners. She hates to be disturbed. It's the curse of having a short attention span. The mayor also doesn't like being in his office. He thinks it's haunted. He's always out in the city and loves to meet new people. How may I help you until your appointment?"

"Well, Peter," said Corin. "We need a hotel for the night, but we are considering jobs and a home here unless we continue traveling."

"I understand! We have many travelers like you who come and go. If you choose to stay here, I promise you will love it. Centerville is a great, peaceful place to live. I can hook you gentlemen up with a hotel right away. How many people are in your party?"

"Ten," said Corin. "Eight men, a lovely woman, and a faerie staying invisible."

"Good to hear she is obeying the rules. We highly respect Antiquities, but unfortunately, there have been some issues with faeries. Come with me, and I will take you to one of our finest hotels. I'll get you checked in, and then I can take you to see the mayor," said Peter.

"I have a question. If Rowan became visible, what would happen?" asked Jack.

"She would be banished from Centerville City," said Peter. "She can be visible in her hotel room or the privacy of a home you may purchase, but nowhere else within the walls of this city."

"Are you a brownie?" asked John Doe.

The little man chuckled. "Call me what you will, but I like to call myself a gnome."

"Are there a lot of gnomes in this city?" asked Corin.

"Oh, gnomes are everywhere. It's just that most of my kind dislike working for humans, so humans hardly ever see us. I enjoy humans and their activities, especially the mayor's outings. Something exciting always seems to happen around here."

"Sounds like this Centerville City is a fun place," said Jack.

"Oh my, yes," said the gnome.

"We were hoping to stay at the hotel beside the park, the Way O' Wings Hotel," said Jack. "Two of our friends are at the park now."

"That's a lovely area. I can allow you to rent the entire third floor until you purchase a home. There are twelve rooms. Follow me, please."

Troll escorted the baby animals and Rowan, in her invisible state, to the park. Although she could not see her own body, Rowan knew how to skillfully navigate and could flirt with the young warrior. She intentionally extended her invisible arm and gently touched Troll's fingers, trying to slide her tiny hand into his large palm.

Troll felt her gentle touch and glanced at his hand.

Rowan gasped, pulled her hand away quickly, and her cheeks blushed. She was glad to be invisible.

"Were you trying to hold my hand?" asked Troll.

"No, of course not!" Rowan stated.

"It's okay to be nervous, you know," he said. "The babies have never been to this park before, but I'm sure they'll be comfortable. I don't mind if you need to hold hands for comfort. You don't need to feel embarrassed. It's not like anyone else will see. Only I will know, and I won't tell a soul."

Rowan's embarrassment grew. She could not bring herself to touch him, but she wanted to. "You're so sweet," she said. *If only you knew the truth about how I feel, but I cannot tell you. You would never have the same feelings for me. It will be wise to change the subject before he figures out why I want to hold his hand.* "Troll, I didn't know you grew up in the wilderness. I wanted to let you know that I *didn't* grow up in the forest. My father and sister live in a magical city called England. I live in my forest now because I earned the responsibility to protect life in the human world. I'm actually a city girl at heart."

"Oh," said Troll. "I didn't know that."

"Haven't you a mother or father?"

Troll did not answer her question. Luckily for him, they arrived at the park. "Look, we're here. Now, your little friends will be safe and sound."

"Oh, good! This park is beautiful. Thank you for coming with me, Troll."

"It's not a problem, Rowan. I'll give you space. You go ahead and show your little friends around. I'll wait for you over here in this maple tree."

"Okay, thank you," she said. "Come, babies, follow my voice."

The baby animals immediately followed Rowan into the park, and Troll climbed the maple tree to wait for her. He sat on a thick branch that was strong enough to hold his weight. He sighed and waited patiently for his faerie friend.

Though invisible, Rowan led her baby animals deep into the park's heart. She hugged each of them. "I'll always care for you and visit regularly. I promise you'll be safe here. Now, go explore your new home. Live happily and play together," Rowan said, smiling as she watched her little friends scamper around excitedly.

All the babies, even the turtle, looked happy to be in their new home.

I'm glad these children are safe. I feel so bad about the forest. Fixing and regrowing all the destroyed trees and plants will take years. I loathe Raw. He must've been the one to start the fires. I have never hated someone, but I have many reasons to dislike him. Mainly because he tried to kill Troll. I have known many humans for centuries, but Troll is my favorite. He is different. He is kind, gentle, protective, and smart. I like Jack, too, but there is something extraordinary about Troll. He makes my heart light up, and my soul feels like a feather. What is so special about him? Am I truly in love with him? I must keep my head. I cannot let him or anyone else know my feelings.

Peter led the foursome to a brick and concrete building with a large cherry wood carved sign above the main entrance that read CENTERVILLE WAY O' WINGS SUITES HOTEL.

"Welcome to Way O' Wings," said Peter. "This hotel got its name from the great bald eagles who used to visit our park. The hotel was a shelter for humans during the early months of World War III in 2026. It was severely damaged and rebuilt after the twenty-first century but is a big part of our city's history. Would you care to see the third floor? It has an excellent view."

"Great," said Corin, "let's go see."

"Follow me," said Peter, leading them inside the first floor.

They gazed in awe at the stunning lobby as they headed to the elevator. All of the door frames were forest green with gold trim. The carpet was a beautiful shade of olive green, and the walls were light blue with a hint of gold glitter. The ceiling was decorated with chandeliers and paintings of beautiful birds with gorgeous large wings.

They boarded the elevator and went up to the third floor. When the doors opened, Corin, Jack, John Doe, and Magnum inhaled sharply upon emerging. The third floor was just as breathtaking as the main lobby. It was the most beautiful hallway any of them had ever been in.

"Well," said Jack. "This is *definitely* better than being down in the mines!"

"It's beautiful," said John Doe.

"It's giving me the creeps," said Magnum. "It's *too* pretty."

"How much?" Corin asked.

"Four hundred and ninety-two gold pieces exactly for tonight," said Peter. "You may pay two hundred and forty-six gold now and the other half tomorrow during checkout. If you rent longer, we'll determine the price with the mayor."

"I think we can pull together that much," said Corin. "I have coins. I can give you three hundred now."

"Very good," Peter said, smiling as he held up his tiny hand.

Corin carefully took Peter's tiny hand and shook it gently, sealing the deal.

"Let's head back to the lobby," said Peter. "I will have the front desk associate reserve the entire floor, and then I'll escort you to the mayor."

Once back on the elevator, Jack and John Doe searched their pockets for gold to assist with the morning payment.

Corin smiled. "Gentlemen, don't worry about contributing. I can handle it."

Peter looked up at them and smiled.

Magnum looked at Peter and licked his lips.

"Good doggy," Peter gulped.

"That's nice of you, Corin, but we don't want you to use up all your money," said Jack. "We have those gold coins from Mayor Caser. I wish I had more."

"With my job being given to those two grunts in Kenny Town, I have no money either," John Doe said, sighing.

"What about Troll?" Corin asked, noticing Peter distracted by Magnum.

John Doe chuckled. "Listen, Troll usually doesn't have money, and if he does, he won't use it. He says he doesn't need it."

"What does he do with it?" asked Corin.

"He donates to people who need it," said John Doe.

"What if one of us needs it?" Corin asked with hungry eyes.

"I'm sure he'd let us have it if it was for a good reason," said John Doe.

"A good reason," Corin said, nodding.

The elevator bell dinged, and the doors opened to the lobby.

Peter was the first one off the elevator. He tried staying away from Magnum. He ran to a tall, redheaded woman at the front desk. "We have guests for tonight."

Corin approached the associate, took the coins he had stolen from Raw's base, and handed them to her. He was meticulous in not giving her the large gold coin from the mayor of Kenny Town. She activated a small computer console and entered their information, reserving the third floor. When she was finished, Corin returned to the others.

Peter thanked her and ran back over to them, avoiding Magnum. "Come, follow me. I know where the mayor is," he said, leading them out of the hotel.

Troll was in the tree, waiting for Rowan. He wanted to give her plenty of time, so he relaxed for a brief meditation period. Just as Troll closed his eyes, he sensed something in the city. It made him feel uncomfortable. He looked toward the unsettling sensation, and his blue eyes fixed on a particular building to the north. Even though it was far away, its negative energy felt very close. The building was constructed in an alternate white brick pattern with a bright blue roof. Troll could not see around the entire structure because the other buildings blocked his view.

I have never seen a building like that before. Is it someone's home or a hotel? It's unique. The structure doesn't match any of the other buildings. I want to avoid that place. There's something there I don't like.

Rowan had finished talking with her animals and returned to the maple tree. She looked up at Troll and grinned at him. Her smile melted away when she noticed how tense he was.

"Troll," she said sweetly. "Is everything okay?"

"Rowan, do you sense anything in this city? Anything negative?"

"Really? Let me see," she said, flying above the tree and focused on sensing any disturbances. "The people are busy, but I can't feel anything unusual." She landed and became visible.

"Rowan, you shouldn't stay visible too long. I don't want you to get in trouble."

"I want to put your mind at ease."

He offered her his hand. "Come on. We can sit and talk before we find the others."

"All right," she said with a big smile, taking his hand. "So, what did you feel?"

"I'm not sure," he said, pulling her up with his strong arms. "I thought it was something bad. It's an uncomfortable feeling. You honestly feel nothing?"

"No," she said, shaking her head. "But if I do, I will let you know immediately."

"Thanks," he said, smiling at her.

She stared into his blue eyes and could not stop her cheeks from blushing.

Golden eyes watched them from the shadows of clustered trees.

Peter led Corin, Jack, John Doe, and Magnum through the city streets. They walked past citizens who waved at them.

"Everyone is very polite," said Jack. "I'm glad they're not afraid of me."

They were one street over from City Hall.

"We should see the mayor soon," said Peter. "It's almost time for your meeting."

"It is?" asked Corin.

"Yes, this is the time Rebecca scheduled, you know."

"We didn't—" said Jack.

"Now that's just irresponsible," said Peter.

"But—she—you—no one told us," Corin said.

"Mayor Lanus!" Peter called to the mayor when he spotted him walking by the Centerville Bank beside a man with Asian features.

"Ah, Peter," said Mayor Lanus, brushing his fingers through his short, silver hair. "Who are your friends?"

"They arrived today, sir, and they're right on schedule. It's time for your meeting with them. They're interested in jobs and possibly purchasing a home. They're currently staying at one of our finest hotels."

"Terrific! Hello, boys. My name is Lanus, Mayor Tucker Lanus. Welcome to Centerville City!" Mayor Lanus said. "Let me present Mr. Sun, the Food Dragon grocery store owner."

Mr. Sun smiled and bowed slightly to them.

Corin and Jack bowed respectfully as John Doe accidentally bowed too fast and head-butted Magnum.

Magnum shrieked, gripped his head in pain, and shot John Doe a dirty look.

"Sorry," said John Doe, rubbing his forehead. "That hurt."

Mr. Sun laughed. "It is very nice to meet you. I take it you gentlemen have never bowed as a greeting before. In my home country, a slight bow is how we say hello. You must work on your bowing."

"Yeah, we'll get right on that," Magnum moaned.

"Nice to meet you too," said John Doe.

"So, gentlemen, are y'all thinking about living here?" asked Mayor Lanus with a strong southern drawl. "Everyone is welcome, magic creatures and scientific beings alike. If any of you are refugees from Franklin City, you're welcome to hide here briefly, but I'm afraid you can't reside here. I must protect my city and its people from the Restrain Corporation. We are against what that horrible group stands for. Are y'all fleeing their violent tendencies in search of a new start?"

"Not exactly," said Jack. *I'd best not mention escaping from the mines.* "We're not from Franklin City—"

"But Franklin City sounds *interesting*," Corin cut in. "I'm not from this planet, so I am unfamiliar. My name is Corin Degodi, and these are my friends: Jack, John Doe, and Magnum."

"Well, you don't look like an alien to me, son, but all y'all certainly are outlandish," said Mayor Lanus, smiling. "A cyborg traveling with humans and—" he paused, looking at Magnum with confusion. "What exactly are you, my dear boy?"

"I'm considered a demon dog by human standards," Magnum told him. "You have nothing to fear from me. I am only here to eat John Doe."

"I'm your master," John Doe said.

"Dinner," said Magnum.

The mayor looked at John Doe from head to toe before staring at him. "Son, are you a wizard?"

"Yes," said John Doe proudly, gripping his trench coat and pushing out his chest. "Does my outfit give it away?"

"A bit," he said, holding back his laughter. "Isn't that outfit a little ridiculous?"

John Doe looked at his clothes. "It's comfortable."

"You will love Centerville," said Mr. Sun. "I have been living here for a long time, running my own grocery store. I have a great life. Everybody does. We're protected. I highly recommend living here and avoiding Franklin City."

"Thanks," said Jack. "So far, the place looks great. We really like the hotel Peter has hooked us up with."

"The Way O' Wings Hotel," said Peter, winking at the cyborg. "It's one of our best."

"Indeed," said the mayor. "But you gentlemen just can't stay at a hotel forever. Suppose y'all are interested in residing here; I suggest you come with me tomorrow and take a gander at homes for sale. There are plenty of jobs here too. Money is easy to come by."

"Well, I'm interested," said Corin. *I want to be wealthy!*

"Corin," said Jack. "I thought you wanted to find your way home?"

"I do," said Corin. "However, Earth is pretty neat. I may want to stay. I wasn't in love with my old job. I wouldn't mind a change in my career."

"That's the spirit, my boy. Walk with me for a minute," said Mayor Lanus as he led them back to City Hall. "Now, listen to this idea. For the last three months, I have been looking to sell one of my homes at an affordable price. Everyone in the city already owns land. They're not interested, but y'all may very well like my home." He handed Corin a small business card. "This is the address. It's a two-story white brick building with a blue roof, five bathrooms, and six bedrooms. It has an extra-large kitchen, a finished underground basement, and a large sociable area to congregate with relatives, otherwise known as a living room."

"Wow!" exclaimed Corin, putting the card into his pouch. "How much?"

"Well, let's not talk numbers yet, Corin," said Mayor Lanus. "Y'all haven't even seen it. I will take you there first thing tomorrow morning."

"I'd love to see it," said Corin with an ear-to-ear grin. *I will have to think of jobs we can do to earn a living here. Can I ask the mayor to create a job for us? What a great idea! I'll start planning.*

"I want to see it too," said John Doe. "Magnum, are you up for it?"

"I might be," said the demon dog, looking hungrily at John Doe. "I'm sure I'll be more than willing to look at a human home once I've had something to eat."

"Would you stop that!" shouted Jack.

"Stop what?" asked Magnum, giving a sly wink with his left eye and a deep-throated chuckle. "Aren't you coming, cyborg?"

"Actually, no," said Jack, turning to the mayor. "Mr. Mayor, I am in desperate need of repairs. What mechanic do you recommend?"

"Oh, an excellent mechanic who has experience working on machines, cyborgs, and all engine types my city has, of course!" said Mayor Lanus, clapping his hands enthusiastically. "You're going to have to walk north on Main Street. That's this road we're on right now. You go north and six streets down until you come to Mastermind Drive. You turn left onto Mastermind Drive and continue on that road until you reach the dead end. A large cul-de-sac. The mechanic's shop is the building in the center. It's called Systems Spark and Flash Mechanics. You can't miss it."

"Great," said Jack. "I'm going to set up an appointment for tomorrow. I want to take care of myself."

"That place is bustling, so scheduling an appointment is a good idea. But I will caution you because you are a cyborg. The city folk may look at you with fearful eyes. Some cyborgs live here, but they've been here for quite some time. Most cyborgs outside of these walls are dangerous."

"We encountered a few people, and they were polite," said Jack. "I promise not to harm anyone."

"Tell the mechanic that I sent you."

"Thank you very much. Guys, I'll see you soon," Jack said, heading north.

"So," said the mayor to Corin and John Doe. "Shall we meet tomorrow at around ten in the morning?"

"Agreed," Corin said, glancing at John Doe.

"But I want to meet with the legendary warlock tomorrow," said John Doe.

"Our warlock, eh? You mean Heeb?" asked Mayor Lanus, glancing at John Doe suspiciously.

"Heeb!" shouted John Doe with enthusiasm. He performed an excited little jig before he realized he was dancing and stopped. John Doe cleared his throat.

The mayor put his hand to his chin and stared at John Doe. "Hmm, perhaps that can be arranged. We'll discuss it tomorrow."

SEVENTEEN

Jack followed Mayor Lanus's directions that he replayed on his data file. Up ahead, he saw Ace, RJ, Jessica, and Finnegan returning on foot from the military base. "Hello," Jack said, waving at them.

"Jack," Ace announced. "Lad, what are you doing on your own?"

"I'm going to the mechanic to make an appointment and be fixed up. Good news! Corin got us a hotel to sleep at tonight. It's called the Way O' Wings Hotel, by the park where Rowan is keeping her animals. You guys can go there now and check in. Corin has already paid half of the rent," Jack explained.

"Really?" asked Jessica. "That was fast. At least there are beds to sleep in tonight, and we got paid for our delivery."

"Wonderful!" said Jack. "You guys head back to the hotel, and I will see you later. I really want to schedule this appointment so I can feel better."

"Good luck," Jessica said. "I hope the mechanic here is skilled and can help you."

"The mayor said this mechanic is the best in the city," Jack informed them.

"That sounds good then," said Finnegan. "Well, see you later."

Jessica and her team continued, heading toward the hotel as Jack continued up Main Street in search of Mastermind Drive.

Rowan couldn't take her embarrassment any longer and turned invisible.

Troll blinked his eyes when she vanished. "Did I say something wrong?"

"No," Rowan said. "I am just tired."

"I bet the others got rooms for that hotel," said Troll. "Come, we'll go together and see."

"No, you go. I won't sleep in a hotel room again," Rowan said, sighing. "I want to go visit my family. Tell the others I went to England but will return tomorrow."

"How are you going to England so fast?" he asked.

"John Doe is not the only one who can open portals." She giggled. "I am just better at doing it. Stand clear."

Troll jumped out of the tree and took a few giant steps back as Rowan became visible.

"Lanua pateat domi meae Anglia." A yellow portal opened before her, and a forceful gust emerged from the whirlwind. Rowan stood durably against the wind with her arms extended.

Dirt, leaves, and branches blew around Troll. He shut his eyes, taking a knee. A ferocious roar emanated from within the windy portal. Troll covered his ears. His heartbeat quickened. *What kind of a portal is that? What's that sound?*

Why is it so windy? Is something going to come through? Troll cautiously opened one eye.

Rowan turned around, facing him. "I'll be back soon," she yelled over the roaring wind. She smiled, waved, and gave him a friendly wink. Rowan faced the portal, jumped into the air, fought the breeze, and flew in. When she vanished, the noisy whirlwind ceased, and the portal shut.

Troll breathed a sigh of relief and uncovered his ears. He stood, brushed his hands through his long hair, and looked where Rowan had disappeared. *That was different from the portal that brought Corin here. Hers was yellow, and he said that the portal was purple and functioned like a giant tornado. Rowans blew outward, but I wouldn't consider it a tornado. Although I have never seen one like that, she is the first faerie I have befriended. Of course, her powers would be different than John's.* Troll could see Rowan's baby animals happily making themselves at home. He smiled, exited the park, and read the street and hotel signs, "MAIN STREET and CENTERVILLE WAY O' WINGS SUITES HOTEL. Did the others manage to get rooms here?"

"Troll!" yelled a familiar voice.

Troll looked to his left.

The tank crew walked toward him.

RJ was waving his arms wildly.

"Hey," Finnegan said. "Jack told us Corin had our rooms ready. Do you know what floor we're on?"

"I have no idea," said Troll. "I just arrived. I was making sure Rowan's animals got to the park safely. I have not seen the others since we entered the city."

"Well, I don't want to stand out here wondering," said Jessica. "Let's go in and ask the front desk associate."

"That's a great idea because I'm exhausted," said Finnegan. "We'll need our rest for our new assignment tomorrow."

"Bright and early at eight-thirty, we're to report back to the military base to assist with preparation for testing equipment. Our salary will also be doubled. It's such a great deal!" said Jessica.

"That's great," said Troll. "I bet if you guys purchased a shop in this city, you'd get lots of good work."

"It's an option," Finnegan said. "I wouldn't mind making this place my new home. Jess, what do you think?"

"Later, Finn," she said. "Let's get checked into the hotel."

The tall, redheaded associate looked up from her computer console and smiled when they approached the front desk. "Welcome. How can I help you?"

"Hello," said Jessica. "Our friends Corin, Jack, John Doe, and a flying dog were here earlier and reserved rooms for us."

"Oh yes, the entire third floor has been reserved for your party," said the associate.

"The whole floor?"

"Yes. There are twelve rooms."

"Twelve? But there are only ten of us—"

"Are you certain?" asked Finnegan.

"Yes, I hope you enjoy your stay. Here are your room keys. I have Mr. Jack staying in room 301, Mr. Corin is in room 302, and Mr. Doe is in room 303—"

"Pardon me, which room is *Mr.* Troll in?" asked Troll.

"Room 305. Are you Mr. Troll?"

"Yes, I would like to share a room with *Mr.* Doe, please. He has a guest, and it's my responsibility to keep them . . . *comfortable.*"

"Oh, certainly," said the associate. "I will ensure they go to room 305."

"So that demon dog is indeed still with us?" asked Ace. "I figured the lad would put it back where he found it by now."

"I think John wants him as a pet," said Troll. "Anyway, I'm not leaving them alone together. I fear Magnum genuinely wants to eat him."

"Speaking of food," said Finnegan. "Anyone hungry? Let's go grab some grub!"

As the rest of the party discussed what food they wanted, Troll noticed Jessica speaking quietly to the front desk associate. *Now, what are they discussing?*

Rowan flew through the portal until she reached the other side of the whirlwind. She fluttered into the open night sky, closed her eyes, and placed her hands together. *"Prope ianuam, gratias pro salute tua. Arcus me domum excipient,"* she chanted. Nimbus clouds formed around her. She opened her eyes, and it began to rain. Rowan laughed as she flew around, trying to dodge the raindrops.

The moon was bright in the sky. A lunar rainbow appeared as Rowan soared under the moonlight with the water's magical rainfall.

She soared to the moonbow and chanted her spell again.

The moonbow changed shape, becoming a tunnel.

Rowan glided into the beautiful lunar rainbow tunnel. "Wee!" she squealed in delight as she let the delicate shades of color dance around her. Rowan loved the sensation of traveling by magic. It made her feel like she was young again, filled her heart with joy, and melted away her worries. She flew for a few minutes until she could see a golden light at the end of the tunnel. It was amazingly bright. She smiled. "This is my exit!" She sailed into the golden light, and the moonbow vanished.

Now, she was soaring above the ocean. She could see fish and other creatures swimming in the clear moonlit water. She flew inland over a white beach and a sprawling city. She headed for a large, lit clock tower in the city's center. Her smile grew when she noticed the time on the clock read four o'clock. *I don't think that's the correct time.* "Hello, Ben!" she shouted, waving her hand.

Behind the big hand of the clock waved a tiny little red arm.

"Let me see your face!" Rowan demanded.

A tiny red face poked out from behind the clock's big hand.

"Hi, cutie! How is my favorite little gremlin today?"

Ben climbed to the other side of the big hand and reached for Rowan. He was twelve inches tall with brick red skin covered in orange warts, a patch of black hair on his head, pointed but floppy medium-sized ears with thick strands of black hair on the tips, a big broad nose, and large brown eyes. He wore a brown over-the-shoulder tunic, a black belt, and brown fabric cuffs tied to his ankles.

He wants a hug! Rowan giggled, flew to him, and embraced the little gremlin. "Are you keeping the Great Clock in tip-top shape?"

He nodded, then gripped back onto the big hand. He climbed it, jumped into a small hole in the glass, and ran up the gears inside the clock to the Great Bell. Ben wiggled his nose after applying oil to the motionless components and belt. The caliber glowed a light orange hue and began to move. The Great Bell rang four times.

"Good try, Ben. It's ten-thirty, though. Isn't it? It would be five-thirty in my forest. That's a five-hour difference."

Ben smacked his forehead and ran outside, jumping onto the small hand. He landed with great force and swiftly moved it from the number 4 to 10. Ben laughed heartily and then climbed onto the large hand near the 12. Once he was at the top, he swung it down to the number 6.

"Well, I could be wrong. Ben, what time is it really?" Rowan asked.

Ben shrugged his shoulders.

"You do not know?"

Ben shook his head.

"Well, shouldn't you find out? You oversee the clock."

Ben just chuckled and reached for Rowan again.

"Oh! You're so cute! Of course, I love you, Ben," she said, hugging the tiny gremlin again. "Do you still have my small double mattress? Let's have a sleepover!"

Jack rounded the final turn displayed on his internal map and observed the quaint cul-de-sac. The NOT A THROUGH STEET sign was rusted, but that didn't remove any charm from the impressive mechanic shop between two other buildings at the very end of the road. A large stained wooden sign over the mechanic shop's door read SYSTEMS SPARK AND FLASH MECHANICS. Jack smiled impulsively, knowing the building would look like a generic industrial steel-clad warehouse with a messy lawn to the untrained eye. Jack was not just anyone. He knew what to look for, and what he saw spoke volumes about the owner.

The garage door was enormous. *Wow! That is big enough to handle any sized vehicle.* The building's frame had a built-in boom crane that could lift a tank with no problem. The lawn was full of workstations: a forge with an anvil set, a heavy-duty welding rig, a table covered in precision measuring tools, and other devices Jack could only guess at. Scrap piles sat along the side of the building, neatly ordered by size and material. *This person is well-organized! I'm curious about the goodies inside if the exterior is this striking. It's a metalworker's heaven!* He approached the door but noticed there was no doorknob and no doorbell. Jack knocked and waited. He heard rustling. *Someone is inside, hard at work, no doubt.* He tapped on the door again, and the rustling ceased. He heard footsteps and stepped back. The steel door opened like a portcullis. "That's cool," he said in his thick German accent.

"Thank you," said a female voice.

Jack's optics grew when he saw the tall, beautiful woman with curly shoulder-length blonde hair, hazel eyes, and marvelous curvy features. Her hands and clothes were filthy. She wore tight, gray coveralls and tiny glasses on her face that she adjusted to gaze at him.

"Can I help you?" she asked.

Jack swallowed, "Um, yes, thank you. I need to meet the mechanic, please. I need repairs."

"You just met her, darling," smiled the blonde. "Welcome to my little shop. I service all robots and cyborgs."

"Y-y-you are the mechanic?" asked Jack, his system overloading and steam ejecting from the exhaust pipe in his neck.

"Of course. I am Meike Stormhild. It's a pleasure to meet you, Mr.—"

"Geyerwulf, Jack Geyerwulf," Jack said, carefully taking her messy hand and bringing it up to his metal lips. "Oh, yeah . . ." He gasped nervously, quickly lifting his faceplate and bringing her hand to his natural lips, kissing it gently.

The black residue on her hand now covered his mouth.

Meike chuckled as she carefully took her hand out of his and pulled a handkerchief from her front jacket pocket. "Here, darling," she said, offering him the cloth. "You have a little something on your face."

"Thank you," Jack said, taking the handkerchief. "You have a German accent."

"Yes, I am from Deutschland. It has been many years since I have heard the lovely voice of another German. I am so happy to meet you. Please, come in."

Jack smiled and happily entered the building.

"Come, have a seat," she said, pulling over an oversized chair for him. "I engineered this chair myself; it's made especially for cyborgs. Sit and tell me what type of mending you need. I would be more than happy to fix them for you."

"Well," he said, sitting down. "Wow, this *is* comfortable! You're very talented. The mayor obviously was not kidding when he said you were the best."

"Oh, Mayor Lanus sent you? That's wonderful! He knows I love to stay busy. I shall thank him later."

"*Ja*, he seemed pretty nice," said Jack. "Well, let me tell you what needs to be looked at. I was recently in a battle, and my entire system needs fixing. I *worked* in the mines for a few years. I need many updates. I'm not as fast as I used to be either."

"Oh, yes, darling, a mine worker must keep updated. You must be a very hard worker. Dedicated, yes?"

"Um, yes, absolutely," said Jack, trying not to think of the torment he was put through in the mines. *How could she understand? She lives in this beautiful city, so secure from the world. This must be a good life.*

"I need to give you my full attention and be absolutely devoted to you. I am very much like you, Mr. Geyerwulf. I love what I do. As your *doctor*, I will be very strict about repairing your body and system. I must insist that you stay here throughout the night. Overnight work is some of my *best* work."

"Overnight?" gulped Jack. "B-b-but I have friends here, and they're expecting me at the hotel. I thought I could make an appointment with you for tomorrow."

"I am booked all day tomorrow, darling; it has to be tonight to get you fixed up as soon as possible. You do want to be back on your feet, yes? There's no way I can let you out of my custody in your condition."

"I didn't realize I was in such horrible shape," he said. "Am I really in such a bad way?"

Meike approached him slowly, removing her glasses and putting them into her jacket pocket. She gently touched his metal chest and smiled at him. "You won't be for long, darling. I am going to take such good care of you."

Jack felt his body heating up. "Ms. Stormhild—"

"Call me Meike, darling."

"Okay, Meike, listen . . . I have not been with a beautiful woman in a long time. I l-lost my wife . . . I have not—"

"Oh, you poor thing. Don't worry. I'm not here to take advantage of you. I have not been with someone in a very long time, too. I do not want to make you uncomfortable . . . but I am *attracted* to you."

"And I am attracted to you, Meike. You're gorgeous and a mechanic! I don't want to sound like a dirty old cyborg, but I *love* having a woman service me."

"And service you, I shall," she said, smiling. "Come; let us begin getting you back to one hundred percent. Then afterward, we shall have a bite to eat and get better acquainted."

"By acquaintance, you mean . . . friends?"

"Do you desire *more* than friends?"

Jack was lost in her lovely eyes and could not answer her question.

"Let us begin," she said, holding up an impact wrench. "It's going to be a long night."

Corin, John Doe, and Magnum returned to the hotel. They walked up to the front desk and were informed that John Doe and Magnum were in room 305 and Corin was in room 310. The associate smiled at Corin as she handed him his keys. "Room 310 is perfect for you, sir," she said, winking.

"It is?" he asked, confused. "I thought I would have a room closer to my friends."

"Originally, you did, but I thought you would like this room more."

"Oh, well, thank you."

"Enjoy."

"Come on, guys, let's get upstairs and get comfortable," Corin said.

"That sounds like a plan," John Doe said, stretching his arms above his head as they boarded the elevator. "Man, I could go for a bite to eat."

"As could I," Magnum chuckled deeply.

The elevator bell dinged, and the door opened to the third floor.

"As soon as we get into the room, we'll call for some room service," John Doe said happily.

"See you guys in the morning," Corin said, walking to his room.

John Doe opened the door to room 305, and they entered. Once the door was shut and locked, Magnum grabbed John Doe and threw him to the ground. John Doe grunted in pain and looked at the demon dog in shock. "What are you doing?" gasped John Doe.

"You're my snack, wizard. Did you really think I was going to be your servant? You should have returned me to my domain. Now it is too late. I like it here, and you will not stop me from ruling this world. I will eat you now and benefit from devouring the powers you are so poorly skilled at controlling. Prepare yourself," Magnum said, looming over John Doe. He opened his mouth wide, but strong hands grabbed his scruff and squeezed. Magnum yelped as his body became limp. "Who—"

"Get off of him," Troll said with a low growl.

"You?" Magnum shrieked.

"Let him go!"

Magnum whimpered as he allowed John Doe to crawl out from under him.

"Thanks, Troll. I didn't expect that," John Doe said.

"You never do," Troll said, gripping the demon dog tightly.

"Release me, p-please," Magnum pleaded. "I won't do that again."

"You best not. Because if you do—"

"You'll kill me, won't you?"

"He'll do worse," said John Doe.

"I do not intend to find out what you would do to me, strong man," said Magnum. "I swear I will not attempt to harm John Doe again. He is my master."

"Good," Troll said, releasing him. "Let this be a lesson to you."

"A lesson I will not soon forget," Magnum said, shamefully curling up in a corner.

Troll turned to John Doe and sighed hard. "What am I going to do with you?"

"I should be the one asking that," John Doe said.

"No, you should be asking what you would do without me," Troll said. "Come on, you need your rest."

"I'm hungry! I need some food," said John Doe.

"Here, I saved you a snack," Troll said, handing John Doe a small box.

"I hope this isn't more rabbit," gulped John Doe as he opened the box.

"No, I know what you like," Troll said, chuckling.

"Macaroni and cheese!" John Doe squealed, removing his hood and pulling down his scarf. "Thank you!"

"You're welcome."

"What am I to eat?" grumbled Magnum.

"You may have my leftovers," said Troll, putting a second box on the ground beside the demon dog. "I'm sure you'll enjoy eating marmot as much as I do."

"Oh, it smells wonderful!" Magnum breathed in merriment.

"Hey, Troll, there is only one bed. Where will you sleep?" asked John Doe with a mouthful of macaroni.

"John Doe, you know I don't need to sleep yet," Troll said, positioning a chair beside the window. He opened the curtains slightly so the evening sunlight came into the room. "It's around seven o'clock. I hope everyone rests up. We need to figure out what we're going to do tomorrow."

"I'm not interested in what the others are doing tomorrow. I have my own plan to meet Heeb," John Doe said, finishing his meal. "Troll, how many nights do you have until you need to rest again?"

"I don't know. Maybe a few more nights? It depends on how active I am."

"You're not going to sleep at all?" asked Magnum, confused. "Is this because of me? Are you watching me all night?"

"No," said Troll. "My sleep schedule is very unpredictable."

Magnum shrugged his shoulders, finishing his meal. He stretched his arms out, becoming comfortable on the floor, and snuggled into the corner.

John Doe removed his coat and boots but left his tunic, scarf, and pants on as he entered the bathroom. He took a shower, dried off, emerged in heart print boxer shorts, and got into the single bed. Sleep immediately found the exhausted wizard.

"I'll see you in the morning," Troll said, shaking his head, grinning. He stood and walked over to pick up and dispose of the empty boxes. He folded John Doe's clothes and left them on the nightstand before he returned to the chair. Troll gazed out the window. He calmed his heart and meditated.

Corin entered his hotel room and turned on the lights. He closed and locked the door, removed his helmet, and took out his journal. He walked over to the bed and stopped dead in his tracks. He dropped his journal and gasped.

"Hi, Corin," said Jessica, sitting on the bed, polishing her boots. She wore a baggy white shirt over her black undergarments. The freshly cleaned parts of her pistol were arranged around her. "Are you ready to come to bed?"

"It's only seven o'clock . . . isn't it too early for sleep?"

She gently set the gun parts on the nightstand and looked at him playfully, "Who said anything about sleeping?"

KRISTINA M. HOFFMAN

EIGHTEEN

This is the best night I have ever had! I am so comfortable yet full of buoyant energy. I will have a restful sleep tonight. I am excited about the meeting with the mayor. Everything will go according to my plans. I like being right. I will do everything I can to make the meeting go my way. I want to stay on Earth! Why go back to my old life and job? I don't miss it anymore. I never want to go back. This is my home now. I can't wait to tell the others my decision.

—From the journal of Corin Degodi
June 13, 2215, 2:15 a.m.

"This is the worst night I have ever had!" barked Magnum.

John Doe was asleep, and the horrible sound coming from his mouth had the massive demon dog tossing and turning with his paws pressed tightly against his enormous, sensitive ears.

Magnum's eyes were wide and bloodshot as he struggled on the floor. The sound was intolerable. Comfort was impossible. Sleep was beyond his reach.

John Doe's snoring became a chainsaw trying to cut through a log of soggy cheese.

Magnum sat up, panicked, and looked around the room. His head was spinning but felt heavy. His temples pounded. He pressed his paws harder on his head, hoping to relieve the pain. Magnum panted uncontrollably.

Another snore erupted from the wizard's mouth. He sounded like a dragon.

"I cannot take it," Magnum growled, standing.

Troll came out of meditation and looked at Magnum. His blue eyes didn't show any signs of exhaustion. "What's the matter?" asked Troll, rising from the chair.

"How can you stand it?" asked Magnum, pacing back and forth.

"Stand what?" asked Troll, confused.

"That sound!" Magnum whined, pointing at the sleeping wizard.

"John?" Troll chuckled. "He always sounds like that when he sleeps."

"He's not sleeping!" shouted Magnum. "He's torturing me! He's enjoying it!"

"He really is unconscious," Troll said calmly. "He has no idea he's bothering you. You get used to it."

"How are you *used* to that awful sound? No wonder you don't sleep! What is it he is doing? Is he possessed? He summoned something other than me that took over his body when he slumbers, right?"

"No, he is just snoring. It is a natural thing people and animals do sometimes while asleep. My inability to sleep has nothing to do with John, really."

"It's pissing me off and keeping me awake! I need to leave! Don't stop me!" Magnum said, turning toward the door.

"Hey, where do you think you're going?"

"I need to flee! I can't bear it! It's worse than death!"

"John's not that bad," Troll said.

"Do you snore like him?"

"No. I've asked John. He said I never snore."

"Well then, let's wake him, and then we can sleep."

"Good luck with that," said Troll. "It's nearly impossible to wake John after he's been asleep for so long."

That agonizing sound . . . it feels like it's penetrating my skull! Tears formed in Magnum's eyes, and he clawed at the door. "I cannot take it anymore! I want out! Let me out!"

Troll walked over. He made sure to have the room's key in his tan sack. "Get a hold of yourself. I'll take you out. Come on." He unlocked the door.

Magnum ran around in a circle, desperate to exit the room and end his suffering.

Troll opened the door. "I'll go to the front desk associate and assign you a different room."

"That won't be necessary," said Magnum. The demon dog ran past him down the hallway.

"Hey, slow down!" Troll followed the demon dog.

Magnum ran to the elevator and hit the button. The door opened. "I'm in no need of a room now. I'll see you later." Magnum cackled as he swiftly entered the elevator.

"Wait!" Troll shouted, running toward him.

The door closed.

Troll could hear Magnum laughing inside the elevator as it descended to the ground floor. He raced to the stairwell and threw open the door. *I hope I can stop him from escaping. He's dangerous and could attack someone.* Disregarding the steps, Troll kicked off the wall and leaped over the railing to land gracefully on the floor below. He repeated the action and landed in front of the entryway to the first floor. He opened the door and dashed into the lobby.

The elevator door opened, and Magnum emerged. He saw Troll running toward him.

A tall, blond-haired man was on duty at the front desk. His eyes widened when he noticed them. "Hey, you two, do not run in the building!"

Troll ignored the associate and leaped toward Magnum.

"Keep away from me!" yelled Magnum, trying to escape, but Troll grabbed his scruff.

"Why are you being difficult?" asked Troll.

"My brain!" yelped Magnum. "I could take no more! I was going insane!"

"Come on," Troll said, pulling Magnum to the front desk. "I'll get you into another room. Corin reserved plenty of rooms."

"I don't want to sleep here. I'll hear the sound!"

"You won't hear him snoring from another room. Calm down," said Troll, turning his attention to the associate. "I'm Troll, and my room is 305. Can my friend here have an empty room that's close to mine? My friend Corin reserved the third floor."

"Certainly," said the associate, assigning a new key. "Sir, please have more control over your pet in the future. Also, running is a liability. Walk while you're in this hotel."

"Pet!" barked Magnum. "I'm not a pet!"

"Shh!" Troll said, tightening his grip on Magnum's scruff as he accepted the key. "Thank you, sir. Now, Magnum, be a good boy, and let's go back to bed."

"Okay, tough guy," Magnum said. "I'll just escape when you're back in the room with John Doe."

Troll dragged him to the elevator. "No, you won't because you and I are sharing this new room, and I can stay up the rest of the night."

"I'm not going to sleep at all, am I?" whimpered Magnum.

"I promise you won't be able to hear John's snoring. Trust me, I'm not going to hurt you. I'll let you sleep. I know you're tired."

They got on the elevator, and as the door closed, the front desk associate lifted his eyebrows and whistled. "I sure am glad he's not my pet."

Magnum resented the associate's comment as the elevator lifted them back to the third floor. Despite Troll's kind words, he felt like a domesticated dog put in a kennel.

The elevator opened, and Troll pulled Magnum to the assigned door. It was beside the room where John Doe slept. He unlocked the door and opened it. It was dark inside the room. He released Magnum's scruff, letting him go inside first. Troll stepped in and locked the door. "You can have the bed," Troll said, flipping on the light switch.

Magnum perked up when the lights turned on. "A-are you serious? I get the bed? Aren't I just a dog to you, human?"

Troll pulled up a chair and sat down beside the window. "No, you are our companion," he said, smiling.

"Does that word mean *friend*?" asked Magnum.

"It does. Now, get some sleep. I won't bother you."

"I never had a friend before. Th-th-tha . . . thank—" Magnum grunted, "I can't believe I'm saying this, but . . . thank you, Troll. You have my highest respect."

Troll smiled again and nodded.

Magnum jumped onto the king-sized bed and rested his head on a pillow. The comforting sound of silence relaxed the demon dog. He closed his eyes and immediately fell asleep.

Troll noticed an alarm clock on the nightstand beside the bed and quietly walked over. He picked up the clock and set it to ring at eight o'clock in the morning. He stretched his neck and shoulders as he returned to the chair. Troll clicked off the room light as he sat down and relaxed his body and mind as he quietly gazed out the window, observing the starry sky.

That morning, Ace, Finnegan, and RJ were the first out of bed and entered the hallway.

Troll heard them emerge and quickly left the room to meet them. He didn't want their voices to wake Magnum.

"Troll," announced RJ. "Good morning!"

"Good morning. What time is it?" Troll asked.

"It's six twenty-five," said Ace. "Come, lad. We heard breakfast was free, so we didnae waste any time and decided to check it out."

"Okay, I'll wake up John, and we'll join you."

"I will wake up Jessica," Finnegan said, walking to her door. As he balled up his fist, ready to knock—

The door flew open.

Corin emerged.

Finnegan gasped in shock.

Corin was wearing green boxers and clutching his jumpsuit between his left arm and chest. His boots were in his right hand. His cheeks were flushed, but he smiled at Finnegan and cleared his throat. "Are we going to breakfast then?" Corin asked.

No one answered. They stared at Corin in bewilderment.

"Great," Corin said. "I'm starving. I'll meet you guys downstairs."

Finnegan's pulse was in his ears. He was unable to blink his widened eyes. He couldn't move. His entire world crumbled as Corin walked past him.

Corin dashed to the elevator. "I'll see you all in the lobby," Corin said, pushing the elevator button. The doors opened. He entered and started dressing as the elevator doors closed.

"Why wasn't he dressed?" RJ suddenly blurted out.

"That moment when ye know you have to take off as soon as possible. He didnae expect us to be up so soon," Ace clarified.

"That doesn't explain why he's half-naked," said RJ.

"Lad," Ace said, putting his arm around RJ. "There's much your young mind still needs to learn."

Finnegan's face turned white. He took a deep breath and gawked at the floor.

He's in shock. His heart is hurting. Troll stared at Finnegan and reached for his shoulder—

"She lied to me. She had her own room," Finnegan muttered.

Jessica suddenly opened the door. She was fully dressed and looked directly at Finnegan. "Oh, Finn. Hi," she said sheepishly. "Are you guys ready?"

"Jess," said Finnegan quietly. "I . . . I . . . you and the spaceman?"

Jessica blushed. "Come on, Finn. Please, don't make a scene."

"A scene—"

"Yeah. I'm starving, and we should go eat. Come on," Jessica said. She slowly walked past Finnegan to the elevator.

Troll could see the tears in Finnegan's eyes. *I can feel his heartbreak.*

John Doe opened his door and walked into the hallway. He rubbed his eyes and stretched his arms above his head.

Jessica got on the elevator, and before the door closed, she glanced at Finnegan.

John Doe yawned, looked at Troll, adjusted his goggles, and reached into the back of his pants. He thoroughly scratched his butt. "Are we ready to have breakfast?" asked John Doe.

"Did you just scratch your ass?" asked Troll.

"Maybe—"

"Wash your hands."

"I was going to," John Doe said, going back into his hotel room. He returned after a few seconds, and his hands were wet.

"Dry them?" asked Troll.

"Not yet," John Doe said as he retreated to the room before he emerged with dry hands. "So, what's going on? Did someone die or something? Why do you guys look so gloomy?"

Finnegan stood motionless, staring at the door.

"It's a door, man. It's nothing special," John Doe said to Finnegan.

Troll quickly grabbed John Doe by his scarf and pulled him down the hall.

"Hey!" gasped John Doe. "What'd I say?"

"I'll explain later, John," said Troll.

Ace approached Finnegan. "Lad?"

"RJ, could you please go with Troll and John Doe? I want to speak to Ace in private," Finnegan said.

"Okay," RJ replied, walking over to where Troll scolded John Doe. "Will Finnegan be okay?" he asked Troll.

Troll sighed. "I don't know."

The alarm clock beside the bed began to beep. Magnum slowly opened his eyes and groggily looked at it. "Eight o'clock," he moaned before he smashed the clock with his large paw. The alarm continued to ring with a pathetic shrill until it finally stopped. Magnum yawned and then returned his head to the comfortable pillow.

Tap-tap

"Housekeeping?" called a woman's voice from the door.

Magnum groaned, turning onto his side.

Tap-tap

"Housekeeping?" she called again.

Magnum put the pillow on his head and pushed his face deeper into the mattress. He quickly fell asleep after the annoying knocking ceased.

The housekeeper unlocked the room where Magnum slept soundly. She turned on her vacuum cleaner, and a loud, intense howling sound immediately woke the sleeping beast.

He stood up in the bed and screamed.

The maid did not hear him over the vacuum but definitely saw him. Squealing, she picked up the vacuum and threw it at him.

The vacuum miraculously remained plugged in as it rammed into his face. Magnum collapsed on the bed, his body bouncing slightly. The vacuum began to suck in his fur. He shouted in terror.

The maid ran out of the room, still shrieking and thrashing her arms about.

Magnum attempted to escape the suction of the vacuum. He bounced around in the bed, whimpering, trying to keep the machine away. He finally fell onto the floor. After freeing his fur from the vacuum's nozzle, he raced out of the room, nearly tripping on his wings.

"I need to get to the elevator!" he wailed.

The maid was ready for him. In her hands was a broom. She swung it directly into his face. With the accuracy of a master broom wielder, she battered him repeatedly over the head.

He yelped, flailing his arms, legs, tail, and wings. He was desperate to get away from the maid.

The ferocious woman did not stop. "The elevator is off limits, you monster!" she screeched.

"Demon woman! Stop hitting me!" he cried.

"I will end you!" the housekeeper declared, hitting Magnum harder.

Magnum bellowed in utter terror. He spread his wings and knocked the maid over. He dashed for the stairs, broke through the door, and raced to the roof. He bolted through the emergency exit and opened his wings as he leaped into the sky.

Corin, Troll, and John Doe exited the hotel's main entrance at that same moment.

"Crazy demon woman!" yelled Magnum, flying over them.

They looked up and saw Magnum heading toward the center of the city.

Corin and Troll crossed their arms over their chests and looked at John Doe.

John Doe mimicked them, crossing his arms over his chest, looking beside him where no one was standing. He moaned, then looked at Corin and Troll. He chuckled. "Oh, you're looking at me, aren't you? Why? I didn't do it."

"I must kill it!" yelled the housekeeper, bursting through the hotel entrance, still carrying the broom.

"Whoa, lady! What are you doing?" Corin gasped.

"You clean *inside* the hotel," said John Doe. "Brooms are to sweep the floor."

"Broom is to kill the beast with wings," said the maid.

"Oh no," said Troll. "Magnum was asleep in his room. I guess he frightened you?"

"Frightened me nothing," spat the woman. "I struck fear into *his* heart. I will get him if he ever comes back!" She marched back into the hotel, growling.

"Wow!" said John Doe. "I think I'm in love."

"Shut up, John Doe," said Corin, sighing hard. He glanced at Troll, concerned. "Well, he's loose."

"He'll be back," John Doe said. "Remember, guys, I'm the only one who can send him home."

"You better be right," said Corin. "I don't want that demon dog to start trouble and give us a bad reputation. I want us to stay on the mayor's good side."

Jessica and her team departed, walking past Corin, Troll, and John Doe.

Finnegan glared over his shoulder at Corin and became lost in his thoughts. *Look at him! He's too busy focusing on his advantages to spare any thought or affection for Jessica. He didn't even acknowledge her just now. What kind of a man is he?*

"We need to be at the military base in twenty minutes. Let's go," Jessica ordered.

"Yes, Jessica," Finnegan said. A lump formed in the back of his throat. He was unable to speak another word.

"It's going to be a difficult day for them," Ace whispered to RJ as they trekked.

"I can't wait to discuss my ideas with the mayor," said Corin. "Especially about buying property in this city."

"Corin, are you certain you want to do that?" asked Troll. "You haven't been here long. You should think about this sensibly before making any decisions."

"Well, we don't have to meet with the mayor until ten o'clock, so I'll keep thinking about it until then."

"We should start searching for Magnum," said John Doe.

"Let's explore the city," Troll said. *I fear Corin's new desire for wealth and status has overcome his rational thought.*

On their search, Corin drifted into his imagination. He saw himself sitting on a giant hilltop of coins. Around his neck was a necklace of rare gems and gold nuggets. He giggled like a schoolgirl and gripped the coins in his pile. Once his hands were full, he threw them into the air, cheering like he had just won a marathon. Corin returned to his conscious mind. *I'll convince the mayor to offer us jobs that are handsomely paid. Hero work is popular in comic books. In fact, finding a dangerous, flying demon dog is the perfect first assignment. That'll show the mayor we're capable.*

"Hey, watch out!" screamed a voice, interrupting Corin's thoughts.

A construction crew was repairing a historic building's roof, and one of the cables broke on a suspended scaffold and flipped it. A construction worker fell but managed to grab the gutter, preventing him from falling four stories down. The yells from the construction crew and people in the city filled the streets. Their concerned voices bounced from building to building.

"Hang on, pal!"

"Don't let go!"

"Oh, man, this is bad."

"We're coming!"

"Someone, save him!"

Troll and John Doe saw the dangerous situation before Corin noticed the accident.

"I'll be right back," Troll said, tapping the amulet in the center of his chest. He inhaled sharply and moaned as the surge of energy raced through his body.

Corin blinked.

Troll vanished.

The gutter bent and the man fell.

Troll leaped into the air, catching the worker. As soon as his boots touched the ground, the scaffold broke, falling toward them.

"Jube haec ego volitare contritum metallum. Glide quam ventus!" John Doe proclaimed.

The scaffold suddenly stopped, surrounded by a white light, hovering inches above Troll and the man he saved.

"Phew! Just in time," John Doe said, wiggling his shimmering fingers.

"Whoa! Thank you so much, sir," said the worker as Troll securely put him down. "I thought I was a goner."

"The scaffold would have crushed you for sure," Troll said. "Let's get out from under this thing."

"I helped!" John Doe yelled, accidentally releasing his spell. "Oops."

The white light vanished, and the scaffold fell.

Everyone winced, but Troll caught it barehanded and set it down gently.

The citizens and construction crew cheered.

"Wow! No way," breathed the worker.

Corin, John Doe, and city residents ran toward them.

"I'm sorry, Troll," said John Doe, over the gathering of people talking at once. "I accidentally let up my spell because I was desperate to be popular and part of the rescue."

"Thank you for helping, John," Troll said, sighing.

"You're welcome!" John Doe sang happily. "Am I admired now?"

"Sure, John Doe," said Corin as he patted the wizard's back. "Wow! I can't get used to how fast and strong you are, Troll. You're a hero." *Bragging rights from our 'first assignment' just fell out of the sky. Forget Magnum! This is so much better.*

"You saved that man!" declared a woman.

"What's your name?" asked a local man.

"Who are you?" asked a child's voice.

"Way to go!" praised another person.

"I was just being helpful," Troll told the people. "Are you all right, sir?" he asked the worker.

"Yes, I am. Thanks to you, hero."

Troll blushed as more citizens arrived and showered him with adoration.

"A hero. That's what I want to be," said John Doe to Corin.

"He can really draw in a crowd," said Corin, seeing dollar bill signs before his eyes.

"He doesn't like to. Look at how embarrassed he is. Troll is a humble and courteous man. He helps and moves on. He never wants a reward for his good deeds. Troll takes pleasure in doing what's right. He has told me, 'It's doing what you love that's truly important.' He loves helping others, but I love being popular and important! Nothing seems to go my way. I'd love it if these people were to worship me."

"Maybe you're trying too hard?" asked Corin.

John Doe looked at Corin and tilted his head to the side. "You might be right. A*m* I trying too hard? I just need to stop trying, then I'll be popular, and women will find and love me."

"I didn't say that—"

"I'll do it!" John Doe said happily.

Corin sighed hard and put his palm on his forehead.

"I'm uncomfortable from so much attention, but my name is Troll."

"Troll? That's an interesting name . . . you know, I don't care what your name is! I'm Reginald Bass. You saved my life. I'm in your debt, sir," he said, shaking Troll's hand in gratitude. "I will tell the mayor and everyone in the city of your heroism."

The crowd cheered again.

"Thank you, Reginald, but I was just in the right place at the right time. I'm glad you are not hurt."

"You are a modest gentleman, Troll."

"Yeah, that's our Troll," said Corin, pushing through the crowd to get to them. "Would the mayor be willing to honor Troll for saving you?"

"Absolutely!" announced Reginald.

"That's not necessary, really—"

"Don't be silly, Troll," Corin intervened. "You saved this man and deserve an award."

"His thanks is good enough for me," said Troll.

"Nonsense. Reginald, we are on our way to the mayor's office. Would you care to come with us and tell him yourself what Troll did here today?"

"I would indeed. I'll get permission from my boss," Reginald said, maneuvering through the crowd to where his coworkers had gathered.

Paydirt! Corin thought smugly.

"But, Corin—"

"Troll, you're such a great guy," said Corin, interrupting him again. "Come here." He pulled him out of earshot from the crowd. "I can see how nervous you are from all that unwanted attention. John Doe and I can talk to the mayor and find Magnum. You should calm down. Look, we need food. Why don't you do me a favor? Here," he handed Troll a grocery list, a small sack of gold coins, and the mayor's card. "Can you please get these items and meet us at the new house? The address is on this card. Radio me when you're on your way."

"Corin, search inside yourself. Have you truly made your decision to stay on Earth?"

"I sure have. I never want to go back to my old life. There was nothing there for me, but there are many possibilities here. Wealth and women—"

"Corin," Troll breathed. "Are you sure?"

"Do you still have your radio?" Corin asked.

"Yes," said Troll, sighing.

"Good, be in touch." Corin patted Troll's shoulder.

"You're buying this property and are moving in today?" asked Troll.

"That's the plan," Corin said confidently. "Wish us luck."

"Well, good luck," Troll said, looking at John Doe. *He'll be all right. He's going to meet Heeb. I know he won't want me around for that.* "John!"

John Doe looked over at Troll through the overfilled street of people.

"I'll be back soon. Good luck with Heeb."

"Troll, wait!" John Doe struggled to get by the excited citizens.

"Corin, I will stop at the arena to set up a match before I head to the grocery store. Jack has been itching to fight me. I'll try to schedule it for tomorrow."

"Oh, don't forget, I'd like to be an announcer," Corin said eagerly.

"I'll let them know," said Troll.

John Doe emerged from the crowd. He removed his sunglass-goggles and stood like a statue. His green eyes were full of concern as he watched Troll leave.

NINETEEN

Rowan woke up with a loud yawn. She yanked off the sheets covered in popcorn, peppermint, sage, seeds, and empty honey and maple syrup containers. "Oh, that was some sleepover," she said. "Where are you, Ben?"

Ben crawled out from under the bedstead with tired eyes. He smacked his lips together and yawned.

"Rise and shine, little guy. It's eleven-thirty in the morning." *It's six-thirty back at my forest. I wonder if the others are awake yet?* "I had so much fun! Now, I have to visit my father. It was wonderful to see you. Next time, we'll have some tea!"

As she turned to leave, the red gremlin gently tugged her wing.

"What is it, Ben?"

Ben held up his index finger and raced to his small hole in the glass. He climbed in, and Rowan heard clanking and banging as he sorted through gears.

"What do you have back there?"

Ben poked his smiling face out of the hole. When he jumped through, he revealed a pair of black high-heeled shoes.

"Oh, Ben!" Rowan gasped in delight. "Are those for me?"

Ben nodded and held them up to her.

"They are vintage, too!" Rowan giggled. "My favorite! Thank you so much, my little friend!" She put on the shoes, picked up the gremlin, and danced in the air, clutching him to her chest. "I love you so much! Thank you!"

Ben's smile grew ear to ear. He snuggled his face into her bosom like a pair of fluffy pillows.

Rowan laughed, picked him up by the scruff of his neck, and kissed his cheek.

Ben blushed and twisted his arms and legs around each other as his tongue hung out of his mouth.

She flew him back to the minute hand of the Great Clock. "You get back to work now," she said, putting him down.

Ben nodded and gave her the British Army hand salute as he held onto the copper hand.

Rowan giggled and curtsied before she somersaulted backward and continued her flight into London. It wasn't long until she came to a bridge. She flew under it and approached a portal resembling a giant pink gelatin mass. "There's the hidden gateway. It smells like strawberries."

The pink glop jiggled as Rowan flew through. She came out the other side into her father's faerie realm—her childhood home. The sky was purple, and the city resembled Victorian London. The buildings were painted bright and warm colors. Her father's grand stone castle was adorned with rubies and crystals around every window and entrance. It sat at the city's heart, surrounded by a forest. "Ah, the dwelling of my younger sister," Rowan said, flying into the trees. "Tiff! Tiffan!" Rowan sang loudly, landing on the forest floor. "Tiffannnn!"

"What are you doing here?" asked a female voice above.

Rowan looked up and saw a green faerie with shoulder-length, curly blonde hair dressed in a dark green crop top and loincloth decorated with twigs and white flowers. She sat on a branch, petting a beautiful golden owl.

"Hello, Tiff," Rowan said, flying to her sister. "How are you?"

"Well, I was having a pretty nice day—"

"Really?" Rowan asked excitedly.

"—but then something ruined my mood." Tiffan's crystal-clear white eyes looked at Rowan with annoyance.

"I'm sorry to hear that, sister. May I ask what disturbed you? Do you need help ridding yourself of the annoyance?"

"I doubt you will be able to assist me with this annoyance unless you decide to leave," Tiffan said, petting the owl.

"Do I really bother you so much? You never see me anymore since I dwell in the human world." Rowan sighed.

"Yes, and that is not fair to me!" Tiffan said, striking the owl in her frustration.

The golden owl flew out of her arms with a reproachful hoot and settled on a higher branch.

"Why can I not live in the human world with you?" asked Tiffan. "I am more than old enough to be responsible. Father just likes you best!"

"Father is very busy," Rowan said. "I'm sure he will give you an assignment like mine someday. It took me hundreds of years to be ready for my mission. It just takes time; you must be patient."

"That's a laugh! I've been patient, Row," Tiffan said harshly. "It's been hundreds of years for me as well."

"I am on my way to see Father. I will speak with him about your dilemma, I promise."

"No! Do not speak a word of this to him," Tiffan demanded. "He'll be furious with me if you do."

"No, he won't. He may wish to speak with you, but that is all. He'd never become angry at you for wanting to better yourself. He's so proud of us."

"*You!* You mean *you*! He's proud of *you*. You're the oldest, and you're the favorite."

"That's not true, sister," Rowan said sadly. "He loves you, and I love you."

"Love is a cheap word people use to get what they want," Tiffan growled. She stood on the branch, spread her significantly longer wings, and kicked off into the sky. She flew as fast as she could through the forest until Rowan could no longer see her.

"Oh, my poor sister," Rowan said, shaking her head. "I wish I knew how to help the anger inside her. She has been such a hothead since our mother disappeared, and it's only gotten worse with age." Rowan flew to the owl and petted him gently. "I apologize that she smacked you, little friend. She did that because of me."

The owl nudged her hand with his head in a friendly manner.

"You're sweet," Rowan said happily as she spread her wings and flew into the air. She soared above the forest, heading toward the castle. She flew to the main gates and noticed they were open.

A male faerie dressed in golden armor waved respectfully at her.

Rowan waved at him and entered her father's courtyard. It was decorated with stunning tall red rose bushes, purple and pink flowerbeds, and a stone path surrounded by glorious marble statues of Antiquities, Egyptian gods, and goddesses. She glided over the beautiful scenery until she entered a window into the throne room.

The throne room was enormous, with silver-colored walls that gleamed brightly in the chandelier light, ornamented with green, orange, and yellow banners, bright Victorian purple décor wall art, bronze statues of unicorns, nineteenth-century terracotta urns, gold and mauve lanterns, and a polished checkerboard ceramic tiled floor. It smelled like a mixed blend of bergamot, jasmine, and sandalwood. She immediately recognized the smell from her childhood. Her mother loved those fragrances. Her father must've discovered some of her oils and incense. Rowan embraced her fond memories before noticing her father wasn't on his throne.

"He must be in his study," Rowan said as she flew to another window above the throne room. She peered inside. The study was a rose-colored, medium-sized room with a lilac velvet carpet, and antique clocks, paintings, and mirrors decorated the walls. On the left was a spiral staircase that led above his desk to the ceiling balcony, where the king kept his private library and grand piano. Rowan saw her father seated at his mahogany desk, working on paperwork with another male faerie who stood beside him. His long red hair and beard had a hint of white highlights, his light green skin was smooth and unwrinkled, and his orange tunic intensified the honey color of his eyes. He looked very healthy for being over six thousand. He wore an antler crown made of tree roots and gold, adorned with gems and infinity markings.

"Hello, Father," Rowan said, landing in front of his desk.

"Row," the king said, looking up from his duties.

"His Royal Highness King Clash welcomes his daughter, Princess Rowan Fae," said the faerie beside the king.

"Thank you, Edward. You may leave now so that I may speak to my daughter in private," King Clash said as he stood tall, walked around his desk, and reached for his daughter.

Edward promptly brought himself to attention, bowed to them, and left.

Rowan fluttered into the king's warm embrace.

"Rowan, I cannot believe how beautiful you've become from living in the human realm. I feared living with the mortals would have aged your youthful beauty, but astonishingly, you appear even younger. Oh, my little Rowan. I have missed you. What brings you here on this wonderful day, my daughter?"

"Father, I have journeyed from my forest to tell you I am helping some new friends. We've traveled to a beautiful human city called Centerville."

"Row, you are not supposed to *interfere* with human affairs," the king reminded her, straightening his posture and putting his hands behind his back. "It is forbidden by many of our oldest laws. You'd best explain yourself, young lady! I don't want to force punishment on my daughter for such a dire crime."

"No, Father," declared Rowan. "I don't consider how I am *helping* them to be interfering. Besides, they're not all technically humans. Among them are a cyborg and a wizard. It all started when I caught a humanoid not from this world on my web. I am simply traveling with them to help him return to outer space. A large portal brought him here from the Andromeda Galaxy. I'm just trying to balance the natural order of things. That's what I am supposed to do, is it not?"

"What?" the king barked, smacking his mahogany desk. "That sounds like nonsense to me. Are you sure it was a portal? Did you say outer space?"

"Yes, sir," Rowan said, gulping.

Above them, hidden in the shadows on the balcony ceiling, Tiffan was eavesdropping. Her eyes glowed yellow with anticipation. *How delightful. If Rowan has abandoned her position . . . perhaps I can convince Father to give me the job. I will have to speak to him about that. By law, if Rowan interferes with humans in a harmful way, she'll be banished from her post. If I can make her believe she is positively assisting the humans, but it's truly a damaging manner—Father will remove her. She'll be forced to live in the faerie realm again and never be allowed to return to the human world. How delightful, indeed!*

"Rowan, I want you to return to your forest and abandon this new mission with the humans. I do not like this. Look at what humans have done and continue to do to the world: they wage massive wars, unchecked polluting of the land and seas, the releasing of genetic abominations, twisting magical energies for dark purposes . . . must I go on? The Earth under our care is growing back into a healthy world full of life. Antiquities cannot trust humans. Only certain humans were trustworthy. But they left. They're considered extinct on the planet Earth."

"Father, that's not true," said Rowan. "There is an indigenous man in their group. He's a living, breathing Native American."

"That's impossible . . . all the indigenous natives of every land departed this world long ago. No one knows where they went."

"No, Father, really. He's the reason I want to stay with them. I certainly am interested in helping my friend from space, but Troll is really special to me."

"You speak so passionately for a human you hardly know. Troll? No trustworthy Native American would ever have such a name."

"His real name is a secret. He gave himself the name Troll because he is skilled at killing trolls. He saved my life, Father. He is a good man."

King Clash met his daughter's gaze and saw the truth in her eyes. He stepped back in disgust. "You have *feelings* for him!"

"I do," she admitted. Tears formed in her eyes. "I don't know how, but I've fallen in love with him."

From her hiding spot, Tiffan snickered to herself. *How fascinating! Falling in love with a human? How embarrassing for her. Foolish Rowan, she's spent too long in the human realm. This could benefit me.*

"This is an outrage!" spat Rowan's father, leaning forward with his arms crossed over his chest. "You only think you're in love! His heart is human!"

"His heart is pure," Rowan bawled.

King Clash watched his beloved daughter cry. He could sense how deeply she felt for the human. His eyes softened, and he let out a long sigh. He stood tall and straightened his tunic. "Does he *share* your feelings?"

"I don't know, Father," she confessed. "I have been afraid to tell him."

"Dry your tears. I will be calm," the king said, taking a deep breath. "You are infatuated with him. That's all, my dear. You must accept this as fact. You're going to outlive him by many thousands of years. He's an infant compared to you. You must convince yourself that this is only a passing fascination."

"Father," Rowan whimpered. "Please, give him a chance. Give me a chance. Please."

The Woodland Faerie King made an aggravated moan when he walked behind his desk and sat on his chair. "I will allow you to help your friends for now but heed my warning, Daughter. If you break any of our traditional rules, you may lose your forest."

"I understand," Rowan said, pouting.

"Now, enough talk of human affairs. Since you are here, I have a mission I wish to bestow upon you. If you can accomplish this task, it will prove that you are still responsible enough to remain with these humans who fascinate you."

"What is it?"

King Clash raised his head and closed his eyes. A red light magically beamed into his palm. Once the light subsided, a golden goblet sat in his hand.

Rowan gasped at the sight of the relic, wiping away her tears. "Oh, Father," she breathed. "Is that *the* Holy Grail?"

"No, my child," he said. "It is *a* holy grail, but not *the* Grail of legend. But it has a purpose. It is called the Kantharos. I'm to have it delivered by a trusting soul. Surprisingly, it needs to be delivered to the area you're located in right now with your friends. I know of Centerville City and the surrounding forest. It must be taken to the forest until the one known as 'The Greater Good' finds it."

"Who is 'The Greater Good?'"

"I'm afraid I cannot tell you. It is a legend that this goblet used to have high handles, and it's destined for an Antiquity to repair it. I am entrusting its delivery to you."

"This is a big responsibility," said Rowan. "Where in the forest do I take it?"

"The exact location is not known. The one destined to have it will find it in the forest. It is your choice where you put it. Now, pay attention. What I am about to tell you is very important. Do *not* allow any mortal to drink from it. Without its handles, I am uncertain what would happen. It could be disastrous. Only 'The Greater Good' must have this goblet. Don't let anyone touch it. It's broken but very powerful," he said.

Rowan hugged her father. "Thank you. I will not fail you."

"I know you won't, my little Rowan," he said proudly. After their embrace, he handed Rowan the Kantharos. "Your mother was the one destined for this mission originally."

"She was? Really?" Rowan asked happily.

"Her soul is happy that you're taking her place. She and I are both honored to be your parents."

Rowan sniffed and allowed tears to stream down her face. She missed her mother deeply. "Please, think of Tiffan. My sister needs affection and hope. Will you help her?"

KRISTINA M. HOFFMAN

King Clash nodded; "I will look after her and give her a mission. Perhaps it will give her a boost of encouragement and confidence."

"Thank you, Father."

How dare she pretend to care! I know how much my sister loathes me. Tiffan growled softly. "I'll make her regret that. *Duc me in silvam sororis meae.*" A green portal opened, and Tiffan flew through.

After four hours of visiting, Rowan hugged and kissed her father. "My stay has been pleasant, but I must return." Rowan clasped the Kantharos, spread her wings to their full capacity, and leaped into the air. "Farewell, Father," she sang, flying out of his royal chamber.

"Goodbye, my child. Good luck. I see a challenge waiting for her. Be strong, Rowan. I know you're capable."

Rowan headed back to the hidden gateway under the bridge. "It's time to return to London," Rowan said, clutching the Kantharos to her chest. "I'll show my father that Troll is pure-hearted. There is hope for the human race."

A green portal opened, and Tiffan flew out. When the portal shut, she saw Rowan and followed her. "Row! Hey! Row, wait!"

Rowan heard Tiffan's cries just before reaching the bridge and stopped. "Tiff?" Rowan glided to the ground.

Tiffan landed beside her.

"You wanted to see me off before I left?" asked Rowan. "I didn't think you liked my company."

"I don't, but I need to tell you something," Tiffan said, looking at the Kantharos. "That goblet . . . did Father give that to you?"

"He did," Rowan said proudly. "It's a new mission in the human world. I need to take it to the forest and leave it there for someone special. It's called the Kantharos."

"Oh? He told you that . . ." Tiffan exhaled. "I can't believe it . . . why didn't he tell you the *real* mission?"

"What do you mean?"

"You see, Rowan, that's not the Kantharos. That actually is *the* Holy Grail!"

"B-but Father said it wasn't—"

"I just heard him tell Edward that he didn't want you to know the truth. Something about not wanting to burden you with overwhelming responsibility. He's just looking out for your sensitivity."

"He didn't really trust me?" *He must've lied because he's upset that I have human friends.* "So, this is the *real* Holy Grail?" Rowan breathed a deep sigh as she looked at the goblet.

"Don't leave it in the forest," said Tiffan. "You could use it to help mortals! Maybe those new friends you mentioned. You're courageous to befriend humans. I would never do that."

"How did you know?"

"I overheard him. He's telling Edward everything."

Rowan frowned.

"Hey, don't worry about him. Legend says the Holy Grail grants the gifts of ultimate happiness to humans and Antiquities. Gifts like eternal life and youth. Use it wisely, my dear sister," Tiffan said, smiling. She brought her hands together, clapping loudly. "I would be lying if I didn't tell you about my jealousy. But I couldn't stand Father lying to you. He's lied to me so many times. It's not fair. Do I want to work in the mortal realm? Yes, but this is *your* mission. I'll talk to Father and see if he'll give me attention and my own mission. We'll just have to wait and see. I can be patient for now."

"Thank you, sister," said Rowan, touching her sister's shoulder.

"Aw, stop that now." Tiffan chuckled, clapping her hands together again, this time even louder. "Go on. You have a job to do. Now, return to the human world because seeing you here annoys me."

"Okay. Thanks," Rowan said, giggling.

"Good luck."

"Goodbye," Rowan sang, jumping into the air, flying under the bridge and through the hidden pink gateway.

Tiffan clapped her hands a third time. A green light flashed behind her, and a giant pterodactyl appeared. It let out a massive roar and drooled before it hovered over Tiffan. It looked at her with red eyes.

"Go after her," Tiffan commanded. "Frighten her, hurt her if you must. I want her to be so scared and confused that she'll easily make mistakes. Return to me after you follow my orders. Don't attack anyone else in London."

The pterodactyl roared after receiving its orders, flapping its wings hard as it flew through the gateway.

"Big sister, your forest will soon be mine. The annihilation of your reputation will be my stepping stone to greatness," Tiffan said, laughing evilly.

Rowan came out of the strawberry-smelling gateway and into London. She flew higher and higher into the air. "I have to give myself plenty of space to open my portal. Let's get my bearings," Rowan said. She was so focused that she didn't see the pterodactyl until it roared behind her. "Wh-where did you come from? Get away!" Rowan shrieked, clutching the goblet to her chest, forgetting her spell, and veering off her flight path. Rowan was too frightened to chant a protective spell.

The dinosaur's massive jaws came at her.

Instinctively, Rowan clasped her wings together and plunged toward the ground.

The pterodactyl did not expect that maneuver and was left confused as it watched her fall. The dinosaur shook its head to regain its concentration and then plummeted after her.

After distancing herself from the pterodactyl, Rowan gathered her composure and opened her wings. The wind lifted her a few feet, and though she could see the flying dinosaur approaching her, she forced herself to concentrate. "I have to say the spell here. I must get back," Rowan said, trembling as she glided on the current. She closed her eyes. "Okay, here goes. *Aperi porta me in salute. Redi me ad amicos et silvam.*"

The same loud and booming sound erupted as when she had cast the previous portal. The whirlwind emerged and blew ferociously at her.

Rowan opened her eyes just in time to see that her head was practically in the jaws of the pterodactyl. Screaming, Rowan tried to pick up speed and flew into the portal through the harsh winds that battered her with the pterodactyl hot on her heels. *I'm not going to make it!*

TWENTY

John Doe walked over to Corin, confused. "Corin, it's almost nine-thirty. Why are you sending Troll away? The mayor will want to speak to him about saving Reginald."

"Reginald is coming with us to talk of Troll's heroism," said Corin. "Besides, you want to talk to the mayor, too, right? You don't need Troll there telling you what to say. I have seen the way he talks to you."

"He explains how I screw up sometimes, but it's all part of learning. He tries to help me. He cares about me. He's like my brother. We haven't found Magnum—"

"Well, Troll's going to care for you by looking for Magnum, and I also sent him to the grocery store," said Corin. *I hate lying to him, but I don't want any distractions on the way to see the mayor.*

"He's going to track him down alone? But Magnum is my responsibility. I feel bad, but Troll does know what I like to eat," said John Doe. "You know what's great? Macaroni and cheese!"

Reginald overheard their conversation as he approached.

"Yes, John Doe," said Corin, patting John Doe's shoulder. "Reginald, are you ready to accompany us?"

"I sure am," Reginald said. "I'm allowed off duty."

"Let's be off then," said Corin.

"The mayor's going to be pleased, I assure you. I hope he'll also grant me a new job," Reginald said, keeping pace with Corin and John Doe on their way to Centerville City Hall.

"You don't like being a construction worker?" asked John Doe.

"I was never a fan," said Reginald. "I always wanted to be a guard and protect the main gates of our city. Maybe now that I've had a life-threatening experience at this job, the mayor will understand that construction work is not for me."

"Wouldn't a job as a guard also put you in life-threatening situations?" asked Corin.

"Perhaps," said Reginald. "But at least then I would be dying for a good cause, not just a job I didn't find worthy. Do you ever want more for yourself? Do you want to feel important?"

"Yes," both men responded.

"I want to be remembered for having proper skills and powerful magic." John Doe sighed. "I want to be the best wizard of all." *But my true desire is to be a god.*

KRISTINA M. HOFFMAN

"I want wealth and power," said Corin. "I want people to know I'm important and be looked upon as a leader." *I want others to feel beneath me to increase my pride.*

"Really?" asked John Doe.

"I've always worked under superiors," said Corin. "When will it be my turn to be the one standing tall? Living here will help me finally reach my goal of being on top. Owning one of the mayor's homes symbolizes power and will show that I have class. I'll finally have status. It'll show that we, as a team, are important."

"Status," said Reginald. "It sounds great."

"I guess so," said John Doe. "I want to improve my magic."

"Why be better when you could be the best?" asked Reginald. "You always need to do your best."

"Troll always encourages me to do my best," John Doe said. "He's never given up on me, although he will run and hide when I perform my magic."

"I can't blame him," said Corin.

"But he always comes out to save me when my spells blow up in my face."

"And you are proud of that?" asked Reginald.

"Well, no," said John Doe. "But I still do my best. That's why I'm here to see Heeb. He can help and train me. I can work harder—"

"You should not have to work at all," said Reginald.

"It does just come naturally to some wizards," said John Doe.

"That's not what I mean," said Reginald. "Why should you work hard when you can just get someone else to do that? Then you can advance without breaking a sweat."

"That sounds great!" Corin exclaimed.

John Doe took a deep breath and stomped in front of Corin, facing the spaceman with his arms extended. "Corin, are you on drugs?" the wizard enquired. "That doesn't sound great! You're not acting like you were before—"

Reginald turned to see why John Doe had stopped Corin.

"No, John Doe," said Corin, chuckling. "I'm just interested in Reginald's advice."

"I don't like it," said John Doe.

"Just take what I said with a grain of salt, okay. Come on, we're almost there," Reginald said.

Corin walked by as John Doe frowned under his scarf. "Well, thanks. I guess?"

When they arrived, the clock in the tower above them struck ten o'clock. They walked up the stairs to the main door and opened it. The mayor stood in the middle of the main hall. In his hand was a document. He took care not to bend the paper as he extended his arms. "Gentlemen, come in. I am happy to see you."

"As are we, Mr. Mayor," said Corin.

"Now, wait a moment," Mayor Lanus said, looking at Reginald. "You, sir. I know you. You work for the Centerville Construction Company."

"Yes, sir. I'm Reginald Bass. Their friend, Troll, saved my life today."

"Really?" asked the mayor, intrigued. "You're friends with a troll?"

"He's a human warrior *named* Troll," said Corin quickly. *I forgot they haven't met!*

"There was an accident, and he risked his life to save me."

"Amazing!" exclaimed Mayor Lanus.

"Mr. Mayor, after my life-or-death experience, I do not believe my job is safe. I feel threatened. I shouldn't need to fear for my safety, and I'd hate to take legal action. I know you own the company—"

"Legal action?" asked Mayor Lanus. "Now, now, sir. There's no need for that. I'm an honest mayor who wants what's best for his community and a responsible business owner. I take pride in that. I can arrange a different and safer position for you. Of course."

"Oh, that'd be great."

"You've shown interest in the past about working as a guard. Haven't you?"

"Captain of the guard," said Reginald.

"Oh, guards need a few years of experience before they're promoted."

"I guess legal action will *have* to take place then. If I were mayor, I wouldn't want a law case looking bad on my career."

"Hmm. That's a good point. My re-election *is* coming up, and I must ensure that I have good ratings," Mayor Lanus said, putting his finger to his chin.

John Doe remained quiet, listening to how Reginald and the mayor spoke. *If Troll was here, he would disapprove of this discussion. It's like he wants the mayor to feel guilty and threatened. Is this blackmail? Just what kind of a weasel is he?*

"Reginald Bass, I hereby promote you to captain of the guard. You start today," said the mayor, gripping the front of his coat with his left hand as his right hand tightly held the document. "I'll personally write up your contract myself. It will be done by the end of the day. Stop by my office later to sign your life away."

"Thank you, sir," Reginald said, smiling. "I'll be on my way then." *Now, that's how you move up in the world! I have no training or experience, but I got the job I wanted because I took advantage of the mayor's public image.* Reginald headed back to the construction site to gather his belongings.

Mayor Lanus is a people pleaser, Corin thought. *I wonder if I can be like Reginald and get what I want? I bet the mayor is a pushover. I'm going to give it a try!* "Mr. Mayor, my friends and I want to introduce a job idea to keep your city safe. I know you have security from the wall and must have armed forces, considering the warning sign outside the city, but does your city need saviors? I don't mean police work, but a group of heroes who can look out for your people and stop accidents like Troll did today."

"My city has never had a group of saviors before. I love it, boy," said the mayor. "*Heroes of Centerville City* is a title worthy of a newspaper headline. I'll write the paperwork and make this an official job title. Suppose you're still interested in purchasing my house? If that's the case, I'll arrange a discounted price to make it more affordable to my city *saviors.*"

"Oh! No, sir! We couldn't possibly—" Corin paused. He tilted his head and lifted his eyebrows. "—unless, of course, you insist—"

"I insist," said Mayor Lanus.

Although John Doe felt terrible, he kept quiet. He didn't want to mess up Corin's chance of purchasing the house.

"Come on, gentlemen," said the mayor. "Let me introduce y'all to the house. It is already furnished and ready for you to move in today if you wish."

Corin and John Doe followed the mayor, heading northeast to the house.

John Doe couldn't help thinking of Troll with every step he took. He missed his partner and was unsure what to say to Corin or Mayor Lanus. He felt tense as they approached the two-story Georgian architectural-style white brick house surrounded by two stunning gardens. The smaller garden was in the front, full of fresh vegetables and fruits. The larger garden circulated around the entire house, with flowers and bonsai trees of every variety.

"She has quite a history. Built sometime in the late 1860s, it was one of the few buildings left standing after World War III. My family has owned this house since we founded Centerville, but I haven't lived here since childhood and have no interest in keeping her. It's time she finds a new family. Let me take you boys inside and give y'all a proper tour," he said while he unlocked the front door.

A figure glanced at them from the shadows around the corner, with yellow glowing eyes behind a rose bush.

The mayor led them inside the foyer, but he referred to it as 'the vestibule.' "Please be respectful and kindly remove your boots before venturing into the house," said Mayor Lanus. He pointed to two decorative chairs against the wall.

John Doe and Corin sat down and removed their footwear. Once their boots had been set neatly under their chairs, the mayor led them into the kitchen on their left. It was lit well, thanks to the natural light through the windows. The bright white cabinetry, fancy chandelier, and dinette made the kitchen inviting. A small bathroom was almost hidden in the corner of the kitchen.

The next room on their left was the dining room. The walls were painted ivory white, making the room appear larger. A big, beautifully set dining table sat in the middle of the room, with ten chairs surrounding it.

The mayor continued the ground floor tour, passing the living room, two bathrooms, and a library in the parlor. The final room had a wet bar. Wines, beers, and liquors of every variety were on the shelves behind the bar. This was what the mayor called 'the sociable room.'

Corin excitedly gasped. *I am falling in love with this house. It's so grand compared to the shoe box I lived in on Orion Three.*

I'm nervous. How much does a fancy house like this cost? John Doe thought, overwhelmed.

They ventured upstairs, where there were five bedrooms and one large bathroom. Each bedroom had one or two single beds, a cherry wood dresser set, and a fireplace decorated in gold trim.

The mayor led them downstairs to the finished basement. Underground, the air became cooler the deeper they descended.

John Doe stopped dead in his tracks. The young wizard inhaled sharply at what he saw. *This is no ordinary basement.* A giant medieval door made of oak planks and large decorative iron hinges was in front of them. John Doe approached the door cautiously. "Is this a dungeon?" His hand trembled as he reached for the handle.

The mayor laughed. "No, that door leads deeper underground into old tunnels. This was used for emergency travel in case of natural disasters. All the homes have these underground bunkers that lead to different tunnels under the entire city. They are ancient and were last used long ago. Unfortunately, our sewers leaked into them, and now they're restricted for sanitary reasons. At least, that's what I believe happened. The previous mayor designated it unsafe, and I have not been through there. The tunnels simply exist now, a part of history."

"It'd be a nice dungeon," suggested John Doe.

Corin chuckled at his comment.

Mayor Lanus showed them around the finished basement. The walls were a mix of red and black brick. It had a workshop area, laundry area, storage, hot water heater, gas furnace, and a sixth bedroom and fifth bathroom.

"A furnace?" asked John Doe. "But there are fireplaces. I thought this was a nineteenth-century house."

"It is," said the mayor. "The fireplaces have all been upgraded to natural gas. It circulates the heat perfectly during the winter."

"Fancy," said John Doe.

Returning to the ground level, John Doe and Corin put their boots back on and stepped outside, where the mayor showed them the extra-large garage. It had rows of large tool cabinets, each organized with expensive equipment, practically an auto repair shop on its own, with just enough room for Jessica's tank.

As they returned to the front of the house, John Doe looked up and put his right fist into the air. "I love it! The house is a very nice abode."

"The house is breathtaking. It has every requirement necessary to keep us comfortable. I think we'll take it," said Corin, removing a large bag of coins from his belt pouch.

"Her," corrected the mayor. "This house is a graceful lady who has seen many years. Shower her with respect." The mayor eyeballed the bag of coins and smiled.

"Oh, I'll definitely shower in her, all right," John Doe said, sniffing his armpits. "Oooohh! I am ripe!"

"Abode . . . I think that is what I'll call her," Corin said to John Doe.

"You're naming your new home?" asked John Doe.

"Sure," Corin said. "My space station had a designation."

"But this is a house . . ."

"It was technically my house."

"Well, that seems strange to me, but if you're into the weird stuff, then I am no one to judge."

"John Doe, have I told you how weird you are?"

"Not today, Corin," John Doe said proudly. "Not today."

Corin sighed hard and shook his head. "We'll take it," he said to the mayor.

"Good," the mayor said avidly. "Oh, I must introduce you to your personal gardener!"

"Our what?" asked Corin.

"We get a free *gardener* with the house? Does he live or just work here?" asked John Doe.

"Both. Follow me. He tends to the gardens and lives in a hut outside. He's never been inside the house," Mayor Lanus said. He escorted them to the house's rear side, and they admired the stunning garden.

"It's obvious this gardener works hard and gives the garden his love and attention," Corin said.

A thin but muscular man dressed in a raggedy red shirt and blue overalls stood holding a large garden hoe. He had long, messy, and matted black hair past his shoulders. His bangs rested over a thick, red bandana across his forehead. He wiped a drop of sweat from his cheek and noticed them approaching. "Hello, Mayor Lanus, who be your guests?" asked the gardener.

"Boys, this is Benjamin Saul Craft. Benjamin, this is Corin Degodi and John Doe. They have bought this house. Isn't that great?"

"Hi, nice to meet you, Ben. It's a great house. We're fortunate to have it. This place looks amazing!" Corin declared. "You must be some gardener and have a serious green thumb."

"Thank you," said Benjamin. "It's a pleasure to meet you. I'm so glad you've bought the house. If you need anything, just ask me, and I will assist you in any way I can."

"Great, thanks," John Doe said excitedly. "I've always wanted a servant."

"No," Corin said. "Benjamin will not be our servant, John Doe. He will be treated as one of us. Welcome to the family, Ben."

Benjamin smiled. "Family? I have never had a family."

"I have the contract ready for you, Mr. Degodi," Mayor Lanus said, handing Corin the document he had been carrying. He removed an ink pen from his pocket and gave it to Corin.

"Good, I want to be the head owner," said Corin. He signed the document on the mayor's back. "I plan on staying here for a long time."

"That's great, Corin," said John Doe.

"Now, your first payment is due in full today on your housing mortgage, but I'll cut you a deal on next month being free *if* your friends can impress me and are worthy of doing business for my city." The mayor put his hand on the signed contract.

"I thought you would discount us on the full payment for Troll's good deed and our new employment?" Corin asked, bewildered. He was so shocked at this sudden turn that he didn't perceive the contract firmly being yanked from between his trembling fingers. *Oh, gods! I didn't read it.*

"Indeed, Troll did a wonderful duty in saving a man's life, but let me explain something to you, son," said the mayor, keeping the signed document close to his chest. He held out his left hand and pointed to Corin's bag of coins. "Reginald did not deserve the job I gave him, and I guarantee he will fail at performing that duty. He has bothered me to give him better work for years. You can't be rewarded for something you have not earned. Those who are can never truly be themselves. They're weak people. Are you a weak person, Corin?"

Corin couldn't speak. He shakily held his bag of coins.

"If you and your friends are to be the city *saviors* and want a discount on the house, then you're going to earn it . . . properly. You have potential, Corin. You made a good attempt at trying to pull one over on me, but I will not be taken advantage of, not by a weak person like you. You're in my world now. I own you. I have jobs for you and your friends," said Mayor Lanus, greedily taking Corin's bag.

John Doe swallowed hard. *Corin, what have you gotten us into?*

Corin was stunned. *The mayor played me. I feel like a fool! Why did I admire Reginald? No . . .* "What jobs would we be doing?" asked Corin, struggling to keep his composure.

"As *saviors*, y'all are more than willing to protect my city against my enemies . . . I have a neighbor who causes me and my city trouble—"

"Franklin City?" asked Corin, gulping.

"You'll discover *who* when I come to you with a mission. Your cyborg seemed like a strong fellow, but I haven't met Troll, so I can't comprehend if they're worthy of being my city *saviors*. If you want to keep this house and not be homeless, you'll do whatever I tell you." The mayor shook the bag and listened to the coins jingle inside. He smiled maliciously. "You owe me quite a bit more than this now, son."

I wanted to live on Earth, but I am feeling anxiety and stress for the first time since arriving on this planet! It's heavy, like a boulder, weighing on my head and shoulders. Corin's heart pounded in his ears. He did not appreciate the mayor pressuring him. *I can't allow anyone to mess up any missions the mayor assigns us. If John Doe summons a destructive monster, we could fail. I can't let that happen. I can't let the mayor take our home. I might have a way of getting enough money for this first payment . . . I just hope this idea works.* "Mayor Lanus, Troll is putting together a match at the arena," Corin said. "He will battle Jack, and I will be their announcer. He's there now making the arrangements. Perhaps you could watch the match to see how skilled my men . . . my friends are? Maybe place a few bets? The money can go toward the first payment."

"I'll tell you what . . . I *will* put money down on the winner." The mayor chuckled. "I haven't gambled in a while. A man versus a machine! The crowd would enjoy watching them test their skills in throwing heavy objects and weapons. I can see it now—who is better? That'd bring in a lot of money. Then your friends can compete against one another in the first match. For the second—"

"Second?"

"Of course, there must be more than one! I think the second match should be an open battle. Troll and Jack will tag team against whoever wants to join in the fight: visitors or citizens. There haven't been arena battles in a long time, and the people crave excitement. Again, if your boys do a good job impressing me, I'll hire y'all and regulate discounts on your house payments." The mayor lowered his eyes when he glanced over at John Doe. "Will you be fighting also?"

John Doe rubbed his nose under the scarf. "I'm interested in magic, not jobs for you or fighting in an arena. I want to meet Heeb, the great warlock." John Doe turned to Corin. "Corin, do you *want* to live here? Should I *not* ask Heeb about helping you back to your home?"

"Not yet, John Doe," said Corin. "I want to stick around a little longer and see if I can fit in."

"That's the spirit, boy," Mayor Lanus said, patting Corin's back. "Working hard and taking responsibility will help you grow into a strong individual, and then you'll fit in just fine here on Earth. As for Heeb, do you know how to get to his place, John Doe?"

"I don't," said John Doe. "I found his store on the map, but I'm bad at directions."

"All you need to do is get to the other side of my city. Heeb's Herbal Remedies is next door to a spa. You can't miss it," said Mayor Lanus. "You know, John Doe . . . I almost wasn't going to allow you to meet Heeb."

"Why not?" John Doe asked, his voice trembling. *Why is this guy so rude?*

"You already believe yourself a wizard, yes?"

"Yeah," said John Doe cagily.

"Heeb is *very* busy, son. He shouldn't be disturbed by wizard wannabes . . . but you *are* a wizard. You should get along famously."

"Thanks?" John Doe had a bad feeling in the pit of his stomach. *Troll wouldn't like him. Is this mayor a bad guy? Did he just play me? I'm sure Heeb is a busy warlock, but is he also not polite? I know he is elderly and wise but also amazingly talented. I was so confident before. Now I am feeling stressed. I wish Troll was here and that Magnum had not flown away. I feel alone, but I need to meet Heeb. I have to. I can't let my dream die.*

"Mayor Lanus, could I see the contract again?" asked Corin. *So, I'll know how much to pay today.*

"Of course, son," said Mayor Lanus, "but understand that I cannot hand you back the paper. Here, I'll hold it up so you can see it." He held the contract before Corin's face, allowing him to look.

Corin sighed, reading the fine print. *I should have read this before!* Corin's face drooped when he saw the ridiculous price. He sifted through his pockets, pouches, and other holders on his belt until he had enough coins.

Mayor Lanus wore a wicked smile on his face. He rolled up the contract and took Corin's money. "You boys, have a good night now and enjoy your new home. Don't feel too bad, Corin. This is just business. I'm sure your warrior friend and the cyborg won't let you down. Money isn't everything." Mayor Lanus chuckled, and as he left, Corin balled up his fists and growled.

"That was not very nice of him," said Benjamin before he returned to work in the garden.

"John Doe, you should meet Heeb. I will go inside and ensure we have plenty of beds tonight. We may need to purchase sleeping bags and pillows for a few days before we can afford proper beds."

"Oh, Troll won't need a bed," John Doe informed him. "He probably won't even sleep inside. It's not his way."

"Thank you for telling me, John Doe. You go have fun. Here, you take the map. I am going to go inside and think for a while. I need to just be alone."

"Thanks," said John Doe, heading north to find Heeb. "I hope Troll is okay. He needs to bring the food. I'm going to be hungry!"

I feel like a fool. I let myself be taken advantage of and am almost out of money. I deserve this. I was trying to manipulate the mayor, but he played me instead. What's wrong with me? I have craved wealth ever since I came to Earth. This planet is rich in minerals that I am not used to, including gold. Perhaps I have an allergy that is causing a strange addiction? Or maybe that is just my excuse.

What if this is a lesson? I don't like losing! It's unfair. I really want to succeed. I guess I did win. I bought a house, have status, and will live here.

But I made a big decision without thinking. Troll was right. I should've thought about it first. How could I do this to myself? No one else did this. Just me. I let my confidence and pride fill my head with arrogance. I thought I was better than everyone else.

But aren't I? This was just a hiccup. I forgot! John Doe knows what happened. He'll tell the others! I know it. Although, he does have memory problems. Perhaps he'll forget?

That's probably wishful thinking.

—From the journal of Corin Degodi
June 13, 2215, 11:30 a.m.

TWENTY-ONE

Troll stood at the Dragon Food grocery store entrance. He looked at the list Corin had given him and sighed. There were a lot of groceries listed. He shrugged his shoulders, went through the automatic sliding doors, grabbed a cart, and began going down the aisles.

He sniffed the air in the store. It smelled sweet and fragrant. His nose led him to the fruits and vegetables. He smiled and checked the list. He tilted his head to the side in confusion and frowned. Corin had not put any fruits or vegetables on the list. Troll shook his head. "We need fiber," he said, grabbing a dozen different fruits and vegetables and putting them into the cart. "I can afford that. I hope I'll have enough to afford the rest. He's got some weird requests on this list," Troll said to himself as he read. "Pies, cookies, crackers, and cereal? Hmm, a lot of wheat and sugar. I don't eat that stuff. Do these foods come in a package? Is that food you must make on your own? I think it's called baking."

Troll sighed as he looked up at the sign above him.

Grocery stores list what is down each aisle on those signs. I'll follow those. Man, I don't eat half of this stuff. How am I supposed to do this? Why didn't he ask John to do this? I feel so unnatural and uncomfortable. I'd rather be in the river fishing for our dinner than do this.

As Troll followed the signs and constantly glanced at the list, he failed to notice that a little old Asian man was watching him.

He was three feet tall, had dark brown eyes, and was partly bald save for a neat line of gray hair wrapped around the back of his head. The old man had an enormous gray mustache draped down his chest, a dark freckle on his cheek under his right eye, and wore an orange hanfu with green sandals on his stubby feet. He walked closer to Troll, holding his hands behind his back.

There are eyes on me. I'm all too familiar with the feeling of being watched. It feels like whoever is staring at me can see into my soul! Troll turned around but saw no one.

"Ahem!" grunted a voice below.

Troll's blue eyes looked down and saw the tiny Asian man looking up at him.

"You're magnificent, my boy," the man said in a thick Chinese accent. "Absolutely impressive!"

"Um," Troll gulped nervously. "Th-thank you?"

"You look like a strong warrior," the little man said. "If you're interested in a quest, I can employ you, but you must first pass a test."

"T-test?"

"Now . . . get ready to . . ."

Without warning, a large monster leaped over a food stand behind Troll and tried to grab the young Native American.

". . . fight!"

Troll's heart jumped in his chest. He reflexively stepped back, dodging the attack. He didn't get a good look at his opponent, but not knowing who his attacker was did not stop him from defending himself. Troll moved incredibly fast, and the aggressor's claws missed him by a fraction of an inch.

His adversary pressed on with its assault and unleashed a flurry of rapid claw swipes. Any of the monster's hits might have taken Troll's head clean off, but he skillfully weaved between the powerful strikes.

The old Asian man watched, barely able to keep up with Troll's quickness.

The fight was in slow motion to Troll. He kept up his evasive tactic, and the monster overextended one of its attacks. Taking advantage of the opening, Troll crouched under the challenger and gave it a left upper punch to the jaw.

The monster's jaw snapped shut. Its sharp teeth pierced its tongue. Bright red blood gushed, running down its chin. Tears sprang from the monster's eyes, and it whimpered loudly.

Troll punched just below its ribs.

His adversary exhaled sharply and roared in pain.

To finish the job, Troll karate-kicked the monster's genitalia.

The monster's deep roar suddenly turned into the gentle squeak of a kitten.

Troll looked at his attacker, expecting it to be a therasapien. He gasped and stumbled back in surprise when he saw the beast was unlike any he had ever seen. It had a big head with thorns bunched together on its crown, broad shoulders, and toned muscles. It was shirtless, exposing large circular umber-colored warts on its dark sienna skin. It wore black jeans, a belt, and no shoes, showing its gruesomely large feet and taloned toes. The sweet aroma of the fruit in the store hid its pungent body odor.

"Wh-who are you? Wh-what are you? What do you w-want?" Troll asked shakily.

It couldn't answer Troll. Its eyes crossed and cupped its privates to protect them from another strike. It sank to its knees and collapsed backward, resting on its rump and moaning.

"He is with me," said the little old man. "His name is Bronze. I'm not surprised you don't know his species. He's not from these parts. He's a Java Island lava monster from Indonesia. You have nothing to fear from him."

"Are you—thieves?" Troll asked, breathless.

"We're not robbers. You are impressive, indeed! You did a marvelous job, son. I am Bi Qu."

"A marvelous job?" wailed the lava monster. He had a strong accent that sounded Australian. "H-he kicked . . . my jewels!"

"You'll recover, Bronze. Don't be such a baby," said Bi Qu, chuckling.

Troll crouched down, grabbed the little man's hanfu, and brought his face close to his own. "Why did you attack me, little old man?"

"Little?" Bi Qu giggled. "Why, son, my condition is called dwarfism, but let me assure you that I only appear little to you now—in this form."

Troll swallowed hard. "What do you mean?"

Suddenly, Bi Qu's eyes changed from brown to yellow.

Troll cried out, released the hanfu, and stood up. He backed away. Every muscle in his body trembled. His first reflex was to run, but he stood his ground.

Bi Qu roared loudly.

Troll screamed when the sound rang through his ears. He was forced to cover them. *His roar . . . it's so familiar. No! It can't be. It sounds like the red dragon John summoned.* Troll's heart raced.

Bi Qu's tiny body glowed a brilliant orange color, and then he transformed. His neck grew long, his limbs stretched out, his hands became giant claws, and great wings pierced his back.

Troll flinched in fear as he stared at the giant twelve-foot orange dragon. Sweat formed on his brow.

"Who is little now?" Bi Qu asked.

"It looks like I'm the small one," Troll said. *My axe . . . I left it with the gatekeeper. Why are these two in a grocery store terrorizing the customers? What should I do?*

Panic flooded the entire store when the shoppers and employees saw the dragon. They chaotically began to evacuate.

Troll could feel their distress.

Store associates ran outside and yelled for the city authorities while customers fled and left their full carts behind. Mr. Sun emerged from his office trying to calm his employees and customers, but when he saw the dragon, he also lost himself to fear and raced out with the frightened crowd.

"I'll stand my ground," Troll bravely told the dragon to keep Bi Qu's focus on him. "I won't let you harm any of the people escaping. As long as no one is harmed, I will surrender myself."

The orange dragon laughed at the young warrior.

Bronze stood up.

Troll breathed in when he saw the full height of the lava monster. He stood around eight feet tall, taller than Jack. Troll was the shortest among them and outnumbered. His right hand slowly reached up to his ear to activate his communicator.

"I wouldn't do that," suggested the dragon. "No need to involve anyone else. Now, return your hand to your side. Nice and slow."

How does he know I have a radio? Troll thought as he obeyed, bringing his trembling hand down to rest on the amulet. He felt his hammering heartbeat.

"That's it. Good little warrior," Bi Qu cooed.

Troll's instincts told him to activate the amulet and run or fight. But he did not move. *They want me for a reason. They don't seem to have any evil intentions. They've not harmed anyone. I'm frightened, but—* "Wh-what do you want with me?" Troll asked.

"You're not running away," said Bronze, surprised. "Bi Qu, can you believe it?"

"Let's see what happens next," said the dragon, raising his head into the air and breathing fire.

Troll gasped loudly when he saw the flames. His eyes trembled. He lost all mobility and couldn't press the amulet. Like the wings of a hummingbird, his heartbeat turned into a remarkably fast flutter. Troll watched the dancing flames pour out of the gigantic mouth. *Fire! Oh, gods! Is he going to burn me or the entire building? Don't come near me! I have to get away—but I can't!*

"He must have balls of steel," said Bronze. "I've never seen a human just stand there like this. He must be brave indeed."

If only he knew my fear. Can he not smell it? It's disgusting! I am so embarrassed. Why aren't they attacking me? What is going on? Is this part of the test?

The dragon stopped breathing fire and looked at Troll. He could see the horror in his eyes. *He is afraid of fire, yet he did not run,* thought Bi Qu. *That could be a problem. Perhaps I can help him overcome his fear, but trust must come first.* "Very good!" said Bi Qu, returning to his human form. He adjusted the orange hanfu and smiled. "Your heart is perfect."

"M-m-my heart?" Troll asked, startled and still unable to activate the amulet. He blinked his eyes several times, trying to calm himself.

"My deepest apologies for attacking you, son. I needed to find the right person," Bi Qu explained. "I can feel it within you . . . goodness, honor, and purity. There's something special about you. I know it, and you're the one I need. Please, the quest is important!"

"What is this quest?" Troll asked, removing his hand from the amulet after his heart finally returned to its normal rhythm. He wiped the sweat from his forehead and sighed with relief. "Do you often hang out in grocery stores seeking warriors to ask them for help?" Troll managed a chuckle as his muscles relaxed through his nervousness.

Bi Qu snickered. "No one was willing to help in my hometown. So, I checked the arena here in Centerville City. Decent warriors come here to keep their skills sharp. However, no warriors were available."

"I just came from the arena and scheduled a match for tomorrow. There hasn't been a battle in a very long time."

"Indeed, I figured the grocery store was the next best place to go. Everyone needs to eat. I figured Mr. Sun wouldn't mind us *interviewing* a few people. It worked, did it not?"

"It seemed like a good idea at the time," said Bronze. "And we *did* meet you."

Troll shrugged his shoulders. "You did run into me."

"It made sense to me," said Bronze. "I love food."

"The quest is a mighty challenge but a short mission. Ultimately, it will be worthwhile because you'll save a precious life," Bi Qu said.

"Someone's life is in danger?" asked Troll.

"Indeed, and I will pay you handsomely for your aid. I'll give you enough to buy all the groceries you'll ever need!"

The three of them laughed.

"What is your name, son?" asked Bi Qu, extending his right hand to Troll.

"I'm called Troll." He took Bi Qu's hand and gently shook it. "Nice to meet you, I guess."

"Troll?" asked Bronze. "That's not a human name!"

"It's my code name."

"What is your real name?" Bi Qu asked. "Or is that a secret?"

Troll quivered as he took his hand back. "I'm sorry, but it *is* a secret."

"Marvelous!" Bi Qu breathed. "You see, Bronze, I told you the one we needed would be secretive!"

"You were right," Bronze agreed. "You've been right about this entire encounter. You're always right. Now, can I get a bag of frozen peas for my jewels? They still hurt; you know—"

"Of course, boy." Bi Qu laughed. "Put some ice on those."

Bronze shuffled over to a cooler, opened it, grabbed a frozen bag of peas, sat down, and placed it on his nether regions.

"This has to be one of the weirdest days . . ." Troll said.

"Now, Mr. Troll—"

"Oh, just Troll, please. You don't need to call me *Mr.* Troll."

"But I must, dear boy," said Bi Qu. "You are not family. I must be respectful. Bronze is like family. He's one of my students, so I don't need to be proper. He will be going with you. You'll need to find three ingredients that I will add to my mixture to cast the spell to save the precious life. Without the three ingredients, I cannot complete the spell, and the life needing our aid will perish."

"If it's a short mission, I'll help," Troll said, reaching for his communicator again. "I should tell my friends. I don't want them to worry."

"No," said Bi Qu. "They must not know. As you have secrets, so do I. Contact them if you need assistance in something other than gathering the ingredients, but do not tell them about this journey. If someone else knows, then the spell cannot be completed. It is very complex and sensitive. Give me your word that you won't ever tell anyone."

"I promise," said Troll.

"Swear on it," said Bronze, glaring at Troll with serious yet sensitive eyes. "We need to know you mean it. The universe must hear you make this official in honoring my master's request."

"What can I swear upon?" Troll asked, looking down at his feet. His eyes drifted from his boots to the red amulet. Troll cleared his throat. He felt a warm sensation erupt from his chest. The skin on his back crawled up to his neck, tickling him. "Okay." *I cannot believe what I am about to say.* "I swear . . . on what is most precious within me—" Troll gulped and placed his hand upon the amulet. He made eye contact with Bi Qu and breathed in deeply. "I swear . . . on my beating heart . . . that I will not tell anyone about this mission." Troll blushed as the warm sensation continued. "You have my oath."

"Purity," Bi Qu said, sighing passionately. He closed his eyes and then fluttered them open. "I *knew* you were special. I am so glad your destiny brought you here. We're going to be great friends. Thank you, Mr. Troll!"

"You're welcome," Troll said as the embarrassment melted away. *That sounded cheesy.*

"That sounded kind of cheesy," said Bronze, laughing.

Oh, gods. Did he read my mind?

Bronze stood up and clutched the bag of peas. "You know, Troll, you've got guts to say something like that out loud in front of others. There are not many people who could do that. I'm okay to work with this guy, boss. Are you ready to leave, Troll?"

"Yes, if we start now, I can return to my friends before they worry. I don't want them to think I have abandoned them."

"Give me your grocery list," said Bi Qu. "I will take care of this for you."

"Thank you," Troll said, handing Bi Qu the list Corin had given him.

Bi Qu studied the list. "Huh, no fiber! What's wrong with your friends?"

"I thought that too!"

"Here is your list, boys," Bi Qu said, handing them a small slip of aged paper. The ingredients were certainly interesting:

ONE TOENAIL OF AN OGRE.
BARK FROM A HAUNTED TREE.
AN ORB WITHIN A WELL.

"Take this map," Bi Qu said, pulling out a rolled-up map from his hanfu pocket. "It's of the forest surrounding this city. Luckily, you boys won't have to go far for these things."

"You mean, these objects are right outside this city in Rowan's Forest?" Troll asked.

"They're not exactly in her . . . Rowan? You know, Rowan? Lovely, isn't she?"

"Yes, how do you know her?"

"I am good friends with her father," Bi Qu said. "Remember not to tell her of this."

"You have my word," Troll said confidently.

"I will have your heart if you break your oath. Remember, you swore your heart to me. If you break your promise, even by accident . . . then your heart must be given to me, or else the precious life will die."

Troll felt sick. "Oh my—" He parted his lips slightly and breathed out as his heartbeat accelerated. "—I didn't know that was—"

"But don't worry," Bi Qu said. "I trust you."

"Me too," Bronze said, taking the map before giving Troll a firm pat on the back. "I'll hold onto this."

Troll stumbled forward in surprise. *Whoa! He's strong.*

"Oops, sorry." Bronze chuckled, putting the cold bag of peas onto his head.

"Oh yeah," said Bi Qu, reaching into his pocket again. "Before I forget, I have summoning stones to give you both. They may prove useful on this expedition. They are yours to keep, even if you don't use them today. Bronze, you get the bumble bee jasper. It will enhance your confidence and instincts. Mr. Troll, I give you the rose quartz. This pink stone will guide your tender heart and give you courage. I can sense you already have a precious stone on you."

"Yes, I wear a green aventurine bracelet under my armor," Troll said, touching the blue gauntlet cuff on his left arm.

"Excellent! Together, those stones will repel your fears," Bi Qu said. "To contact me in an emergency, just raise your summoning stones and state my name." He handed them their stones and nodded. "You boys, be careful, and please don't come back empty-handed, or that life will be lost forever."

"We'll meet you back home, right boss?" Bronze asked, shaking the bag of peas in front of Bi Qu's face.

"Yes, I will be there," Bi Qu said, snatching the bag of peas. "I'll purchase this for you and take it home."

"Why, boss?"

"Because I refuse to allow anyone to eat your *crotch peas*, dear boy! Now, off with you! Have a good journey. I'm going to get busy with Troll's groceries . . . I say now . . . are there any employees left? Hmm. I may have to find them and apologize sincerely to my friend, Mr. Sun. I've known him for years, but he has no idea I'm a dragon! I kept that a secret. I'll just let him know the dragon has gone. This may take a while. Good luck, gentlemen. Adventure is waiting for you."

"Are you ready?" Bronze asked Troll, heading toward the door.

Troll swallowed hard. "Yes, but I'm a bit nervous," he said as he put the rose quartz into the small sack on his belt and followed Bronze.

"You have no idea how much this means to us," said Bronze as they exited the grocery store and headed to the South Gate. "My master knew you'd be here. He described you to me and everything. He just had to test you to make sure you are worthy."

"He knew I was here?" asked Troll.

"Yes, he knows everything. I think he's an oracle. He knows your wizard friend is seeking Heeb as well. Heeb and Bi Qu are very close friends. They're like brothers or very close cousins."

"That's so interesting," said Troll. "It—It's almost like this was destined to happen. I can feel deep inside that I'm supposed to do this."

They approached the South Gate where Jeer sat. The goblin saw them coming and folded his arms across his chest. "You need something?" Jeer asked.

"Hello," said Troll. "Can I please have my axe and grenades? They're in the storage unit C2. I am leaving the city briefly, but I promise I'll be back soon."

"Fill out the forms," Jeer said as he pushed papers toward them. "Write your name, when you leave, and what weapons you sign out." He rustled through the storage unit, looking for Troll's weapons. "Warrior's axe, ah, here it is. Grenades, yes. Here they are."

"I just need my pack, ammo, holster, and Beretta shotgun, please," said Bronze. "They're in unit B3."

"You have a shotgun?" Troll asked as he filled out the documentation.

"Yes, she's an antique too; she's a side-by-side, twelve gauge. I call her Amber. I use her to hunt," Bronze said proudly. "I think she'll help us if we run into trouble in the forest. Don't worry, I'm very professional with her. Do you not like firearms?"

"Oh, I have no problem with them," said Troll. "I don't use them often. My axe suits me just fine."

Jeer grumbled nonsense as he handed them their belongings. He sat in his chair, glared at them, picked up a book, and opened it to a random page, pretending to read.

"I think he wants us to go," said Bronze as he snapped his pack to his belt.

"Gee, what gave me away?" Jeer sarcastically stated and opened the gate.

"Thank you," said Troll, walking outside the gate. "We'll be back soon."

"Don't rush and give me something to do," said Jeer gruffly.

"Come on, Troll," Bronze said, chuckling as he headed toward the trees.

Troll stopped and turned around as the enormous gate closed. He glared at the wall surrounding the city. Troll shut his eyes, breathed deeply, opened them, and exhaled slowly. "I'll be back soon, guys."

"Don't worry, warrior," said Bronze. "You're doing a noble thing. Remember, this is destiny. Do not feel bad. Your friends are safe here."

"I hope so." He turned away from the city and walked into the forest with Bronze.

TWENTY-TWO

John Doe arrived at Heeb's Herbal Remedies shop. He stood on the front step with his hands clasped against his cheeks and gawked starry-eyed at the sea-green storefront. He approached the big bay window, pressed his nose against the cold glass, and gazed into the shop. He saw organized shelves with rows of herbal packets. A section of large pots on the floor contained hibiscus, amaranth, elephant ears, and agave plants. Small, full jugs of elixirs were kept in a display case. John Doe was so captivated by Heeb's shop that he almost ignored its surroundings.

Mayor Lanus had mentioned a spa next door, and he was indeed correct. The spa was in a white and black building, but John Doe could not see inside because the windows were frosted. Two decorative trees in pink pots sat on the step beside the glamorous red front door. John Doe's attention was taken away from the spa when his nose caught the scent of freshly picked strawberries, apples, and corn. There was a small farmer's market in the alley between Heeb's shop and the spa.

John Doe glanced back at the spa. *Oh man, I could go for a relaxing back massage! How wonderful it would feel if a beautiful woman's soft and gentle hands rubbed oil all over my body. I have not been touched by a woman in such a long time! I miss my lover.* His imagination teased him as he pictured a voluptuous woman oiling her hands and winking at him. "I have to check this place out!" he exclaimed, drooling into his scarf. He slowly opened the door and peeked inside. "Hello?" John Doe walked in. He expected to see gorgeous women responsible for the beautification process, but there were no human employees.

The owner and sole worker of the spa was a giant cephalopod resting on a table, working its appendages into the backs of many Centerville citizens.

John Doe cried out when he saw the enormous mollusk.

The locals smiled, lying still on their bellies, allowing the sea monster to do its work.

"Ah, a new customer," gurgled a gregarious voice with a strong Brooklyn accent.

John Doe gasped when he realized he heard the cephalopod, but its beak had not moved. The giant sea monster had communicated with its mind.

"What'll it be, stranger?" asked the cephalopod telepathically. "A back massage? A shoulder patting, perhaps? Maybe you'd prefer a nice oiled—"

"I want nothing to do with a telepathic sea monster touching my bits!" John Doe shouted and swiftly turned around, dashing out the door.

"Gee, what's his problem?" the cephalopod questioned.

"I don't know," replied a customer. "He's certainly missing out. You're the best!"

John Doe ran to Heeb's shop and sat on the small step before the building. "Well, that was something I've never seen before. The only thing that came close was that giant spider I pulled through a portal a year ago. Boy, Troll hated fighting that thing," John Doe said to himself, shuddering as he attempted to slow his rapid breathing.

"Where do you think such a creature would come from, might I ask?" asked a voice behind him.

Alarmed, John Doe leaped to his feet. He quickly spun around, as fast as his heart jumped. His hands glowed with magical energy.

A tall, older man stood in the doorway. He had long dark brown hair pulled into a ponytail and a well-groomed beard. He wore a fine indigo robe, a thin multi-colored neckerchief, and red sandals decorated with emeralds and pink gemstones.

"Sorry, lad. I didn't mean to startle you. The sunken city of Brooklyn just did not suit such a splendid creature with great talent," said the man. "Now, could I perhaps interest you in some herbal supplements?"

"A-are you Heeb?" John Doe asked steadily, relaxing his hands and allowing the magical energy to diminish.

"I am indeed. I can tell you are not from here. Welcome to Centerville, young man. I see you are a wizard-in-training."

"In training?" John Doe grumbled. "No, sir! Now look, I *am* a wizard!"

"Are you now? Says who?" Heeb smiled.

"Says *me*!" John Doe yelled. "I am John Doe, and I'm a wizard. You can ask my partner, Troll."

"Partner? Is he a fellow wizard, or is he indeed *a* troll?"

"Neither," John Doe said. "He is my friend. He's a Native American warrior."

Heeb looked into John Doe's eyes with sudden interest.

"Did you say Native American?" Heeb inquired.

"Yes, I did. Are you hard of hearing, old man?"

"Old man?" Heeb laughed. "Listen, boy, I may be much older than you, but that does not give you any right to disrespect me. I am over one hundred years old and still have a baby face under this beard."

"Y-you're really over one hundred years o-old?" John Doe asked nervously. "I heard you were legendary . . ."

"Indeed, I am," said Heeb, grinning. "Now, John Doe, I can see you are a young and rude man. I have met many like you. Nevertheless, I am interested in hearing about your Native American friend."

"Aren't you more interested in training me?" asked John Doe.

"Why?" asked Heeb. "I thought you said you *are* a wizard. Why would you need training from me?"

"Because you're a great warlock," John Doe stated passionately. "I have . . . some . . . to still learn. Would you be willing to train me?"

"Hmm, perhaps," uttered Heeb. "But first things first, John Doe. Tell me more about Troll. Is that indeed his true name?"

"Well, it's not his real name. It's a code name. I don't know his real name. Even though we have been together for a couple of years now, he's never told me his real name, and I have never been very interested in learning it. He's always there to help me and whoever we meet."

"He is generous then?" probed Heeb.

"Yeah," said John Doe. "He's a great guy. He has a big heart."

"Ah, I bet he does," said Heeb, grinning. "How old is he now?"

"Twenty-four," said John Doe.

"Wow, twenty-four years old already—"

"Wait! What do you mean 'already?' Do you know him?" grilled John Doe.

"I can't say that I do. I think I would remember someone named Troll. Is there anything else about him? Anything unusual?" Heeb pried as he sat on the front step.

"He has blue eyes," John Doe said. "I have never seen another Native American with blue eyes before. But since I've not actually ever seen another Native American . . . I'm just assuming that's rare."

"That is *extremely* rare," said Heeb. "But not what I was thinking . . . anything else about him that is out of the ordinary?"

"He's strong and fast. He has super strength! He can lift an amazing amount of weight and runs at impossible speeds, probably as fast as a cheetah or pronghorn. That's why he became my partner. He's also saved me from numerous monsters. Just yesterday, he fought a dragon and rescued me and our new friends from a crazy Spanish-speaking jaguar mutant."

"A jaguar mutant? A therasapien?" asked Heeb.

"Yeah," answered John Doe. "He was tough. It took Troll a while to beat him. I've never seen such a creature before."

"Their species are created by the Restrain Corporation."

"Oh yeah, Troll knew that too!"

"Interesting. It's a good thing your friend was there."

"Yeah. Troll is a good friend."

"Tenderhearted?" asked Heeb.

"Yes! Speaking of his heart . . . he does have a red gem or amulet-looking thing in the center of his chest."

Heeb's brown eyes twinkled.

"I always thought it was a part of his armor, but it seems to be a part of him."

Heeb stood, took John Doe's right hand, and shook it determinedly. "I *will* train you, John Doe."

"R-really?" John Doe interjected in shock. "B-but—"

"No buts. We begin today! Come into my shop for a spot of tea, and then we shall begin."

"Wait, what's the rush, and why the sudden interest after I told you about Troll? In fact, now that I've told you so much, I feel really weird about it. I feel like I've betrayed him. Oh no!"

"I agree to train you if you introduce me to your young friend," Heeb said eagerly. "I must meet him."

"What do you want with him?" demanded John Doe, trying to sound aggressive. "If you wanted to know stuff to harm him, you'll have to go through me. I won't let you hurt him!"

"You really care for your friend," Heeb said with a hearty chuckle. "That is good. I always knew that he—" Heeb cleared his throat and adjusted his posture. "It is good to have friends. Believe me, I will not harm him. I'd never hurt anyone with a pure heart."

"Were you about to say something else?"

"Of course not! Now, come in. I hope you like seafood," Heeb said, touching the doorframe. A small puff of pink smoke emerged between his fingertips once his hand came in contact with the wooden frame.

"Wouldn't that disturb your neighbor?" asked John Doe.

"The cephalopod? Disturbed? No, John Doe. He enjoys eating seafood too, you know," Heeb said, opening the door to his shop.

John Doe stopped in the doorway and glanced inside.

Heeb's shop was an average living area with white walls, turquoise-colored curtains on the windows, a red brick fireplace, a small kitchen with a regular table and chairs, and normal-looking candles and glassware.

I expected something more magical. This is disappointing. It looks like a grandma's house. Where did all of the herbs and potions go? This isn't what I saw through the windows before . . .

"Is something wrong, son?" asked Heeb.

"No," said John Doe, trying not to sound dissatisfied. "I thought this was where your magic shop was. I figured, as a warlock, you'd disguise your magic shop as an herbal store, but this . . . looks like an ordinary house."

"I opened a portal to my home when I touched the doorframe. You're too important of a guest to just walk around my little herbal store. I would be a rude trainer if I didn't invite you to my residence where you can be comfortable. Isn't that nice of me?"

"Well, yeah," said John Doe, scratching the side of his neck under his scarf.

"Good," said Heeb. "Enter so I can shut the door. You're letting the bugs in."

"Oh, sorry," John Doe declared, quickly stepping into the house.

"And I *do* sell potions," said Heeb. "But they're all created by the herbs I also sell. My herbal store is legit, as well as my magic shop." Heeb shut the door, and the regular appearance of his home melted away. The living area became a stunning granite-surfaced space with a high ceiling and a decorative archway. There was a roaring fire in an ornate fireplace, shelves full of magic books lined the walls, various potions in glass containers sat on a low coffee table, and an open wooden armoire full of capes, hats, and wands. The table and chairs in the kitchen morphed into a stone table decorated with human and animal skulls, dragon horns, and spikes.

John Doe took a deep breath. He was in awe of the marvelous transformation. "Now, *this* is a house!"

"You may have it one day," Heeb said as he clapped his hands twice.

The fabulous room changed back to the regular setting.

"Where did it go?" John Doe asked, looking at Heeb, his sad expression hidden under his scarf and hood.

"That's the home you desire one day, John Doe, but I want my home to look like this. Humble, comfortable, and tidy. Come into the kitchen. I'll make us tea."

"Wait a minute," said John Doe gruffly. "That was a mirage?"

"Certainly," said Heeb filling a pot with water from the tap. "I wouldn't have my living space look like that."

"But, you're a warlock. Don't you want to live in a fancy mythical dwelling?"

Heeb ignored John Doe's question as he cast a fire spell. *"Fermentum urna."*

The water boiled instantly.

Heeb poured the hot water into two mugs and placed tea bags into each cup. "This is my own personal brew. I hope you like it," Heeb said, handing one of the cups to John Doe. "Cream, sugar? Honey or lemon, perhaps?"

"Sugar," said John Doe.

Heeb passed him the sugar container.

John Doe opened it and poured a significant amount of sugar into his cup.

Wide-eyed, Heeb grabbed the container from John Doe and closed it, returning it to his shelf. He cleared his throat, took his cup, and gestured to the kitchen wall. "Come, let's go into my basement. I'm sure you'll find it more to your liking." Heeb waved his hand at the wall, and it magically turned into stairs leading down into a deep chamber.

They walked to the basement.

John Doe was impressed by the décor: spider webs, stone slabs, a large fireplace with a cauldron, a library with shelves of magic books, and a display case of potions. "This place is real, right?"

"Very much so," Heeb said with a chuckle. "Just because my home life seems pretty normal doesn't mean my work life can't be a little more spectacular."

"Hello there," rang out a female voice.

John Doe jumped in surprise; his eyes darted around the room, but he saw no one. "Who was that?"

"It's rude not to say hello back," said Heeb roughly to John Doe.

"Oh!" John Doe gulped. "Hello there . . . strange voice in this room."

Heeb burst out into laughter.

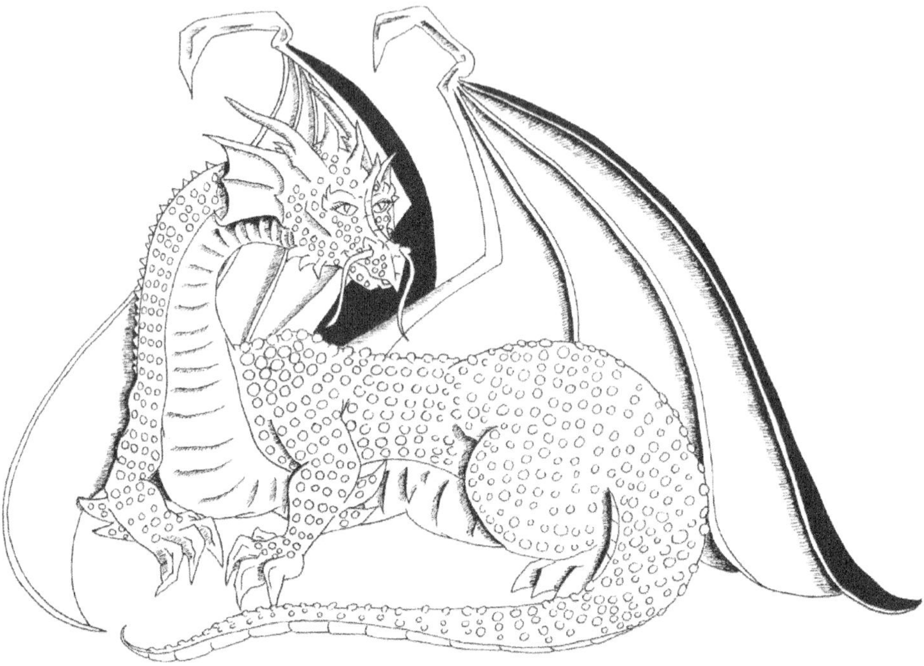

"Hello dearie, and welcome." An immense blue dragon manifested before them, filling most of the room.

"Wow!" exclaimed John Doe, looking at her in awe.

"John Doe, this is my longest friend, Silvia," Heeb said. "Silvia, this is John Doe. He's my new apprentice."

"So nice to meet you, dear," Silvia said. "Heeb is a wonderful warlock. You'll learn much from him."

"Silvia is my roommate, but don't let the mayor know."

"I accidentally set fire to his hair once, and he was so taken aback he exclaimed in front of the whole city that I couldn't live here anymore. I was appalled."

"He has a temper, that's for sure," said Heeb.

"He can hold such a grudge. It was years ago!"

"Anyway, Silvia, this young wizard is friends with a big-hearted man we know of," Heeb said, winking.

"Really?" she gasped, her eyes lighting up. "*That* young man?"

"You *both* know him?" John Doe asked.

"Never heard of *him*," Silvia said quickly as she slowly motioned to the other side of the room.

John Doe removed his sunglass-goggles, looking puzzled.

"A bit of dragon humor," Heeb said, chuckling as he patted John Doe's back. "Come on, lad, let's get started on your first lesson: opening portals."

"I know how to do that. Watch!" John Doe said excitedly. He put his sunglass-goggles on a stone table and held his hands before him. *"Oscail doras misticiúil, tabhair amach mo bhealach isteach."* His hands shined, and a small portal opened.

"Oh my," said Heeb. "John Doe, is that a *random* portal?"

"It's okay. I'll reach in and grab something," John Doe stated, shoved his arm inside, and felt around.

"That *is* just a random portal, isn't it? You have no idea where that portal goes. John Doe, this is dangerous," Heeb said, panicked.

"Troll tells me that every day."

"That's not a good thing, John Doe."

John Doe felt the coarse fur of an animal brush against his palm. He grabbed it. "I got something!" John Doe said eagerly, pulling with all his might.

The large head of a werewolf emerged; it roared and snapped at John Doe.

"Oh! My lords!" Heeb yelled when he saw the bloodthirsty beast. "Put it back!"

"I can't!" shrieked John Doe. Panic gripped him, and he accidentally let go of the werewolf's scruff.

The werewolf began to climb through the portal, snarling at John Doe and ready to attack.

John Doe backed away in fear, dropping his cup of tea. The mug shattered on the hardwood floor.

Silvia used her tail to strike the werewolf in the face. The blow forced it back into the portal.

Heeb quickly raised his glowing hand toward the portal and moved his forefinger and middle finger to his thumb until they touched.

The portal closed.

John Doe let out an explosive sigh of relief, pulled down his scarf, and smiled. "See, I'm a natural!"

"You, sir, are a novice!" bellowed Heeb. "You need *real* training, John Doe! You will *not* open another portal until I say so!"

"Does this mean I can't have another cup of tea?" asked John Doe.

Heeb growled, grabbing John Doe's scarf and roughly pulling him over to the large stone table where his sunglass-goggles were. "I can tell this will be a rough lesson, John Doe, but you will master this even if I must beat it into you."

"Um . . . about my tea?"

"Good lords, he's odd! Even for a wizard," sighed Silvia.

TWENTY-THREE

Troll and Bronze followed Bi Qu's map through the thick woods. They stepped over large stones and carefully maneuvered around trees and shrubs. The trees around them altered the deeper they trekked. Their leaves became sharp, their bark bristly, and their colors changed from brown to gray.

Troll noticed the familiar scent of Rowan's Forest had vanished. The smell of decomposition replaced all aromas. The air around him was getting muggy, and the sunlight began to fade. Troll looked up at the canopy. He could barely tell that it was daytime. His heart skipped a beat when they heard ghoulish laughter.

"Wh-what is that? I think we're in the h-h-haunted forest," warned Bronze, trembling. He held up his gun and aimed it toward the tops of the trees. "Where d-d-did that laughter come from? Was it above us?"

"I can't tell," said Troll, sniffing the air. "It sounded like it came from all around us."

"I don't like this," said Bronze nervously. "Why does it have to be bark from a haunted tree anyway? What's so wrong with a normal tree? I hate ghosts! You can't punch or shoot them. They creep me out."

A bush close to them shuddered, and Troll aimed his axe at it.

Bronze yelped in fright, shooting his gun into the air.

Startled by the sudden blast, Troll screamed and threw himself to the ground in front of the bush. He looked over his shoulder at Bronze with his eyebrows lowered. "Are you crazy?" Troll shouted.

"I was scared! I'm so sorry. What's that behind you?"

Troll shivered. Staying on his belly, he bravely glanced at the bush. He could hear someone breathing from within it. A hot breath that surprisingly smelled like pine erupted from it. "Who's there?" Troll asked. "I know you're in there."

The bush stopped moving. A green man with a skin tone that was slightly lighter than Rowan's stood up from inside the shrub. He was tall and skinny, with webbed ears. His brown hair was short and thinning, showing off the curvature of his head. His golden eyes were very pronounced from his wondrous skin tone. "Can a man not have a few moments alone to relieve himself?" murmured the green-skinned fellow as a sudden zipper sound was heard from within the bush.

"Oh, gross! I'm near his *thing*," Troll grunted in disgust as he stood up and backed away.

"You're nowhere near my privates, and I didn't get any urine on you, young man," stated the green fellow. "How rude!"

"Sir, did you hear a ghost laughing?" asked Bronze.

"That's certainly an odd thing to ask a stranger in the woods!" declared the man. "What were you trying to shoot at? A ghost? You cowardly fool, you're trying to shoot at ghosts!"

"It was a reflex," said Bronze, ashamed.

"Who are you two, and what are you doing here?"

"We're on a quest," said Troll, holding his axe at his side. "I'm Troll."

"You are very short and handsome for a troll," said the green-skinned man. "I thought you were human."

"I *am* a human. My *name* is Troll."

"Fascinating," said the man. He looked at Bronze. "And you, sir?"

"I'm Bronze. Nice to meet you. Sorry about disturbing you. I was just scared," admitted the lava monster. He noticed he still had his firearm aimed up at the trees. He lowered his shotgun and chuckled with embarrassment.

"These woods are not safe," said the man as he stepped out of the bush. He was well-dressed in a dark forest green tunic with violet trim and dark brown trousers. The toes on his brown shoes were curled with little leaves sprouting from the ends. "My name is Vicar. You may address me as Vic. Is there anything I can help you find?"

"We shouldn't tell anyone about the ingredients we need," Troll whispered to Bronze.

"Um, do you know if any of these trees are haunted?" Bronze asked Vic.

"Why, yes, there are quite a few. That's why these woods are dangerous. Come on, I will take you to an incredibly haunted section of the forest, but I won't stay with you. I won't risk my soul being ripped from my body."

Bronze gulped loudly, and his entire body trembled. "Our souls ripped from our bodies? Are you serious?"

"Yes," said Vic. "The ghosts there are evil. Follow me."

"Can I see the map, Bronze?" Troll asked.

"Sure." Bronze handed Troll Bi Qu's map.

Troll studied the map as the putrid air surrounding them became stronger. He could sense negativity as they walked further into the forest. His heartbeat quickened in his chest.

A dense fog suddenly surrounded them. The air on their flesh felt sticky and cold.

"Gross! I feel clammy," said Bronze.

"I will go no further," said Vic, pointing at the fog. "You boys, be careful in there. Don't allow the ghosts to touch you. If they do, your body will become absorbed, and your soul will belong to them."

"Absorbed?" asked Troll.

"Good luck," Vic said, turning around and leaving the way he had led them.

"I'm so scared," said Bronze as Troll handed him the map.

Troll clutched his axe. "Come on, let's find the tree we need. I'll cut off some bark, and we'll get out of this creepy place."

"Are you nervous too?" Bronze asked as he chewed on his talons.

"I'd be lying if I said no," Troll responded. He took a deep breath and walked forward.

It became challenging to see in the thickening fog. They crept cautiously and discovered a packed-down dirt path. The negative energy intensified.

We're being watched. I'm so tense. I hate this feeling. Troll tried to breathe in another mouthful of oxygen to calm himself, but the air was like soup. "My heart is pounding," Troll said aloud.

"M-m-mine too," Bronze said, trembling, as he walked behind Troll, close to the warrior's backside. He squeezed his firearm but kept his finger away from the trigger. He didn't want to accidentally shoot Troll or himself.

"Look," Troll said.

There in front of them was the largest, most frightening dark tree either of them had ever seen. They approached the gnarly tree with utmost caution. The tree had jagged black bark growing all around it. The leaves were dead but looked like sharp knives aimed at the dirt below. The bushes and flowers around the tree were dead. Mushrooms grew in a circle surrounding it.

"I don't like this," Bronze said. "That is a faerie circle . . . the willow-o'-the-wisps might be watching us. Do you think that's the tree? I really don't want to go near it."

"My instincts say yes. Wait here," Troll said bravely and headed toward the terrifying tree. As he walked closer, he noticed something odd about its bark. He stopped at the mushroom circle. He was just a few feet away when the fog cleared, and his eyes adjusted. Troll gasped in shock.

There were three faces embedded in the bark of the dark tree. All three faces looked horrified, with their mouths gaping open.

Now I understand what Vic meant about bodies being absorbed. Troll swallowed hard. He stared at them. He couldn't peel his eyes away. He was petrified.

"Troll, what's the matter?" asked Bronze. The lava monster dared not go any closer to the tree.

"Th-th-this was a mistake." Troll respired. "Coming to . . . w-we shouldn't be here—"

"Troll, cut some of the bark so we can leave," Bronze said with shaking knees. "I have a bad feeling!"

Troll closed his eyes. "I have to calm down." He breathed in through his nose and gently out of his mouth. He opened his eyes and raised his axe above his head. He looked at the tree bark above the trapped beings. "Just cut the bark. You can do it," Troll encouraged himself.

"Ssssttoooppppp!" hissed a voice very close to the tree.

Troll drew in a deep breath and didn't move a muscle.

"OooooOoooooohhhhhOooohhhhhh!" screeched the voice.

"It's a ghost!" Bronze squealed as he aimed his shotgun at the tree.

"Please don't shoot me!" Troll exclaimed.

"I'll try to talk to it," Bronze said, keeping his aim as he approached the tree.

"Talk to it?" Troll asked breathlessly. He remained perfectly still, clutching his axe over his head. "What are you talking about?"

"It might work. If I speak Ghost, it may leave us alone," Bronze chirped.

"Wait a minute, you were just scared out of your skin . . . and now you want to talk to it? Do you even know how to speak the Ghost language? Bronze . . . seriously, don't make it angry."

"Don't worry, Bi Qu taught me. Don't move," Bronze said, clearing his throat.

"That is easy for you to say," Troll said as his arms trembled and his muscles burned.

"Blaahhhhh!" Bronze suddenly bellowed.

"Huh?" came a voice extremely close to Troll's body.

Troll twitched in surprise when he felt a cool breeze near him.

"Uughhhhh! Oooo! Blahhh!" shouted Bronze.

"My mother is a *what*?" shrieked the voice near Troll. "How dare you!"

"Great job not making it mad, Bronze!" Troll yelled.

Beside the purple-haired warrior, the form of a ghostly woman manifested.

Troll gasped again when he saw her out of the corner of his eye.

The ghost glared menacingly at Troll but made no move to touch him. "I can feel how tenderhearted you are," she told him, transforming into a small glowing ball of light. She circled his body intimately, starting at his ankles, floating around his toned waist, and stopping at his massive chest.

Troll shivered, sweating buckets.

She changed back into her ghostly form and stared into his blue eyes. "Ah, yes! Your spirit *is* pure! Your dumb friend isn't as virtuous as you are. I will have your soul!" she hissed in ecstasy, reaching for Troll's heart.

"No!" Troll screamed, swung his axe, and struck the tree above the frozen faces.

"My tree! You hurt my tree!" she cried, flying away from Troll to the top of the tree. "Deal with this warrior, but do not harm his heart. I will kill the stupid one!" she roared, charging at Bronze.

Bronze squawked in terror and ran away from the ghost.

Who was she talking to? Troll thought as he pulled his axe from the tree. He looked up, and the tree had massive glowing red eyes. They looked at Troll with evil intent, raised a branch, and struck his midsection.

Troll shrieked as he was thrown into the dirt. The air was knocked out of his lungs.

"You're a troublesome little brat," said a voice within the tree. "Came here to obtain my bark, did you? I overheard your friend. You cannot have my bark. Soon, my lady will obtain your soul and embed it within me!" The tree raised its branch again and forcefully brought it toward Troll.

On his back, Troll raised his axe, and the blade sliced through the wood with ease.

The tree cried in pain, quickly pulling its remaining branches away from the warrior.

Troll stumbled to his feet but kept his axe firmly clutched in his right hand as he brought his left hand to his chest. He watched the evil tree. His hand hovered over the red amulet. Troll closed his eyes and listened to his heartbeat. He tapped the amulet and inhaled sharply. Troll opened his eyes and threw his head back as both hands gripped the axe. The veins in his neck pulsed wildly, and he dropped to his knees.

"I do not know what is going on with you, brat. But your soul will be mine!" the tree said, extending its branches in the direction of Troll again.

Troll screamed as adrenaline raced through his entire body.

The tree branches lunged for him like deadly spears.

Troll became silent, smiled, and ran at a tremendous speed. His legs pumped madly as he circled the evil tree rapidly.

The deadly branches missed him entirely as it couldn't keep up with Troll's swift movements.

Troll leaped, landing on a branch next to the radiating red eyes. Before the tree could defend itself, Troll had taken a thermite grenade from his pouch and pulled the pin. He shoved the grenade into its left eye, jumped down, and ran away from the hollering tree as the grenade exploded, scattering shards of smoldering bark and tiny fireballs.

The ghost abruptly ceased chasing Bronze and gasped. *"Nooo!"* she shrieked, gripping her throat, transfixed with pain from her bond with the evil tree. "My sanctum! No! How could you?" She slowly floated away from Bronze and over toward Troll. Her shuddering arms reached for him before she hesitated and turned into the ball of light and soared overhead.

The tree shrilled in pain as it was set ablaze from the grenade blast. The flames were small initially but strengthened and spread quickly within seconds. "I'm on fire! No! Put me out! I'll die—" the tree exclaimed hysterically.

"If you promise to behave yourself and never harm anyone else, then I will douse the flames," Troll shouted through his rapid breathing and cracking voice as he counted heartbeats to center himself. Troll knew he had to maintain control of his mind and phobia.

"Never!" roared the tree as it launched sharp, knife-shaped leaves at Troll.

Troll lost count. His heart was racing. He stared at the merciless fire. Sweat poured from his forehead. He tried to run, but his feet felt like concrete. His face flushed as his traumatic childhood memory stole his vision.

Those horrible flames.
The fire spared nothing, and the farmhouse turned into ash.
"No!" Troll sobbed, extending his hand.
The fire was so hot.

"Troll, look out!" Bronze yelled as he wrapped his giant arms around Troll and rolled out of the tree's reach.

The sharp, knife-shaped leaves stabbed the ground where Troll had been.

"Damn!" yelled the tree in frustration.

"Are you okay?" Bronze asked, leaping to his feet.

Troll was on his back, trying to control his erratic breathing. "Th-thank—you, Bronze," Troll said, blinking his eyes as the terrifying memory faded from his vision.

Bronze offered him his hand.

Troll took it willingly, and the lava monster pulled him to his feet. Troll brushed off the dirt from his neck and back.

A piece of the dark tree bark was stuck on Troll's armor, and Bronze carefully picked it up. He showed Troll. "Look," Bronze said with an ecstatic smile. "We have the bark. That's the first item. I can't believe it."

"What about me?" the tree howled in agony as the fire engulfed it. "I'm burning! I'll die here. You purple-haired brat! Look what you've done to meeeee—"

"Don't look," Bronze said, grabbing Troll's shoulders and turning him around.

"If I could possess your pure heart right now, I'd have enough power to overcome the flames and thriveeeee—"

"I'm a-afraid," Troll whispered.

"Don't be. We won," Bronze cheered.

"I'm afraid . . . of fire," Troll admitted.

"Really?" asked Bronze, looking at Troll surprised. "Well, you did great. You could've run away, but you faced it."

"I just froze," Troll said, tears burning his eyes. "That always happens. I get so scared. I can't move. I'm not a hero. I'm a coward and an ignoramus."

"No!" shouted Bronze. "You're not! You need some help getting over your fears. I won't tell anyone you were afraid, and I promise you are not an ignoramus, and to hell with whoever said you were."

Like a shooting star, the ball of light suddenly plummeted to Troll's chest. "You are mine!" she yelled, reappearing in her ghost form. Her fingertips phased through Troll's amulet.

Troll screamed, and Bronze attempted to punch the ghost, but his fist went through her.

The tree's prolonged shrieks faded to silence as it died.

The ghost moaned, then evaporated into a breeze.

Troll fell to his knees, breathing hard and clutching the amulet as the crackling sound of the burning tree amplified.

"Are you all right?" asked Bronze.

"I think so," Troll said apprehensively.

"That was close!" Bronze said.

Three new voices erupted over the sound of the snaps and cracks of the burning wood.

"Oh my! We are free," cried a relieved voice.

"We are alive," said another.

"Our souls are back," praised the third voice.

Troll and Bronze looked back at the burning tree.

Out from the flames walked three human beings. Their bodies appeared transparent at first, then became whole the further away they walked from the dead tree. All three humans were young males wearing hunting gear.

The faces I saw! Troll thought as Bronze helped him stand.

"You freed us, good sirs," said the first human as they approached Bronze and Troll. "Thank you so much! My soul has been trapped there for years. You were brilliant to ignite the tree, good sir. That was pure genius."

"Breathing feels so good. We're released from that nightmare. Thank you, brave ones. Especially to you, sir knight. Your clever thinking saved our souls," said the second person to Troll.

"Thank you," said the third man, tears pouring down his cheeks. "I'm so grateful!"

"You're welcome," Troll said, taking a deep breath, unable to control his intense flash of emotions. Tears streamed down his face when he blinked his blue eyes.

"See," said Bronze, smiling. He put a friendly hand on Troll's shoulder. "You are a hero, and you're smart."

I am a good person. I feel confident. Troll embraced the feeling and let it wash over him.

"Come on, guys," said Bronze. "Allow us to lead you out of this awful place, and then we'll continue our quest."

"Bronze, we cannot return to Centerville," Troll whispered. "Let's take them to Rowan's Forest."

"You're right. They could gossip about your heroism, and then Bi Qu's spell won't work."

"And that precious life will be lost," Troll said woefully.

"You'll also have to give up your heart," Bronze said. "I wonder what Bi Qu would do with it?"

Troll shuddered as he imagined the tremendous orange dragon devouring his heart.

TWENTY-FOUR

Troll and Bronze followed the map to a clearing outside the haunted forest. It showed a house in the center of a field. Bi Qu had written the word OGRE and drawn an arrow pointing to it. They stepped out of the trees and gazed in awe at the grassland. It was a relieving transition from being in the dark and frightening forest.

The sun's warm rays tore Troll's attention away from the map. "That feels wonderful!" he interjected. Troll exhaled and closed his eyes. He breathed in deeply. The air in the open field was savory and sweet. He opened his eyes and smiled.

"How are we supposed to get a toenail from an ogre?" Bronze asked, intruding on Troll's moment of peace.

"I don't know," Troll said, gulping when he remembered the mission. His heart trembled at the thought of the giant ogre. "But we'll figure something out."

"What time do you think it is?" asked Bronze, rolling up the map.

Troll looked at the position of the sun in the blue sky. He allowed a gentle hum to escape his lips as he invited the comforting warmth of the sunlight. Troll couldn't stop himself. He closed his eyes again.

The image of fire appeared in his mind.

If what I fear is as warm and heavenly as the sun's rays, is it really so terrifying? Troll saw the burning farmhouse. His heart pounded.

"Troll?" Bronze touched his shoulder.

Troll gasped at his touch and opened his eyes as the memory left his mind.

"Are you okay?"

"Yes." Troll chuckled nervously. "It's around one-thirty. Let's voyage on."

They slowly walked toward the center of the field.

"I left my friends four hours ago. They must be worried sick about me," Troll said. "It does not take four hours to go grocery shopping. I wonder what they're doing right now. I hope they're okay. I feel so guilty that I cannot contact them. I miss John Doe—"

"John Doe? Is he your best friend?"

"Yes, he's like my younger brother. I hope he's all right. He's a wizard, and I know how dangerous the world can be for Antiquities."

"You're magical," Bronze told him. "I feel it radiating from you like the warmth of a fire. It's alluring. Plus, I saw your ability with my own eyes. You were blinding fast, like the wind."

"I am not an Antiquity. I possess no magical abilities," Troll said, surveying their surroundings. "Whatever you're feeling isn't me."

"Has anyone else ever shared with you that they feel a mysterious power coming from you?" asked Bronze.

"I don't think so," Troll said. "John Doe has been my partner for two years, and he's never brought it up."

"I learned how to feel magic in others from Bi Qu."

"We'll have to save this conversation for a later date, Bronze. We need to get back to focusing on our mission. We must figure out the best way to approach the ogre's home. I suggest caution and stealth in dealing with this target. It would not be wise for the ogre to see our approach."

"Don't ogres eat humans?" asked Bronze, giving Troll a concerned look.

Troll swallowed hard and nodded. "Yes, humans are one of their favorite foods." *My life is in grave danger here. I've luckily never had to fight an ogre, but thinking about defending myself against one today makes my heart shudder.*

"Ogres do not usually eat monsters like me," said Bronze. "Maybe I should take care of this guy myself? I have Amber. I bet being shot between the eyes is the last thing he'd expect."

"The skin of an ogre is tough, like a crocodilian. Their bones are hard, like iron. Your bullets may be like mosquito bites—" Troll began to cough uncontrollably. "Ugh! I can . . . smell . . . him." Troll groaned and covered his nose and mouth. A putrid odor, comparable to rotten cabbage dipped in sewer sludge, violated his nostrils.

"You can smell him downwind already? We haven't even ventured close to his house yet. Strange, I cannot smell him—"

"Let's travel low and slow. We can't let him detect us. I suggest we use soil to neutralize our scent." Troll rubbed dirt on his exposed arms.

Bronze groaned as he spread dirt on his chest and belly. "If only this was mud."

"It may not stick very well, but it'll help to prevent him from finding us right away," Troll said, applying dirt to Bronze's back.

"You let me lead this time," said Bronze. "If the ogre sees me, I'll tell him we're selling something. Didn't humans in the past go door to door to homes selling large pamphlets or magazines?"

"I remember something like that," Troll said, thinking about his history lessons. "Can an ogre read?"

"Oh, that's a good question," Bronze said, slapping his right palm into his forehead. "I didn't think of that."

The ogre's massive one-room cabin appeared as they cautiously approached the center of the field. The house was made from the logs of old pine trees. It had a covered porch, two windows, and a front door.

Troll stayed behind Bronze. He removed his axe from its sheath and clutched it firmly.

Bronze kept his hands tight on his Beretta, his index finger on the trigger.

A loud rumbling came from the ogre's porch, followed by a piercing screech.

"Wh-what is that?" Troll groaned.

"What a dreadful noise," said Bronze. "How annoying."

"It's t-tearing . . . apart . . . my m-mind!" Troll screamed, dropping his axe. He covered his ears and whimpered in agony. His entire body quaked until Troll's legs gave out, and he collapsed into the fetal position. Tears raced down his cheeks.

Bronze quickly ripped small strands of fabric from his pants, balled them into balls, and plugged his ears. He glanced at Troll, concerned for his young human friend. "The ogre is snoring. I will try to plug your ears, but I do not know if it will help you," Bronze said as he shredded two more pieces of cloth from his pants and rolled them into balls.

Troll continued to cry out in pain. His strength kept his hands locked around his ears, making it difficult for Bronze to insert the rolled fabric.

"You're sensitive to his snores because you're a human. You'll never reach the porch like this. You stay here. I'll cut his toenail, and we'll leave." Bronze said as he managed to carefully tuck the fabric between Troll's palm and ear.

"P-please . . . hurry," Troll begged.

"Hold on, Troll." Bronze quickly made his way to the porch. He cautiously snuck up the stairs and saw the enormous, fat ogre asleep in a gigantic wooden rocking chair. "*Pee-yoo!* Saying he smells unpleasant is a serious understatement," Bronze whispered to himself as his eyes watered.

The ogre was a horrible mountainous mass of unwashed, flabby flesh in tattered tan clothes. The top of his head and chin were bald, and he didn't have eyebrows or eyelashes. His rough skin looked like red leather. His shoes and socks were off and placed beside the rocking chair. Beside his seat were seven large dark bottles. Four were empty, and three were full of ale. The ogre abruptly stopped snoring. He kept his mouth closed, and his head fell to his right shoulder as his left hand and thigh twitched. The ogre scratched inside his nose, then licked his giant, disgusting lips as he exhaled.

"Oh good, he didn't wake up," whispered Bronze.

Troll's ears rang as he breathed hard on the ground. He rolled onto his back and brought his hands down from his ears to rest on the earth. "What a relief . . . he stopped snoring. I don't think I . . . could have taken any more . . . torture," Troll said, slowly sitting up. He left his axe and clumsily crawled over to the porch steps. Troll struggled to stand. *I'm too weak. Maybe I shouldn't do this? But I won't fail the precious life we've been chosen to save.*

Bronze heard Troll move in the grass. *If I can hear him, then the ogre surely will.* Bronze looked up at the sleeping ogre. So far, the beast had not stirred. The ogre being drunk might be their saving grace. Bronze raced to Troll and saw him leaning on the bottom step. "What are you doing, Troll?" Bronze whispered. "Stay here. It's too dangerous."

"I need to help you," Troll whispered back. "I can feel it within me. I need to do this. I have strength if I touch my amulet. It will help us."

"Where is your axe?"

"I left it. I cannot lift it yet." Troll sighed and shut his eyes. "Please, get it for me. I will regain my strength."

"Okay," Bronze said, climbing down the large stairs.

Troll leaned into the ancient wood of the massive stairs and tapped the amulet on his chest. His heart throbbed as his eyes opened wide and adrenaline pumped through his body. The muscles on his arms and legs flexed. He pushed his chest out, and his head flew back as energy surged through him.

Bronze picked up Troll's axe and turned around. He stared in awe at Troll's body. "Wow! I have never seen anything like that before," Bronze said, bringing the axe to Troll. "Here, now, be careful."

"Thank you," Troll said as he took his axe and smiled. "Let's get that toenail."

"I'll watch the ogre. You cut," Bronze said.

They climbed the large stairs and approached the sleeping ogre.

Troll walked up to the ogre's disgusting feet. The smell was horrific, like festering feces. His stomach churned. Troll removed the fabric from his ears and used them to plug his nostrils. *This is gross but better than breathing in stinky feet.* Troll kneeled before the ogre's big toe and was glad he kept his axe sharpened. He carefully yet forcefully cut into the thick toenail with his axe. It was like carving into a piece of sheet metal.

Bronze watched the ogre's face nervously. *Please don't wake up.*

After two minutes of frightful tension, Troll finished cutting off the toenail. He took the piece and slipped it into his sack. He stood up, returned his axe to its sheath, and gave Bronze a thumbs-up.

Bronze smiled, returning the gesture. He then waved at Troll to assure it was safe to leave.

Troll slowly walked toward Bronze as the ogre adjusted himself in his sleep. He lifted his left foot and unintentionally kicked Troll's back, knocking him over.

Troll gasped and managed to catch himself before faceplanting.

The ogre stirred when he felt the gentle graze of his foot touch something small.

Troll clenched his teeth together as he fearfully looked over his shoulder.

The ogre yawned, and his eyes fluttered open. He leaned forward, looked at his feet, and exhaled when he saw Troll. "Ah! A tender morsel! How delightful. I'm hungry! Hold still, little one," said the ogre, bringing down his left hand to grab Troll.

Troll's arms, neck, and face glistened with sweat that rinsed off the dirt smeared on his exposed flesh. He trembled as he rolled onto his back, not taking his eyes off the ogre. *I can't move . . . he's going to eat me alive!* Troll's heart pounded like a jackhammer.

"Oh no," Bronze said, raising his shotgun and aiming it at the ogre's forehead. He pulled the trigger.

"Darn bugs are out early today," the ogre aggravatedly stated as Bronze's bullet bounced off his impenetrable skull. He brought his left hand away from Troll and up to his face as if to swat away a fly.

Bronze swore under his breath.

"Aim for a soft spot," Troll cried. "His neck!"

The ogre hovered his right foot above Troll. "Don't move, little snack. I will crush your bones and suck out the juices."

Troll screamed as the colossal foot brutally compressed him. The antique wood fractured from the ogre's foot-stomping force, and Troll plummeted through the porch.

"Oh, I ruined my entryway!" blubbered the ogre.

"Troll!" Bronze yelled, shooting his shotgun. This time, his bullet penetrated the ogre's throat, severing his jugular vein.

The ogre touched his neck wound, as his blood rapidly streamed down his torso. A moan escaped his lips as his eyes rolled into the back of his head. The ogre's lifeless corpse crumpled from the rocking chair, and the entire porch collapsed in a loud, shattering crunch.

"I killed him," Bronze cheered. "Oh no, Troll!" He cautiously approached the giant hole. "Troll, can you hear me?"

"That hurt," said Troll, his voice muffled. "Help me! I'm trapped . . . under one of his legs."

"I'm coming," Bronze said, jumping into the hole. He reached under the oversized leg. His muscles strained as he lifted, and his eyes squinched shut.

Troll crawled out, and Bronze dropped the leg.

"Are you injured? How the hell did you survive that?"

"I don't think I'm hurt," Troll sighed with relief, removing the cloth bits from his nostrils. "Euu," he said, covering his nose with his left hand. "If his porch had not been so frail, he would have crushed me. Let's get out of here."

"Troll, I'm relieved you're unharmed, but I'm so confused! How do you not have any broken bones or cuts?"

They climbed out of the collapsed porch, jumped into the field, and swiftly raced to the forest.

"This," Troll said, pointing to the amulet as they ran. "Remember how I said I can't control it?"

"Yes."

"Well, I don't know how it works, but it heals my wounds and protects me."

"Magic." Bronze breathed as they took shelter in the trees.

"No," Troll said quickly. "It's not magical."

"Hey, your armor is cracked," Bronze said, pointing at Troll's chest plate.

"Oh, that happens," Troll said. "It's okay. I'll fix it."

Bronze pulled out Bi Qu's map and studied it.

Troll leaned against a tree and slid down the bark until his rump hit the soil. "I'm so hungry. I have some dry food, but I don't think you'd enjoy it. Does the map show anywhere to eat?"

"You'd best repair your armor before thinking about hunger, Troll. Centerville City has some diners and cafés. We could return?"

"If I go home now, my friends may notice me," Troll said, gently resting his left hand on his amulet. "I can't risk them finding out." *I can't risk my heart—*

"Hey," Bronze said, bringing the map to Troll. "Look, there's a tiny village nearby. I bet they have a place to eat, and it's on the way to the mountain."

"The mountain?" Troll pulled out a rag and the small container of magic polish from his tan sack to repair his armor.

"Yes, that's where Bi Qu has labeled the final ingredient."

"Give me a few minutes to catch my breath and repair these cracks," Troll said, unlatching and removing the clasps around his amulet. "Please don't be startled by this." He took off his chest plate.

"Startled by wha—" Bronze gasped. His pupils shrank when he saw the amulet embedded in Troll's chest. "Is that part of your body?"

"Sort of," Troll said. He squirted the polish onto his rag and rubbed it on the armor. As the crack vanished, Troll returned the vial and rag to his sack. "I don't know how this happened to me," Troll explained, putting on his chest plate and attaching the locks around his amulet. "But I'm grateful it saves my life, though I am unsure *how* it works . . . and *why*."

"Maybe one day you will," Bronze said. "I wonder if that is why Bi Qu knew you were the one to help us?"

Troll shrugged and stood. "Come on, let's get to that village. I'm starving." *I wish I was just an ordinary person . . . living a normal, peaceful life. I hope that one day I can.*

TWENTY-FIVE

Troll and Bronze came to a small village surrounded by a ten-foot-tall ornamental wrought iron fence. They casually entered through the open gate and wondered at the lack of guards. The village was incredibly tiny compared to Centerville City and Kenny Town. It had an antique railroad station with tracks long since closed and dismantled. At the center was a law enforcement building, bank, church, park, school, and recreation facility enclosed by nature preserves. Good energy floated in the air. It was a very peaceful place. Humans and Antiquities lived together in harmony. A few people were walking, going about their daily lives. A group of unhappy children were gathered around a deflated ball in the nearby park. An elf went to them, took their ball, and placed it to his lips. The ball filled with air magically. He returned their ball, the children thanked him, and they happily returned to their game.

"What a nice place," Bronze said. "I like it here. This is where I'd like to retire someday. Maybe have a wife and kids. What say you, Troll?"

Troll let out a playful laugh at Bronze's carefree and innocent abruptness. *Wife and children? A real family?* "I don't know if I'd be a good father and husband, but I would certainly try."

"Look," Bronze said, pointing to a small restaurant. "It's a Chinese food joint! Let's eat there."

"Okay, do you think they'll have crickets and shrews?" Troll asked as they walked to the door.

"What?" Bronze asked, surprised.

"Oh yeah, I don't have the same eating habits other humans do." Troll chuckled sheepishly as he ran his fingers through his lavender hair.

"I'll say," Bronze snorted.

They walked inside and were immediately overtaken by the aroma of ginger, onion, garlic, fish, and sesame oil. They salivated. The restaurant was full of customers enjoying their meals. Only two seats were available at the bar. Troll and Bronze sat on the swivel bar stools and glanced at the menu.

"Let's see . . ." Troll pondered. "Oh, sushi. I haven't had fish in a long time. I will try that. Tuna, avocado, and cucumber sound good. That'll be refreshing and hydrating. Ah, they do have some pan-roasted crickets. Excellent!"

"Troll, even I don't eat insects like that . . . and I'm a monster," Bronze said, fascinated and entertained by Troll's taste. "I think I'll order a bowl of cooked vegetables with noodles and a big piece of raw salmon."

They placed their orders with a friendly green-skinned waitress with bright pink hair.

After she left, Troll sighed, rested his elbows on the table, and put his forehead into his hands.

"What's the matter?" Bronze asked.

"I miss Rowan. She's my faerie friend. Our waitress reminded me of her. Rowan owns the forest I traveled through to get to Centerville."

"Oh! She's *that* Rowan?" Bronze blinked. "I didn't know you knew the princess."

The waitress brought them glasses of ice water.

"Thank you."

"No problem, cutie," the waitress said, winking at Bronze. She skipped back to the kitchen.

He blushed and hid his face under his large hands, giggling shyly. "Oh! Did you hear her? She's getting a good tip from me. She thinks I'm cute; bonus, she's adorable and polite! No one ever thinks a big brute like me is attractive. Aw, I'm embarrassed."

Troll laughed at Bronze's reaction, put his hands on the table, and relaxed into his seat.

"How does she remind you of Rowan?" Bronze asked.

"It's not her personality but her looks. Rowan is special," Troll said, looking at his hands. He twiddled his fingers and thumbs out of nervousness. "She has a lovely laugh, is always in high spirits, and is funny. She makes me feel warm inside. I like being close to her. She's also brave and supportive. She even stood up for me once. She hardly knows me, but she's very kind. Being near her is like being engulfed by an invigorating embrace. You forget the bad situation and are too distracted to feel fear or pain. It's a powerful magic that lets you know you're safe."

"It sounds like you love her," Bronze said, sipping his water.

"I might have a slight crush on her, but I know a relationship would be painful in the end. I'm a human. I'm a young child in comparison to her. She's a faerie who will outlive me. I think I'll know when I fall in love with the person meant for me. I'll feel the warmth and glow in my heart as it flutters uncontrollably. The desire to gaze upon the one I love, to see her and only her. To love and protect her with my entire being. I just haven't found her yet," Troll said, blushing.

Bronze sighed gently, rested his chin on his fists, and batted his eyes at the warrior. "You're so passionate and romantic! I'm such a sucker for tenderness. I might be falling for you," Bronze said sarcastically, letting out a belly laugh.

Troll laughed through his embarrassment from sharing his feelings. He forced himself to sip water as their waitress returned with their meals. She set down their plates and gave each of them a fortune cookie. "Thank you so much," Troll said, ready to eat with chopsticks.

"Yes, thank you," Bronze said, picking up a fork.

"You're welcome, gentlemen," said the waitress as she danced back to the kitchen.

Troll picked up a piece of sushi in his chopsticks and sniffed it before putting it into his mouth. "Oh!" Troll exhaled heartily when the heavenly flavor hypnotized his taste buds. "It's so good," he said, carefully chewing.

"It is pretty good meat," said Bronze, chomping on the raw fish. "Freshly caught, too. How nice."

"I can't believe it!" yelled a voice from the kitchen as Troll and Bronze gulped down the food they were chewing. The kitchen door swung open, and Bi Qu stared at them. "What are you boys doing here?"

"Bi Qu?" Troll asked, confused.

"Boss, you own this restaurant as well? I didn't know that," said Bronze.

"Have you finished the mission?" Bi Qu asked, pounding his hands on their table, almost knocking over their glasses.

"We have two of the objects," Bronze said happily. "We're doing great. We were just hungry."

"Hmm, I'm impressed. I thought it would've taken you longer to get the ingredients. What's the final object you seek?"

"The orb," said Troll as he ate another piece of sushi.

Bi Qu sighed hard as he pulled up a chair and sat with them. He stared intensely at Troll. "That is going to be the hardest one to get. It is heavily guarded. Is your will strong enough, Mr. Troll?"

"Who guards the orb?" asked Troll.

Bi Qu pulled out a scroll from his hanfu. He opened it, and the scroll unraveled over the table and onto the floor. It rolled to the front door, where it stopped.

"Whoa. This looks bad. Is it guarded by an army?" Bronze began to breathe quickly.

Bi Qu cleared his throat, put on small reading glasses, and glanced at the writing on the scroll. "It says, 'NATURE PROTECTS THE ORB.'" He removed the glasses and began to roll up the extra-long scroll.

"That's it?" Bronze questioned before he began to violently cough. His vision faded in and out, and he gripped the table, feeling dizzy.

"Bronze, are you okay?" Troll gasped, putting a supportive hand on his shoulder. "Did you choke?"

"No," Bronze managed to say. "I feel weak, though. Like I'm catching a cold or something."

"Drink some more water," said Bi Qu. "That will help."

Bronze swigged the rest of his water.

Bi Qu sighed, his eyes heavy with worry. "I will fill that glass for you. I'll be right back." Bi Qu left the scroll, took Bronze's glass, and returned to the kitchen.

"Are you sure you're all right?" Troll asked.

"Yes," Bronze said, clearing his throat. "I'm okay now."

Bi Qu returned, handing Bronze the refill. He returned to his task of rolling the scroll. "You boys, eat up, then get back to work. Time is now of the essence."

"It is?" Bronze grumbled.

"*Shí,* I didn't think the precious life would need my spell so quickly, but I need those ingredients before nightfall," Bi Qu said. "If not . . . it'll be too late."

"We won't let that happen," Troll said, standing. "We'll get the orb in time!"

"Mr. Troll, you're not like other men . . . I knew you were destined for this quest. Don't ever second guess yourself. Follow your heart," Bi Qu said, looking into his blue eyes.

"Hey, let's open our fortune cookies!" Bronze cheered, opening the package. "I can't wait to read mine! I love these!"

"My fortune cookies do not lie, gentlemen," Bi Qu said, finally getting the scroll rolled up and returned it to his hanfu. "Let's see what they say. Quickly now, so you can go."

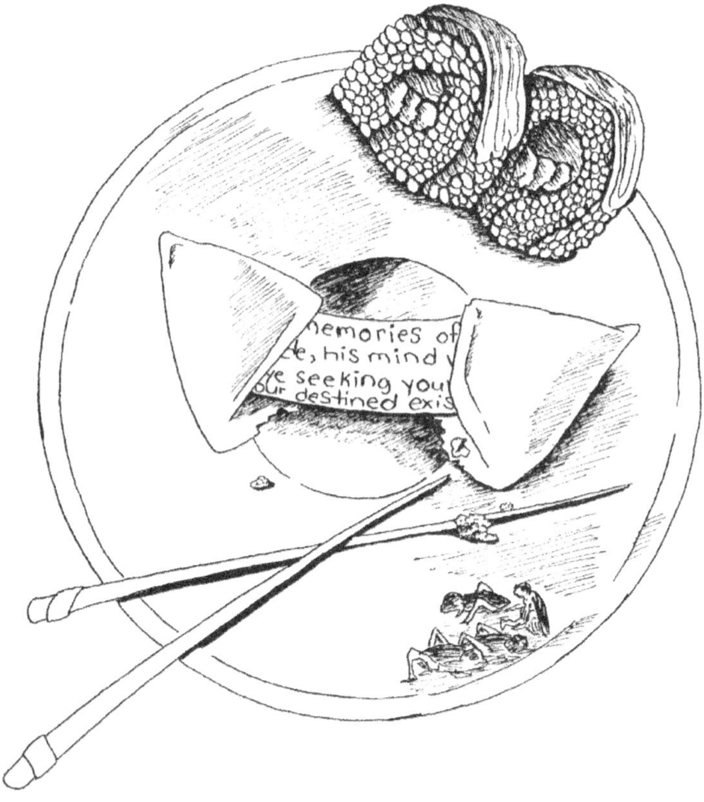

Bronze removed the cookie from the package and smashed it in his hand. He pulled out the little slip of paper and licked up the cookie crumbs on his palm. He squinted his eyes to read the small print. "Mine says, 'YOU WILL

ACCOMPLISH GREAT THINGS IF YOU BEGIN THE JOURNEY NOW.' Oh, that's very similar to what we're doing today." Bronze said proudly. "I like that."

Troll opened his package and snapped the cookie in half to open it. He was not ready to eat it, so he placed the cookie on his plate and read his fortune out loud. "It says, 'YOUR MEMORIES OF THE DARK, YOUR YOUTH FORSAKEN. BEWARE THE GLOWING BLADE; HIS MIND WILL RE-AWAKEN.' What is this? A poem?" Troll gulped but continued to read. His hands trembled. "It keeps going, 'PROCEED WITH CAUTION WHEN NEW ENCOUNTERS START. BEWARE THE EYE SEEKING YOUR HEART.'" Troll's heartbeat increased. He took a deep breath. "I don't like this . . . 'ADVENTURE WILL TAKE YOU A GREAT DISTANCE. DO NOT FEAR. THIS IS YOUR DESTINED EXISTENCE.'" Troll exhaled sharply, dropped the paper onto the table, and looked at Bi Qu in shock and horror. "What does this mean?"

"Bi Qu, what's going on? That's not a normal fortune."

"Did you write this?" Troll demanded.

"I don't write them," Bi Qu admitted. "They're magic. The paper starts out blank. The paper gives you a message once you hold the cookie in your hand. Mr. Troll, you didn't just get a fortune . . . you received a prophecy."

"Is it truly possible that a person is destined to exist?" Troll whispered.

"Wow! I'm a little jealous, but not really. That sounded pretty scary."

"You boys finish your meals," Bi Qu said. "Then get out of here. You have four hours until sundown, and Mr. Troll, remember you need to get back to your friends."

"I don't feel hungry anymore," Troll said, staring at the slip of paper. "What does all of that mean? Is that going to happen right now?"

"No," answered Bi Qu. "Fortunes are perplexing in hinting at events that may not happen for days, weeks, months, or even years. Try not to worry and eat. You'll need your strength, especially for the challenge you're about to face." Bi Qu departed to the kitchen.

"I have a bad feeling," Troll said, picking up a few crickets with his chopsticks and putting them into his mouth. The sweet taste almost washed away his fears. Troll eyeballed the piece of paper again. He opened his small sack and put the fortune inside.

TWENTY-SIX

Rowan flew as fast as she could. She saw the opening at the end of the portal. She was almost to Centerville. *I have to make it!*

The pterodactyl on her tail reached for her with its sharp talons and beak.

Rowan shrieked and put all her energy into maneuvering away from the pterodactyl. She kept a powerful grip on the Kantharos as her hands and body glistened with sweat. Her heart pounded wildly.

The dinosaur opened its mouth as wide as possible, ready to snap off Rowan's feet.

Rowan exploded out of the portal. *"Claudere!"* She could hear the pterodactyl's frustrated roar end abruptly as it slammed shut. Rowan turned invisible and squealed as she fluttered down Centerville's streets. She soared over a male merchant selling knapsacks at the marketplace.

The little merchant heard her wail but saw no one. He looked above in fright. "What is it, Magical Sky?" he called, his arms outstretched.

Rowan calmed herself as she glided through the city. She wiped the sweat from her forehead and slowed her breathing. "I can't believe I made it," Rowan said, flying to the park where her baby animal friends lived. Sighing with relief, she landed and sat under the maple tree where she and Troll conversed. Rowan became visible so her animal friends could see her. "Come to me, children."

The baby animals heard her voice. They stopped their exploration of the park and ran to her. She held her arms out and happily embraced them. The little turtle was the last animal to come up to Rowan. It waddled to her leg and extended its head to look at her. Rowan cooed, picked up the turtle, and kissed its cheek.

"Oh, my little friends," Rowan said, sighing with relief. "I am so glad to see you! I was in such danger. I do not know how that dinosaur came to be in England. I thought all the dinosaurs thrived in the Southern States wetlands. He did have wings, so perhaps he migrated?" She shrugged her shoulders and leaned against the tree. "I am safe now," she told herself, unclenching her grip on the goblet. "What a relief the Holy Grail isn't damaged. Look what I have, little babies. My sister told me that anyone who drinks from this will be blessed and possibly gain longevity or eternal youth."

The animals looked at the goblet with puzzled expressions.

"My father said it could harm mortals, but Tiffan said he lied because he didn't want me to be burdened. I want to trust my sister. We've never gotten along, but I want that to change," Rowan said as she studied the goblet. "It's so beautiful. How could something this pretty harm anyone?" She stood up and remembered the merchant. "He had knapsacks at his shop. I'll go get a knapsack to keep the goblet safe. I have just the right person in mind who should drink from this. Goodbye, for now, little friends. I will be back later to check on you. I love you all."

The baby animals watched Rowan vanish. They sniffed the spot where she had sat and glanced around at one another, concerned for their adoptive mother.

Rowan flew to the marketplace and grabbed a knapsack from the merchant's table. *I'll just borrow this!* she thought happily as the same male merchant gawked in surprise when he saw the knapsack rise into the air and vanish.

"Thank you," Rowan sang.

"Y-y-you're welcome, Magical Sky," said the frightened merchant.

Magical Sky? I like that! Rowan turned visible on her way to the South Gate. "I want Jeer to see me coming."

Jack Geyerwulf had an exhausting yet satisfying night full of repairs and intimacy. He was on cloud nine as he headed to the Abode after Corin had radioed him the address. As Jack followed the directions in his database, he saw Rowan. She carried a knapsack and headed toward the South Gate. "Hey, Rowan!" Jack called.

She did not stop. "Jeer! Jeer!" Rowan shouted.

Rowan has terrific hearing. She heard the dangers in the forest. How could she not hear me now? I don't know her well, but I know when a woman is distracted. She wasn't even invisible! Something must be wrong. I'd best go after her.

The goblin gatekeeper, Jeer, sat relaxed at his desk as he read a newspaper. He reluctantly glanced up to see Rowan approach. He sighed, folded his newspaper in half, and set it aside. He stood and crossed his arms over his chest, glaring at Rowan. "Just what do you think you're doing flying around? You should be invisible!"

"Sir, I'm sorry I broke the law, but I must show you something important! You're the only person who is worthy of this gift."

"A gift?" asked Jeer. "Just what are you up to, faerie? I know your kind all too well. Nothing but trouble! Do you *want* to be banished from Centerville City?"

"No! I am not up to trouble. I know you are always in a bad mood, and I wish to make you feel better."

"Really? How are you going to do that?"
"With this!" Rowan showed him the Kantharos.
"A cup?"

"This is not just a normal drinking goblet, Jeer," she said, soaring to the fountain. She filled the Kantharos with water and flew back to him. "If you drink from the Holy Grail, you will be happy. I cannot bear to see you so irritated a moment longer."

"Really?" Jeer asked, shocked. "No one has ever gone out of their way to help my mood. I'm surprisingly touched by your kindness. So, this drink will cheer me up then?"

"Yes, sir," Rowan said, putting the goblet in his hands.

Jeer looked at the Kantharos and then back at Rowan. He grinned and brought the Kantharos to his lips.

Jack reached the South Gate just as Jeer took a sip. "Hi, Rowan. What are you doing over here?"

"Oh, Jack! You're just in time. Our friend Jeer is about to be the happiest goblin in Centerville City."

"Is he the *only* goblin in Centerville City?" Jack asked. "What's he drinking?"

Jeer suddenly choked, dropped the Kantharos, and fell to his knees. He looked at Rowan with frightened eyes as his left hand gripped his throat. Jeer reached his right hand to her before he pulled it back and grabbed his stomach.

"He's choking!" Jack cried, rushing over to help the goblin.

Jeer opened his mouth; it appeared he may become sick. A tiny squeak escaped the goblin's lips, and his legs began falling to pieces. Literally—

"Wh-what's going on?" Rowan asked, fearfully and confused.

Jeer's legs broke into six pieces and crumbled to the ground. The six pieces began to sprout dark green fur and moved independently. Jeer gasped again and emitted another squeak as his arms also fell to pieces. The six fragments that used to be his arms hit the dirt with a thump, immediately growing fur.

"What is *happening* to him?" Jack asked Rowan.

Rowan backed away in fear, trembling. "I don't—th-this was not supposed to happen! I d-don't know what's happening—I'm so sorry!"

Jeer's torso and head were next, breaking into twenty-four pieces. Again, as soon as the pieces hit the ground, they grew green fur.

Rowan and Jack watched, horrified, as all thirty-six furry pieces that were once Jeer twitched around and grew long brown arms and legs. Eyes appeared next, then horrible, wide-open mouths with sharp fangs; finally, tiny horns spread all over their furry bodies like a demonic pox.

"What are these things?" Jack asked.

"I don't know! This is entirely my fault!"

"We can fix this. We just need to gather all these little guys and take them to the warlock John Doe is obsessed with. He has to know what to do."

"I hope so," Rowan said with tears pouring down her face. She walked up to the swarm of little critters and keeled down to them. They were each about the size of a squirrel. "Jeer, if you can understand me . . . we're going to help you."

The little critters looked up at her and smiled.

"You're not angry with me?"

They looked at one another and then back at Rowan, their beady eyes narrowed. They laughed maniacally as one lunged at her.

Rowan yelped and fell over. She tried to crawl away, but the critters charged at her. "Jack!" Rowan exclaimed in fear.

Jack rushed over and swatted his arms at them. "Stop, little Jeers! Stop it! Don't hurt Rowan. We're trying to help you!"

They did not listen. Instead, they grabbed the desk and broke it apart with surprising strength. They used the wooden shards from it to strike Jack.

Being made primarily out of metal, Jack was not harmed but provoked. "Cut that out!" he yelled in anger. "I don't want to hurt you."

Rowan attempted her root spell to stop the critters. *"Amicae radices funes flunt!"* Tree roots popped out of the ground and tried to wrap around them, but the critters were too small and quick to get caught and ran into the city.

"Come on," Jack ordered, grabbing Rowan's hand. "We have to go after them. They're going to hurt someone!"

Screams filled the streets as the little critters attacked whoever they came across.

"Inform the mayor! They are invading my shop!" a storekeeper cried. He gazed in horror as five critters destroyed his clothing store, and one danced erratically with a mannequin.

"They're in my hair!" shrieked a woman as she plucked three critters from her head and threw them to the ground. "Little perverts!"

"Hey! That's my sandwich!" yelled a law enforcer. "That's my *personal* sandwich, and I want it back!" he chased the little critter. "Give it back right now!"

The critter ate the sandwich and growled at the human before vomiting the undigested food back onto the law enforcer. Horrified, the human ran away.

Jack radioed Corin as he chased after the little critters. "Corin, come in!"

"Yes, Jack, what is it?" Corin replied.

"We have a problem!"

"Oh no, what now?"

"Rowan gave that goblin gatekeeper something weird to drink, and he changed into several evil critters. They are terrorizing the city!"

"Try to detain them."

"That is difficult, Corin."

"Just don't harm them! Where are you? I'll get John Doe, and we'll come help you."

"Where's Troll?"

"I sent him to the grocery store."

"I think we'll need his help!"

"Troll, did you copy that?"

Static—

"Troll?" Corin asked again over the radio.

Static—

"That's so weird," Corin said. "I wonder what happened to him?"

"I don't know, but one of the critters is trying to eat a baby!"

"Jack! Jack!"

Jack ignored Corin's voice in his ear. He rushed over to a struggling mother trying to pull her infant away from one of the critters. The woman screamed in fear as the critter enlarged its mouth to devour her wailing child.

Jack grabbed the critter, and it released the baby.

The mother held her child tightly and ran away.

Jack accidentally squeezed too hard and crushed the critter in his hand. He stared at the blood as the other thirty-five critters winced. They had felt their friend die. All of their angry eyes were on the cyborg. Jack swallowed hard and looked over at Rowan. He felt her eyes turn into daggers. "I didn't mean it."

"Jack, you killed a Jeer," Rowan stated in shock.

The thirty-five remaining critters rushed at Jack. They tore at his legs and scrambled to remove the screws that kept his joints together. Some of the little Jeer critters even climbed up his back. They roared with anguish and loathing.

Jack, genuinely scared, panicked and flailed his limbs. He used his strength to throw the little Jeers from his body before he pressed the button on his wrist and changed his left hand into his energy gun.

The critters bared their fangs and charged him again.

Jack reflexively fired his energy gun. As the smoke cleared, Jack was horror-struck at the smoldering corpses of the Jeer critters. He had destroyed them all. He lifted his faceplate and looked at Rowan with sorrow, his eyes full of despair. "Wh-wh-what have I done?"

At that moment, the mayor, the riot police, and the Centerville City military arrived and surrounded Jack with their weapons aimed.

"You! Cyborg!" the mayor yelled. "You are under arrest!"

"Corin," Jack said.

"Yes, Jack?"

"I'm in trouble."

"Number 1-1-9-8-9, come in please," the therasapien said into his radio as he hid in the shadows.

"Yes, 7-8-9-0," Unna's voice rang. "What do you have to report?"

"I lost sight of the purple-haired warrior after he arranged to fight in an arena match tomorrow."

"Are his companions still in Centerville?"

"Yes, madam. They've all separated, but I feel they will be reunited in prison. The cyborg and faerie have been arrested for the murder of a gate-keeper."

"Was the gatekeeper a human?"

"No, an Antiquity," he answered.

"They must be a criminal gang."

Heeb and John Doe strode past the concealed therasapien.

"I see one of them now! I will stalk and report back later."

"No, if their friends have been arrested, there's no need to continue following them. I'd rather you search the entire city and find the warrior. I was informed he has knowledge about therasapiens. He might have spotted you and taken cover."

"No one can hide from me! I will find him!"

"Very good, contact me when he is located. 1-1-9-8-9 out."

"I really appreciate your help, Heeb. Troll never radioed me about finding Magnum, so I'm glad we're on the hunt!"

"I'm only helping you because that demon dog could be dangerous. I take it you brought this creature here from another one of your portals?" asked Heeb.

"Yes, sir," said John Doe. "He's really cool. He's tried to eat me a few times, but I'm definitely his master."

"Your enthusiastic naiveté frightens me. Every lesson we've attempted has ended in disaster."

"You can't win them all, but let me tell you—in detail—about my mastery of opening portals! It all started with my interest in centaurs—"

Heeb rolled his eyes. It was around five-thirty, and he was exhausted from spending such a long time with John Doe. "I will cast a location spell," Heeb said, interrupting John Doe's story. "I want you to watch me do it. Learn my movements. Listen to the tone I use when I chant. I don't want you to say a word. Not one word. Just stand there. Look pretty."

John Doe nodded. "I can be pretty."

Heeb stepped back and put pressure on his left foot. He stepped sideways and raised his arms. Heeb balled his hands into fists, brought them to his face, and opened his fingers wide. "Map of Centerville City, appear before me. *Ad canem daemonium collcandum.*"

Like tiny stars, a cloud of glowing dust swirled into a giant flat map that floated before them. Each twinkling celestial body represented a location in Centerville City. One in particular glowed brighter than the others. "Found him," said Heeb, smiling. "He's at Centerville City Hall."

"Wow!" John Doe breathed, looking at the magical map. "This is amazing! I've never done this. I can't wait to try it. I wonder why he's there?"

"Let's find out."

"Aren't we going to train anymore?"

"John Doe, I'd rather help you find your demon dog than spend another moment training you."

"I'm glad you care so much!" John Doe exclaimed, hugging Heeb.

Heeb exhaled when John Doe's arms unexpectedly gripped him. He flicked his fingers, and the starry map vanished.

John Doe squeezed him.

"Okay, John Doe," Heeb said, sighing. "You have to let go if we are to find him."

"Right," John Doe cheered, releasing the warlock.

"How does Troll tolerate you?"

"Well, he doesn't really—"

"I'm not surprised," Heeb said under his breath.

Mayor Lanus and Reginald trudged by listlessly. Their faces were aggravated, and their bodies were tense.

"—I know that guy with the mayor. Troll saved him earlier," stated John Doe.

"What did Troll save him from?"

"Dying."

"Where are they going? It looks like they're on their way to the South Gate. Come, John Doe, I want to see what is the matter," Heeb said, swiftly following them. "Hello, Mr. Mayor!"

John Doe hurried alongside Heeb.

Mayor Lanus heard Heeb but ignored him.

That's unusual. We usually get along exceedingly well. Something terrible must've happened. The closer Heeb got, the better he could see how drawn the mayor's face was, his mouth a thin, serious line. "What is wrong?" Heeb asked, catching up to them.

Mayor Lanus stopped and glanced at John Doe. "*Your* cyborg friend!" the mayor snarled, pointing at him. "He is going on trial at six o'clock in the Centerville Courthouse. You best show up if you and your other friends want to see his sentencing."

"Jack . . . is being locked up? For what?" asked John Doe, flabbergasted.

"Y'all want to see what he did? Come here!" yelled the mayor. He led them to the South Gate and saw where Rowan had left the Kantharos on the ground. "Do not touch the goblet. It could be cursed," warned Mayor Lanus.

"Is that safe to touch?" John Doe asked Heeb.

Heeb kneeled and studied the goblet. "It should be safe, so long as you do not drink from it."

Mayor Lanus cautiously picked up the Kantharos and handed it to Heeb. "Can you get rid of this evil magic? Get it out of my city! Dispose of it into the forest. It brings shame to our glorious landmark and culture."

"Yes, sir. I think I know what this is, and it *does* belong in the forest. How did it come to be here?" Heeb questioned.

"Some insane faerie who claimed this magical goblet was the Holy Grail cursed Jeer. She turned him into little monsters, and *his* cyborg friend helped her kill them," shouted the mayor again, pointing at John Doe. "They are both murderers and will stand trial in court to have their sentences."

"Whoa, I'm in shock." John Doe breathed. "They would not have killed him on purpose."

"*They?* You mean you know the faerie as well?" asked the mayor.

"Um . . ." John Doe gulped. "It depends on the faerie. I know a lot of Antiquities—"

"Whatever!" Mayor Lanus screamed.

"Mayor Lanus, Jeer's death might've been an accident. Don't be so quick to call them murderers before the trial," suggested Heeb.

"Just get rid of it," Mayor Lanus ordered, looking deeply into Heeb's brown eyes. He turned to Reginald. "I want you to organize a team and guard this gate until I can find a replacement for Jeer. Make sure these two Antiquities put that goblet into the forest."

"Yes, sir," said Reginald, opening the gate. "I'll find two good men to be on my team."

"Good," said the mayor as he glared at John Doe. "I'll see you in court." He walked away, heading to City Hall.

"Come on, John Doe. Let's do as he asked."

Still in shock, John Doe followed Heeb into the forest.

"I know this goblet needs to be left here, but in no specific spot," Heeb said. "Though I would like it to be out of sight. This artifact is powerful and should not fall into the wrong hands. Wait here. I'll be right back."

"Okay, so you're not going to hide it?"

"No, just wait there."

"But will an animal eat me?"

"You'll be fine, John Doe!"

"I have a bad feeling."

"Nothing will eat you, although I've heard rumors of a new female red dragon in our area. It's said that she's large and mean and has been terrorizing the neighboring cities."

"*Red* dragon? Female? Female dragon? Did you say a *red* dragon?"

"Hush now, let me dispose of this," Heeb said as he securely tucked the Kantharos into a tree trunk. "There, that should be a good spot." He returned to a very nervous-looking John Doe. "Are you all right?"

"Yes. Just a little anxious about dragons."

"Don't worry about dragons. I am friends with Silvia, after all. They're not so bad. Now, come on, let's get your demon dog, and I'll try to convince Mayor Lanus not to sentence your friends to death or whatever he is planning."

"To *death?*" John Doe squeaked, tucking his chin further in his scarf.

Magnum was at Centerville City Hall sniffing a fire hydrant. *Such a fascinating canine smell this impressive red pillar has! I have never seen or smelled anything like this before. Has every dog in the city indicated this spot as a territorial dominion? The aroma is intoxicating. I could stay here all day.*

"Magnum," called John Doe behind the demon dog.

Magnum grunted and looked over his shoulder to see John Doe and Heeb.

"Master, I have discovered this wonderful statuette. It smells like other dog creatures. It is some kind of totem, yes?"

"Um, it's not what you think," John Doe said and looked at Heeb. "I feel uncomfortable."

Heeb covered his mouth and held back his laughter.

"No," said Magnum. "It's *exactly* what I think. It is great! I really like it."

"Magnum, you can't run off like that again."

"It wasn't my fault. A demonic woman was after me," Magnum said, sniffing the fire hydrant again. "Oh, blissful! You could get drunk from the smell. You both should try this."

"No," said Heeb.

"We need to go inside for a trial. Apparently, Jack and Rowan killed someone."

"That eccentric cyborg and goody-two-shoes faerie actually killed someone?" Magnum asked, taking his nose away from the fire hydrant. "I am exceedingly enthusiastic about attending. I hope they're given a death sentence. Let's go in and watch!"

"Your friend is great," said Heeb sarcastically.

Corin entered the crowded courtroom. The walls were tall and dark, decorated with antique oil paintings of judges. Their painted eyes stared at Corin, following his every move, judging him. The air was stale and sticky. It smelled like old wood furnishing, and cheap shampoo had been used to try and hide the mustiness. Large windows allowed in beams of sunlight that revealed small particles floating in the air. Corin's stomach turned. The space station was always clean, and dust didn't exist. The room was loud, full of people talking. Corin heard the frustration in their voices and saw the scowls on their faces. The feeling in the room was very stressful. Corin tried to calm himself as he sat in the front row. His chair creaked loudly. It was made of hardwood that immediately felt uncomfortable under his rump. The room was very warm, but the angry citizens sitting behind him, gossiping about Jack and Rowan, made the room feel even hotter. Corin slumped in his chair so the enraged residents wouldn't engage with him.

A security guard paced back and forth at the front of the courtroom, staring at the empty seats where a jury would be seated.

"What a hideous carpet! The mayor needs to hire a fashion designer!" John Doe exclaimed from in the hallway.

Heeb, John Doe, and Magnum entered the courtroom.

"Please keep your voice down," Heeb said.

Corin saw them. *Oh, thank goodness!*

"There's Corin," John Doe said, leading them.

Mayor Lanus entered through a door behind the witness stand wearing a black robe as they sat beside Corin.

"Is he the judge for their trial?" asked John Doe.

"I think so," said Corin.

"Jack and Rowan are screwed," John Doe said, sighing heavily.

Twelve individuals walked through the main doors and sat in the jury box. The trial was getting ready to begin.

"Let me try to talk to the mayor," Corin whispered, hurrying to the front of the courtroom bench.

"I wouldn't . . . let me talk to him later," Heeb whispered.

"Oh, man. I don't think Corin heard you," John Doe said, slapping his palm onto his forehead.

"Excuse me, Mayor Lanus. May I please speak with you?" asked Corin.

"Make it quick," the mayor said, tugging on his robe.

"I'm sure all of this is a misunderstanding, sir. Jack and Rowan would never kill anyone on purpose. It had to be an accident."

"You didn't tell me a faerie was in your party, Mr. Degodi," said the mayor sternly.

"What does it matter? I thought all Antiquities are welcome here."

"They are, but faeries are troublemakers. She was supposed to be invisible. Fae-folk who remain invisible can't cause any problems. She's trouble, Corin, and if you want to live in my city, you best rethink your choice of friends."

"Mr. Mayor, if Rowan and Jack are found guilty, I should be too."

"You didn't do anything, boy. Don't be so foolish. You want me to spare your friends if they're found guilty? I will . . . but only if you tell the faerie to leave my city."

"If she goes, my friends and I go too. I'll destroy our contract—"

"That's not how things work," stated Mayor Lanus. "I know you crave status, power, and wealth, but you'll never have those things with a faerie around. You want to be rich, don't you?"

Corin swallowed hard but nodded.

"I'll put you and your friends to work as soon as possible, but only if you aren't friends with that troublemaker. Now, go sit down. The trial needs to begin," said the mayor, exiting the door behind the stand.

Corin blinked several times, drying the tears in his eyes. On his way back to his seat, he touched the radio in his ear. "Troll, can you hear me? Come in, please."

Static—

Damnit! Where are you, Troll? I really need to talk to you.

"Corin, is everything all right?" asked John Doe as Corin sat down.

"John Doe, could you try to contact Troll? I think something is wrong with my communicator. I can't get through. Maybe you can?"

"I'll try," John Doe said. "Troll? Hey, Troll, can you hear me?"

Static—

"I'm only hearing static."

"That's all I could hear also."

"I really hope Troll's okay. It's not like him to be gone this long and not contact me. He tells me everything. I don't know where he could be!"

"He was going to set up a match at the arena, and I asked him to grab some food at the market, but that was this morning. Do you suppose that the therasapien followed us? What if he snuck into the city and did something to Troll?"

"Magnum," John Doe said, turning to the demon dog. "I need a favor."

"You now ask a favor of me? You, who does not keep his word?"

"You're not still sore about the fact that I won't send you home, are you?"

"Of course. It bothers me that you lord it over me. But lucky for you, I like this dimension. Not that you care," Magnum muttered. "So, what do you want?"

"Well, I'd like you to fly around the city and look for Troll."

"John Doe, we just found your demon dog. You cannot ask him to go alone in the city again," Heeb expressed, annoyed.

"Yeah," agreed Magnum, fiddling with his talons. "Besides, I'm not Troll's babysitter! A large man like that with purple hair stands out in a crowd. Inform the mayor and have his people look for him. Oh, wait, he can't. Because he's busy punishing your other two stupid friends."

"Magnum, please," John Doe pleaded.

The demon dog sighed hard. "Fine!" *I only do this because I respect Troll.* "I'll fly around and see if I can find the purple-haired fool. If you ask me, he should be tied to a tree! But who's asking for my opinion?" He flapped his large wings and leaped into the air, flying out an open window.

"I hope he can see Troll," Corin said. "I'm worried."

"I think we need to worry about Jack and Rowan, too. What's going to happen to our friends?" John Doe asked fretfully.

A side door to the courtroom opened, and armed military men walked Jack and Rowan to the stand.

Jack was restrained by hefty alloy rigging shackles around his wrists and ankles.

Rowan also wore small iron chains around her slender wrists and ankles. Her empty knapsack had been confiscated.

"If a penance is applied to Jack, I can try to pay it after court," Corin said.

"What about Rowan?" asked John Doe.

"Well, she's a princess . . . I'm sure she has wealth she hasn't told us about. Rowan is an honest faerie," Corin said. "She'll do the right thing and confess it was all *her* fault."

"All her fault?" asked John Doe, confused. "Corin, we don't know what—"

"This court is now in session," announced a bailiff. "All rise for the honorable Judge Lanus."

Everyone stood as the mayor walked into the room behind the stand. His black robe had been adjusted, and he wore a white barrister's wig. "Be seated. Let's get this over with," Judge Lanus said, sighing loudly.

Corin's shoulders felt tense. He heard some mumbling whispers in the crowd. He glanced around the courtroom at the angry citizens.

Judge Lanus scowled, looking through the paperwork about the case. "Rowan Fae, approach the podium. Charges and allegations are failure to disguise appearance within city borders, failure to follow civic safety regulations, endangering citizens with an unknown magical artifact, and manslaughter. Rowan Fae, how do you plead?"

Rowan stood up but didn't go to the podium. "Not guilty. I did not know my sister lied to me. My father told me the Kantharos could harm mortals, but he did not say how. My sister, however, told me the Holy Grail would bless a person. She told me the Kantharos *was* the Holy Grail. I only made myself visible to help Jeer. I wanted to see him smile. I did not know Jeer would transform into all of those little critters."

"Spontaneous utterance!" said Judge Lanus.

"What is tha—"

"Proceed!"

"Jack *did* kill them, but it was to protect the good people of this city."

"Rowan," Jack gulped, practically trembling in his seat.

"Shut up!" Judge Lanus yelled at Jack.

"I d-d-don't think you're aware of this, b-but you're not helping me by admitting that I *did* k-kill him," Jack stuttered timidly.

"Be silent!" exclaimed Judge Lanus.

"I'm sorry, Jack," Rowan said quickly. "I only want to speak the truth."

"Silence, both of you!" Judge Lanus shouted, striking the gavel. "If you continue your disobedience, I'll hold you both in contempt! Rowan Fae, take your seat. Jack Geyerwulf, approach the podium."

Jack rose apprehensively and shuffled to the podium at the front of the courtroom.

Rowan sat with tears in her eyes.

"The charge is possession of a concealed weapon, discharging an illegal weapon in city limits, the murder of an innocent citizen of Centerville City. How do you plead, Jack Geyerwulf?"

"I plead not guilty to the charge of murder," Jack said. "I was acting out of self-defense and trying to save people. There were plenty of witnesses who saw the entire thing. They'll tell you that it was just an accident. I didn't mean to kill all of the little Jeers."

"Take your seat, Mr. Geyerwulf. Witnesses, prepare to describe what y'all saw," ordered Judge Lanus.

Jack slowly returned to his seat, slumping over with his elbows resting on his knees as he held his head in his metal hands.

The mother whose child Jack had rescued sat on the witness stand. She looked anxiously into the crowd and then frowned at Jack.

"Madam, state your name," said the judge.

"Judy."

"Judy, explain what you witnessed."

"Th-th-that cyborg c-c-crushed a piece of Jeer in his hand."

"Don't you remember that I saved your child?" Jack asked calmly.

"I can't remember . . . I'm too nervous!" Judy cried.

"I'm terrified of being in this courtroom, too," Jack admitted.

"I'm not afraid of that," she admitted. "I'm afraid of you!"

"Please don't be scared of me . . . I saved your baby. It was going to be eaten . . . you have to remember. I grabbed the small monster so you could run away with your child."

"I remember the crushing sound of Jeer's tiny bones," she said as she wept.

"I just squeezed him—it was an accident, I promise."

"No badgering the witness!" commanded the bailiff.

"I wasn't. I'm sorry," said Jack.

"Next witness," called the judge.

The law enforcer whose sandwich had been taken by a Jeer critter sat on the witness stand.

"State your name," instructed the judge.

"Bruce."

"Bruce, explain what you saw."

"I was on my lunch break, you see. Then I saw that faerie and cyborg with Jeer before he transformed into these . . . little . . . terrors, and one of them ran up to me and took my sandwich! I didn't even get to take a bite!"

"But you saw me trying to protect the people, right?" asked Jack.

"Well, my memory is a little fuzzy. I am an officer of the law, so I'm very busy. I might have been helping another person at the time."

"I saw the little Jeer throw up on you, and then you ran away," stated Rowan.

"That is—debatable. I can't quite remember . . ." Bruce looked at Judge Lanus. "Oh shit, am I fired?"

Judge Lanus sighed hard and rubbed his eyebrows. "You may step down, Bruce."

"I deserve a free lunch after this," Bruce complained as he returned to his seat.

"It must be hard to find good help nowadays." Jack chuckled.

"Shut up!" barked Judge Lanus.

After multiple witnesses shared their information, the judge allowed all twelve jurors to reach a unanimous decision for a verdict.

"Your honor, we find Rowan Fae and Jack Geyerwulf guilty," a jury member read from a slip of paper.

"Oh no," John Doe whimpered.

"This is terrible," Corin said, exhaling in shock. *He said he'd spare them! What the hell? Say something you—*

The entire courtroom erupted in chatter.

"Order! I will have order! Order, I say!" Judge Lanus yelled, slamming the gavel multiple times to regain courtroom control. "I have heard enough. There are enough witnesses and evidence to prove that the cyborg and faerie are in the wrong. Rowan Fae, I find you guilty on all charges, and you are hereby banished from our fair city. Jack Geyerwulf, I find you guilty of second-degree murder, and you will spend the next twenty-five years in prison . . . unless you can pay the penance."

Rowan gasped. "I'm banished? I can't stay with my friends? This can't be happening."

"How much is Jack's bail?" Corin asked, loud enough for Judge Lanus to hear.

"Six hundred thousand coins! You, sir, you're one of his colleagues," said Judge Lanus to Corin. "Are you taking responsibility for him?"

"What?" Corin inhaled, embarrassed that Judge Lanus made the people in the courtroom aware of his connection to Jack and Rowan.

The courtroom was suddenly quiet.

Corin immediately felt sick when he saw everyone staring at him. He couldn't think and blurted, "Oh, my gods, I will be broke forever."

The courtroom grew loud again from the voices of angry people in the crowd.

"Is that all you are concerned about?" asked Heeb.

"N-no, of course not," Corin said nervously.

"I could bust him out of jail," John Doe suggested. "That'd be easier."

"John Doe, don't help me," Jack said.

"I *will* pay his penance, Your Honor," Corin said dolefully over the crowd. "I won't be able to right away, but I can give you what money I have left until I can work to pay the rest. We promise this will not happen again."

Judge Lanus gave a smug look when he saw Corin's misery.

"His friends won't need to pay anything," Meike Stormhild said, standing a few seats behind Corin.

Judge Lanus's smug expression immediately changed to surprise when he heard Meike's lovely German voice ring out through the crowd.

"May I approach the podium, your honor?" Meike asked.

"Ms. Stormhild, of course. I will allow this."

"Thank you," she said, walking to the podium. "I, for one, know this cyborg did not mean any harm. I embedded a microchip into his throat to show that he was under my care before he met with Rowan and performed this . . . messy ordeal. I promise you he will be under strict surveillance. If he causes any problems, I will be the first to know about it and will report him."

"Thank you, Ms. Stormhild," Judge Lanus said, swallowing his pride. "I am willing to qualify this as a special case of house arrest. He's in your hands."

Jack looked over at Meike, shocked. "You installed a microchip in my throat?"

"Yes, darling. You were in my care, after all. I'm a responsible mechanic. Your Honor, will this cyborg be participating in the arena?"

"That is correct, Ms. Stormhild. I have that information from the arena manager. His friend Troll set up their match for tomorrow at ten o'clock in the morning. What are you suggesting?"

"I'm suggesting, instead of his friends paying, that he earns the penance fighting in the match. All his earnings will automatically go to City Hall because you own the arena."

"I like that. What a brilliant idea. Jack Geyerwulf, I need you and Corin Degodi to meet with me in my private office immediately to go over the arena's rules," said Judge Lanus, slamming the gavel. "Court is adjourned! Everyone, get out!"

"I'll wait for you in the hallway, darling," Meike told Jack as she, John Doe, and Heeb followed the crowd out of the courtroom. The bailiff removed Jack's shackles and allowed him and Corin to follow the mayor through a backroom.

"I'm banished . . . my friends . . . I failed them. Why didn't they try to help me?" Rowan whispered to herself as tears poured down her face. The bailiff removed her bonds and led her to the hallway.

"This is the nastiest carpet I've ever seen!" John Doe hollered in the main hall.

"Yes, we know of your disgust for the carpet!" Heeb exclaimed, irritated.

"I'm going to rip it up."

"Don't do that, John Doe. I'm going to the powder room. Please don't vandalize the carpet!"

"No promises."

Mayor Lanus stripped off the black robe as they entered his office. Even though it was a big room, Corin and Jack felt cramped from how much tension they felt. The walls were golden yellow with black trim, decorated with framed certificates and awards. It surprisingly smelled like hot sauce.

They stood before Mayor Lanus's sleek black desk. The mayor put his hands together and sat in a synthetic vinyl executive chair. "Gentlemen, I have a proposition."

"I thought we were going to go over the arena rules?" asked Jack, confused.

"My city has not had a decent arena match in years. I own the arena, as you know, and we need to put on a hell of a show if we're to bring in enough to pay for your penance."

"I am looking forward to my fight against Troll," said Jack.

"But are you both worthy?" asked the mayor. "Are you skilled enough to work for me?"

"We didn't know you owned the arena until today. Sorry if you think we're not worthy to be in the match, but we're both outstanding fighters."

"Corin, you haven't told him?" asked Mayor Lanus.

"Told me what?" asked Jack.

"Corin signed a contract when he purchased my old property. If you and Troll impress me, I'll hire your group to work for me and regulate discounts on your housing payments. I need assistance with espionage. Corin knows he must do as he's told, or you'll all end up homeless and poor."

Corin looked at his feet shamefully.

"I'd rather be banished with Rowan," said Jack.

"Oh, I can't allow that. If only Corin had read the fine print. When he wrote his signature, he signed all of your lives over to me, except for Rowan."

"But only if they impress you in the match," stated Corin. "You said you'd hire us as your city *saviors*, and that's all we agreed upon."

"No, Corin, it wasn't." The mayor chuckled.

"It wasn't?" Corin gulped.

"You signed a magic paper," Mayor Lanus explained. "Remember how I told you faeries are trouble? They taught me how to craft magical paper from the wood of a Tree of Life. I banished them from my city afterward to keep their secret for my benefit. I mean, for my city's benefit. If you had read before signing, you would've noticed that it's clearly labeled at the top that the contract is made from a Tree of Life."

"But what does that mean?" asked Corin.

"It means my mind fills out the contract, and I can change it at will. Right now, it says that you and your friends, Jack, John Doe, and Troll, are my indentured servants if Jack loses the arena match against Troll tomorrow."

"What!" Jack exclaimed.

"You're terrible!" Corin cried.

"My boy, you tried to take advantage of me before I decided to teach you a lesson in earning for yourself. I'm doing you a favor."

"What is he talking about, Corin?" asked Jack.

"I am . . . I was trying to save us money because I want . . . status," Corin said disgracefully.

"Mayor Lanus, if I win the match tomorrow, destroy the contract, and we'll leave this horrible city. You'll never hear from us again," directed Jack. "You tricked Corin! We don't need to live in your despicable house."

"I like that," said the mayor.

"Then let's sign the contract and be done with this," said Jack.

"Only one signature is enough," Mayor Lanus said. "But let's up the ante because y'all still need to bring in a crowd that will pay your penance. As I said before, you must put on one hell of a show. I can't allow Troll to just let you win once you tell him about our deal. I have something in mind for your warrior."

"What do you want with him?" growled Jack.

"Reginald told me about him before the trial, and he heard John Doe say they are like brothers. If Troll loses the match, then all of you are free from the contract and allowed to leave Centerville, except John Doe, because he will be my servant. I knew he was servant material when I met the foolishly dressed wizard. If Troll really cares for his friend, he will fight his heart out trying to win to save him from solitary servitude."

"That's not fair!" Jack screamed.

"Would Troll really be willing to give up his own freedom and ours just for John Doe's benefit?" asked Corin. "He wouldn't . . . would he? He'd sacrifice John Doe for us, right?"

"Corin, would *you* sacrifice your parents if they were in a deal like this?" Jack asked.

"I guess not," Corin sighed.

"It's all in the fine print now, boys," cheered Mayor Lanus, holding up the contract. They watched the ink glow red, and the wording changed right before their eyes. "You boys are going to make sure that I win lots of money no matter what!"

"If I win, we're spared, but John Doe loses," Jack said.

"And if Troll wins, we all lose," said Corin.

"How are we going to tell the others?" asked Jack.

"Let me do that," Corin said. "You need to prepare yourself for the arena tomorrow."

"Get out, boys." The mayor cackled. "It's been a pleasure doing business with you."

"Come on, Jack," said Corin as they left Mayor Lanus's office, slamming the door.

"Don't slam my door, you'll piss off the ghosts! I hate it in here. Damn ghosts, always putting hot sauce in my coffee."

Jack and Corin walked down the hallway to meet the others outside the courtroom. John Doe and Rowan were having a discussion as they approached. Rowan sadly looked at them.

"Corin, you can't help me?" Rowan asked, walking to them. "John Doe told me you offered to help Jack but not me. This isn't fair. I didn't kill Jeer. I was tricked. I just wanted to help him. I made a terrible mistake." Filled with anger and betrayal, Rowan sobbed uncontrollably.

John Doe stared at the ground. "I'm sorry, Rowan. I don't know what to say that would be helpful," admitted the young wizard, scratching his blond hair.

"Maybe we could speak to the mayor again?" suggested Jack. "I was so upset I didn't even consider defending Rowan's sentence."

"I wish Troll was here," Rowan wept.

"Well, Troll's not here," said Corin. "He left."

"What?" Rowan asked, sniffing and taking in a deep breath. "Where did he go?"

"We don't know," said John Doe. "We can't reach him by—"

"Maybe he left because of *you*!" Corin accused Rowan, getting very close to her face.

Rowan was startled by his accusation.

"Corin, I'm sure he's around here somewhere," said Jack.

Heeb walked over to Rowan. "Hello dear. My name is Heeb. I'm so sorry for this terrible verdict. You do not deserve this. I assure you, the mayor is grieving and taking his pain out on you. Something similar happened in the past with Mayor Lanus and another Antiquity. I know him well and will speak to him on your behalf."

"You won't need to do that," said Corin. "Rowan, it's best if you leave."

"What?" gasped his companions simultaneously.

"Just think about it. Rowan will be safer in her forest. She won't have to be invisible just to avoid trouble."

"Trouble? Are you calling *me* trouble, Corin?" Rowan asked.

"Corin, why are you saying this?" asked John Doe. "I mean, Rowan and I don't see eye to eye, but I don't want her to leave. She is Troll's friend. It'll break his heart."

Corin ignored John Doe and casually took Rowan's hand in his. *I can't tell her the truth, but I want her to be safe. I don't want her anywhere near that horrible mayor. I'll do exactly what he asked and push her away.* He pulled her close and brought his lips to her large left ear. "We won't be able to find work and make a living with a troublemaker around," Corin whispered. "I'm sorry, Rowan, but it's best for all of us if you just go. Return to your forest and protect it. Again, I'm sorry."

"Please, no," Rowan begged as Corin released her hand and walked away.

"Corin, what did you say to her?" asked Jack.

"I told her that for her own safety, she should go."

"Corin, you *liar!* Tell them what you really said!" Rowan yelled.

Corin turned around and gave Rowan a stern glare as he took a small cloth and a pen from the pouch on his utility belt. He scribbled an inscription on the fabric and handed it to her. "This is the address to our new home, the Abode. Jessica and the others should be there by now. Go say goodbye and then leave. I will tell Mayor Lanus to give you a couple of hours so you can prepare to leave—for good."

"Corin . . ." Jack sadly hung his head. *This is probably for the best. She's in danger here, and I don't want her to know our troubles. It might make things worse. We can't endanger her.* "I'm going to miss you, lovely Rowan."

"I guess this really is goodbye," said John Doe, sighing.

Rowan violently cried. She tried to run out of the hallway, but Heeb swiftly yet gently took her hand. "Wait! Troll will want to see you . . ."

"I have no friends here! I don't want to stay!" she sobbed.

"If you leave now, you will regret it," Heeb said. "Things are *not* what they seem, and you *do* wish to see him. I *know* it."

Rowan nodded. "You're right. I'd also like to see Jessica and the others. They traveled here with us. I'm sure Jessica will say goodbye. Thank you, Heeb. I'm going to go find them."

"Travel invisible," Heeb told her. "You do not need to be abused any longer."

"Thank you," she said and then glanced at Corin.

"Please, Rowan, let me talk to the mayor," begged Heeb. "Do you give me permission, Your Highness?"

Corin gazed at Rowan sadly and then looked away.

Rowan nodded her head as tears poured down her face again. She turned invisible. "Yes," Rowan whispered.

"As you wish. Take heart, lady. Your friends aren't betraying you this day. The truth will be revealed in the future. I know it hurts now, but go and be well."

"Thank you, Heeb."

"We're still friends, Rowan," Jack called when he saw his faerie friend disappear. "I'm so sorry!"

Rowan pretended to not hear Jack's comment. She flew into the courtroom and out one of the windows as Magnum flew inside through another.

"No sign of Troll in this entire city," Magnum told John Doe, entering the hallway.

John Doe sighed hard. "Troll. Where are you?"

Meike approached them and slapped Jack's rear, which caused a loud clank.

He shrieked in surprise.

"Thank you, ma'am, for helping Jack," Corin told Meike.

"It is my pleasure," Meike said. "Jack, you must accompany me back to my residence. Will you come peacefully, or do I have to restrain you?"

"I'll come peacefully, Meike, but do I have to live with you forever?" Jack asked, worried. "I am still uneasy about discovering the microchip you installed without my permission."

"No, darling, you won't have to stay with me permanently. But tonight, you will have to be punished."

"P-p-punished?" Jack asked, gulping a lump in his throat. "What kind of punishment?"

"Darling, that will be for me to decide," she said, batting her eyes and taking lipstick out of her coveralls. "You might even *enjoy* it." Meike applied the lipstick and tapped the case. It transformed into a metal collar. She snapped it around Jack's neck.

"Good luck, Jack. She's into the weird stuff." John Doe said.

"Is it a control collar?"

"Indeed, darling. You need guidance, after all."

"I don't know—"

"You're not getting out of this." Meike laughed as she pulled out a remote control and hit a red button.

Jack suddenly felt warm and very sensual. He moaned. All the tension he had felt in the mayor's office and courtroom melted away.

Meike smiled.

"Okay, so, back to your place?" Jack asked excitedly. "I'm willing! Let's go!"

"Corin, my boy," said Mayor Lanus, walking through the hallway. "Come have a word with me."

Corin slunk away from his companions and went to the mayor.

Heeb saw Mayor Lanus call Corin over. *Just what is going on? What are you up to, Mayor Lanus?*

"I did what you asked," Corin said regretfully. "Rowan is leaving. I only ask that you give her time to prepare for her departure. She has many friends to say goodbye to."

"Not to worry," said Mayor Lanus. "So long as she's out of the city by tomorrow morning, everything will be fine. You know, I didn't think you'd actually follow my orders. I thought you'd be faithful to her, but boy, you've got gold fever pretty bad and should probably seek help. You're going to be just like me one day, Corin Degodi. You should feel pride in that."

"Gold fever? What's that?"

At that exact moment, John Doe heard a voice in his ear. "Who could that be?" John Doe asked, puzzled. He gently touched the bud in his ear. "Hello?"

"Hi, John," Troll's voice came through on the receiving end of John Doe's radio.

"Troll?" John Doe cheered, gaining the attention of all his comrades.

Corin's heart leaped in his chest.

"Quick! Tell me what defense I can use against a water-element creature," said Troll.

"Um, let me think . . . . Oh! Fire will work. Anything that causes heat or an explosion. Why? Where are you? Troll?"

"Fire?" Troll asked, grunting in pain. He screamed.

Static—

"What did he say?" asked Corin, approaching John Doe. "Where is he?"

"What kind of danger has he gotten himself into now?" asked Jack.

"Who is this person?" asked Meike. "I am fascinated by your concern."

"It's our friend, Troll," said Corin. "I sent him to get groceries, and he must've gotten into trouble."

"This is the same Mr. Troll who'll fight Jack in the arena tomorrow?" Meike asked.

"Yes, unless he's gotten himself into something that he can't handle," said Corin, disheartened.

"Troll has been able to get himself out of pretty much anything he's gone up against," John Doe said confidently. "I have faith in him, but I'm also scared for him. We are always together. This is the first real challenge he's been in without me."

"It won't do us any good standing here worrying about him. John Doe, we should head back to the Abode."

"Corin, can we bring Heeb home too?" John Doe asked childlike.

"I'm not a puppy, John Doe, but I would love to see the Abode, and I am honored you're inviting me."

"Of course, you're welcome to visit," said Corin. "Jack, you go with Meike. We'll see you tomorrow at the arena. Good luck tonight."

"He's surely going to need it," Meike said, hitting a green switch on the remote.

The collar around Jack's neck sparked, shooting an electrical current through his torso. "I think I'm going to like this visit." Jack chuckled.

Corin turned to face the mayor. "Mayor Lanus—"

The mayor had left.

What is gold fever? I don't want to be like him. Corin shivered.

TWENTY-SEVEN

Troll and Bronze headed up the mountain a few miles from the village. After an hour-and-a-half of hiking into the thinning air, Troll stopped and looked behind them to see their progress. He marveled at how beautiful Rowan's Forest looked from this elevated location. The brilliant sun shined from the clear blue sky, and the trees swayed in the gentle wind.

In the distance, Troll could see the defensive walls of Centerville City just barely poking out over the edges of the rich greenery of the woods. Further away, a cloud of smoke hung thickly over another city surrounded by a much taller wall.

That must be Franklin City.

"Hey, Troll," said Bronze, pointing upward. "I think we're almost there—look at this."

Before them was the start of a narrow stream. The water appeared normal until they noticed it left the earth, hovered into the air, and flowed up the mountain.

"The water current is actually defying gravity and flying. I have never seen anything like that. That's incredible magic, right?"

"It's amazing," Troll said breathlessly.

Bronze suddenly gripped his throat and coughed violently. He kneeled, covering his mouth. The cough sounded much worse than it had at the restaurant. He lost his balance and cried out through his coughing.

"Bronze!" Troll yelled, panicked. He grabbed him and held on so he wouldn't roll downhill. "Are you okay? Can you breathe?" Troll helped him sit.

Bronze uncovered his mouth, looked into his palm, and gasped. It was covered in bright red blood.

"Wh-what's—wrong with—me?" Bronze asked, his breathing raspy. "I feel—dizzy again."

"I wonder if the altitude is causing that? Has this ever happened before?"

"No," Bronze responded. "I'm a little nauseous now. Maybe it's just my nerves. I've never coughed up blood before, Troll. I'm scared."

"Where is this orb so we can get out of here?" Troll asked. "Hand me the map. I'll carry it."

Bronze handed Bi Qu's map to Troll.

Troll glanced at the map. "We need to get you to a medicine man."

"Just let me rest for a bit," said Bronze, trying to calm himself.

"All right, but if you start coughing up blood again, I'll get you help," Troll said as he kneeled down and put a supportive hand on Bronze's shoulder. He allowed Bronze to rest for several minutes.

"I'm starting to feel better," Bronze said, his breathing returning to normal. He stood up slowly. "I can make it. Let's continue. If we follow this magical stream, it'll take us to the orb."

"Okay. Just be careful. Listen to your body. If you need help, tell me."

"Agreed."

They followed the magical stream to where the mountain leveled out into a meadow. Trees, flowers, and foliage didn't grow in the grassy field but encircled the vast area. In the very center of the grassland was an ancient stone well, and the enchanted water flowed directly into it. Hovering above the well's mouth was a clear volleyball-sized orb.

They breathed in amazement.

"The orb is glorious!" said Bronze.

"It's also probably dangerous," Troll said nervously, folding the map and putting it into his sack.

"What do you suppose is holding it up? A barrier?"

"Perhaps. I think this entire area is a barrier. Look how the forest circles around this place."

"You're right. Nothing is growing near that well besides grass. Could this be a covenstead where witches meet?"

"I don't want to find out."

"Come on, let's grab the orb."

"Wait! Didn't Bi Qu say it was an orb *within* the well? He didn't say above it. I think that crystal clear orb may be a trap."

"You could be right, Troll."

"I'll go first and look in the well."

"Be careful."

Troll approached the ancient well cautiously, staring at the crystal orb. He took a deep breath, leaned over, and gazed inside.

Floating on the water was a small, beautiful white orb.

Troll suddenly felt a warm energy inside of his chest. It felt as if a star had burst in his heart. He placed his hand on the amulet, and his breathing increased.

The white orb glowed.

"You cannot claim my orb," a deep voice erupted above him.

Troll yelped and backed away from the edge of the well. "Who are you?" he asked, keeping his hand on the amulet.

"I am the guardian," said a voice from the floating crystal orb. It changed from clear crystal to deep blue. "If you touch the white orb within the well, I will kill you."

"It's a water-element creature!" announced Bronze. "What do we do?"

Troll swallowed hard and looked back at Bronze. "I don't know magic, but John Doe does. I can radio him."

"Wait, you can't tell your friends about our mission," Bronze said.

"No, but Bi Qu did say I could contact them if I needed help with anything other than the items. I don't know what to do against a water-element creature, but John will," Troll said, tapping his radio. "John Doe."

"Do you think your radio signal will reach Centerville?"

Troll shrugged his shoulders. "John Doe, come in."

"Hello?"

"Hi John," Troll said.

"Troll?" John Doe's voice yelled through the communicator.

"John, I need you to think. Quick! Tell me what defense I can use against a water-element creature."

"Um, let me think." John Doe gulped. "Oh! Fire will work."

"Fire?"

The stream crafted a watery hand. It grabbed Troll's ankle and pulled him off his feet. Troll gasped in surprise and grunted when his back hit the ground. Troll looked over his chest and screamed as it dragged him upstream.

"Anything that causes heat or an explosion," John Doe said. "Why? Where are you? Troll—"

Static—

"Bronze, it's pulling me to the well!"

"Oh no! I'm coming," Bronze cried, running to help him.

"Stay back! If you come any closer, I'll drown the boy in my magic well," the water-element creature warned, jerking Troll's body up the stone side of the well.

Bronze stopped, balled up his fists, and growled. "Troll, I don't know what to do!"

"I didn't touch your orb! Let me go!" Troll shouted at the water-element creature. He grabbed at the earth, trying to stop the creature's pull.

"You cannot be trusted!" the water-element creature said, dangling Troll's foot over the well's mouth.

"Fire. John Doe, please be right," Troll said as he grabbed his belt and yanked an explosive grenade out of his pouch. "Oh please, don't kill me!" He pulled the pin, braced his core muscles, and exhaled. He performed an abdominal crunch, lifted himself to his foot, and dropped the grenade into the well. Troll inhaled sharply, lowered himself as much as possible, and strained his leg muscles against the magical, watery hand.

The grenade exploded, projecting the white orb from the shattering well. It landed with a thud nearby in the grass.

Troll shrieked as he was thrown directly into Bronze's arms. "Good catch," Troll told his large friend. "Oh, benevolent Ra, am I all here?"

"You're lucky to be. I thought you would lose your leg," Bronze said, looking Troll over when he put him down.

"So did I." Troll breathed a sigh of relief.

"Look, the water stopped," Bronze said, pointing at the stream.

Troll walked to the white orb and crouched down to observe it. Thankfully, it was undamaged. He went to pick it up, and it glowed at the approach of his hand. Troll felt the same warm sensation in his chest. He stood and backed away, grasping the red amulet again.

The orb stopped glowing.

Bronze watched the crystal orb. It continued to hover above the destroyed well. Bronze gasped when its surface color changed to green.

"Troll, it's not an ordinary water-element creature."

As Troll made eye contact with the green orb, vines rose from the ground and wrapped around his toned muscular torso. He cried out in agony as they squeezed and pulled him to his knees before they locked around his arms and legs. "Help!" Troll yelled, being forced onto his back as a vine encased around his head and covered his mouth and nose. *I can't breathe!*

Bronze took his shotgun from its holster and aimed at the green orb. He fired.

The bullet struck.

The orb made a tingling sound, and its color changed from green to a furious red. Fireballs shot out of it and streaked through the air at Bronze.

Bronze yelped, dodging the fireballs. "I think it's a multiple-element creature!"

Troll groaned, flexing his muscles. The vine around his wrist shredded, freeing Troll's right hand. He reached for his chest, but another vine secured around his bicep to stop him. He moaned, struggling against the strength of the vines. *I can't give up!* Troll pulled his hand to his chest. His finger grazed the smooth red amulet. *I have never used the power of the amulet this often before. I don't know what it'll do to me.* His hand trembled. *Is it dangerous to use it this much?*

The vines tightened.

Troll whimpered. *They're squeezing the life out of me. I have to use it!* He forced his palm on the red amulet and screamed as adrenaline raced through him. *The power . . . I can feel it surging through me . . . it's flooding my veins and into my . . . heart.* Troll flexed his muscles again, and the vines shredded from his body. He performed a rising handspring from his prone position, landed on his boots, drew his axe, and approached the white orb.

This time, the orb did not glow.

Troll picked it up and put it into his sack.

The fireball-shooting orb noticed Troll and hissed. It stopped firing at Bronze. Its surface color changed to yellow and abruptly released a bright, blinding light as strong as the sun.

Troll and Bronze shielded their eyes.

The multiple-element creature cackled evilly and changed its color to deep blue again. The still stream transformed into a tall demonic humanoid creature made entirely of water.

Bronze cautiously opened his left eye. "The water changed into a river demon!"

It charged at Bronze.

He screeched and shot at the demon. It had no effect. The river demon grabbed Bronze's shoulders and shoved his head into its watery body. Bronze held his breath, but the magical water forcefully invaded his nostrils and mouth. He dropped his shotgun and thrashed his arms and legs. The river demon held him firmly in place.

Bronze was drowning.

Troll raced over to the blue orb and struck it with his axe. The multiple-element creature made another tingling sound, and its color turned orange.

The water demon's body collapsed, making a loud splashing sound, freeing Bronze from his watery prison. "Sweet . . . oxygen," Bronze choked as he coughed water out of his lungs, fell to his knees, and struggled to breathe fresh air.

The orange orb shot a lightning bolt at Troll's axe and knocked it out of his hand. "Now you have no weapon!"

Troll pulled Raw's severed tail from his belt and thwacked it against the orange orb.

The multiple-element creature made a whirring sound of utter confusion when it noticed what Troll had struck it with. It roared and blasted a lightning bolt straight at Troll's amulet.

Troll gasped when the red amulet moved his body faster than ever. It forced him to fall backward, landing hard on his back. With his breathing erratic, Troll stared at the lightning soaring over him. "Th-th-that would have stopped my heart!"

Bronze sat on his haunches, lifted his shotgun, and fired at the orange orb. His bullet struck and knocked it off balance. It growled, changed to red, and blasted fireballs at Bronze.

"I have an idea," Troll said, returning Raw's tail to his belt and his axe to its sheath.

"What is it?" Bronze asked, dodging the fireballs.

Troll took off his chest plate, held it before him, and aimed it at the red orb. "I hope this works." He charged at it. Once close enough, he jumped into the air, pushed his chest plate forward, and lodged it into the hole designed for his amulet. Troll broke through the magical barrier that allowed the multiple-element creature to hover and landed hard on the ground near the damaged well.

The red orb continued to blast fireballs under the chest plate. Troll could feel the metal getting hot. He kept his body weight on his armor and dragged it to the still stream. He pulled it into the water, and the fireballs stopped.

The multiple-element creature screamed, its colors faded, and it died.

Troll sighed with relief and rolled over onto his back, breathing hard.

"That was brilliant," Bronze said. "How did you know that would work?"

"I didn't—but I'm so glad—it did! John gave me—the idea. He said that fire—could be used against water. So, I figured—at that moment—while it—was being fire—would be—vulnerable to water. It destroyed itself," Troll explained between breaths.

"Bi Qu was right. This was *not* easy."

"I'm exhausted! I never want to fight another magical entity without John Doe again," Troll said.

"Do you have the orb we were seeking?"

"Yes," Troll said, still lying down as he removed it from his sack and showed Bronze.

"Awesome, now we can go back to Centerville."

"I'm so relieved," Troll said, slowly sitting up. He retrieved his chest plate from the water.

Bronze began to have another violent coughing fit.

Troll dropped his chest plate on the ground and grasped Bronze's shoulders. "Are you okay?"

"I think so." Bronze breathed as his coughing subsided.

"You don't look so good."

"I'll be fine. Should we take the multiple-element orb to Bi Qu as well?"

"You think he could use it? I believe it's dead."

"You never know," Bronze said as he reached into the water and pulled the crystal orb out. "It might make a nice paperweight." He shoved it into his pack.

THE UNIQUE CAMPAIGN

TWENTY-EIGHT

Jessica and her crew sat in the Abode's living room for quite some time, tediously waiting for the others after completing their job at the military base. Finnegan sat in a wooden rocking chair with his elbows on his knees, RJ and Ace sat on a pink acrylic loveseat, and Jessica paced behind a tan nylon sofa.

"I appreciate that Corin radioed us the address and insisted we make ourselves at home, but they've been gone a long time," complained Finnegan as he stood.

"Aye," said Ace. "I hope they're all right and didnae get into trouble."

"I'm hungry," RJ said as his stomach growled.

"I'm sure everything is fine," said Jessica, walking to one of the large windows. She saw Benjamin outside in the garden, removing weeds before hoeing new rows for planting in the dry soil.

I need privacy with Jess. This can't wait a moment longer. I hope this distracts them. "Jess, can we talk?" asked Finnegan, touching the triangular corner of a thin mesh screen on the wall. His touch activated the mesh, and a moving picture appeared.

"Oooh!" RJ coed. "I love watching view-screen!"

"What's on, lad?" asked Ace, turning his attention to the screen. "Change the channel."

"Okay," RJ said, running up to the screen and touching the corner as the image changed several times.

Finnegan gave Jessica a serious look.

"What is it, Finn?" she asked, concerned.

He took her hand, and they retreated to the parlor.

Rowan remained invisible as she flew through Centerville City and wiped away her tears. "I hope Heeb can talk to that horrible mayor, but do I *want* to stay in a place where I'll never be welcome? I don't know if it's worth my sorrow. The least I can do is say goodbye to the others." *Troll . . . where did you go? I know you're strong, but I can't bear it if anything happens to you. If you're facing something dangerous on your own, please be safe.* She arrived at the Abode and became visible on the front porch.

Benjamin saw her appear but wasn't startled. "Greetings, faerie ma'am," he said.

Lost in her thoughts, Rowan didn't see him in the garden. She screamed and jumped. "You scared me! Who are you?"

"I'm so sorry! I'm the gardener," Benjamin said, nodding.

"Corin hired a gardener for his new house?"

"Apparently so," he said, extending his hand. "It's nice to meet you."

Rowan stared at his hand and then looked into his blue eyes. *I sense something about this man. I don't know what it is about him. It's difficult to describe, but I haven't felt anything like this before. I'm nervous to take his hand.*

"Ma'am?"

Rowan gulped, rubbed her hands together, and put them behind her back. "I hope I don't offend you by not shaking your hand, sir. I don't know your name; please forgive me for being shy."

"Oh, no need to apologize. My name is Benjamin Saul Craft," he said when he saw her discomfort and lowered his hand.

"I'm Rowan. I'm just here to say goodbye to my other friends. I must leave the city and am very emotional about it."

"Your four companions are inside."

"Thank you," she said, walking inside.

"Good day, Rowan," he said softly.

Rowan followed her ears to the living room, where RJ and Ace laughed hysterically at an entertaining program featuring a family making smoothies out of rotten fruit.

"I don't trust him," Finnegan said to Jessica. "You just met him!"

"I like him."

"Jess, I *know* you. We've always been close. Corin's presence has created an awful feeling in my gut."

"What? Go ahead and say it, Finn. You're jealous!"

"Yes, I'm jealous, but that's not my only reason. Corin's bad news! There's something about him—I don't know what it is, but he's trouble!"

"I thought you'd be happy for me."

"I'd do anything to make you happy."

"Hi, friends!" Rowan said, loud enough for everyone in the living room and parlor to hear.

"Lass!" announced Ace when he saw her. "We didnae know what became of ye. How are you?"

"I came to say goodbye," Rowan said somberly.

"But you just got here," said RJ.

"Well, I mean goodbye for real, RJ," Rowan sighed. "I have been banished from the city by the mayor, and I must leave tonight unless John Doe's warlock friend can help me. I got in trouble, and Corin—" She sniffed as a tear trickled down her cheek. "—said awful things to me. Jack and John Doe just sat there . . . after all I did to help them come here . . . I thought they were my friends."

"Rowan," Jessica said softly, rushing to her.

"Jess, we're not done—"

"Later, Finn. She needs us," Jessica said as she embraced Rowan. "I'm so sorry, dear!"

"You're being serious?" Finnegan asked Rowan.

Rowan nodded.

"This isn't a joke! Jessica, don't you see? See what they did to her? Rowan is distraught and hurt. She was his friend! Think of what Corin could do to you!"

"Finn, I said we'll talk about this later!" Jessica huffed, rubbing Rowan's back. "We need to be supportive. Rowan, please sit down and relax. You don't have to go anywhere."

"The mayor wants me out," Rowan said, crying as she gently withdrew from Jessica's embrace. "He hates me, and I got Jack in trouble. They think we murdered Jeer. I know Troll would understand, but no one knows where he went or what happened to him. He just disappeared!"

"Jeer? The grumpy goblin? He's dead? How did that happen?" asked Ace.

"It was an accident!"

"Troll is gone?" asked Finnegan. "Again?"

"It's unlike before. Troll was protecting us in the forest then," said Rowan. "Corin sent him to the grocery store, and he never returned."

"So *that's* why the refrigerator is empty," said RJ. "I'm starving."

"Please, not now, RJ!" Jessica said sternly. "Rowan, I'm sure Troll is okay, and I know he'd want to see you. Look, no one knows you're here. You can stay here until morning."

"I don't want to stay where I am not wanted, and Corin does not want me here."

"What about Jack and John Doe?" asked Ace.

"Jack's been ordered to stay with his mechanic, and John Doe is John Doe."

"Was Jeer really murdered?" asked Jessica.

"No! I visited my father and was given a magical goblet for a mission. My father warned me it could harm mortals, but my sister lied and said the goblet was the Holy Grail! I foolishly believed her and thought I could help Jeer be happy. I would *never* murder anyone, and Jack was only trying to help protect the people. This is all so unfair. Maybe my father was right about humans all along? I never should have gotten involved in human affairs. I've lost my new friends I considered a second family. Without their friendship, returning to my forest is going to feel . . . lonely. I'll have to learn how to cope with my isolation."

"I thought ye loved your forest, lass?" asked Ace, walking over to her.

"I do. I'll admit, I've missed it and all of my nature friends, but talking to my trees and animals is very different than the relationship I built with the boys. In all my years, I've never experienced a bond of friendship as deeply as I have these past few days with them."

"But caring for your forest is a noble job," Ace said, hugging her. "And yer good at it, and ye love it."

Rowan leaned into his hug. "You're right. Thanks, Ace."

Ace took Rowan's hand and led her to the tan sofa. "Now, be comfortable for a wee bit and relax, lassie. No need to be rushing off in a hurry," Ace said.

"RJ and I were watching funny entertainment programs. Would ye like to watch with us?"

"I'd like that."

"Jess," Finnegan whispered.

"What?" she asked, annoyed.

"You believe her, don't you? Just look at her. Those tears! She speaks the truth, and you know it."

Jessica balled her fists and stared at Rowan.

"Trust your gut, Jess," Finnegan said.

Finnegan, I don't want to look at you. I'm so angry! I want to believe Rowan. I do believe her . . . I do, right? Corin . . . he was so kind to me. So gentle. I wanted our romance to be real. I hoped he was a good man. I do not want to believe he's not who I think he is.

After watching a view-screen program, Rowan stood and hugged RJ and Ace. "I really shouldn't stay. This will be the first place the mayor will send the authorities. Plus, I'd like to check on my baby animals. I must be sure they're happy. I *am* responsible for them."

"They'll be plenty happy here, lass," said Ace. "Do nae worry about them. You did them a wondrous deed, bringing them here where they'd be safe. Don't go yet . . ."

"Thank you, Ace, but I don't want to be here when Corin arrives," she sweetly said to him and walked to Finnegan. "Goodbye, Finnegan," Rowan said, extending her arms. "Too macho for a hug?"

"Of course not," he said, taking her in his arms. "I agree with Ace and think you should stay. We won't let Corin run you off, and Troll will want to see you. He's not like the others. I think he's a fool, but the boy has a good heart."

"Please, Troll is not a fool. He's not! He's just different . . . like me, and I don't want to trouble anyone any longer," Rowan said as tears rolled down her face and she pulled away from Finnegan.

Finnegan shamefully looked at his feet.

"Take care of yourself," Jessica told Rowan and clutched her again.

"You take care of yourself, too," Rowan whispered before they released.

Jessica nodded.

Rowan wiped her tears, opened the front door, and walked outside. She gently shut the door behind her and sighed. "I don't want to leave."

"You're going so soon?" asked a voice.

Rowan gasped and saw Benjamin holding his gardening hoe. "You startled me again."

"I promise I'm not trying to do that. You said your farewells then?"

"I did. Now I have to go to the park and see my animals."

"*Must* you depart?" Benjamin asked.

"I *need* to," she said. "I was ordered to leave the city, and I will do that. I just wish my friends would have been good to me. I wish the one person I wanted to see was here. I hope he's safe."

"What is his name?" Benjamin asked. "I can deliver your message when he arrives."

"Would you?" Rowan asked, perking up.

"Certainly, I wonder if I have met him yet?"

"His name is Troll. He has purple hair."

"I have not met anyone with purple hair, but the moment I see him, I will tell him you wish him well."

"Thank you so much, Benjamin," Rowan said, smiling.

"Good day to you, Rowan," he said, returning to work.

Rowan smiled and turned invisible. *Heeb, I want to stay. I won't leave until morning. Please help me.* She jumped into the air and flew toward the park.

TWENTY-NINE

Bronze and Troll swiftly journeyed back down the mountain.

"We've made excellent time and still have a full hour before sunset," Bronze said happily.

"I'm relieved. I can't wait to see my friends," said Troll. "I hope I didn't make them worry too much. I wonder if Bi Qu got all of the groceries?"

Bronze started coughing again. He sounded like he was trying to hack up his lungs. He collapsed to his knees and was unable to get up. His vision went black, and he could barely breathe. "Troll, what is wrong with me? Why can't I walk or see?"

Alarmed, Troll grasped Bronze's shoulders and kneeled down to him. "Hang on. I've got you," Troll said, taking Bronze's right arm and pulling it over his head. "Lean on me. We're almost to Centerville."

"I'm glad we're almost there. I don't know what's going on," Bronze said, struggling to stand. "I feel like I'm fading away."

"Stay with me," Troll said, using his strength to support the lava monster, taking careful steps toward the South Gate.

"My vision is coming back," Bronze said. "It's fuzzy, though."

"Psst."

"What was that?" Bronze asked, panicked.

"I heard it, too," said Troll. "Who's out there?"

"Psst."

"There it is again," said Bronze.

Troll gripped Bronze tightly. "Is anyone there?"

"Come here, buddy," a voice whispered.

"Who's there? Show yourself!" Troll demanded.

"Do you mean to harm us?" Bronze asked, swallowing hard. "I sure hope not."

"Are you guys interested in something?" asked the voice.

"Depends on what *something* is," said Bronze.

"No, we're not interested in whatever you're selling. Leave us alone! I have to get my friend to a medicine man."

An old, short, olive-skinned goblin emerged behind a large tree near the South Gate. He was bald, had dark green warts all over his body, and honey-colored eyes. His ears were pointed but harshly torn from age.

"What do you want?" Troll asked.

"No need to be alarmed. I'm Olea. Can I interest you in something I discovered?" asked the goblin. "Someone left it in my tree trunk, but I don't need it. I will give it to you in exchange for a few gold coins. Interested?"

"No," said Troll. "Please, leave us alone."

"Well, wait a minute," said Bronze. "What is it?"

"Bronze, you need medical attention! There's no time to barter with a tree goblin," Troll declared, feeling anxious.

"I'm okay at the moment, really," Bronze said, pulling out the bumblebee jasper stone. He squeezed the stone and held it to his chest. "I won't need a medicine man."

"Are you sure?" Troll asked.

Bronze nodded.

Troll sighed. "Okay, just be careful. He might try to swindle you," Troll said, letting him go.

"Oh, not me, sir. I'm not the swindling type," said Olea.

Bronze stepped clumsily toward the goblin.

"Behold," Olea said, pulling a shiny golden goblet from the tree trunk. "Someone from your city put this here. A warlock, I believe. Why would he do that?"

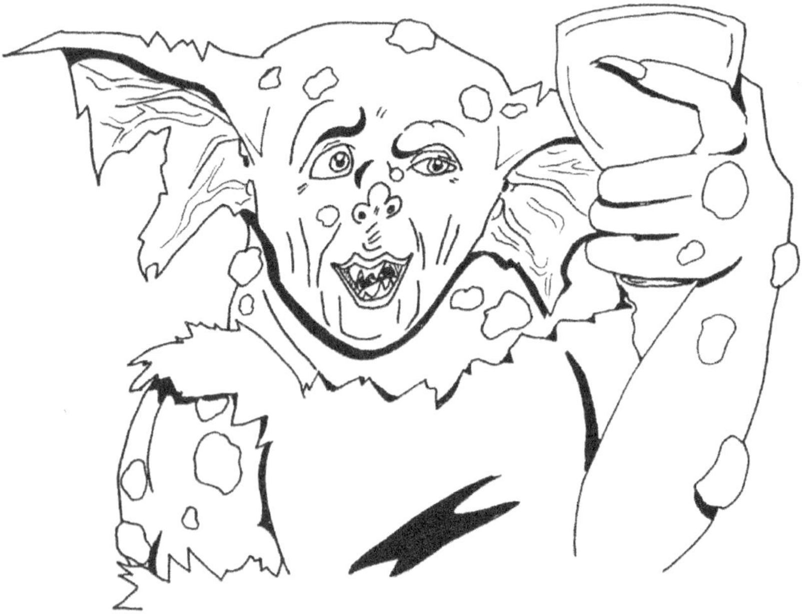

"I have no idea," said Troll. "I don't even know what that is."

"Is that the Holy Grail?" asked Bronze.

The goblin shrugged his shoulders. "It could be."

"How much?"

"Bronze, you don't need that," said Troll. "We have to get back to your boss."

"For you, sir . . . twenty gold," said Olea with a smile showing all of his rotten teeth.

"All I have is fourteen," Bronze said, sighing deeply. "I really wanted it—"

"I'll take it! It's better than nothing. I have to eat and don't want this in my trunk."

"It's a deal," Bronze said happily, giving the goblin his coins and taking the goblet. "Thank you, Olea! This is wonderful."

"Whatever," said Olea, returning to his tree.

"Troll, look at this. It's pretty!"

"Yeah, it's pretty, but we must get to Bi Qu," Troll said as Bronze tucked the goblet into his pants pocket. The lip of the goblet remained visible, as it could not fit all the way inside. Troll helped Bronze walk to the locked steel gate, but Jeer was nowhere in sight.

"Jeer?" Bronze called through the gate frame. "Hello?"

"Who goes there?" asked a human, brandishing his sword through the gate.

"Hey, you're the human I rescued," Troll said, surprised. "Reginald, right? It's me, Troll. Can we come in?"

"Troll!" Reginald exclaimed happily, immediately putting his sword into its sheath and unlocking the gate. "Yes, come in, your friend too."

"Can we sign in? I'd like to go see my boss," said Bronze.

"Sure," Reginald said, bringing them the logbook from Jeer's demolished desk. "I'll have to take your weapons. You know the rules."

"Of course," Troll said, handing Reginald his axe and the pouch of remaining grenades.

"Bye, Amber. I'll see you later for hunting," Bronze said, kissing his shotgun's barrel and handing it to Reginald. "Is Jeer taking a break?"

Reginald didn't answer his question. He was distracted by the goblet in Bronze's pocket as they filled out the paperwork. "Hey, what's that there?"

"Oh, that's my treasure," Bronze said. "I'm going to give it to my boss."

"You are?" Troll asked, noticing Jeer's desk in pieces. "There was a struggle here." *As much as I'd like to ask about what happened to Jeer's desk, I don't have time. I must get Bronze and the items to Bi Qu.*

"Yeah, he's done so much for me. At first, I thought I'd keep it for myself, but no . . . he deserves it," Bronze said, smiling. "Come on, I'll take you to see him."

"Troll, I'm putting your weapons back into storage unit C2. Bronze, your gun and ammo will be in B3," Reginald said, unlocking the units and carefully placing their belongings inside.

"Thanks for letting us in, Reginald," Troll said, putting Bronze's arm around his neck and helping him walk.

"Not a problem," Reginald said, taking out his sword again and saluting.

As they walked away, Reginald sat on Jeer's chair, which collapsed under him. He screamed, landing on his rump and dropping his sword. "Oh! Apparently, I need a new chair!"

Bronze coughed the entire way to a Chinese restaurant. "We're here. Go in through the back door," he wheezed raggedly.

The smell of salty food floated outside the building. Troll resisted salivating, but Bronze couldn't help but drool. "Mmm! Roast duck, fried rice, and sesame chicken. My favorites! Isn't it a shame that you can eat as much as you want, but later, you're always hungry again?"

"Does Bi Qu own many restaurants?" Troll asked.

"Oh, I'm not sure," said Bronze, scratching his head.

They entered the back door into a storage area. Bronze carefully bent down and grabbed a handle in a floorboard. He grunted and lifted a giant trapdoor. "Come on. His divination office is down here."

They walked down a flight of stairs into an underground chamber.

Troll gasped in awe at the room's layout. "What a big space!"

The walls were made of stone, lined with several wooden bookcases full of books. Hundreds of wax candles lit the room. Each gave off a lustrous yellow light that cast flickering shadows in every direction along the tops of old bookcases, prism-decorated chandeliers, and tall floor candelabras in each corner. A large stone table sat in the middle of the enormous room. A big white circle had been drawn in chalk on the concrete floor around the table. A pre-war vintage globe of the Earth sat beside a mahogany desk where Bi Qu sat in a fancy green leather chair, puffing on a carved ivory pipe. He looked at them and smiled.

"I have never seen so many books in my life," Troll stated.

Bronze coughed again. "Master, I hope we're . . . on time. I think . . . I'm sick."

"Ah!" Bi Qu breathed, putting his pipe gently onto its stand. He walked to them. "Gentlemen, it's good to see you. Bronze, I need you to lie on the table. Your cough sounds terrible. Don't worry, I'll take care of it," Bi Qu said, snapping his fingers.

A giant iron cauldron appeared beside Troll.

Bi Qu snapped his fingers again and ignited a fire under the big pot.

Troll inhaled sharply and stepped back.

"Jumpy?" asked Bi Qu, chuckling.

"Yes," admitted Troll, opening his small tan sack. "We got every item."

"Excellent! Mr. Troll, I can't thank you enough," Bi Qu said, taking the objects. He pulled a flask from his robes and poured an orange liquid into the cauldron. Bi Qu carefully added the three ingredients to the mixture.

"What is that?"

"My elixir. This is what's going to save a precious life."

Bronze coughed up blood.

"Is he going to be all right?" Troll asked, concerned.

"He will be now," Bi Qu said, lifting his hands above the pot as the elixir began to boil. The orange liquid turned yellow. "With this potion, hear my plea. Heal my friend's cancerous anomaly."

"Was it *his* precious life all along?" Troll drew in a deep breath as he watched the yellow liquid transform into a gas.

The gas traveled to Bronze's nostrils. He breathed in the yellow fume deeply.

Troll's eyes widened in amazement.

"Thank you, Troll," Bi Qu said, hugging the warrior. "You saved my friend's life."

"I . . . he . . . you're welcome. You didn't say, *Mr.* Troll?"

"That's because you are family now!"

Bronze slowly sat up and looked over at them. "Boss, you knew I was dying? Why didn't you tell me?"

"Because I didn't want to get your spirits down, son," Bi Qu said. "I am so proud of you. You went out and accomplished what many would have just given up on. You were sick and near death, but you never gave up. You never know what you can accomplish if you don't give up."

Never give up. Those words entered Troll's soul.

"Thank you, boss," Bronze said as his tears streamed. He jumped off the table and hugged Bi Qu tightly. "I'm so happy!" he cheered, reaching for the warrior. "Troll!" Bronze grabbed Troll's chest plate and pulled him into the embrace. "I love both of you guys!"

"You're welcome." Troll chuckled. "Hey, don't forget to give Bi Qu your gift."

"Oh yeah," Bronze said when he released them and pulled the goblet out of his pocket. "Here, boss. I bought this for you."

"Bronze!" Bi Qu cried when he saw the goblet. He quickly took it and set it on the table. "Where did you find this?"

"It was outside the city in the forest. A goblin sold it to me. He said someone put it in his tree trunk. Isn't it beautiful? I thought you'd like it."

"This was meant to be delivered to 'The Greater Good' in the forest earlier today, but it wasn't there when I went to retrieve it. Thank you, Bronze."

"You're welcome. Oh! Here, boss. A new paperweight." Bronze pulled out the dead multiple-element orb from his pack. "This thing tried to kill us, but Troll stopped it. We figured you might want it."

"Thank you. Great work, both of you!" Bi Qu said proudly, taking the orb.

"I'm hungry. Can I go to the restaurant now?" asked Bronze, childlike.

"Of course," Bi Qu said with a hearty laugh as he put the crystal orb on a bookshelf. "Enjoy."

Bronze smiled. "Troll, I think we made a good team. Thank you for saving my life. You're a great person, and remember, you are brave."

"Thank you, Bronze," Troll said, extending his hand.

Bronze took Troll's hand and shook it gently. "If you ever need my help, I will be there, my friend. You have my oath."

"Thank you," Troll said.

As Bronze ran upstairs, Troll turned to Bi Qu. "So, you have a secret name as well? 'The Greater Good?'"

Bi Qu smiled at him. "We all have secrets, my boy."

"May I ask you something?"

"Certainly."

"Bronze told me he could feel magic radiating from me, but I am not an Antiquity. This amulet in my chest gives me strength, speed, and healing abilities. Do you know what it is?"

"To be honest, I do not know what that gem is, but I, too, feel a powerful aura surrounding you. It's appealing. Antiquities may feel attracted to you because of it."

"Attracted? Do you mean in love?"

"It's possible, but I wouldn't worry about it."

"If anyone's worried, it's probably my friends. I need to get back to them."

"Indeed. Oh! Before I forget! Here," Bi Qu snapped his fingers, and a large refrigerator appeared. He opened the door and pulled out a large sack full of food. He handed it to Troll. "I got everything on your list and a little bit more. I included a bundle of money, jewels, and gold. I told you I'd pay you well."

"Thank you," Troll said, throwing the sack over his shoulder.

"No, son. Thank *you.* We're family and will meet again. Keep that rose quartz I gave you."

"I'm afraid I didn't use it during this journey."

"Who said your journey was over?" Bi Qu asked, winking. "Your adventure is just beginning."

THIRTY

In the garden, Benjamin heard the approaching voices of the new homeowners, expressing their hunger and exhaustion. Grimacing, he stood straight and wiped the sweat from his brow under the red bandana. Benjamin plastered on a smile as they came into view. He waved his left hand in salutation as his right hand gripped the gardening hoe. "Greetings, friends," Benjamin said.

"You're supposed to call us your masters," said John Doe.

"What!" exclaimed Heeb. "Did you really just say that to this man?"

"He's our servant," replied John Doe.

"He is not," said Corin, rolling his eyes. "How are you, Benjamin?"

"I'm fine. The garden is coming along nicely."

"Benjamin, it's the most professional garden I've ever seen," said Corin. "You're doing a great job. Why don't you take a break and get some rest?"

"I cannot do that. I must tend to the garden."

"Do you have anxiety, my boy?" asked Heeb, eyeing the gardener with concern.

"Anxiety?" Benjamin asked, confused.

"Yes, you work and work, never taking breaks. Are you anxious about something?"

"I do not think so."

What an interesting fellow. He's a master gardener! The garden is breathtaking, but I've never seen him in the city. "Benjamin, when did you move to Centerville? Are you a new resident?" Heeb asked.

"I have always been here," answered Benjamin.

"Always?" asked Heeb. "I have lived here for many years, and I do not remember seeing you—"

"I tend to the garden," said Benjamin, turning away from Heeb's intense gaze. He carefully rested the hoe aside to treat the soil with his hands.

I'm feeling a very peculiar sensation. It's coming from Benjamin after he took his hands off that tool. How odd! It feels like magical energy. "What's your name, son?" Heeb asked.

"Benjamin Saul Craft," said Benjamin, not looking up from his work.

Heeb bit his bottom lip and lowered his eyebrows in thought.

"You okay, Heeb?" asked Corin.

"I have a bit of indigestion," Heeb said, grinning.

"Don't throw up on me," John Doe said, scooting away from Heeb.

"I wouldn't dream of it," Heeb chuckled, slowly leaning toward John Doe. He gripped his stomach as his skin turned as green as an emerald. "Though . . . if I had a choice . . ."

"That's not funny," John Doe said petulantly.

Magnum, Corin, and Benjamin burst into laughter.

Heeb also laughed. His skin returned to its normal color, and he looked at Benjamin again. *I won't mention the unusual energy I'm sensing until I have more information.*

Jessica walked outside. "Corin, can I speak to you?"

"Sure."

"Come inside."

This is the perfect time for me to talk to Mayor Lanus. "Pardon me, John Doe. I will be right back." Heeb snapped his fingers, and a black staff made of wood and steel, crowned with a jade gemstone, appeared in his right hand.

John Doe looked at the staff in awe. "Oooh! That's pretty!"

"Apertum porta. Urbs praetorium," Heeb chanted.

A green portal opened, and Heeb stepped through.

Rowan landed in the park and became visible. "Come to me, my children."

The baby animals heard her call and ran to Rowan.

Tears filled Rowan's eyes as she cuddled and kissed them. *I know you'll be safe and happy.* "I'm going to miss you all. I'm not allowed to be here anymore, so I have to go soon, but maybe . . . one day . . . I'll be allowed to return. But if not, you all live happy and long lives. I love you all." *I can feel it as they nuzzle me. They genuinely love me and their new home. I'm so glad and grateful that something benefited from this adventure with mortals.* Rowan looked at the baby turtle, and a tear left her eye as she blinked. It landed on the ground, and she remembered how Troll battled with the therasapien, saving her from being ripped to pieces when she tried to retrieve his axe. Rowan gasped and stood. "I can't leave yet! I need to see Troll!"

The baby animals watched her in awe.

"I'll stay invisible until I find him. No one will know I am here. I will return to the Abode, and when he comes, I will tell him how I feel."

Mayor Lanus locked his office door and turned to see Heeb stepping out of a green portal with his staff. "Hello, Heeb. What brings you here? Can it not wait until morning?"

"Mayor Lanus, I beg you to reconsider Rowan Fae's fate."

"What does her banishment mean to you, Heeb? She's a faerie, and they're troublemakers. She broke the law and murdered my friend."

"She did not *murder* Jeer. His death was an accident because her cyborg friend was trying to defend himself and save others. You are punishing her due to your grief."

"Heeb, I do not want to have this conversation. Will you please leave!"

"No," Heeb said, tapping his staff. A freestanding mirror appeared.

Mayor Lanus frowned at his reflection.

"You have abused your power before in this same fashion. Do you remember this?" Heeb waved his hand over the mirror.

The mayor's reflection changed several years prior. "What is this?" he asked.

"Just watch."

Mayor Lanus watched his younger self laughing and having fun at a city celebration. Music played, colorful kites flew, and citizens drank lemonade. Behind him was Silvia, wearing a pink apron, blowing fire onto a barbecue. A group of cheering children lined up with plates in their hands to get food from the blue dragon. A tiny spark flew into the mayor's hair and caught fire. The residents watched in horror as Mayor Lanus thrashed his arms wildly, screaming as the flames grew. Silvia grabbed a cup of lemonade and poured it on his head, dousing the small blaze. Everyone cheered, calling the blue dragon a hero.

Mayor Lanus growled, his cheeks turning red. "Dragon!" he screamed angrily, pointing at Silvia. "I knew I never should've allowed you to barbecue at this carnival! You are a liability my city does not need! You are no longer allowed to live here! You're banished!"

The vision of the past vanished, and the mayor's reflection changed back. "How dare you—"

"You were unjust to Silvia due to your embarrassment then, as you are being unjust to Rowan because you are grieving now. Others should not be so harshly punished because of personal feelings. You are our leader—"

"Her banishment stands," Mayor Lanus said coldly.

"If she cannot live here, neither will I," said Heeb, tapping his staff. The mirror vanished. "*Portum apertum. Sedes.*" The green portal opened.

"Where do you think you're going? You cannot leave!"

"Oh, I can, and I will. I'll close my business in sixty days . . . unless you consider your future as mayor and the good of this city and its people, human and Antiquity alike. Let me know if you change your mind, and I will consider staying," Heeb said, stepping through the portal.

The green portal shut as soon as Heeb disappeared. Mayor Lanus was left alone with his clenched fists and his bitter feelings.

"Did you or did you not turn your back on Rowan when she needed you?" asked Jessica to Corin after he stepped into the kitchen.

"Jessica, you weren't there. You don't know what happened. Rowan and Jack accidentally killed the goblin gatekeeper. Rowan *admitted* to her guilt. The mayor made the decision and forced her to go."

"That doesn't mean you turn your back on a friend. I can't believe you would do that."

John Doe walked by them and opened the refrigerator.

Jessica gestured to John Doe. "I could see *him* doing that. But not you, Corin."

John Doe shut the refrigerator and looked at Corin. "This is empty."

"Troll never returned with the groceries," said Corin, annoyed. "He disappeared, remember?"

"No," said John Doe, walking outside. "Benjamin, can I eat something from the garden?"

"No," said Benjamin. "It is not ready. Don't touch anything."

"But I'm hungry," John Doe whined.

"That's not my problem."

The green portal returned, and Heeb stepped through.

"That was fast," said John Doe.

"Did I miss anything?" Heeb asked, sitting on the front steps.

"Only the growling of my stomach," moaned John Doe.

"Hmm, I'm hungry too," Heeb said, closing his eyes and calmly meditating. *I won't allow hunger to disturb my concentration. I must piece together what I am sensing from Benjamin. I feel some kind of block keeps me out of his mind. This is strange! I'll try again later.*

"Heeb, can I open a portal to a burger bar?" John Doe asked impatiently.

"A what?" asked Magnum.

"A burger bar is a restaurant that only serves burgers," John Doe explained. "It's good!"

"It is probably not good *for* you," Heeb said, coming out of his meditation. "It's just take-away food, full of grease and fat."

"*Delicious* grease and fat," said John Doe.

"Oh! That *does* sound good!" Magnum breathed, licking his lips.

"What sounds good?" a voice asked behind them.

"Troll!" John Doe gasped, recognizing the voice immediately.

Troll walked up to the front porch with a large sack of groceries. He smiled. "Hi, John."

John Doe raced over and hugged him. "Where have you been?"

"I was busy," Troll said. "I'll explain later."

"You'll explain now," said Corin, having stepped outside as soon as he heard John Doe yell Troll's name. "We've been worried about you!"

"I was just helping a friend," Troll said when he recognized the house. *I remember seeing this place in the distance when Rowan and I were at the park. I had felt negative energy erupting from here, but I'm not experiencing that now. How strange.* Troll brushed aside his confusion and handed the sack to John Doe.

"Is this food?" asked John Doe, looking into the sack.

"It sure isn't a sack of bricks," said Troll. "Yes, John, it's all the groceries Corin asked me to buy."

"Oh, thank you! Team, we can eat! We're not going to die!" he cheered as he dragged the bag through the front door and into the kitchen.

"That was an unusual 'welcome home.'" Troll chuckled.

"Sorry," said Magnum. "He's just thinking with his stomach."

"No offense taken. I know John all too well. I know how worried he must have been. I didn't mean to concern anyone."

"Well, we're glad you're back," said Corin. "A lot has happened while you were away."

"Where are Jack and Rowan?" asked Troll.

"Troll," Corin said hesitantly. "Rowan had to leave."

Troll frowned. "Why? What happened?"

"She got in trouble with Mayor Lanus, and he banished her back to her forest. She killed the goblin gatekeeper with an object her father gave her. Apparently, Jack helped her, but it was an accident. He's with the mechanic doing time for his crime. Jack has to fight in the arena tomorrow against you, too. He owes the mayor money, so if he beats you—"

"I don't understand," Troll interrupted, stepping back. His breathing increased as his blue eyes filled with turmoil. "All of this happened when I was—"

"How was your quest?" asked Heeb, slowly approaching Troll. "Forgive me, son. I am Heeb."

"Oh, nice to meet you, sir. How do you do?"

"Very well, thank you. Oh, such manners," Heeb said, smiling. "I have been waiting to meet you. It is an honor. So, how was the mission?"

"Mission?" gulped Troll. *This warlock is quite forward and makes me very nervous. How does he know about where I've been? I can't tell him anything!*

"Allow me," said Heeb, gently stroking Troll's hair. He took a strand in his hand, sniffed it, and let it slip through his fingertips. Heeb grinned. "It went *well*. That's wonderful."

"How?" Troll asked breathlessly as he brushed his hair behind his ear.

"Magic." Heeb chuckled and winked at the young warrior.

"John Doe wishes he could be that good." Magnum laughed and entered the Abode. "Hey, John Doe, what meals are you preparing?"

"I can't cook!" John Doe screamed.

"You were on a mission?" Corin asked Troll.

"No," Troll said nervously. "It wasn't—"

Benjamin stepped forward. "Your faerie friend wishes you farewell. She asked me to deliver the message to a man with purple hair." He locked eyes with Troll. "I am Benjamin Sauuulll . . . Cccrrraft."

Troll whimpered when his eyes met Benjamin's. He felt extraordinary energy pierce through his entire body. His eyes widened in fear as the jolt paralyzed him. He became a living statue and could not break eye contact with Benjamin's bright blue eyes.

"Son, are you all right?" Heeb asked, trying to gain his attention.

Troll's bottom lip trembled, his neck and jaw muscles strained, but he could not speak.

Benjamin's eyes penetrated into Troll's being like a drill. He tightened his grip on the gardening hoe as his breathing became faster. He slowly walked toward Troll, not breaking their mutual gaze. It was almost as if a magical spell had put the gardener's body into slow motion.

"What's wrong with you two?" Corin asked, uneased.

"What's going on?" Heeb wheezed.

Benjamin continued forward. "Who . . . are . . . you? How can . . . I—"

Troll's breathing was sporadic and panicked. *Oh, my gods. I can't move! I can't blink! I cannot speak! Who is this person? My sight . . . it's like a kaleidoscope! There are rainbow colors surrounding this person's aura . . . how?*

"—I see you . . . in a light . . . a halo . . . of glowing colors," Benjamin strained to say.

Benjamin and Troll shared the unusual sight alteration toward one another. But that wasn't what frightened Troll. He watched Benjamin's colorful aura transform into a glaring bulbous form with multiple appendages. Then Benjamin spoke to Troll with such eeriness. "I . . . can . . . see . . . your . . . heart!"

The comment hit Troll like a bullet to the chest. The impact was so strong Troll couldn't breathe. His eyes trembled and filled with tears.

Heeb noticed Troll's struggle to take in oxygen. He gently reached out with his mind to investigate what was troubling the young warrior. The warlock was utterly unprepared for the waves of primal terror radiating off Troll like crashing ocean waves. The shock of experiencing that much raw fear sent Heeb's mind reeling back in a wild panic. His rational brain screamed at him to run away from whatever Troll saw. His fear blanked any helpful spells or lore that might've helped. He could do nothing but watch the young warrior suffer.

Troll's relentless fear became a hand that squeezed his erratic heart. A faint, red light erupted from within the amulet, but Troll didn't notice. *Someone, please help me . . . what is happening? Is this my end? Please . . . my heartbeat! My heart . . . .*

TO BE CONTINUED

ABOUT THE AUTHOR

KRISTINA M. HOFFMAN is an artist who has always wanted to be a science fiction/fantasy author and illustrator. She has made up stories with her wild imagination since she was a small child, and she's been drawing since she was old enough to pick up a pencil. Kristina worked as an art teacher, and her art has been featured in multiple galleries, online studios, magazines, and art shows. In September 2023, Kristina had her first successful Kickstarter campaign to assist in funding DESTINED EXISTENCE: THE UNIQUE CAMPAIGN. Kristina lives with her husband, Jay, and their cats in West Virginia.